FLESH AND BLOOD

ALSO BY THOMAS H. COOK

Sacrificial Ground
Elena
Tabernacle
The Orchids
Blood Innocents

FLESH
AND
BLOOD

Thomas H. Cook

G. P. PUTNAM'S SONS
New York

G. P. Putnam's Sons
Publishers Since 1838
200 Madison Avenue
New York, NY 10016

Library of Congress Cataloging-in-Publication Data

Cook, Thomas H.
Flesh and blood/Thomas H. Cook.

p. cm.
ISBN 0-399-13409-3
I. Title.
PS3553.055465B55   1989   88-12645 CIP
813'.54—dc19

Printed in the United States of America
1 2 3 4 5 6 7 8 9 10

For Justine Cook and Bryan Furman

We read in this hand
how it hath healed a
bitter wound; and in that,
how it hath locked the
door against a cry.

LOUISE IMOGEN GUINEY
Goose-Quill Papers

FLESH AND BLOOD

1

As his eyes moved about the apartment, shifting from one cluster of party guests to another, Frank realized what a good job Karen had done with the place. He'd been living with her for well over a year now, but it seemed that he'd only just noticed the way everything fit together, the brocade sofa and softly muted oriental carpet, the thick burgundy drapes and polished antique furniture. He assumed that everything around him had some sort of name or was from some particular place. Maybe the buffet table at the end of the room was Chippendale. Maybe the carpet at his feet had been handwoven in some remote, but oddly prestigious, village of the Middle East. Karen would know the name, know the place. He sometimes thought that she'd been born with such distinctions already in her mind, a refinement that was beyond him, and which he could never reach because he'd come out of a dusty rural world of hardscrabble Southern farms and hand-me-down clothes. He remembered rough hands and coarse speech, hard biscuits and redeye gravy. The taste and feel of his past never seemed to leave him, and none of the glitter of Karen's high-rise Manhattan world could ever change it.

"Well, I understand that you and Karen are quite an item these days," someone said.

Frank glanced up from his seat and saw a large man in a dark blue velvet coat. His long, slender fingers were wrapped so delicately around the crystal stem of his champagne glass that for an instant Frank felt like taking it from him before it slipped from his grasp.

The man sat down beside Frank and offered his hand. "I'm Zachary Chapman," he said, "an old friend of Karen's."

Frank nodded politely. "Nice to know you."

"I've been in Europe for the past two years," Chapman said, "so this is the first time I've seen Karen in quite some time." He shook his head sadly. "I wrote to her when Angelica was killed, but I wasn't able to come to Atlanta for the funeral."

Frank said nothing.

He looked at Frank intently. "No one knows how Karen survived it."

For an instant, Frank remembered the first time he'd seen Angelica's body sprawled in the little weedy field where Toffler had dropped her. He could still remember the heat of that long Atlanta summer, thick, stifling, the kind that grew around you like a choking vine.

"Angelica was such a beautiful girl," Chapman added. "I met her when she was only nine, but even then, she was very beautiful."

Angelica's face swam into Frank's mind, her eyes staring up at him from the littered ground where they had found her body, her hair splayed out around her head like a fan of spun gold.

"But then, I hear," Chapman said, "her beauty was part of what killed her."

"Yes," Frank told him. All around him the other people were laughing quietly, and for a moment he felt his own mind as something entirely out of place among them, alien and detached, like something floating in their midst, yet utterly withdrawn. Within a few feet, perhaps thirty people chatted politely while they ate and drank leisurely in the spacious living room. He could hear their voices quite plainly, and yet they seemed vague, bodiless, and as he let his eyes wander from one face to the next, each seemed to blend featurelessly into the other, become a soft white haze.

"And you're the man who caught her killer," Chapman said brightly.

"It was my job," Frank said crisply.

"Did he die?" Chapman asked.

For a moment, Frank thought he meant Caleb, his partner, and he saw Toffler's hand grab for the chisel and plunge it into Caleb's back, saw Caleb tumble forward as Toffler clung to him, the chisel rising and falling again and again in the steamy air. Then he realized that Chapman was asking about Toffler, had Toffler died.

"No," he said.

Chapman looked surprised. "Why not?" he asked. "The South being what it is." He smiled. "I mean, that area's not exactly known for being lenient in such things."

"Toffler was insane," Frank said dully. "At least that's what the jury thought." Across the room, and through the milling, well-dressed crowd, he could see Karen making the rounds, talking to each guest in turn, the perfect hostess. She seemed happy, unexpectedly happy, and he wondered why he found her happiness so disquieting, something he had not bargained for when he'd fallen in love with her that summer, then followed her to New York. Now her happiness made him restless and uneasy, and he yearned to return to someplace where the cliffs were higher and more dangerous, where the fall was quick and clean.

"Is that what you think?" Chapman asked.

Frank turned toward him. "Pretty much," he said. He could see Toffler quite clearly in his mind, a blond young man with piercing blue eyes who sat beside his lawyer, staring toward the witness stand while Frank meticulously described what he had done to Karen's sister, how he had injected her with lye until she'd finally died, and then dropped her body in a vacant lot and thrown a fistful of dirt into her beautiful dead face.

"Any chance of him getting out?"

Frank shook his head wearily. "Not much," he said, turning his eyes back to Karen. She was wearing a long dress of dark red silk. It was sleeveless and deep cut, and it made the most of her smooth white skin. Still, he preferred the way she'd looked the first day he'd met her, the faded jeans and spattered artist's smock which now seemed like little more than relics from the past.

"But it could happen, couldn't it?"

"There's always a chance," Frank said, without looking at him. Karen drew the glass from her lips and laughed lightly at something the man in front of her had said. His name was Lancaster, and Karen thought a lot of his work. She hung it in the gallery she'd bought on Madison Avenue, and sold it for what she told everyone were steadily increasing sums.

"I guess that's a policeman's nightmare, isn't it?" Chapman said.

Frank looked at him. "What?"

"That someone like Angelica's murderer would get out."

"Yes."

"And come after you, I mean."

"That, too."

Chapman's eyes narrowed. "And what would you do if that happened?"

"I'd kill him," Frank said. He could sense a peak rise beneath him, lift him up toward what he needed, a raw and dangerous edge. "I'd kill him," he repeated. "Without a second thought."

Chapman laughed, but a little nervously. "I don't expect that an attitude like that would get you very far among New York's finest," he said hesitantly.

"I'm not a cop anymore," Frank said. In his mind he saw the shabby little basement office he'd rented on West 49th Street. There was a gray metal desk and a few chairs he'd picked up at the Salvation Army store only a few blocks away. There was a sofa, a telephone and an answering machine. It was all bargain basement, except for a single beautiful brass lamp, a gift from Karen, which gleamed brightly in the grayish air and made everything around it appear just a little more dreary.

"Really? What is it that you do, then?"

"Private work."

"A private eye?"

"Yes."

"Well, that must be exciting," Chapman said enthusiastically. "I don't believe I've ever met a real flesh-and-blood private eye."

"Well, it's not all that interesting," Frank said with a dull smile. He'd tried to sign on with the New York Police Department, but after what he'd done to Toffler, beating him almost to death in his spattered little artist's studio, he'd been officially marked VP, violence prone, the kiss of death as far as getting another job was concerned. So he'd finally gone through the paper chase of getting a private investigator's license, spent his last dollar on the office, and set up shop. Not much had come in until Karen started talking him up among the smart set. After that, he'd had reasonably steady work.

"So you like the work?" Chapman asked casually.

"It'll do," Frank said quietly as his mind did a quick run through his cases. He'd been hired by a fancy jewelry store to catch a thieving clerk, by a wealthy Park Avenue doctor to find some dirt on a man who was suing him for malpractice, and by a matron on Central Park West whose dog had disappeared on the Sheep Meadow and which she suspected had been kidnapped by her malicious son. "It's not what I'm used to," he added, "but it'll do for now."

Chapman looked as if he were about to start another round of questioning when a tall, slender woman sat down beside him.

"Good to see you again, Zack," she said. "Are you back in New York for good?"

The two of them began to chat amiably together, and Frank took the opportunity to let his eyes drift about the room again. The walls were a light pink with white trim, and Karen had decked them with paintings she'd collected over the last year. Her taste had softened a great deal since she'd moved to New York, the old somberness giving way to light pastels. Frank had watched it happen painting by painting, and it was as if Karen had decided to dull the edges of her life, to surround herself with steadily more passive colors, the sort that fought against the darker vision that he thought must still prowl about inside her head. It was her right, of course, given all that had happened to her, but something in it gnawed at him nevertheless, and he often found himself turning away from the gay street scenes and unobtrusive bowls of fruit that now watched him from every wall and made him feel faintly rancid in their midst.

"This is Frank Clemons," Frank heard Chapman say suddenly.

He turned toward the woman and nodded.

"I'm Imalia Covallo," the woman said.

"Glad to meet you," Frank said.

"Frank's a private eye," Chapman announced.

Imalia looked at him wonderingly. "Really?"

Frank nodded dully.

The woman smiled quietly. "Well, if I ever need any detective work—"

"I'm in the book," Frank said coolly.

For a time the three of them continued to talk together. Then Chapman and Imalia drifted away. Others came in their place, joining Frank for a little while on the sofa, then moving off into the crowd. He knew some of them, and some of them he didn't, but as the hours passed, he found that it didn't matter either way. Toward midnight he wandered into the back bedroom and stretched out on the bed, fully clothed, his long legs dangling over the shining brass rail. He thought of Karen, still out with her guests, and then of Sheila, the ex-wife he'd left in the South, then of that unfathomable female presence which seemed to follow him everywhere, a distant, ghostly figure which the slightest touch dissolved.

He was in the twilight of half-sleep when Karen finally came into the room. She sat down on the bed beside him and shook his shoulders softly.

"That was less than polite, you know," she said.

He rubbed his eyes with his fists. "What was?"

"Coming in here while we still had guests."

"I'm sorry," Frank said. "I was tired, that's all."

"Was it the quality that bothered you?"

"The quality of what?"

"The guests."

"No," Frank told her. "They are fine. Your friend Chapman— he seemed like a very nice man."

Karen looked somewhat relieved. She leaned toward him, touching first his shoulder, then his neck. "Why don't you get undressed," she said tenderly. She smiled. "I will, too."

He sat up slowly. "I thought I might go out."

"It's three in the morning, Frank," Karen said, almost pleading.

He looked at her gently. "You know how it is."

"No, I don't, Frank," Karen said. "I've never known."

He stood up silently. "I won't be gone long."

Karen shrugged helplessly. "All right," she said. Then she

quickly got to her feet, walked to the bathroom and firmly closed the door.

Behind the door, he could hear the water running for her shower. She always took showers after a party, as if the champagne and pâté had somehow gotten under her nails or into her hair. For a while, he stood in the darkness and listened hazily to the falling water until at last it stopped. Then he knew that she'd be coming out soon, that she'd have the same questioning look in her eyes. He wished that he had an answer for her, something that would explain why, in the end, he always seemed to drift away. But there was nothing to say, nothing at all, and so when he heard the door of the bathroom open, he quickly threw on his coat and rushed away.

Park Avenue was almost entirely deserted, and as he headed downtown, he could feel the deep winter chill in the wind that swept down it. The isolated streets looked eerily blue and deserted in the early morning hours, as if, at some time during the night, a terrible alarm had sounded and everyone had fled across the bridges, filling the outer boroughs as they emptied midtown. It was the sort of solitude he wanted, but only for a little while. And so, after a time, he turned west and headed into that part of the city where the streets came alive again, and stayed alive, no matter what the hour. The ghostly blue gave way to garish blasts of neon light, and a steady flow of traffic moved up and down the major avenues. Along Eighth Avenue, the whores leaned in tavern doors, their faces lit by the marquees of the porno theaters. While they worked the sidewalks, their pimps ran poker games or sold crack in the cheap hotels which lined the adjoining streets. It was only a fifteen-minute walk from the luxury condos of Park Avenue, but it was another world, teeming, immediate, a place where people still put something vital on the line. Over the last year it had become the only part of the city in which he felt at home, and there were times when he drank alone in the dank, smelly bars, or stood in the dark corners of the slum hotels, or walked slowly through the gray, spectral streets, and felt such a sudden, surging love for the people who surrounded him that he wanted to gather them all into his arms and lift them up into that peculiar light their own dark lives deserved.

2

"I didn't hear you come back last night," Karen said as she turned toward him. Her hair shimmered in the light that streamed in from the large bay windows at the front of the room.

"I didn't want to wake you," Frank said. He sat up and rubbed his eyes wearily.

"How long were you out?"

"Almost dawn."

She ran her fingers up his bare arm. "Why don't you stay home today? I could have Felix handle the gallery. We could go to the park, or to a movie, anything."

He shook his head. "No."

She looked at him worriedly. "Frank, I'm beginning to get a little concerned about—"

He stood up quickly, silencing her, and walked to the window. He could see a large blank canvas reflected in it, and a little stool and an artist's palette. They had all been resting together unmoved for several months, the colors unmixed, the canvas smooth and white.

"Why don't you stay home," he said cautiously, knowing that she did not want to be reminded of it. "You haven't painted anything in a long time."

Karen's body stiffened visibly. "I'm not in the mood," she

said, a little sharply. "I'll know when I'm ready. You don't have to keep pushing me."

Frank drew back the glass door that led to the terrace and felt a cool winter breeze sweep across his body. In Atlanta, she had painted in a dark, windowless room, and he could see it very well in his mind, spattered walls and stacked canvases, an old desk covered with sketches, a rickety wooden easel. It was a place where something happened, and in its willful disarray it had given off something he admired, a deep and unimpeachable commitment.

"Well," Karen said as she got out of bed, "if you don't want to stay home today, I'll go to the gallery." She walked stiffly into the bathroom and closed the door.

Once again he heard the shower. Once again, he imagined the water as it flowed over her. There had been a time when the sound of it had lifted him toward a strange and furious ardor. But now, he could only think of the bare canvas, the unmixed paints, and the listless life they represented, the fact that she no longer put her hands to anything that mattered. He could feel a kind of dull anger building in him at the thought of such privilege, and to choke it off, he simply did what he had always done.

"I'm going to work," he said.

An old woman was sleeping soundly at the bottom of the stairs when Frank got to his office. She was wrapped in a thick tangle of old clothes, worn one layer on top of another, her body serving as the only closet she had. He had found her in the same place for the last few mornings, and he'd gotten used to stepping quietly over her and then moving down the narrow brick corridor to the door of his office. By nine in the morning, when he officially opened for business, she had already gathered her few belongings in her arms and crept silently up the cement stairs. A few days before, he had stood at the small window and watched her leave. For a few minutes, she had picked at her clothing, meticulously preening herself for the new day, and as he'd watched her, Frank had wondered at the kind of appalling personal history which had finally landed her on the streets. Whose daughter was she? Whose mother? Whose sister? What web of binding ties must have been severed for her to end up so alone?

A wave of warm, musty air swept out into the corridor when Frank opened the door of his office. It was pungent and faintly sweet, as if, during the night, a strange jungle rot had eaten into everything. He held the door open to clear it out, then closed it against the outer cold.

His desk sat at the back of the room, gunmetal gray and solid as a monument. Several manila folders were scattered over it, and for a time he busied himself going through them. They were the files on cases he'd completed and for each of them he calculated the remainder of his fee, then typed up a letter asking for payment. The money usually came in full and without complaint a few days later, each check in its own monogrammed envelope. Sometimes there was even a polite little thank-you note on embossed stationery. During all the time he'd been a homicide detective in Atlanta, he'd never received a formal thank-you note from anyone. But from time to time, he remembered now, after he'd finally tracked down and convicted the one who'd killed a mother or husband or child, after all the evidence had been presented and all the appeals exhausted, someone would walk slowly up to him in the corridor outside the courtroom and without a single word draw him into a grateful embrace. At such moments the world had seemed to open up, and he'd been able to know with an absolute certainty that he had done something good.

The phone rang as he was putting the last of the folders into the green metal filing cabinet behind his desk.

He picked it up immediately. "Frank Clemons," he said.

"Frank?"

"Hello, Sheila."

There was a moment of silence, and Frank could tell that she was trying to keep herself together.

"This is always the hardest time for me," she said finally.

"I know."

"You, too?"

"Yes."

"She would have been twenty yesterday, Frank."

"I know."

"I went out to her grave. I took some flowers."

They had buried her in a small cemetery outside Atlanta, his daughter, Sarah, who, at sixteen, had walked off into the woods along the Chattahoochee River late one summer afternoon and swallowed a fistful of sleeping pills.

"Twenty, Frank," Sheila repeated.

"Yes."

Sheila started to say something else, but broke it off.

Frank could hear her crying softly from a thousand miles away.

"Are you in Atlanta now?" he asked after a moment.

Sheila cleared her throat gently. "Yes. I just came over for a couple of days."

"Still living with your father?"

"No. I got a small apartment near the courthouse. I finished stenography school. I have a job."

"Good."

"I'm glad I left Atlanta. It was never right for me."

She'd moved back to their hometown in the Appalachian foothills of Alabama, and sometimes Frank imagined her still young and restless among their speckled granite cliffs and narrow twisting streams.

"I'm glad you moved back, Sheila," he said.

"I'm a country girl, I guess," Sheila said with a small, painful laugh. "I can't believe you live in New York City now."

Frank said nothing.

"Are you happy there?" Sheila asked tentatively.

"You know me, Sheila."

"I'll never get over it, Frank."

"No one ever does."

"But this week, it was worse than it's ever been."

Frank shook his head in the dense gray air of his office. "There's nothing to do about it."

"But go on living."

"Nothing else, Sheila," Frank told her. He didn't know what she wanted from him, only that she wasn't getting it. It seemed best not to string it out. "Well, say hello to your father for me," he said.

"He doesn't let me talk about you, Frank," Sheila said flatly. "He doesn't let me mention your name."

"I'm sorry to hear that."

"Well, you know how fathers are."

"Yes, I do."

There was a long pause. He could hear her breathing, almost feel her breath in his hair.

"I have to go now, Sheila," he said finally.

"All right," Sheila said, "I'm sorry. I just wanted to . . ."

"I know."

"It's the one thing we'll always have together, Frank."

"Yes," Frank said as he hung up, but he wondered what else could be said of two people who had nothing left in common but their grief.

The old woman was still curled up in her swirl of ragged clothes when Frank left his office a few minutes later. Her shoulders twitched painfully as he stepped over her and moved up onto the street.

It was nearly eight in the morning, and the construction site across the street was already spewing out a deafening noise. Huge cranes lifted tons of steel girders from the trucks that lined the street, their diesel engines roaring steadily over the normal din of traffic and street cries. Within two years it would be completed, and a huge luxury condominium would rise over the squat brick tenements which now surrounded it. It would tower over everything, transform dilapidated candy stores into chic boutiques, festoon the adjoining streets with fancy restaurants and gourmet bakeries, line the sidewalks with limousines from Ninth Avenue to Broadway. From their littered stoops, the people of the old neighborhood watched in dismay as the colossus approached them. In a little while they would all be gone, swept away like driftwood before a tidal wave.

The sidewalk along 49th Street was decked with battered metal cans and huge black garbage bags, and like everyone else, Frank had to walk down a narrow stretch of walkway to keep from wading into them. Some had already been cut open and rifled during the night by people looking for the beer and soda cans they could redeem at the local food stores for five cents apiece, and because of that, waves of soiled paper and rotten vegetables sometimes swept all the way to the gutter. Each

morning the street looked the same, and every time he walked
along it, Frank remembered the sedate, tree-lined neighbor-
hoods of Atlanta, remembered their gently swaying dogwoods,
and wondered why—compared to this—he could not stand them.

At the corner of Eighth Avenue and 49th Street, Frank stepped
into a small deli, took a table in the back and ordered a cup of
coffee. Across the street he could see the local liquor store, its
windows crowded with bottles, and he felt the old hunger again,
as he always did in the early morning. To keep it down, he
glanced to the left, trying to focus his attention on something
besides his need. Two men were sitting at a small table, one gray
and somewhat chubby, the other young and very thin.

"You think I don't know, Paulie?" the older man asked resentfully. "Huh? You think I don't know where it went?"

The young man said nothing. He had a long ponytail of light
brown hair and it swayed rhythmically across his back as he
shook his head.

"I'll tell you where the fuck it went," the older man cried.
"Up your fucking nose, that's where my goddamn money went."

The young man remained silent, his eyes averted, staring at
the small glass of tomato juice that rested on the table in front
of him.

"What happens to you is your business, Paulie," the old man
said. "But nobody takes me down with them, you understand?"

The young man nodded slowly, but did not look up.

The older man took a deep breath, as if to calm himself, and
when he spoke again, most of the anger had left his voice.

"Paulie," he said, almost pleading. "Paulie, you got to be so
fast to keep out of the shit, you can't believe it. You can't believe
it, Paulie. Christ, you stop a second, it fucking buries you."

A few minutes later, Frank walked back out onto the street.
The noise swept over him, hard, thundering, and for an instant
he thought of the dogwoods again, so white and pink in the
Atlanta spring. Nothing in his life had ever seemed more false.

For a while, he walked aimlessly along the avenue, glancing
into the shop windows or watching the people as they lounged
about or walked hurriedly by. He wanted to begin something,
but he did not know what, and it struck him that he had already
lived too long in a state of helpless waiting. He didn't know

what he'd been waiting for, but only that when it came, it would be wrapped in something else, that he wouldn't recognize it until, like a hand in the dark, it suddenly gripped him from behind.

It was after ten by the time he headed back down 49th Street toward his office. The garbage cans had been emptied by then, and the swollen black bags were gone. The old lady who slept at the foot of the stairs wasn't there anymore, either.

But Imalia Covallo was.

3

She was standing stiffly against the brick wall at the bottom of the stairs, and if it hadn't been for the pale white skin and luminous black eyes, Frank would not have recognized her. The sleek velvet dress of the night before had been replaced by a long denim skirt and matching jacket. Her hair was no longer pulled tightly along the sides of her head and gathered in a small bun at the back of her neck, but fell loosely across her shoulders. The pearl necklace was gone, along with the gold bracelets, and Frank could not help but notice that she looked better without them, less the figment of someone else's imagination.

"Good morning," she said quietly. "I took your advice, I looked you up in the book." She noticed the faintly puzzled look in his eyes. "My street clothes," she explained. Then she smiled tentatively. "You do remember me, don't you?"

"You were at the party last night," Frank said.

"That's right," she said. "Imalia Covallo."

Frank said nothing.

She looked at him with an odd, almost childlike, innocence, and despite the fact that she was over forty, he thought instantly of his daughter, Sarah, of that bewildered look she'd often had as she gazed silently out the front window.

"I suppose I look as if I'm in disguise," Imalia said, then looked at him so strangely that for a moment Frank suspected she was precisely that, a creature hid beneath another face.

"Well, not exactly in disguise," Imalia added quickly. She glanced toward the narrow corridor that led to his office. "This is where you work, isn't it?"

"Yes."

"Most people get to work at nine," she told him in a voice that was gently scolding, yet straining to be light, playful, to warm the air around them.

Frank said nothing.

"It's not exactly the high-rent district, is it?" she added. "For a moment I thought I must have gotten the address wrong. You know, with your living with Karen, I thought . . ." She stopped, as if against the wall of her own awkwardness. Her eyes darted downward quickly, then back up to him. "I didn't mean to suggest that . . ."

"Are you here on business?" Frank asked crisply.

"Well, as a matter of fact, I am," Imalia said, now suddenly very formal. "Last night, at Karen's, Zack mentioned that you were a private investigator."

"That's right."

"Well, I think that's what I need."

Frank stepped around her and headed toward his desk. "Okay," he said. "Come in."

The air inside the office was still faintly musty, and Imalia sniffed at it uncomfortably as she closed the door behind her.

"Have you been here long?" she asked after a moment.

"A few months."

"And before that, you were a policeman?"

"Yes."

She glanced silently about the room, and from the look in her eyes, Frank couldn't tell whether she approved or not, but only that some final judgment was being made.

After a moment, she looked back at him. "It looks like a place where a secret would be safe," she said.

Frank sat down behind his desk and lit a cigarette. "What can I do for you, Miss Covallo?" he asked.

Imalia slipped into the rickety wooden chair which rested a

few feet from Frank's desk. "I don't exactly know where to begin," she said. "It was such a shock." She nodded toward the half-empty pack of cigarettes on Frank's desk. "May I have one?" she asked.

Frank slid the pack over to her.

Imalia lit the cigarette, then sat back slightly in her seat. "Obviously, I've never dealt with anything like this before."

"What is it, exactly?" Frank asked immediately.

Once again, Imalia seemed to hesitate slightly, as if she could not get to the words she needed.

"Well," she said finally, "I suppose you could say that it's about murder." Suddenly, a high, trembling laugh broke from her. "Sorry, sorry," she said quickly as she broke it off. "It's an odd problem I have, nervous laughter." She shook her head angrily. "I hate it. It makes me look like a hysteric."

Frank leaned toward her slightly. "Who was murdered, Miss Covallo?"

"A woman," Imalia told him. "A woman named Karlsberg, Hannah Karlsberg."

"A relative?"

"No. An employee."

Frank took out a small green notebook, flipped to the first page and wrote Hannah Karlsberg's name at the top. "When did this happen?"

"Two weeks ago."

"Where?"

"Here in New York," Imalia said. "Seventy-sixth Street. You may have read about it. It was in the *Post*, but I don't think it made the *Times*."

"What was the address?"

"Three fifty-seven Central Park West."

"Do you know the time?"

"Early in the morning," Imalia said. "That's all I can tell you."

"And you said she was an employee of yours," Frank said.

"Yes."

"What do you do?" Frank asked.

Imalia smiled quietly. "You don't know?"

Frank shook his head.

"I'm a designer," Imalia explained. "I don't want to sound arrogant, but, the truth is, I'm very well known. . . ."

"What do you design?"

"Clothes. Very fine clothes."

Frank wrote it down. "And what did Miss Karlsberg do for you?"

"She worked for me in several different ways," Imalia said. "She'd been doing it for many years." She took a long draw on the cigarette, then blew a thin column of smoke into the air. "Many years," she repeated, her eyes darting to the left. "There's no calendar on your wall. Don't you need a calendar?"

"How many years?" Frank asked.

Imalia hestitated slightly. "Does that matter?"

"I like to know as much as I can," Frank explained.

Suddenly Imalia looked reassured. "Yes, of course. I'm sorry." She took another long draw on the cigarette. "Hannah was a very valuable employee. She had worked for me for over twenty years."

"As what?"

"First as a seamstress, then, later, as a floor manager. For the last ten years she'd been my most important assistant."

Frank wrote it down quickly, then looked back up at Imalia. "This next question may seem a little strange, but it's important."

Imalia stiffened slightly, as if bracing herself against it.

"Is there any doubt that it was a homicide?" Frank asked. "I mean, could she have killed herself, something like that?"

"Hannah was slashed to death, Mr. Clemons," Imalia said darkly. "She didn't do that to herself."

Suddenly, Frank felt his fingers squeezing more tightly around the pen, felt its point bearing down more firmly on the page as his energy began to flow through it, building steadily with each passing second, the way it always did when suddenly, from out of nowhere, something mattered.

"Then the police have been looking into it," Frank said.

"Yes."

"Have they talked to you?"

"Yes, several times."

"About what?"

"Just if I knew anything about Hannah," Imalia said. "Which

I really didn't. She kept to herself. That's just the way she was."

"Do you have any idea about what the police think?"

"None whatsoever," Imalia said. "I guess they're a little like Hannah. They keep things to themselves."

"But have they told you anything at all about their investigation?"

"Only that nothing was missing from Hannah's apartment."

"Did she have anything worth stealing?" Frank said. "Not everybody does."

"Well, she had jewelry," Imalia said. "And I don't mean the sort of junk you buy at Woolworth's. Her jewelry box was open, but nothing had been taken."

"How about a safe?"

"The police didn't mention it. I don't think she had one."

Frank took a map of New York City and spread it out across his desk. It was a police sector map, and it indicated that Hannah's address was in the Midtown North Precinct. "Do you know who's in charge of the case?" he asked.

"Quite a few policemen came marching through my office," Imalia said. "They have a way of all looking the same." She smiled. "It's those polyester jackets." Then the smile vanished, her face softened, and her voice took on a gentle, apologetic quality. "I don't mean to be snide, I really don't. It's just that Hannah was very loyal to me, and I want her to have a decent burial."

"Burial?"

"Yes."

"She's not been buried?" Frank asked unbelievingly.

"No," Imalia said. "And that's why I've come to you."

Frank looked at her, puzzled.

"The police won't release the body until a relative claims it," Imalia explained.

"Did Miss Karlsberg have any relatives?"

"I don't know," Imalia told him. "That's what I want you to find out." She shifted uneasily in her chair. "She mentioned a sister once. Maybe she had a sister. I don't know."

Frank wrote it down, then glanced back up at Imalia. "Do you have any idea why the police are trying to hold on to the body?"

"No."

"Have you asked them to release it?"

"Yes, of course. Right away."

"And what did they say?"

"That for now, they required a relative," Imalia said. "Otherwise, they won't release it."

"Who's in charge of the case?"

"A man named Tannenbaum, I think," Imalia said. "At least he's the one I've spoken to a few times." She looked suddenly puzzled. "They wanted to know if Hannah had any enemies at work, things like that. They wanted to know what she did at work, who she knew at work. That's what Mr. Tannenbaum was always asking about."

"Leo Tannenbaum?"

"That sounds right," Imalia said. "Do you know him?"

"We've had some contact," Frank told her without elaborating. It had been a missing-person case. Kidnapping was suspected. Maybe murder. Frank had talked to a few people in Midtown North, Tannenbaum among them. A few weeks later the missing person had turned up again with a trunk full of souvenirs he'd bought in Honolulu.

"Anyway, that's the name, I believe," Imalia said. "We spoke a few times. He seemed to be in charge of everything. The whole investigation, I mean."

"Sounds like he asked the usual questions."

Imalia shrugged. "I suppose so," she said. "But he kept looking at me like he hated me. Like he wanted to hurt me in some way."

"Why would he want that?"

"I don't know," Imalia said quietly. "I really don't." She took a quick puff on the cigarette. "I told him that Hannah worked for me, but that I didn't know her that well. What else could I say? It was the truth."

"And so you couldn't help them?"

"I don't think so," Imalia said. She shook her head. "I didn't know much about Hannah's personal life. She was an employee. I was her, well, her boss. You know what that is. You don't always have any other kind of relationship." She shrugged helplessly. "She'd worked for me for a long time. At this point, I only want her to have a decent burial. I think she deserves that."

She took a final drag on the cigarette, then snuffed it out in the small tin ashtray on Frank's desk. "This really isn't a personal thing," she added, as her eyes shot up to him. "She wasn't my surrogate mother or anything like that. She was a very valuable employee, and because of that, I don't want the police to keep her body locked up in the morgue."

"They may have their reasons, Miss Covallo," Frank told her.

Imalia stared at him icily. "If they have such compelling reasons, then why won't they tell me what they are?"

"I don't know," Frank admitted, "but I don't think they'd hold on to it for no reason at all."

"Perhaps," Imalia said, as if giving in to his professional judgment. "But I have no confidence in the police, Mr. Clemons . . . Frank." She looked at him closely. "May I call you Frank?"

He nodded.

Imalia smiled slightly. "As far as I know, they've made absolutely no progress in finding whoever it was who killed Hannah."

"You haven't given them much time."

"Two weeks," Imalia said with a sudden sharpness. "It's disrupting everything."

"Disrupting?"

"My life," Imalia said. "The people who work for me, do you think they like being questioned? This has been going on for two weeks. How much longer will it take to put Hannah to rest?"

"Miss Covallo, if a murder isn't solved in twenty-four hours, it may not be solved for years. It may never be solved."

"Are you saying that you don't want the job?" Imalia asked bluntly.

"No," Frank said. "But if you wait a few more days, you might save yourself some money."

"I don't care about your fee, Mr. Clemons," Imalia said softly. "I can afford it." She glanced away from him, as if in an effort to control herself. "I just want Hannah to have a decent burial. That's all I want."

Frank closed the notebook. "All right," he said. "I'll do what I can."

Imalia turned back toward him, and for a moment, an odd, pleading quality came into her face. Then, in an instant, she swept it out again and stared at him stiffly, her head lifted slightly in an attitude of hard command. "I hope you can help me. Please try."

"I can only let you know what I find out," Frank replied firmly. "I can't do more than that."

"Money is no object."

"That may be true," Frank said, "but if you start spreading too much of it around, you'll start buying lies."

Imalia did not seem convinced. "I just want you to know that whatever it costs, I'll pay it," she said. Then she stood up and walked to the door.

"I'll talk to Tannenbaum," Frank called to her. "I'll let you know what I find out."

"I'd like to be able to reach you, too," Imalia said. "When you're not here, I suppose I can reach you at Karen's?"

"Most of the time."

"Anywhere else?" Imalia asked. She smiled tentatively. "Some private haunt?"

"I go to a little after-hours drinking place sometimes," Frank told her reluctantly.

"Telephone number?" Imalia asked matter-of-factly.

"Not for this kind of place."

Imalia's eyes darted away from him shyly. "I guess I don't know much about places like that," she said, embarrassed.

"It's at the corner of Tenth Avenue and Fiftieth Street," Frank said. "Second floor. It's open from two until dawn."

"I'd only come in some sort of emergency," Imalia assured him. Then she allowed her eyes to wander over his office once again, her head turning slowly to the left so that her face was caught suddenly in the dusky light. "This place," she said, "it's like a cave, like a room in the underworld." Then she turned abruptly and walked away.

4

The large brick facade of the Midtown North precinct house sat
in the middle of the street, huge and unmoving, like a gigantic
red watchdog. Blue and white patrol cars lined the sidewalks
left and right, along with several police scooters and an array
of unmarked cars, usually dark blue or dark green, all of them
bearing a police code on their license plates which identified
them almost as clearly as their dusty, unwashed blackwall tires.

A long wooden desk stretched for nearly the entire width of
the front room, and several people stood at various points along
its length, some staring sourly at the bleak world which surrounded them, their hands cuffed behind their backs, their upper
arms grasped loosely by the cops who stood next to them. To
the right, a continuous stream of people moved in and out of
the building, cops, witnesses, complainants, women with black
eyes and broken arms, pimps and gamblers in bright-colored
jackets, chubby, middle-aged detectives who ponderously
mounted the stairs toward the separate units of Vice, Narcotics,
and Homicide.

To his right, Frank could see several wooden benches, and as
he stood waiting to get the desk sergeant's attention, he allowed
his eyes to move over the people who occupied them. A skinny
junkie nodded half-consciously at the far end of the bench, her

pale, washed-out face slumping more and more deeply forward until she finally caught herself and jerked backward abruptly. An old woman sat next to her, obliviously riffling through a suitcase at her feet. It was filled with a thick pile of sodden magazines, and the woman was carefully going through them, slowly peeling back one page at a time. Down the line a well-dressed man stared vacantly toward the opposite wall. The collar of his shirt was torn, as well as the left knee of his trousers, and he looked as if the street mugging he'd just suffered had irrevocably changed the way he saw the world, invested it with a capacity for unimaginably sudden danger.

"Hello, Clemons."

Frank turned toward the desk sergeant. His name was Calvino, and he ran the desk like a ringmaster, moving frantically from one knot of people to the next, answering the phone, screaming commands through the small brown speakers that hung here and there throughout the building.

"Is Tannenbaum in?" Frank asked.

"Yeah, upstairs."

"He still working the Hannah Karlsberg case?"

"Far as I know," Calvino said. His eyes scanned the scarred double doors of the precinct. Three men had just slammed through them, followed closely by three times as many cops.

"Shit," Calvino hissed. "It's a paper storm today." His eyes shot over to Frank. "Upstairs," he said hastily. "Tannenbaum's up there somewhere."

Frank made his way up the creaking wooden staircase which led to the second floor. The railing had been smoothed down by the thousands of hands that had grasped it, and the steps sloped downward at the center. A steady stream of people had moved up and down this single staircase, and as he made his way toward the top, Frank could feel an odd kinship with all of them, not only the weary cops who had tramped up to their desks, but the people they'd pushed ahead of them or pulled up from behind, murderers and arsonists, drunks and thieves, that sea of felons whose murky depths, it seemed to him, knew no restraining tide, but whose disordered lives struck him as deeply interwoven with his own, part of some thin, tenuous connection which still drew him to the world.

Tannenbaum was sitting at his desk in the Homicide bullpen, a *Daily News* spread out before him. He wore an expensive jacket and shiny leather shoes, and because of them, Frank assumed that the Internal Affairs Division had been over his books more than once, found nothing, and so now assumed that he was simply one of those people who preferred a suit from Paul Stuart and shoes from Botticelli to a week in the Bahamas or a narrow little house on Staten Island.

"Hello, Leo," Frank said as he stepped up to the desk.

Tannenbaum glanced up from his paper, then back down at it. "Did you read this, Frank? Last night in Queens, two cops shot each other. Lovers, can you believe it? Both of them married. God knows how many kids between them." He looked at Frank. "It's the sort of thing that makes my heart soar. What about you?"

Frank drew a chair over to Tannenbaum's desk and sat down. "A couple of weeks ago a woman was killed up on Seventy-sixth Street." he said. "Her name was Hannah Karlsberg."

"That's right."

"You still working that case?"

"Well, it's way too early to close it, Frank."

"Are you in charge of it?"

"More or less," Tannenbaum said. "Why?"

"I've been asked to look into it," Frank told him.

"Really?" Tannenbaum said. "Who asked you to do that?"

"A paying customer," Frank said.

Tannenbaum laughed. "Come on, Frank, this isn't television. Cops and PIs work together, you know that." He smiled thinly. "Let's face it, you can't do much without us. At least not when we're talking about murder." He winked playfully. "But, hey, give the devil his due, you know. I mean, when it comes to catching some politico in his girlfriend's undies, you guys have it all over us."

Frank said nothing, and so Tannenbaum continued, happily shooting one finger after another into the air as he ticked off the singular disadvantages of a private investigator who chooses not to share his information with the police. "I love reminding you guys that you don't have a crime lab. You don't have a fingerprint file. You can't do ballistics, run hair and fiber samples, or put so much as a fingernail clipping under the infrared. I hate to tell you, but you can't swab a vagina for semen or trace the blood type of the freak who put it there. You can't do soil chemistry, Frank, or footprint molds, or work up a composite of the human face." He leaned forward. "Am I making my point?"

Frank stared at him expressionlessly.

"You can't do autopsies, work up psychological profiles or look into anybody's past by way of our computers," Tannenbaum continued authoritatively. Then he stared evenly into Frank's eyes. "So what it all adds up to is this: when it comes to a murder case, you need me a hell of a lot more than I need you."

"Covallo," Frank said. "Imalia Covallo."

"She's your client?"

"Yes."

Tannenbaum smiled. "That's what I figured." He leaned back in his chair. "And so she figures you can collar the guy who killed Miss Karlsberg."

"She only wants you to release the body," Frank told him, "so the woman can have a decent burial."

"Anything else?"

"No."

"She's not interested in who killed her?"

"She's leaving that to you."

Tannenbaum nodded. "Well, it's understandable, her concern. About burying her friend, I mean. I don't like keeping bodies in the cooler, myself. What else did she have to say?"

"Just what the police told her."

"Which was?"

"That you didn't want to release the body," Frank said. "And that you didn't have to unless a relative demanded it."

"That's the law, Frank," Tannenbaum said. "Did she say anything else?"

"That Karlsberg was a loyal employee."

"And she wants you to find a relative, right?"

"Yes."

Tannenbaum shrugged. "Okay," he said. "Maybe I can help you." He took a manila folder from the top drawer of his desk and shoved it into his jacket pocket. "Come on, let's go for a walk," he said as he stood up briskly. "I could use a street-dog."

Once outside the precinct house, Tannenbaum turned up toward Ninth Avenue, then headed north, toward Central Park.

"Precinct atmosphere's beginning to get on my nerves, Frank," he explained. "Did that ever happen to you?"

"All the time."

"I can take the streets, but the cophouse is a sewer," Tannenbaum added. "Was it like that in Atlanta?"

"It's always like that, if you have a taste for working alone."

Tannenbaum took a deep, relaxing breath. "When are you going to get rid of that hillbilly accent? I figured that'd be history by now."

"Things cling," Frank said.

"You should hear my brother-in-law," Tannenbaum said. "Sounds just like a goddamn redneck." He laughed. "He tells me you guys have a liquor down there named Rebel Yell. Is that true?"

"Yeah."

"Can you get it up here?"

"Never tried."

Tannenbaum looked at him seriously. "What, you don't get sentimental about the old home place?"

Frank said nothing, and the two of them walked silently to Columbus Circle. Tannenbaum bought a frank from a street vendor, then strolled over to one of the benches at the edge of the park and sat down. He lifted the hot dog slightly before taking the first bite.

"I'd miss these," he said.

Frank leaned back on the bench beside him. A young woman walked by quickly, then darted into the street. She reminded him of Karen's sister, and for a moment he wanted to run after her, warn her, say the one thing he'd always wanted to say to his own daughter: *Be whatever you like, but do not be a victim.*

Tannenbaum took a sip from a can of soda, then carefully wiped the corners of his mouth with a napkin.

"I hear you live with a pretty classy woman," he said.

Frank continued to watch the young woman as she threaded her way through the thickening traffic.

"Does she know Covallo?" Tannenbaum asked.

"Yes."

"So this business between you and Covallo, it's strictly professional?"

"Yes, it is," Frank said coolly.

"Hey, I got to ask, Frank," Tannenbaum said, almost apologetically. "If you're going to be in on this case, I don't want any secrets between us."

"She came to me this morning," Frank said. "She was at a party at Karen's last night. I'd never seen her before. Does that satisfy you?"

"No problem, Frank, believe me," Tannenbaum said. He took another bite of the hot dog and chewed it rapidly, his eyes darting right and left as he watched the street. "Nothing personal," he added after he'd finished. "It's just that I can't let anybody burn my case. You were a cop, you know what I mean." He took the manila folder from his pocket and offered it to Frank. "Here. Check this out. It'll get you started."

"What is it?"

"Lab report," Tannenbaum said. "The basic stuff."

"I'm not working the case, Leo," Frank reminded him. "I'm just trying to get the body released."

Tannenbaum continued to press the folder toward him. "Take it. When you've read it, you'll know why we're holding on to the corpse."

Frank tucked the report under his arm. "Where's the body?"

"Still in the cooler," Tannenbaum said. "The problem is, we got a few wrinkles."

"What kind?"

"It's all in the report," Tannenbaum said. "As far as the body, we'll probably hold on to it for as long as we can." He shrugged. "Unless you come up with some long-lost cousin."

"What about children?" Frank asked immediately.

"No heir apparent of any kind," Tannenbaum said. "Not even your friend Covallo could come up with a bloodline that was still pumping."

Frank glanced at the flat manila envelope then back up at Tannenbaum. "What about pictures?" he asked. "In her apartment? People?"

Tannenbaum shook his head. "There were a few hanging on

the wall. One with Imalia Covallo. It was taken midtown somewhere. And there were a few of Karlsberg herself, mostly travel
stuff."

"With anybody?"

"Alone. Probably got a local yokel to snap them for her."

"How about phone numbers?"

"She had a few in a little book," Tannenbaum said. "We
called them all. Business associates of one kind or another. Your
client was in it, and a few other people like her."

Frank looked at him questioningly. "What do you mean, people like her?"

"People in the rag trade," Tannenbaum explained. He looked
at Frank evenly. "You know anything about the rag trade, Frank?"

The tenements of Cabbage Town swam into his mind, that
small dilapidated village of clapboard flats that had bordered
his old neighborhood in Atlanta, a world of sweat and dust and
cheap beer that had squatted in the dark shadows of the adjoining textile factories for over a hundred years. He had sometimes glanced toward it as he sped by, seen the half-naked children
playing in the weedy fields, or the old people swaying idly in
their rotting swings, but he had never turned down one of its
narrow, broken streets or hesitated for even the briefest moment
as his car continued on.

"Not much," he admitted.

"Well, Hannah Karlsberg worked in it all her life," Tannenbaum said. An edge of bitterness swept into his voice. "It's a
real intense business atmosphere, Frank," he added coolly. "Very
competitive. Cutthroat, you might say."

"Where does that lead, Leo?"

"Well, it adds an extra dimension," Tannenbaum said. "We
could look into the woman's personal life, maybe come up with
something kinky, somebody who gets rich on double indemnity,
something like that."

"Have you found anything like that?"

"Not yet, and we assume it's a dead end. If there was something funny on that score, you can be sure the insurance people
would have been nice enough to give a call and supply a neat
little motive." He smiled knowingly. "They're very cooperative
when it comes to things like that."

Frank nodded. "Anything else?"

"The professional angle," Tannenbaum added. "A business beef of some kind, maybe a disgruntled employee. According to Covallo, Hannah had chewed out a few people in her day."

"Do you have anything really solid on that score?" Frank asked.

Tannenbaum smiled. "Why are you asking, Frank?"

Frank said nothing.

"We don't have anything solid at all," Tannenbaum told him. "We know she wasn't robbed." He shrugged. "If you want to know the truth, it looks like a lone psycho right now." He nodded toward the report. "Read that, you'll understand." He finished the hot dog in one final bite, then washed it down with the soda. "Got to get back to the cophouse," he said as he stood up. He looked down at Frank and smiled. "You PIs live the life of Riley, if you ask me. No schedules, no snotty little superiors, practically no paper work." He shook his head slowly. "The life of Riley. I mean it."

"What about her apartment?" Frank said. "Can I get in there?"

"Why not?" Tannenbaum said. "We've been over it from top to bottom." He shrugged casually. "It's not a pretty sight," he added, "but you've been there before, right?"

"Yes."

"You'll need an escort," Tannenbaum added. "Will I do?"

Frank nodded. "When?"

"I can fit it in this afternoon," Tannenbaum told him. "Around three okay with you?"

"Yeah."

Tannenbaum touched his finger to his hat, then turned to walk away.

"Miss Covallo," Frank said quickly. "She says you don't like her much."

Tannenbaum turned toward him instantly, his eyes slowly darkening. "Is that right?"

"That's what she said."

"I don't know a thing about Covallo, Frank," Tannenbaum said. "But I know about the rag trade. I know plenty about that." His face suddenly took on a slowly boiling resentment. "My mother worked her fucking heart out in one of those goddamn sweatshops they used to have down on the Lower East

Side. You know what she got out of it? Nothing. They used her for a while, then they flushed her down the toilet." He shook his head. "Sometimes, between you and me, I hope there is a God. A real God, mad as hell. You know why? So you can say to a guy, 'Don't do this. Don't do this, you fuck. Because if you do, you'll rot in hell.' "

He turned quickly, as if to hide his face, and as he walked away, his long black overcoat flapped wildly in the cold, hissing wind.

5

It was only a few blocks back to the office on 49th Street, but Frank walked it slowly, taking his time. The cold winter air was refreshing, and it reminded him of his first weeks in the city. It had been a happy time, those first days when he'd spent his time discovering New York with Karen as his guide. He could recall long, lingering afternoons in the park or strolling through the galleries on Madison Avenue or down in Soho. Karen had never seemed closer to him, and this closeness had appeared to lend both their lives a strange, somber happiness.

But although, as the days passed, the dark memory of her sister's murder had slowly disappeared from Karen's mind, it had clung tenaciously to Frank's, and there were nights when it all came back to him with a sudden, irreducible fury, and he saw Angelica's body sprawled across the weedy lot, her hair spread out around her head, a clump of dirt lodged beneath her tongue. Then, in an instant, Caleb was dying in his arms, and an instant later Toffler was beneath him and he was plunging his fists downward again and again until Toffler's cold blue eyes had been transformed into small bloody pools. He had felt a terrible joy at that moment, and the memory of it disturbed him now as much as it had in the days following Toffler's arrest. To escape it, he let his eyes drift up toward the towering buildings and the vast, unpopulated blue which hung above them. Slowly, as he walked southward down Ninth Avenue, the immense brick high-rises gave way to the ancient tenements of Hell's Kitchen until, at 50th Street, an entire city block had been torn down, and looking across the shaved ground of the construction site, Frank could see the little iron gate that led down to his office.

Two young men in denim jackets were leaning next to it, their short-cropped blond hair all but gleaming in the light. They eyed Frank suspiciously as he moved toward them from the corner of 49th Street. One of them tucked his hand beneath his jacket, and in his mind Frank could see its stubby, pale fingers wrapped around the grip of a .38. They could be anything, and as he continued to walk toward them, he tried to find some small detail that would clear things up. In the heart of Hell's Kitchen, they could be a couple of undercover cops working out of Midtown North, or they could be two mean-tempered Westies, members of a local gang of mostly Irish thugs. Frank hoped they were cops, but as he came steadily nearer and stared into their eyes, he thought Westies a better guess. They had the look of men who would, according to the word on the street, smoke absolutely anybody for two thousand a pop, and as he came up to the iron gate, he felt his own hand tense suddenly and crawl upward toward the .45 he kept tucked at his back.

He was almost on top of them before he stopped, his eyes locked on the hand beneath the jacket. He could feel his heart leap forward as the hand jerked out suddenly. It was empty, and in its emptiness it struck him as naively vulnerable.

"Got to get through," Frank said quietly as he nodded toward the gate.

"Oh, sure," one of the boys said. "Sorry."

"No problem."

The two young men moved quickly to either side of the gate.

"Excuse me," one of them said.

"No problem," Frank repeated, this time with a quick smile.

He passed between them and headed down the stairs and then into the narrow corridor which led to his office. Something deep within him was disappointed, and he realized with a sud-

den astonishing sorrow that some lost and aching part of him—
the same part, he thought now, that must have finally triumphed
over everything else in his daughter—had wanted the pistol to
jerk out from behind the flap of denim and fire and fire until
he couldn't hear it anymore.

Once behind his desk, Frank turned on the antique lamp and
spread the lab report Tannenbaum had given him beneath it.
It was written on the sort of unadorned police form that he'd
seen a thousand times before, and, as always, it gave a concise
account of what the autopsy had revealed. Fact by isolated fact,
the last few hours of Hannah Karlsberg's life began to emerge,
however ponderously, from the flat scientific language.

She had begun the day as a "well-developed Caucasian female" of approximately seventy years of age.

Although she had been suffering from no deadly illness, she'd
had a "slightly enlarged liver," and her lungs had shown "marked
signs of deterioration, particularly alveolar inflexibility, con-
sistent with a diagnosis of advanced emphysema."

At the moment of her death, her heart had weighed four grams,
her brain seven.

She had eaten a late dinner which included chicken and as-
paragus tips. Toward midnight, she'd had a cup of tea.

She'd had no alcohol, no drugs. She'd taken no medicines in
the past twenty-four hours.

At around two in the morning, someone had attacked her.

She'd fought him off with her bare hands, and because of
that, they were now marked with "slits and cuts indicative of
defensive wounds."

She had not succeeded in defending herself. She had died at
approximately two o'clock in the morning.

Her body had remained undiscovered for around twelve hours,
long enough for rigor mortis to come and go. Once dead, her
body had not been moved, but had simply remained, face down,
so that her blood could follow gravity downward through a
dense maze of steadily collapsing tissue and into the inevitable
state of "fixed frontal lividity," which it had reached by the
time the medical examiner first observed it.

She had not been raped, either before or after death.

But something had been done to her which seemed no less perverse, and as soon as he read it in the flat language of the report, Frank realized why Hannah Karlsberg had not yet been buried. "Right hand severed at the wrist."

Someone had cut off her right hand and taken it with him.

Those were the facts, but they seemed fleshless to Frank, as they always did, and so he sat back for a moment and tried to imagine their human face. In his mind he could see Hannah as she ate her dinner, see her grow weary as the night wore on, see her go to bed, then rise suddenly at a sound, lift herself up, startled, and walk into the living room. A few seconds later, perhaps in total darkness or in the light she'd turned on suddenly to see her way, the blade had swept down upon her.

But what had happened during the next few appalling seconds was always the part that remained essentially unimaginable. The room must have filled with the sound of her body as it spun about in the throes of its defense. A chair must have tumbled over, a lamp must have crashed onto the floor as the air filled with the pink spray of her blood. There must have been a cry of some kind, either a wrenching, unbelieving scream, or simply a low, helpless groan. Somewhere in the building, beside, beneath, above her, another human being must have heard some part of this, questioned it for a single sleep-numbed instant, then dismissed its darker possibilities as grimly unthinkable and turned back to the pillow, the late show, or the book. Whatever small hope still remained for Hannah Karlsberg had died at that moment, and a few terrible seconds later, she had died as well.

Only the pictures were left, and Tannenbaum had included them in a separate envelope. They showed nothing but the aftermath of what had happened, and each time Frank went through the slender stack of such photographs, he had the dreadful sense that everything that was redeemable in life, everything that sweetened or enlivened, gave it meaning, inevitably came a few seconds, minutes, days or years too late.

Hannah Karlsberg lay on the carpeted floor of her living room. Her head faced the camera, the left eye open, staring, the right pressed closed against the blood-soaked carpet. One arm rested parallel to her body. The other seemed to reach frantically for something above her head. Her legs were spread wide apart, the balls of her feet rising like small pink mounds from the floor. The heel of one of them was dark red where she had stepped into her own blood. She was dressed in a dark blue terry cloth robe that had been slit open from the back. Flaps of skin and small white chips of severed bone could be seen beneath the wide slit, and as Frank stared down at Hannah's butchered body, he was once again struck by the awful vulnerability of the flesh, by how tenuously it maintained its tiny grip on life.

There were eleven photographs in all, and after Frank had slid the last of them back into the envelope, he reached into the bottom drawer of the file cabinet behind his desk and took out the bottle of Bushmills he kept there.

He'd been fighting off the first shot since early morning. He'd wanted one during the predawn walk to Times Square, and he'd been around the neighborhood long enough to know that he could have gotten one easily enough, despite the fact that New York State required the bars to close at 5 A.M. What New York State wanted was very different from what some of its more desperate citizens required, and a great many of them tended to gather in the small after-hours drinking holes that dotted the west side of the city from 34th Street to Central Park. Frank preferred the one on Tenth Avenue at 50th Street because it was dark and quiet, and each customer seemed to sense and respect the noble isolation of the other, the hard determination of its grip.

He took the small glass that rested, bottom up, on the neck of the bottle and poured himself a round. It went down smoothly, as it always did, as the very first one had long ago. Even then, when he was fifteen, there'd been no sudden grimace or wrenching cough, no knot of older men laughing at his inexperience from the other side of the room. That first drink had been as good as the last one, and after it, he'd felt nothing but the soft, uplifting ease which had slowly overtaken him, and which he'd instantly realized he could neither surrender to entirely, nor entirely live without.

The phone rang suddenly and Frank quickly capped the bottle and answered it.

"Frank Clemons," he said crisply.

"Frank, it's Karen."

He could remember how the sound of her voice had once thrilled him, how he had longed to hear it during the sweltering summer days in which he'd hunted down her sister's murderer.

"Hi," he said.

"I was thinking of taking you to dinner tonight," Karen said brightly.

"Sounds good," Frank said. He glanced to the right and allowed his eyes to linger on one of her paintings, the one he'd bought himself in Atlanta and which had seemed to capture her entirely at that time, a ghostly vase of flowers that appeared by some odd play of color to be radiantly fading.

"No special occasion," Karen added. "Just for fun."

"Okay," Frank said.

"How about a very nice place?"

"Wherever you say."

"Irini's on Thirty-eighth Street?"

"All right."

"Around eight?"

"Okay."

"Good, see you there."

Frank hung up the phone. For a moment, he thought about going back to the photographs, but instead he returned to the report, and read it once again, this time more slowly. He had been through dozens like it in the past. Meticulously, he had copied their details into the little green notebooks in which he recorded the progress of his cases. He'd collected scores of them over the years, and after he'd moved from Atlanta, his brother, Alvin, had boxed them up and sent them to New York. They now rested in the corner of the room's only closet, and each time he thought of them, or started a new one, the full fury of each death swept over him. One face after another swept into his mind, lingered there for an instant, torn, slashed, exploded, and then swept out again, only to be replaced by another, until the whole grisly parade was over, and he could go on to the next body sprawled by the river, or slumped behind the wheel, or, as in the case of Hannah Karlsberg, face down in the morning light, face down in her own apartment high on the fourteenth floor, with all the city's noise and movement oblivious beneath her, and nothing above her but the empty sky.

6

Hannah Karlsberg's apartment was in a large brick building on the corner of 76th Street and Central Park West. It was an old building, but from the look of the outside, the recently installed windows and sandblasted brick facade, it had been well maintained.

A doorman in a large black greatcoat with enormous brass buttons waited under the outer canopy. He looked as if the whole play of the street and the sidewalk had come to bore him inexpressibly, and his eyes seemed to come alive only as Frank drew uncomfortably near the front door of the building.

"May I help you?" he asked sternly.

Frank took out his identification, a small laminated card with his picture on it, along with the official seal of New York State and his private investigator's license number.

The man glanced indifferently at the card. "If you're going to start pumping me for dirt on anybody in this building, forget it," he said.

"Hannah Karlsberg," Frank said.

The doorman looked at him intently. "I guess you know she's dead."

"Yes."

"Well, you should talk to the police," the man said.

"I already have."

"So you don't need me, right?"

"Were you on duty the night she was murdered?" Frank asked.

"No," the man said. He shrugged. "Nobody was on duty. This building's regular doorman died about two weeks ago. Nobody had replaced him yet. The murder made them do that right away." He smiled broadly. "Meaning me."

"So you never met her?"

The man shook his head. "To tell you the truth, this doorman outfit is just for show," he said. "I'm with a security company. I'm just here until they get a permanent doorman." His lips curled downward. "I wouldn't work this kind of job full-time. All that bowing and scraping to the tenants. I'd rather sit in a warehouse in Brooklyn." He smiled. "Crates of computer parts don't snap their fingers at you, or make you haul your ass out in the rain to whistle them up a cab."

"I'm here to see the apartment," Frank said.

"You allowed to do that?"

"Not without an escort," Frank told him.

"I can't leave the lobby."

"I mean a cop," Frank said. "I'm waiting for one."

"Fine with me," the man said. "You want to wait inside?"

"Thanks."

The lobby of Hannah Karlsberg's building looked like a great many others on the border of Central Park. Most of the furniture looked as if it had been selected with only one idea in mind: to convince the privileged residents that they had achieved a certain place in life, one from which, in all likelihood, they could never be dislodged. There were large, gilded mirrors and richly detailed oriental carpets. The walls were paneled in dark mahogany, and the floors were made of a polished green marble. The air itself smelled as if it had been recently cleaned, and Frank wondered how often Hannah had breathed it quietly, calmly, with no hint of what lay ahead.

Tannenbaum arrived a few minutes later. He flashed his badge to the doorman, then joined Frank in the lobby.

"You're punctual, Frank," he said. "That'll get you a long way with Midtown North." He walked hurriedly to the elevator. "She lived on the fourteenth floor. Apartment A."

A strip of yellow paper with black lettering hung across the door: DO NOT ENTER CRIME SCENE. Tannenbaum inserted the key, opened the door, then leaned under the paper and walked into the apartment.

Frank followed along behind him.

"Well, this is it," Tannenbaum said, as Frank joined him in the foyer. "It's a mess, of course. It always is with this kind of thing."

A few yards beyond the small foyer, Frank could see the thin slants of grayish light that came through the nearly closed louver blinds. A line of reddish stains ran in a rough diagonal across the dark brown blades, and as Frank's eyes drifted downward he saw a large pool of dried blood which spread out across the carpet only a few feet from the window. The figure of a body had been drawn around the stain in white chalk, and from its position relative to the stain, it was obvious that Hannah Karlsberg had died of wounds to her throat and chest.

Tannenbaum strode into the living room, stopping just to the right of the chalk outline. "Did you notice the door?" he asked, as he turned back to Frank.

"You mean the jimmy marks?" Frank asked.

"That's right," Tannenbaum said. "Very crude. I mean, not exactly what you'd call a cat burglar."

"Were both locks jimmied?"

"No, just the bottom one," Tannenbaum said. "We figure the top one wasn't bolted." He shrugged. "Who knows why?"

"Is there any other entrance?"

Tannenbaum shook his head. "Just the fire escape outside her bedroom window, but it looks clean. Her window was locked. No marks outside it. Looks like he just got lucky with that bottom lock."

Frank walked slowly into the living room. Earlier, in his office, he had imagined an overturned chair and a shattered lamp. Instead, he saw an overturned magazine rack and a heavy glass coffee table whose top had been knocked off its deep green marble stand.

"Looks like she fell into it," Tannenbaum said as he stepped gingerly over the edge of the table. "There were blood stains and small pieces of flesh on one corner." He glanced about the room, his eyes taking in the pattern of blood drops that dotted it. "She moved around a little," he said. "You can tell that from the walls."

All four of them had been splattered with blood, along with the ceiling. The knife, in its flight, had sent arcs of blood high over the killer's head, and some of it had reached the high speckled ceiling which now looked down upon the even bloodier scene below.

Frank walked to the far right of the room and nodded toward the corridor that led back into the remaining rooms of the apartment. "Anything back there?" he asked.

"No," Tannenbaum said. "It's clean as a whistle."

Frank said nothing, and Tannenbaum looked at him curiously. "Want to see the rest of the place?" he asked.

"Yeah."

"Follow me."

Tannenbaum turned swiftly and led Frank down the corridor and into the back bedroom. The bed was made up neatly.

"She must have been up late that night," Frank said as his eyes moved over the bed. He looked at Tannenbaum. "Did you notice the number of cigarettes in the ashtray in the living room?"

Tannenbaum pointed to another ashtray which rested on the small white table beside the bed. "That one's full, too. Same brand as the pack we found on the floor of the living room."

"Was it her brand?"

"We checked that out. It was."

"She had emphysema," Frank said. "Had she always smoked like that?"

"We hear she'd been trying to quit," Tannenbaum said. His eyes lingered on the ashtray. "Looks to me like she was a little nervous that night." He shook his head. "If she were a younger woman, I'd figure some sort of romantic problem, you know. Maybe she was waiting for her married lover, something like that. Maybe they had words. Things can get very nasty in a situation like that."

Frank nodded.

Tannenbaum walked to the bedroom window, parted the blinds and peered out. "Of course, the jimmy marks wouldn't go with that theory," he said. "But still, when I saw the bed all made up, despite the fact that she died early in the morning, I thought that it could have been someone she knew." He turned back to Frank. "I mean, people don't wait up for psychos."

"Not the ones they don't know, at least," Frank said.

Tannenbaum laughed. "But the way I see it now, she was maybe dozing on the bed while the guy was trying to get in."

Frank looked at him doubtfully. "Wouldn't she have heard it?"

"Maybe not," Tannenbaum said. He pointed to a pair of headphones which lay on the floor next to her bed. "She could have been using those things. They're like speaker systems for your ears. If she were using them, she might not have heard anything until it was too late."

"Was a record on the stereo?" Frank asked.

"She had a CD player," Tannenbaum said. "And the answer is, yes. Classical. Loud, too. Beethoven's Ninth." He shrugged. "In any event, she was up late." He stared at Frank intently. "What would keep you walking the floor till the morning light, Frank?"

"Love can do it," Frank replied. "Money. Family troubles."

Tannenbaum released the blinds and they clattered shut. "Nobody heard a thing, you believe that?"

"Not unless he gagged her."

"Lab says no for the gag," Tannenbaum said. "And he couldn't have drugged her first. Not the way she was dancing around the living room."

"Who've you talked to?"

"We've canvassed the whole building. The people right downstairs were taking a much-needed vacation in Saint Thomas. The woman in the one next door was shacked up with her boyfriend for the evening. That leaves the one across the hall."

"And?"

"The sublessee hadn't moved in yet," Tannenbaum said. "So, what can you do in a neighborhood like that?"

Frank shook his head. "Not much."

"When she hit that fucking table," Tannenbaum said, "that made a big noise, you know?"

"Yeah," Frank said.

"As for screaming," Tannenbaum added, "the M.E. says he might have gotten her vocal cords first." He smiled. "What do you think, Frank, a lucky punch?"

"I don't know."

Tannenbaum shrugged. "Well, maybe time will tell," he said as he headed back out of the room.

Frank followed him slowly into the room across the hall. It was set up as an office. There was a small wooden desk, a bookshelf filled with books about the fashion industry, and a tall antique oak filing cabinet. A computer rested on top of the desk, along with a small portable typewriter. A box of Hannah's personalized stationery lay open beside the typewriter, light blue paper headed with an elegant gold script: *Hannah Karlsberg, Fashion Consultant.* It did not list her address or phone number.

"Far as we can tell, absolutely nothing was taken," Tannenbaum said. "She had nice clothes, nice jewelry, and this computer would be worth a few bucks on the street."

"How about money?"

"There was three hundred dollars in the top drawer of her desk," Tannenbaum said. He pulled the drawer open and pointed to the small black tray inside it. "It was laying right there, right in the open."

Frank glanced about the room. One wall held an enormous framed painting of an island paradise where brown native people lounged happily by the river, while the one opposite it was decked with an enormous handmade quilt. There were also a few photographs. One showed a large, middle-aged woman as she posed stiffly in front of the Eiffel Tower. Frank nodded toward it. "Is that her?"

"Yeah," Tannenbaum said. "Like they say, at a happier time."

Frank's eyes moved from one photograph to the next. Hannah in Venice, Hannah in Rome, and finally, Hannah standing on one of the serpentine ramparts of the Great Wall of China.

"She got around, no doubt about it," Tannenbaum said.

"Traveling like that," Frank said, "it's expensive."

"She made a good dollar," Tannenbaum said. "We checked with your client on that. According to her, Hannah was pulling down over a hundred thousand a year."

"She spent a lot of it on this place," Frank said.

"She had a lot to spend," Tannenbaum said quietly as he ran his fingers over the elegant oak desk. "But like they say, it don't buy happiness."

"You figure she wasn't happy?"

Tannenbaum shrugged. "Who is? Money or no money."

Frank stepped to the door and glanced back toward the living room. The chalk outline of Hannah Karlsberg's body spread out before him, the single outstretched arm reaching desperately, as it seemed to him now, for some final hopeless hope.

"What else can I do for you?" Tannenbaum asked.

"How about letters? Postcards?"

"We went bottom up on that," Tannenbaum told him. "Unless you're talking about recent snapshots. She had a box of those, but then just about everybody does."

"Is it still here?"

"Yeah," Tannenbaum said. He walked to the closet on the right side of the room and opened it. A small wooden chest rested on an upper shelf. He took it down and handed it to Frank.

Frank took the box and opened it. A thin scattering of glossy color photographs stared up at him.

"Oh, and since you're looking for lost heirs," Tannenbaum said, "you might be interested in this. It came in today. She left everything to the American Cancer Society." He laughed. "You think they got any button men over there, Frank, people they send out to smoke a rich benefactor once in a while?"

Frank said nothing. He closed the box softly and walked back into the living room. The light from the window flooded in all around him, glaring hazily in the luxuriously framed pictures and awards which she had used to decorate the rose-colored rear wall.

"She took pride in herself," Tannenbaum said as he joined him in the living room. He glanced about randomly. "This place. The way she did that wall. Pride."

Frank's eyes drifted down to the wide red stain which rose like a gaping wound from the pale blue carpet. Nothing had ever looked more out of place. It was as if something had crept through the window, some creature from another world, and taken her in a single murderous instant that nothing could reclaim.

7

Frank didn't bother to return to the apartment before heading for Irini's later that night. He knew that his own rumpled brown suit wouldn't fit the elegant decor, but the other one, which hung in Karen's closet, was not in significantly better shape, and he'd refused, absolutely refused, to allow Karen to refurbish his wardrobe. She'd claimed it was her way of investing in him, and that in return she expected a percentage of his business after it got rolling. For a moment he'd actually considered it, but only for a moment, then his senses had returned to him and he'd simply thanked her softly and said no. To her credit, Karen had never brought the subject up again. She'd even suggested that maybe wrinkled jackets and slightly shiny trousers were what people expected, and that anything a little brighter or with a slightly more recent cut would arouse a certain disquiet in his prospective clientele.

In any event, the suits had remained unchanged, and as he stepped into the salmon-colored foyer of Irini's and fell under the disapproving gaze of the tuxedoed maître d', he realized that it wasn't really Karen's money he'd refused, but the crisp, cool tone of her style, and that he still preferred the look of a slightly battered man to anything he saw in the flashy magazines.

"May I help you, sir?" the maitre d' asked quietly.

"I'm meeting somebody."

"Who might that be?"

"Karen Devereaux."

The maitre d' looked at him unbelievingly. "She's expecting you?"

"Yeah."

"This way, please."

Karen was sitting at a table in the far right corner of the room. She was dressed in a dark blue silk blouse and a long black velvet skirt, and as he moved toward her, Frank realized that he would never know a more beautiful woman, that she had fallen into his life as miraculously as a flaming meteor, and that it would never happen again.

She smiled brightly as he sat down. "Hi," she said.

Frank dropped his hat in the chair beside him. "Nice place."

"You like it?"

He smiled. "It's fine."

She leaned toward him. "You look tired."

"It's been a busy day."

"A new case?"

"Yeah."

"Want to talk about it?"

Frank allowed himself to laugh softly as he shook his head. He knew that soon he would be alone again, but he did not know when, or how, or why, but only that while he remained with Karen, he wanted her to love him.

She laughed lightly. "You never want to talk about them. Were you that way with Sheila?"

"Sheila never asked."

"Did you like that better?"

He shrugged indifferently, the smile fading despite his best efforts to hold on to it. "It doesn't matter."

Karen's face grew somber. "The way you say that sometimes, Frank," she said, "the look in your eyes when you say it, it's as if you mean that nothing matters, nothing at all."

Frank picked up the menu and opened it. "What's good?"

"Have whatever you like," Karen said dully.

Frank lowered the menu. "I don't want to start it off like this."

"Why not? It's become our usual routine."

"That's what I don't like."

"It takes two to make dinner conversation," Karen said curtly. Her eyes darted away from him. "Or anything else, for that matter."

She meant kids, and he knew it. She wanted a child. Perhaps she wanted his child, but he suspected that the exact identity of the father mattered least of all in her immediate calculations. She wanted the experience of child-bearing, of parenthood. She wanted to be a mother, but he knew that he would never be a father to anyone again, never know that exquisite joy, or expose himself to the dark brutal emptiness that had followed in its wake.

He folded the menu. "Order for me, Karen," he said. "I don't know what these things are."

She stared at him resentfully. "Are you proud of that?"

"No," Frank said. "It's just a fact. I don't have any particular feeling about it. Why? Does it embarrass you?"

"You know better than that," Karen snapped. "Don't try to make me out to be some New York snob, Frank. It won't work."

Frank said nothing.

"Is that what you did with Sheila?" Karen asked accusingly. "Did you try to put her in some little square, nail her down, so you could go your own way?"

Frank glanced away, and drew in a long, slow breath.

The waiter stepped up almost immediately, and Karen ordered herself a Black Russian and him a shot of Bushmills.

"So," she said crisply, "I ordered for you."

Frank nodded slowly.

For a long time, the two of them sat in silence. Then suddenly, Karen leaned forward and thrust out her arm. "Feel this, Frank," she said brightly, trying to start the dinner over again. "Feel this material."

Frank felt the cuff of her blouse. The material was soft as liquid, and for a moment he half-expected it to dissolve at his touch.

"And look at the color," Karen added enthusiastically. "Doesn't it look like it has a glow of some kind?"

"It's very beautiful," Frank said.

"You met the designer," Karen told him. "She was at the party last night."

Frank said nothing.

"Imalia Covallo," Karen added. "Very tall. She sat near you for a while. Do you remember her?"

"Yes," Frank said.

"I bought this in her shop this morning," Karen said. She sat back and lifted her arms gracefully. "It's called the 'Imalia Covallo Look.' "

"She has a shop?"

"Oh yes, very exclusive."

"Where is it?"

"Where else, Fifth Avenue," Karen said. "You have to have an appointment to get in." She laughed. "It's all very haute couture and all that." She lifted her nose to the air in a broad, mocking gesture. "So precious, dahling."

"You made an appointment?" Frank asked, almost unbelievingly.

"Yes, at the party," Karen said. "She's really very nice." She ran her fingers up the sleeves of her blouse. "And the clothes, Frank. You should see the clothes."

Frank let his eyes move over the shimmering blouse, its intricately woven fabric and radiant sheen. "It's very nice," he said again.

She smiled sweetly. "Think we can begin again, Frank?" she asked.

For a moment, he didn't speak. Then, at last, he lied.

"Maybe," he said.

It was almost ten by the time they got back to the apartment, and for a while, the two of them sat on the terrace and watched the lights of the city. There was a distinct chill in the air, but the view was worth it. It swept in toward them from up and down the long glittering canyon of Park Avenue, and as he sat in the white wicker chair and listened to the distant traffic down below, Frank remembered his tiny porch on Waldo Street in Atlanta, the metal lawn chair he'd kept there, and the wall of city lights which he'd watched night after night. He could feel his old discontent rising again, reaching into his voice, his eyes, making itself visible to those who were around him.

"What are you thinking, Frank?" Karen asked suddenly.

He turned toward her. She was sitting across the small glass table which rested between them. She was wrapped in a thick sweater, her long, slender fingers tucked beneath its ample sleeves. "Nothing," he said.

"I don't believe that."

"Nothing important," he added.

"I don't believe that, either," Karen said. She drew her arms around her sides, hugging herself tightly. "A cold night," she added. Then she smiled. "We could warm it up a little." She drew out one of her hands and offered it to him. "Want to?"

He took her hand and followed her into the bedroom, and for the next few minutes, they moved into each other with the sort of wordless, sweeping tenderness that had once touched him inexpressibly, which had altered the atmosphere around him, softened the hard corners of the world, made life for one electrifying instant worth every dime you paid.

She was sleeping soundly, as she always did, by the time the last small waves of his contentment had ebbed away. He got up silently, his feet pressing into the lush carpet, as he dressed quickly and went out.

It was a little past four in the morning by the time he got to Tenth Avenue. He made his way up to the second floor and knocked on the door. A large man with beefy red hands opened it immediately, recognized Frank, and stepped aside.

"Delivery fucked up today," he said. "Got nothing but some rotgut shit from over to Killarney."

"That'll do," Frank told him as he walked into the room.

The room was nearly empty, but Frank knew it would begin to fill up steadily as people made their way from the legal bars to the after-hours ones. Some people would go home, of course, take the closing of the bars as a signal to call it a night. But the serious souls would wander on, up this street, up these stairs, or others like them, and sit down behind their small square tables and order a few more rounds. It was not a place for Tequila Sunrises, of course, or Banana Daiquiris, or anything with a little pink umbrella stuck in it. But for a stiff jolt, it was as good a place as any.

Frank took a small table near the back of the room and ordered a shot of Irish. He took it down quickly to rub off the chill of the walk, then ordered another and sipped it more slowly, carefully controlling his own strange uncontrol.

The standing bar was to the left, and the owner was behind it. She looked Puerto Rican, but Frank had heard she was from Ecuador. She was close to sixty, and her hair fell over her shoulders in a ragged silver tangle. She spoke in quick, broken sentences. Everybody called her Toby, but no one knew why. It was said that the gin mill had put her two sons through college, and that one of them now worked downtown in the district attorney's office, but that was the sort of ironic tosspot fantasy that Frank had often heard in such places but had never once believed. During all the months he'd sat at his table, she had never said a single word to him, but from time to time he would catch her eyes as they shifted toward him with a distant, odd affection, as if, through long experience, her heart had learned to trust the lonesome drinker best.

Frank took a long pull on the glass, then tapped it lightly on the table and called for another. A tall thin man in dark glasses accommodated him immediately, and Frank leaned back in his chair and let his eyes wander from table to table. They wandered for a long time, as the minutes stretched one by one into the early morning hours, and the people came and went, singly or in couples, the tone of the bar changing by small, almost imperceptible, degrees with each arrival and departure.

It was nearly seven in the morning when the last of them had left, and the first grayish light seemed sadly stranded outside the front windows. At last, it seemed to sweep in suddenly, like something pushed through a door, and short black shadows thrust their way toward him from across the room.

The bar was entirely empty now, except for Toby, who was wiping the last of the glasses, and a large man who sat near the front window, his hat on his lap, a single glass still poised in his hand. For a time, Frank watched him silently, then suddenly the man turned directly toward him, his large black eyes staring straight into Frank's.

"You are leaving soon?" he asked.

Frank nodded.

"Good," the man said. "I like to be the last."

He had some sort of accent, faintly English, with its soft *a*'s. He had pronounced last "lahst," but he did not look English. Even in the gray light, Frank could make out the darkness of his skin, the thick black eyebrows and full purplish lips. He sat very erect, his head held up so that his chin remained parallel to the surface of the table. He wore a large double-breasted suit which he had carefully buttoned over an even larger stomach. "The last to leave this place," he added, by way of explanation. Then he eased himself from his seat and walked ponderously over to Frank's table, his immense frame shifting left and right like an old tanker.

"My name is Farouk," he said as he stopped beside the table. He smiled tentatively, but he did not put out his hand.

"Frank Clemons."

"You come here often," Farouk said. It was a statement of fact, not a question, although there was something quizzical about it, a distant curiosity. It was as if he had been studying Frank for some time, as he no doubt studied other regulars at the bar. "I have seen you here," he said. "In such a place, it is good to be observant."

"Yeah," Frank said. He nodded toward the empty chair at the opposite side of the table. "Care to sit down?"

Farouk nodded heavily, his great bald head like a smooth dark orb in the still shadowy light. "I have seen you here many times," he said as he sat down, his speech still determinedly formal, as if learned from rules rather than from listening to the usage of the street. "You're often the last to leave."

"I don't sleep very well," Frank explained.

Farouk's dark eyes studied his face solemnly for a moment, then a small, thin smile broke over his lips. "Sleep is not worth much. It is dull."

"Yes, it is."

"Better to be out and on your feet," Farouk said with a slight, dismissive shrug. "You have a job?"

"Yes."

"And a bed?"

"That, too."

"With a woman in it?"

"Sometimes."

"And children?"

Frank shook his head. "No."

Once again Farouk nodded silently. "What is your work?"

Frank hesitated instinctively. "You ask a lot of questions," he said.

"I am a curious person," Farouk told him. "But so, I think, are you."

Frank stared at him silently.

"That is my guess, that you are a curious person," Farouk added. "Shall I tell you why?"

"Go ahead."

"It is a matter of color," Farouk said. "You are often here. Which means not simply that you cannot sleep, but that you prefer the night."

Frank nodded.

"The night is dark, full of shadow," Farouk went on. "Those who prefer it, they are in love with the mysteries of the world." He smiled cunningly. "It is the obvious which they cannot stand. They hate what is clear, what is too easily revealed." He sat back, eyeing Frank proudly. "I am right, yes?" he asked as he folded his large arms over his chest.

"Yeah," Frank said. "Yeah, you're right."

Farouk leaned forward slightly. "So, now I ask again. What is your work?"

"I'm a private investigator," Frank told him.

Farouk nodded, as if confirming something, but did not seem impressed. He took out a pack of cigarettes and offered one to Frank.

"No, thanks," Frank said. Instead, he lit one of his own and sat back slightly. "What do you do?"

Farouk placed a cigarette in an ivory cigarette holder, then lit it. "I put myself at the service of others," he said as he blew a column of smoke across the table. "I lend assistance in difficult matters."

"For a fee?"

"One does not live on air."

"Of course," Frank said. He took a sip of whiskey.

Farouk cocked his head slightly. "You're not from New York." Again, it was a statement. "Your accent. Southern?"

"Atlanta," Frank said. "But I live here now."

"In this part of the city?"

"My office is on Forty-ninth Street."

"Hell's Kitchen. Not a place for everyone."

"The rent's low," Frank said. He drained the last of the whiskey from his glass.

"May I offer you another?" Farouk asked immediately.

Frank looked at him with suspicion.

"It is always in my interest to know a person in your profession," Farouk said, "as it is probably in your interest to know a person in mine."

Frank said nothing.

"It would be my pleasure to buy you a final drink," Farouk told him. "If you wish, you may think of it as a business expense."

"I think I've had too many already," Frank said. He glanced toward the window, his eyes squinting against the morning light.

"Coffee, then?"

"All right."

"Excellent," Farouk said. He motioned to Toby. *"Traenos dos cafés turcos."* Then he turned back to Frank. "Do you speak Spanish?"

"No."

"I am a student of languages," Farouk said quite casually. "It is important in my profession. Especially in New York. An international city, yes? One should know different languages."

Frank nodded.

"Different coffees, too," he added with the same casualness. "Have you ever had Turkish?"

"Not that I know of," Frank admitted.

The thin smile once again broke over Farouk's face. "Then you will be pleased to try it," he said.

Toby brought over the coffees a moment later, set them down firmly, gave Farouk a quizzical look, then retreated back to the bar.

"My wife," Farouk said, as if in explanation.

"Toby?"

"From time past, my wife," Farouk added. "As they say, 'to

keep her from oppression.' " He took a quick sip of the coffee. "For a time, we lived together. But for many years now, we have not. I prefer a place of my own. It suits my nature." One thick black eyebrow arched slowly upward. "You are married?"

"Not anymore."

Farouk nodded toward the cup. "Try it."

Frank took a slow sip. "Strong."

Farouk smiled cheerfully. "Which is the point of it, I think." He leaned forward slightly, folding his thick arms over the table. "I suppose you have a case?"

"A few," Frank said, then suddenly realized that the others did not engage him anymore, that for the immediate future, lawyers could meet whomever they wished in the motels of New Jersey, that clerks could steal jewelry, and painters forge paintings, that all humanity could spread queer and bounce paper throughout the vast green land without any fear of him.

"Up on Central Park West," he added. "A murder."

Farouk's eyes narrowed in concentration. "A dead woman, I think. It was in the *Post*. About two weeks ago?"

"How did you know which murder?" Frank asked immediately.

"You are a private investigator," Farouk said. "Which means your fee is . . . what . . . thirty-five, forty dollars an hour?"

"Something like that."

"At any rate, substantial," Farouk said. "The average person cannot employ you. It must be a person of means. The woman you speak of, she alone in recent days could have known people of such wealth."

"Well, you're right," Frank said. "It was the case in the newspapers."

"I presume you are familiar with Midtown North?"

"Yeah."

"I might have been of some assistance in an introduction."

"I already know the guy who's in charge of the case."

"And who is that, if you do not mind my asking."

"Leo Tannenbaum."

Farouk nodded. "Ah, yes."

"You know him?"

"Yes, I do," Farouk said. He finished his coffee in one sip, then took out a small notebook. "Who was the woman?"

Frank said nothing.

Farouk looked at him evenly. "Unless I am of assistance, there will be no charge."

"I don't think I need any assistance," Frank said firmly.

"That is not true, I assure you," Farouk said, just as firmly. "Shall I tell you why?"

"Go ahead."

"Because of your nature," Farouk said. "You are always moving. Your fingers on the table, your feet, your eyes, always moving." He smiled knowingly. "This tells me that there are certain things which you do not do well. Things which involve stuffy rooms, papers, files, too much reading, too much sitting down. You do not bother with these things, and yet, they can be of great assistance."

"What makes you think that kind of work would be helpful in this case?" Frank asked.

"If memory serves," Farouk said, "this woman was in the garment trade, yes?"

"That's right."

"Do you know much about this business?"

"No," Frank admitted.

"I could find out about all her business dealings," Farouk said. "I could find out what she owned, what she recently acquired. It is quite possible that such information would be of assistance. But if it is not, I can assure you that there will be no charge for my services."

Frank continued to watch him, not entirely convinced.

Farouk eyed him piercingly. "For you, it is a human thing, murder. You want to deal with it face to face, one person to another. You like to hear the voice, see the eyes." He smiled. "I admire this." Then he shook his head. "But it is naive."

"Why?"

"Because much is hidden in words and pages. In such things, for example, even the dead still speak."

Frank looked at him intently. "You mean the victim?"

"Yes," Farouk said. "And I might be of some assistance in finding what is hidden."

Frank considered it for a moment, but remained unconvinced. "There's another problem," he said.

"And what is that?"

"I don't know you," Frank said. "For all I know, you could leave here and boost a few cars on the way home."

Farouk frowned. "Such a petty crime," he said contemptuously. "Surely you already think better of me than that."

Frank looked at him evenly. "No, I don't."

"Then what would raise your estimation?"

"A reference might help."

"Would one from the police do?"

"Maybe," Frank said. "If I knew the cop."

"Perhaps Detective Tannenbaum?"

"Would he stand up for you?"

Farouk smiled. "He would say that I do not boost cars."

"Anything else?"

"That I do not run cons, or play the Murphy man on the Avenue," Farouk added. "He would say that I am competent, and that I am honest." The faint smile which had been lingering on his lips disappeared suddenly. "He would say that I can be ruthless, but he would add that I usually discover the thing I'm looking for." He leaned forward and eyed Frank intently. "Are you ruthless?"

"Some people think so."

"And are they ever right?"

"Sometimes."

"Then you know that it cannot be an act," Farouk said. "When you tell a man that you will harm him, he must know that you will do it." He leaned back in his chair and folded his arms over his chest. "They are not so smart, the ones who work the streets, but there is one thing they can recognize very quickly, a coward in their midst, a man who will not act as he speaks."

For a moment, Frank watched Farouk's face silently. He knew that he had been disturbingly right about a few things, especially one of them, the most critical at the moment, his disinclination to follow paper trails. It was a problem that had plagued him in the past, causing him to overlook obvious motives and connections while pursuing more obscure and darkly passionate ones. He had never liked cases where money was involved, insurance claims or business dealings, and throughout his career, he had avoided as many such cases as he could. But as he sat in the dark bar, he realized that to find a lost or distant relative might require exactly the sort of work he did not want to do. And yet, something in the case drew him irresistibly toward it, and he knew that he wanted to do it right, to overlook nothing, no trail that might lead him further in.

He took a quick drink, then returned the cup to the table. "Do you have any more questions about me?" he asked.

Farouk shook his head. "No."

"Why not?"

"You work in Hell's Kitchen, but it is not the low rent that draws you there."

"How do you know?"

"You come to this bar, even though the drinks cost the same as any other bar," Farouk said. "And you work in Hell's Kitchen even though you don't have to." He smiled. "That is all I need to know about you."

For a moment, the two men looked at each other silently.

In his mind, Frank searched for some final reason to work alone, as he preferred, but the nature of the case argued for an assistant, one who knew the ins and outs of the vast bureaucracies that kept track of births and deaths, money, travel, property, the cleaner lines of life.

"All right," he said finally. "I could probably use a little help here and there."

Farouk smiled broadly. "You will not regret it."

"What do you need to begin?"

"The woman's name," Farouk replied immediately. "I do not remember it from the papers."

"Hannah Karlsberg," Frank said.

"And her address?" Farouk asked.

"Three fifty-seven Central Park West."

"And the apartment number?"

"Fourteen-A."

"Yes, yes," Farouk said, "that would be on the front, facing the park."

"Yes, it is."

Farouk looked at him pointedly. "So you have been to the apartment?"

"Yes," Frank said. "Earlier today."

"And the death," Farouk said. "It was with a knife, I believe."

"Yes, it was," Frank told him. "But I'm not looking for the killer."

Farouk looked surprised. "What then?"

"The police won't release the body until a relative asks for it."

Farouk nodded. "Then you're looking for a brother, sister, child?"

"Yes."

Farouk smiled broadly. "Ah, then I can be of great assistance," he said confidently. "I will start with birth certificates, then deeds." His eyes narrowed in concentration. "Property is a great betrayer."

"I don't have much to go on," Frank said. "Right now, the only thing I know about Hannah Karlsberg is that she's dead, and that the police won't release her body."

"But that is not routine," Farouk said. "This holding of the body. Do you know why they're doing that?"

"Probably because her hand was cut off," Frank said. "Severed at the wrist." He took a long draw on his cigarette. "It looks like the killer took it with him."

Something in Farouk's large brown face drew strangely concentrated. "And they are hoping to find the hand?"

"That's what it looks like," Frank said. "And I can see how they're thinking. Anybody crazy enough to steal a hand might be crazy enough to keep it."

"So they hold the rest of the body as a matter of evidence," Farouk said.

"With one piece missing," Frank told him, and suddenly he saw the stump of Hannah's arm as he knew it must look in the darkness of the morgue, ragged, caked with blood and with bits of shattered bone dangling from strings of torn flesh.

He was still thinking of it when he felt Farouk lean toward him and lightly touch his arm.

He glanced up quickly. "What?"

Farouk did not answer, but only stared at him quietly for a moment. Then he pulled himself ponderously to his feet. "Home," he said as he walked away

8

Karen had already gone to the gallery by the time Frank made it back to the apartment. He showered quickly, changed his shirt, and went out again. The winter cold seemed to have deepened during the night, and before returning to his office, he walked into one of the cluttered hardware stores along Ninth Avenue and bought a small electric space heater. It was purring softly behind him a few minutes later as he looked up Imalia's number, then dialed it.

A woman answered immediately. "Imalia Covallo Designs."

"Is Ms. Covallo in?" Frank asked.

"May I ask who's calling?"

"Frank Clemons."

"Just a moment, please."

A flurry of harpsichord music suddenly came through his receiver, high and tinkling, and as he listened to it, he tried to imagine Imalia's office, the thick carpet, sumptuous curtains and unimaginably soft textures which were inseparable parts of her world.

"Hello, Frank," Imalia said. "I'm surprised to hear from you so soon."

"I like to keep people informed," Frank told her.

"You mean you already have some information?" Imalia asked anxiously.

"Not very much," Frank said. "But it seems the police are hitting the same blank. I was hoping you might help me break through it."

"How?"

"Maybe just by talking," Frank said. "I need to talk to any-body who knew her, and right now you're at the top of the list."

"But as I said," Imalia told him. "I really didn't know much about Hannah's personal life."

"You might be surprised how much you knew," Frank said. "I've seen it happen, believe me."

For a moment she seemed to hesitate. "Well, all right then," she said finally. "How about lunch?"

"Okay. Where?"

"There's a place on Madison Avenue," Imalia said. "Bolero. Do you know it?"

"No."

"Madison and Fifty-first," Imalia said. "Say, two this after-noon."

"Fine," Frank said.

"Don't go into the dining hall," Imalia said. "Just ask for me. I have a private room."

The private room was on the second floor, and Imalia was already waiting for him when the maitre d' opened the narrow mahogany door and let him in.

"Mr. Clemons," he announced.

"Thank you, Philippe," Imalia said.

She was sitting behind a small enameled table which had been covered by a lace tablecloth. A crystal bud vase with a single white orchid rested in the middle of it.

"Thanks for being on time," she said. "I like that in a person." She glanced quickly at her watch. "I've already ordered for us. I hope you don't mind."

"No," Frank said. He sat down in the chair opposite her and took out his small green notebook.

"What's that?" Imalia asked, nodding toward it.

"I write things down," Frank told her. "I don't trust my mem-ory."

"And then what do you do with your notes?"

He decided to tell her what she wanted to hear. "When the case is finished and I've been paid, I burn them."

Imalia smiled tentatively. "I didn't mean to question you," she said. "It's just that I've always been very careful about my privacy."

"Most people are," Frank said dully. He took out his pen and held it over the notebook. "You said that Hannah had worked for you for over twenty years?"

"That's right."

"That's a long time."

"Yes, it is," Imalia said.

"And she never mentioned any relatives?"

"Only a sister," Imalia said. "And only in passing." She shrugged. "I mentioned it to the police when they refused to release Hannah's body."

Frank let his eyes drift over Imalia's face. She had obviously taken very good care of herself. Her skin was smooth, white, and for the most part unlined. Her eyes seemed bright and youthful, and yet, from time to time, a strange weariness swept into them, lingered there for an instant, then dissolved.

"That's the only relative she ever mentioned," Imalia added.

"What did she say about her?"

Imalia shook her head. "Nothing much." She thought about it for a moment. "I remember that someone was talking about cremation, that in some places that was the way bodies were disposed of. And Hannah said something about it."

"What did she say?"

"Something like, 'Cremation, yes, like my sister.' "

"And that was all she said?"

"Yes."

"So you got the impression that her sister was dead?"

"Dead, yes," Imalia said.

"And that's all she ever said during the twenty years she worked for you?" Frank asked.

"That's all I remember her ever saying."

"Twenty years," Frank said. "So she was with you almost from the beginning?"

"More or less," Imalia said. "I began everything from a small warehouse in Queens. It was just a big empty building, nothing but floor space." She laughed. "I set up the metal tables myself. I lifted the bolts of cloth off the truck myself." A sudden vehemence rose into her face. "So you see, nobody gave me anything. It's important for you to understand that."

"But Hannah wasn't with you at that time?" Frank asked.

"Not at the very beginning, no." Imalia said. "I handled practically everything myself for the first few years. But to tell you the truth, I wasn't very successful. I needed someone with more experience. Someone who really knew the business from top to bottom. I was a designer, but I didn't know everything there was to know about the trade. That's why I hired Hannah."

"How did you happen to know about her?"

Imalia thought about it for a moment. "From Tony. He mentioned her."

"Tony?"

"Tony Riviera," Imalia said. "He still works for me."

"And he first introduced you to Hannah?"

"Yes."

Frank wrote down the name. "I need to trace Hannah back a little. That's the only way I know to find her sister."

"But what would that matter, if the sister were already dead?"

"Well, for one thing, if she had children, they would be blood relatives of Hannah's."

"Yes, of course," Imalia said. She took a quick sip of water. "Well, all I can remember is that she'd left the place she'd been working at."

"Why?"

Imalia shrugged. "I don't know. Some disagreement with the management, I suppose." She stopped and looked at him closely. "Do you know very much about this business?"

"No."

"Well, it's very volatile," Imalia said. "It's extremely competitive, of course. But beyond that, it's volatile. There are lots of enormous egos in this business. People get into fights. They leave places, or get fired from them."

"The place where she worked before, do you know where that was?"

"Some small-time manufacturer," Imalia said, "in Brooklyn, I think. At least that's what Tony said."

"You don't remember the name?"

Imalia thought a moment. "Something about imports. I can't remember. But it would be in her personnel folder."

"Where could I get a hold of that?"

"At my administrative offices," Imalia told him. "They're on Thirty-sixth Street. Two oh four West Thirty-sixth Street. Tony should have it. That's where his office is."

Frank wrote it down quickly, then looked back up at her. "You and Hannah worked well together, I guess."

"Yes, very well."

"You never had any serious arguments?"

Imalia laughed lightly. "You don't suspect me, do you?"

"No," Frank said. "But I'm not looking for her killer. I'm just trying to get some idea of what kind of person she was."

"Yes, of course," Imalia said. "About your question. Well, yes, we got along. As I said before, we weren't personally close. But then, not many people are, are they?"

"No."

"But professionally we got along very well," Imalia added. "Hannah was a dedicated person, and she was a competent person."

Frank flipped back through his notes. "You said she began as a seamstress."

"Well, not exactly," Imalia admitted. "She worked on the floor, but that was only to let her get a fix on how the whole operation worked."

"Then what was her real job?"

"She kept track of things," Imalia said. "She handled shipments of raw textiles, calculated what we'd need for any particular garment, all sorts of things like that. She was a troubleshooter, an overall manager."

"Did she hire people?"

"Sometimes."

"And fire them?"

"That, too."

"Did she ever come to you with any particular problem?"

"Business or personal?"

"Either one."

"Well, if she'd had personal problems, I doubt that she would have brought them to me. But business? That's different. If she'd had real problems in that area, I suspect she would have come to me." She shrugged slightly. "That's not to say that Hannah wasn't able to handle most things herself. She was. But still, if some matter arose that was really important, I think she would have come to me."

"Had she done that recently?" Frank asked immediately.

"Not about business exactly," Imalia said. "But a few weeks ago, she asked me to come by her apartment. A magazine was doing a story on home design." She stopped. "Have you been to Hannah's apartment?"

"Yes."

"Very well decorated, don't you think?"

"It was very nice."

"Well, this magazine, *Homelife*, was planning to do a little photo layout on it. You know, how to live elegantly in limited space, that sort of thing."

"And they were doing it on Hannah's apartment?"

"Yes," Imalia said. "And so she asked me to drop by and see if there was some little touch that might be added." She shook her head. "There wasn't. It was all perfectly done." She took a quick sip of wine. "Simply beautiful."

Frank's eyes darted away from her and down to his small green notebook. "I'm going to have to look further back in Hannah's life," he said. "There are no immediate relatives as far as anyone can tell." He flipped back a page of his notebook. "You said something about a personnel file."

"Yes."

"Will I have any trouble getting that?"

"Not if I make a phone call," Imalia said. "When do you want to pick it up?"

"How about this afternoon?"

Imalia glanced to the left and motioned for the waiter.

"Bring me a phone, please," she said, after he'd stepped briskly up to the table.

The waiter disappeared for a moment, then immediately returned with a white telephone.

"Thank you," Imalia said. She dialed a number. "I'll make the arrangements now," she told Frank while she waited for an answer.

"Good," Frank said.

"Hello? This is Ms. Covallo," Imalia said into the receiver. "Get me Mr. Riviera, please. Hello, Tony? Someone will be dropping by the office this afternoon. He works for me. He's clearing up a few things about Hannah. Do whatever he asks. Show him anything he wants to see. Yes. Yes. Fine. Goodbye." She hung up the phone, motioned once again for the waiter, then had it taken away.

"All right," she said after he had gone. "Just ask for Tony Riviera. He's been running things since Hannah's death."

"Did he know her very well?"

"As well as anyone," Imalia said. "But I think Hannah lived very much on her own." Her eyes widened somewhat, as if trying to gather in some distant additional light. "Some people are like that."

Frank thought of the wooden chest with its stash of photographs. "It's like she didn't have a past."

"What do you mean?"

"The pictures she kept," Frank said. "There weren't any from when she was younger. Family portraits, that sort of thing."

A sudden intensity swept into Imalia's face. "Yes, well, maybe she didn't like her past," she said crisply. "Do you like yours?"

Frank did not answer, and Imalia continued to stare at him intently.

"Do you know anything about mine?" she asked after a moment.

"No."

"Well, suppose I give you a taste of it," Imalia said, almost fiercely. Then she stood up. "Let's go for a ride, Frank. I want to show you something."

The limousine was already waiting downstairs and Imalia led him to it quickly.

"I wasn't born on Park Avenue," Imalia said as they headed southward down the wide boulevard. "The name tells everything. Covallo. Guinea. Wop. Greaseball." A high, thready laugh broke from her. "Little Italy. That's where I came from. The princess of Prince Street." She turned her eyes toward the window. "If you had been brought up in New York, you'd know all about it."

She seemed to wait for him to ask a question, and when he

didn't she looked back toward him. "Things weren't so bad. I don't mean that. I grew up over a little social club, the kind where the old men sit and drink espresso and talk about the world, you know, *alla siciliana.*"

Frank nodded.

"I could have been a big fat Italian mama by now," she added, this time almost coldly. "You know the type, stuffing vermicelli down the throats of my fat little husband and our fat little kids." Her eyes narrowed into dark slits. "But not Imalia Covallo," she said determinedly. "I wasn't made to live like that, and then whine my life away to the father confessor the way my mother did." She took a deep, tremulous breath, then called to the driver. "Joseph, One oh seven Prince Street."

She sat back and remained silent, almost sullen, until the limousine finally came to a halt in the heart of Little Italy.

"We don't have to get out," she said. "I never get out."

She leaned toward the window and pointed to a small brick tenement. "That's it," she said.

Frank gazed at the building silently.

"Third floor," Imalia said. "I used to sit out on that fire escape. My father was inside, chewing the last of his calamari. My mother was lighting votive candles. My brother and sister were romping around, driving everybody crazy. That's when I'd sit out there and look out toward upper Manhattan and dream of it. I didn't know what it was. But I knew I wanted it." She smiled as she turned toward him. "Not everybody did. My brother, Angelo, he just wanted to be a punk for some local *capo.* And that's exactly what he is. He's got the alligator shoes to prove it. My sister wanted to see Jesus. And I guess she sees Him every day, she and the rest of the Carmelites." She shook her head. "But I wanted something else." Her hand swept out suddenly, indicating the luxurious interior of the limousine. "And I guess I got it." She gave a final quick glance at the tenement, eased herself back into the seat and drew in a long slow breath. "Okay, Joseph."

The car started instantly, moved along the tight grid of streets, then headed back toward midtown.

"I said that there was nothing really personal between Hannah and me," Imalia said finally. "Do you remember that?"

"Yes."

"In a way, I'm not sure that that's entirely true."

"What do you mean?"

"Well, we weren't close, that's for sure," Imalia said, "but there were times when I think she saw something in me that was like herself. I don't know what it was. Maybe the way I'd sort of lost contact with my family. Evidently, she'd lost contact with hers."

"Yes."

"Maybe that was it."

"Maybe."

She seemed on the brink of saying more, but stopped herself. "By the way," she said, "we haven't discussed your fee."

"It's the standard," Frank told her. "Around three fifty a day."

"When do I pay you?"

"When I've found a relative," Frank said. "Or failed to find one."

"Do you think that's likely?"

"I don't know."

She shrugged. "Well, just do your best," she said softly. "That's all anyone can do."

He left Imalia at the front of her office, then continued south through the thickening afternoon crowds. The smell of street hot dogs, shish kebab and roasting chestnuts filled the air around him. Several Salvation Army volunteers stood stiffly in their worn blue uniforms, ringing their bells softly as the holiday crowds swarmed in and out of the luxurious shops and towering department stores of midtown Manhattan. He turned west on 47th Street, then south again on Fifth Avenue, elbowing his way to the enormous marble library on the corner of 42nd Street. An escape artist was pulling himself through a tangle of chains, and each time he dislodged some part of his thin, wiry body, the crowd that had gathered on the steps in front of him applauded loudly. Farther down, an armless man was drawing sidewalk murals with his toes, and farther still, at the corner of 41st Street, a group of black children was break-dancing on strips of flattened cardboard.

He turned west again on 38th Street, and finally stopped at

the center of the Garment District. A bust of Golda Meir stared out across a small cement courtyard, and Frank took a seat on one of the benches near it. Across Seventh Avenue, he could see the small, modest memorial which the Ladies Garment Workers had erected to honor the generations of textile workers who'd manned the sewing machines and fabric cutters of the industry. It was the bronze figure of a man at a sewing machine, his fingers holding to a bit of fabric while his feet pumped at the wide steel pedal. He looked oddly content, happy in his work, and as Frank gazed at the figure from a few yards away, he could not see the raw competitiveness and volatility which Imalia Covallo had described. The man seemed buoyant and unwearied, and because of that, it was easy to picture him rising happily at the end of the day and walking briskly home to a full dinner and a joyous family.

He pulled out a cigarette and lit it. It was nearly four in the afternoon, and the crowds were swirling about the courtyard in a chaos of moving bodies. Young men pushed bulky racks of clothing through them, waving their arms as they lumbered forward. Frank took a deep draw on the cigarette, leaned his head back slightly and closed his eyes.

He opened them again only a few seconds later, and allowed them to settle on the building across the street. Over the shoulder of the statue, he could see the building's revolving door as it turned ceaselessly, emitting a steady stream of well-dressed men and women. They looked oddly similar, all freshly washed and stylishly dressed, so similar that for an instant he did not even recognize Karen as she stepped quickly out of the building, then paused a moment and waited until Lancaster joined her on the street. They laughed lightly, then turned to cross the wide, bustling avenue, moving directly toward him across Seventh. She was only a few yards away before she suddenly caught sight of him, and for an instant, her face seemed to darken. Then, just as suddenly, it regained its light, and after a moment of hesitation she rushed up to him, with Lancaster following somewhat sheepishly behind.

"Hi, Frank," she said brightly.

Frank nodded.

"What are you doing around here?"

"Working a case."

She touched Lancaster's shoulder. "You know Jeffrey."

"Yes."

"Hello," Jeffrey said.

Again Frank nodded.

"Jeffrey is thinking about doing some designs," Karen said. "I was just introducing him around Fashion Avenue a little. I thought some of the designers might be interested in his work. It would do very well for clothing."

Frank dropped his cigarette to the sidewalk and crushed it with the toe of his shoe. "Good luck," he said to Lancaster with a quick smile.

"It's a real decision for me," Jeffrey said. "The old prostitution question."

"Every artist has to face it," Karen explained. She shrugged. "It's just something that goes with the territory."

Frank said nothing. For a moment his eyes were drawn back to the bronze statue, to its idealized portrait of a man at home in his work, at one with his labor, happy with how his hands served his heart.

"We've been making the rounds in the building across the street," Karen said.

Frank turned toward her. "Any luck?"

Karen and Jeffrey exchanged glances, as if trying to decide who should answer.

"I'd say so," Karen said finally. "I think we made some progress today." She looked at Jeffrey. "Don't you?"

"Yes," Jeffrey said. He wore gray pleated trousers and a dark blue jacket and white, open-collared shirt. His manner was quiet, calm, diplomatic, and in their short acquaintanceship, Frank had never seen him play the tormented, desolate artist, which, it seemed to him, was also something that too often went with the territory.

"Yes, I think we made some progress," Karen said, a little nervously.

"The fact is," Jeffrey said with a slight, self-conscious laugh, "I need money, and doing fashion designs might be a way of getting it."

"Not to exclude your other work, though," Karen said quickly.

Jeffrey looked a little embarrassed by Karen's speedy defense. "Well, that's the plan anyway," he said.

Karen turned back to Frank. "Listen, Frank," she said. "We were thinking of having dinner and then a show." There was a moment of awkward hesitation, then she went on. "Well, how about joining us?"

"No, thanks," Frank said.

"I wish you would," Jeffrey said. "We've never gotten to know each other, really."

"I have this case," Frank said quietly. "I have to meet a guy." His eyes drifted over to the bronze statue once again, drifted down the rounded shoulder and along the rolled-up sleeve to where the hand pressed downward into the flap of cloth.

"Well, we wouldn't have dinner until six or seven," Karen told him.

"No, thanks," Frank said. He looked back toward her, and for a moment lost himself in the face, not as he saw it now, but as he had seen it the first time, so silent, dark, grave. He could feel something in him sinking slowly toward the bottom. "I have this case," he added.

"We'd really like to have you," Karen said.

He shook his head. "I can't do it, Karen," he said softly.

Her eyes stared at him with a sudden, inexpressible resolve. "Okay," she said.

He offered her a thin, resilient smile. "But you have fun, though."

"I'll be back home before midnight," she said, as if to reassure him. "Will you be home by then?"

"I guess."

"Good," Karen said. "See you then." She turned quickly, her long, slender arm curling for just a moment around Lancaster's waist as she led him up the avenue toward the spinning lights of Times Square.

9

The directory in the lobby of the building listed Imalia Covallo Enterprises in bold white letters. It was on the twenty-second floor, and its outer office was elegantly decorated. Beautifully designed fabrics covered the walls, some framed like paintings, some simply hung in large pleated waves that seemed to flow in a gently rolling stream along the four lavender-colored walls.

There was an enormous antique desk at the far end of the vestibule. A woman with long dark hair sat behind it. She smiled sweetly as Frank stepped up to her.

"I'm here to see Mr. Riviera," he said.

"Is he expecting you?"

"Yes."

"And your name?"

"Frank Clemons."

"Just a moment, please," the woman said. She picked up a phone and said something into it. Then she turned back to Frank. "He'll be right out. Take a seat if you like."

Frank remained standing for the few seconds it took for Riviera to join him in the foyer.

He was older than Frank expected, probably in his sixties, and he had close-cropped white hair along the sides of his head. He wore thick wire glasses, and behind the lenses his eyes were

an unexpected pale blue. His skin was brown and slightly wrinkled, but he looked strong, robust, someone who could give
orders well.

"Mr. Clemons," he said cheerfully. "Tony Riviera." He thrust
out his hand and Frank shook it.

"Imalia says that I should help you in any way I can," Riviera
said, "but she didn't exactly say what it was all about."

"Hannah Karlsberg," Frank told him.

"What about her?"

"Her murder," he answered, before he could stop himself.

Riviera's face seemed to tighten somewhat. "Aren't the police
handling that?"

"Yes," Frank said.

"But you're not with the police?"

"No," Frank told him. "I'm sort of looking into it on my own."

"On your own?" Riviera asked unbelievingly.

"That's right."

Riviera stared at him evenly. "I see." For a moment his body
seemed to hang in suspension. Then, suddenly, it jumped to life
again. "Well, Imalia wants you to be given full cooperation,"
he said. "And around here, Imalia Covallo makes the rules." He
did not seem to resent that fact so much as fully comprehend
it. "Well, let's go back into my office," he added immediately,
"and we'll look into how I can help you."

Frank followed Riviera through a labyrinth of corridors until
they reached a spacious office near the rear of the building. The
grayish-purple light of late afternoon flooded through a tall line
of windows behind Riviera's desk. Down below, Frank could
see the enormous black roof of Macy's. It looked like an immense
parking lot which someone had built above the city.

"Now," Riviera said as he sat down behind his desk, "what
can I do for you?"

Frank eased himself into one of the two chairs which sat in
front of the desk and took out his notebook. "How well did you
know Hannah Karlsberg?" he asked.

"I gave all this sort of information to the police," Riviera
said. "At first, they were thinking that someone she worked with
might have done it, some disgruntled employee." He looked at
Frank quizzically. "I guess that's the usual theory."

Frank said nothing.

"But Hannah got along with everyone," Riviera added. "That's what I told them. She was aloof, but she was well liked."

"How well did you know her, Mr. Riviera?" Frank asked.

"Relatively well," Riviera said.

"How long had you known her?"

"Well, I really didn't get to know her until she came to work for Imalia," Riviera said. "But I'd seen her once or twice when I used to do a job or two on the Lower East Side."

"So you knew her before she came to work for Ms. Covallo?" Frank asked.

"Sort of. When I was a little boy, I'd see her around Orchard Street," Riviera explained. "But this was years before she came to work here. I hadn't really known who she was in those days." He smiled. "I don't know if you could really tell much from recent pictures, but when Hannah was a girl, she was a real *shayna maidel.*"

Frank glanced up from his notebook. "A what?"

"*Shayna maidel,*" Riviera repeated. "It's Yiddish. It means 'pretty girl.'" He laughed softly. "Despite my name," he said, "I'm Jewish." He leaned forward slightly. "I am a Sephardic Jew, Mr. Clemons, a Spanish Jew." He waited for Frank to respond in some way, and when he didn't, Riviera continued. "I always like to clear that misunderstanding up."

"What misunderstanding?"

"That because my name is Riviera, that I'm a Puerto Rican or a Mexican or something like that," Riviera said. "The fact is, people have a tendency to treat Hispanics as if they're ignorant menials." His eyes narrowed sternly. "I long ago learned that in this country, you can't allow people to think that." He flattened his hands on the polished wooden surface of the desk and pushed them toward Frank. "Do you see those knuckles? Do they look a little strange to you?"

"Yes."

"I broke them quite a few times when I was growing up on the Lower East Side," Riviera said. "Antonio Riviera, that was me. The blacks didn't like me because I was a Jew." He shrugged. "And as for the Jews, they were mostly Ashkenazi, Eastern European Jews. They didn't like me because I was Sephardic, and

Sephardim are supposed to think of themselves as superior." He smiled cunningly. "Usually they do think of themselves as superior," he said. "And usually, if I might add this, they're right." He leaned back in his chair. "So, now that the record's straight, go on to your next question."

"How did you happen to meet her?" Frank asked.

"Why all this going back into the distant past, Mr. Clemons?"

"I like to get some kind of history," Frank told him.

"Why is that?"

"It helps me know the person," Frank said.

"And that helps you what?"

Frank shrugged. "Feel something for them."

Riviera smiled appreciatively. "It's not all that different in fashion, you know?" he said. "When I start to design a dress, the first thing I do is imagine a beautiful woman in it. Not just a model, not just a clotheshorse, but a real woman, as you say, with a past of some kind. Very elegant, perhaps. Maybe even a little dangerous. Perhaps a spy." He laughed. "Who knows, perhaps even a murderess?"

He took a deep breath, and let it out in a sudden burst. "But you know how it is in life. You walk down the street and there's your dress, your beautiful, elegant dress, draped like a set of kitchen curtains over some old hound who never in her life did anything more dangerous than book a cruise to Martinique." For a moment he fell into an odd sullenness, then, with a shrug, he came out of it. "But that's the thing about the fashion business," he said dismissively. "If you have any mind at all, you develop a certain contempt for your best customers."

Frank quickly wrote it down, then glanced back up toward Riviera. "How did you happen to meet Hannah?"

"I was doing some work for a guy named Bornstein in those days," Riviera said. "I was a bundle-boy back then, a kid who carried bundles of finished garments out of the sweatshops. I worked for Bornstein in various ways. He was a big *macher*— a big wheel, you might say—in the garment shops. A sort of broker, if you know what I mean."

"I don't."

"He was hired by the people who owned the shops to keep them supplied with workers," Riviera explained. "When you got piecework production, a high task-rate, and a lot of cash sunk in the machinery, you don't like to see the machines sitting idle. It was real important to keep that bobbin on the move. Bornstein brokered for the owners, made sure they had a steady supply of people."

"Brokered?"

"It worked this way," Riviera went on. "If you had a problem, maybe some girl who all of a sudden got sick, got married, sewed her fingers together, anything like that, you had to get a replacement right away. If you own a garment shop, every second a machine is idle, you're losing money." He laughed again, this time almost coldly. "The needle trade runs on speed. Fast fingers. Fast brains."

"And it was Bornstein's job to get replacements?"

"To keep the shop full of workers, that's right," Riviera said.

"And Hannah worked for him?"

Riviera shook his head. "No. At that time Hannah was in the shops. You know, at the machines, like just about every other nice Jewish girl on the Lower East Side."

Suddenly, for the first time, Frank saw Hannah Karlsberg in her youth, a young girl stooped over a sewing machine, her fingers dancing around the needle as it incessantly hammered the stitching home.

"Now, like I said," Riviera continued, "I did a few odd jobs for Bornstein back in those days, and one afternoon I was going to meet him at Battery Park, and when—"

"What year was this?" Frank interrupted quickly.

"Well, that was the winter of 1935," Riviera told him. "Cold goddamn winter it was, too. I remember the way the place looked that day. Very run-down. There were Hoovervilles all over the city back then. Little shantytowns on the wharfs. And Battery Park was pretty dreary. It was cold, too. It looked like the bay was going to freeze over. I remember there was a bunch of guys standing by a fifty-gallon drum. They'd made a fire in it and a huge blaze was coming out of it. They were huddled around it to keep warm."

"And this was in Battery Park?" Frank said, as he wrote it down.

"That's right," Riviera said. "And when I got there, I could tell that Bornstein was trying to pick up this young girl." He laughed heartily. "I mean, I was a kid, but I'd been on the streets for a while, and knew about things. And I could tell that Bornstein had a real eye for this girl." The laughter trailed off. "He ran through quite a few girls in those days, let me tell you. He did a little agenting on the side, you know, actresses from the Yiddish theater who had hopes for Hollywood. I think he may have even pimped a little, set up an out-of-town buyer with something for his big weekend in the city." He shook his head. "Bornstein was into everything."

"And Hannah?"

"She was just sitting next to him on a bench in the park," Riviera said. "When I came up, she left. Bornstein kept an eye on her as she walked away. He was really pissed. 'The rabbi's daughter,' he said. 'She don't spread her legs for nobody.' " He grimaced. "Bornstein was a crude bastard, a real crude bastard. I didn't like working for him, but in those days, you had to take whatever came around."

Frank said nothing.

"I mean, it was the early thirties, like I said," Riviera added. "Hard times, let me tell you. People today, they don't know what trouble is." He frowned contemptuously. "They're soft. They got no guts. There are some things they won't do, you know?" He laughed mockingly. "But you couldn't live like that back then. Not on the Lower East Side. You couldn't afford it. Like they say, the wolf was at the door."

Frank wrote it down in his notebook, then glanced back up at Riviera. "You said that Bornstein called Hannah 'the rabbi's daughter'?"

"Yeah."

"Was that true?"

"Yes."

"Did he have a synagogue in New York?"

"Yeah."

"Which one?"

"I don't remember the name of the synagogue," Riviera said. "But it was on the east side. Down on Fifth Street someplace, I believe." He thought a moment. "Somewhere around the Bowery. That's where she came from."

"How did you know about her father? Did she ever mention him?"

"No. She didn't talk much about the old days," Riviera answered. "Only old fools sit around doing that. But she did mention that she'd grown up on Fifth Street, and from what Bornstein said that day, I knew she had been a rabbi's daughter."

"What about relatives?" Frank asked. "Did she ever mention any?"

"She had two sisters," Riviera said. "That's all I know."

Frank felt his fingers tighten around his pencil. "Two sisters?" he asked immediately.

"Yeah," Riviera told him. "You didn't know that?"

"No."

Riviera shrugged. "Well, now that I think about it, I'm not surprised," he said.

"Why?"

"Because Hannah put all that behind her," Riviera said.

"Her sisters?"

"That's right," Riviera said bluntly.

"Why?"

"Because she'd moved up in life, you know what I mean?" Riviera said. "Who knows what she'd left behind? Who wants to be reminded of some little hovel off the Bowery?" He smiled knowingly. "Sometimes it's not enough to have come up in the world, made a different future for yourself. Sometimes that's not enough, you know what I mean? Sometimes you want a different past. Of course, that's the one thing you can never get."

"Was Hannah like that?"

"A little, maybe," Riviera said. "A lot of people are. But some aren't. Miss Covallo goes the other way. Did she take you on her little tour of Prince Street?"

"Yes."

"She likes to do that," Riviera said. "Remind people where she came from. Hannah didn't. I don't know why."

"What do you know about her sisters?"

"Nothing really," Riviera said. "I don't think they were in very close contact."

"How did you know about them?"

"From Bornstein."

"What did he say?"

"Well, as Hannah was walking away, Bornstein smiled that shitty little smile of his. Then he looked at me, and he said something like, 'All three of them need work. What you bet I *shtup* them all?' "

Frank looked at him, puzzled. *"Shtup?"*

"That's Yiddish," Riviera explained. "It means 'fuck.' "

Frank felt a wave of contempt roll over him like a line of fire.

Riviera looked at Frank curiously. "Is this all for history?" he asked.

"Well, no one has claimed Hannah's body," Frank told him. "It's still at the morgue." He glanced down at his notebook. "I was thinking that maybe some relative would—"

"Claim it?" Riviera interrupted. "Give it a nice Jewish plot in a nice Jewish boneyard?"

"Something like that," Frank said. He glanced down at his notebook. "Did Hannah ever mention her sisters?"

"Not after she came to work here," Riviera said. "Maybe they moved away. Maybe she broke off with them. Maybe they died." He shrugged. "I mean, who knows what goes on between sisters?"

Frank wrote it down quickly, then looked back up at Riviera. "And that was all you heard?" he asked. "What this Bornstein said?"

"That's the first and last I ever heard about the Karlsberg sisters."

"How about a brother?" Frank asked.

"Never heard of one."

"Nephews? Nieces?"

"Nobody."

Frank turned to the next page of his notebook and changed the subject.

"Did Hannah have a regular schedule?" he asked.

"Of course," Riviera said. "The fashion business is a tight ship."

"Do you have a record of it?"

"Absolutely," Riviera said. "I kept her itinerary myself. It was one of the jobs Hannah gave me."

"What was her job, exactly?" Frank asked immediately.

"She was Imalia's right-hand woman," Riviera said. "She handled a little bit of everything. She even did some of her own designs. They always came out under Imalia's name, but they were Hannah's." He pointed to a square of cloth which had been framed and hung on the office wall. "She did that one, as a matter of fact."

It was a swirl of eerily darkening reds, and as Frank looked at it, he realized that it had the effect of drawing you steadily down into its deep ebony center.

"It's very nice," he said.

"Sold very well last season," Riviera said appreciatively. "One of the most successful designs we've had."

Frank glanced back down at his notebook. "So Hannah did most of her work in this office?"

"That's right," Riviera told him.

"So she must have known everyone who worked here?"

"Yes, of course."

"Do you know of anyone she was particularly close to?"

"You mean, someone who might know more about her private life?"

"Yeah."

Riviera shook his head. "I'm not sure she had much of a private life," he said. "I think she was one of those people who put everything into their work. She was always here. All hours." He pulled out a drawer, removed a large gray ledger and slid it across the table. "Here's her office log. You can see for yourself."

Frank took the book and opened it. A maze of lines and figures swept up toward him.

"It may take you a while to figure it all out, Mr. Clemons," Riviera said, "so I'll give you the bottom line."

Frank looked up from the ledger.

"Hannah worked a full day, every day," Riviera said with an odd weariness. His eyes glanced down toward the book and lingered there. "She had a nice apartment, I understand."

"Yes, she did," Frank told him.

Riviera looked up, surprised. "You've been there?"

"Yes, with the police."

"Nice, I hear."

"Very nice."

Riviera looked at Frank determinedly. "Well, let me tell you something, Mr. Clemons. She deserved it." He turned slightly, and glanced out one of the enormous windows. "In the business, you hear a lot of bullshit about this person being self-made and that person being self-made. Then, later you hear that Papa floated them a loan of maybe a million or two. Or maybe some uncle did it. You know, from the ready cash." He shrugged. "It doesn't matter where they got it, because you know that if things had gotten tight, no palooka loanshark would have come around to rearrange anybody's knees." He turned back toward Frank. "You call that self-made?"

"No."

Riviera smiled, but his eyes remained deadly cold. "I like my knuckles, Mr. Clemons. I respect them." He lifted his hands up into the soft evening light. "I look at these hands, and I think, 'Well, Tony, no bullshit here.' " He lowered them slowly back down on the table. "And that's the way it was with Hannah, too," he said. "She crawled out from under that synagogue using nothing but her bare hands. Everything she had, she got for herself." A strange fierceness swept into his face. "Who's to say that that's not beautiful, hm?"

Frank said nothing.

Riviera massaged his hands gently. "There's only one god-damn thing Hannah didn't deserve," he said, "and that's the way she died."

Frank saw her face again, first in the photographs in the small wooden chest, then bathed in the hard light of the morgue.

"Where did she work before she came here?" he asked.

"Before here?" Riviera asked hesitantly. "What difference would that make? She's been with Imalia for over twenty years."

"I'm running a few things down," Frank told him.

"You're reaching way back."

"Sometimes you have to."

"Well, I can't be of much help on that," Riviera said. "All I know is that one day Hannah showed up here."

"How about a personnel folder?" Frank said insistently.

"Imalia wants you to have that?" Riviera asked, surprised.

"Yes."

For an instant, he hesitated once again. Then he turned quickly, walked to a file cabinet, and pulled out a dark blue folder.

"This is all I have," he said as he handed it to Frank. "It's Hannah's original application. I noticed it a few days ago when I was cleaning out her desk. To tell you the truth, I was a little surprised by it."

"Why?"

"Because there's not much on it," Riviera said.

Frank opened the folder and glanced down at the nearly empty page.

"She didn't list any employment between 1936 and 1955," he said.

"No, she didn't."

"Or references."

"That's right," Riviera said.

"You mentioned this man, Bornstein," he said. "Is he still alive?"

Riviera waved his hand. "No. He died years ago. He was a legend in the trade. They gave him a big send-off. Lots of flowers. Fancy hearse."

"Did you go to the funeral?"

"Sure, I did," Riviera said. "He gave me my first steady work."

"Did Hannah go?"

"If she did, I didn't notice her," Riviera told him. "But there was a big crowd for Bornstein's funeral. He was ruthless. And in this business, that gets you a lot of respect."

Frank wrote it down. "Do you know of anyone else who might have known Hannah in the thirties?"

"Well, you could always check out that synagogue I told you about."

"I will."

Riviera thought for a moment. "But maybe I have a better idea," he said. "Especially if you feel like a little *schmoozing*." He smiled. "There's this housing project down in Chelsea. People down there will talk your head off."

"What housing project?"

"It's called Consolidated Housing," Riviera said. "It's on the West Side. Ninth Avenue at 23rd Street. There're a lot of old needle-trade survivors around there. They sit around the social room and bullshit about the old days." He shrugged. "Some of them might have known Hannah back when she was a working girl."

Frank wrote down the address.

"As far as anybody around here," Riviera added, "I don't think you'd find much. I mean, the police have tried, but I don't think they came up with anything."

"Did you tell them about the housing project?"

Riviera shook his head. "No. But I don't think they'd have been interested in going that far back. I mean, they figure Hannah's death for some kind of psycho thing. At least that's what they told me."

"Or something to do with her business," Frank added.

"There's always that possibility."

"Did they question many people around here?" Frank asked.

"Quite a few," Riviera said. "And just like you said, they were looking for some sort of beef at work. Somebody Hannah had fired, something like that." He nodded toward Frank's notebook. "But if you're working a different angle, you ought to check out those old farts in Chelsea before you do anything else." He laughed. "You won't have any trouble getting them to talk. All they've got left is memory, and, believe me, they work that pushcart up the whole street." He stood up, as if dismissing Frank authoritatively.

Frank remained seated, his notebook still open.

Riviera looked at him curiously. "Is there anything else? I mean, are you through?"

Frank nodded slowly. "Yeah, I guess I am," he said.

Riviera swept his arm toward the door. "Come, then," he said. "I'll walk you to the elevator."

"Thanks."

Within a few seconds, the two of them were back in the lobby.

"We do nice work here," Riviera said, as he pointed to the graceful waves of strangely radiant cloth that swept along the walls.

"Yes, you do," Frank said.

"It's a rough business, no doubt about it," Riviera added. He smiled. "But what comes out of it is good."

10

The large square building on 23rd Street was constructed of plain red brick and surrounded by long stretches of corroding storm fence. A cracked cement walkway led to the entrance.

An old woman stood at the front door, her body wrapped in a large cloth coat, her head covered with a thick scarf which she gathered at the neck and held with a gloved hand. She shrank back slightly as Frank approached, and he nodded to her quickly, then stopped before he came too close.

"Is this Consolidated Housing?" he asked

"Yes," the old woman told him.

"I'm looking for the social room."

"Inside and to the right," the woman said. She continued to eye Frank suspiciously. "You looking for someone in particular?"

"No," Frank said. "Just anybody who lives in the building."

The old woman turned and pointed through the glass doors to a wide tiled corridor. "There are always a few people in the common room," she said. "First door on the right."

There was a small cluster of people near the back of the room, all of them sitting around a long rectangular table. Several of them watched Frank curiously as he approached.

"Sorry to bother you," Frank said as he stepped up to the table. He took out his identification. "I'm a private investigator, and I'm trying to find out a few things about a woman some of you might have known."

A large woman with brightly painted lips turned toward him. "So what do we look like, *Information Please?*"

"It would help me to find out a few things," Frank said. "She's dead."

An old man jerked his head up quickly. "Dead?"

"Yes."

He laughed. "In that case, I probably know her." He looked at the others and smiled. "It's the live ones, I got no connection."

The woman poked him lightly in the ribs. "You know why, Izzy? Your connection is too short."

The others laughed, and Frank laughed with them.

"Sit down," the old man said. "We'll talk. We love to talk."

Frank sat down.

"I'm Izzy Berman," the old man said. He nodded one by one to the two other people at the table. "This is Clara Zametkin, and this guy with the little Irish cap, he's Benny Shein."

"Glad to meet you," Frank said.

Berman leaned forward slightly, cocking his ear. "Now who was this woman you're talking about?"

"Her name was Hannah," Frank said. "Hannah Karlsberg."

The three people exchanged glances, then shook their heads slowly.

"She worked in a sweatshop on Orchard Street," Frank said.

"When did she do that?" Benny asked.

"Early thirties."

Benny looked at Clara. "You should know her," he said. "You were down there."

Clara thought about it. "Karlsberg," she repeated softly, "Hannah Karlsberg." She looked at Frank. "I don't think so."

"She was a rabbi's daughter," Frank added. "Someone told me that he had a synagogue around Fifth Street and the Bowery."

Suddenly the old woman's face seemed to grow softly illuminated. "Hannah Karlsberg?" she asked again.

"The rabbi died," Frank said. "And that's when she came to Orchard Street. She had a couple—"

"Kovatnik," the old woman blurted. "Her name was Kovatnik, Hannah Kovatnik."

The two old men exchanged glances.

"Hannah Kovatnik?" Benny said. "You're talking about Hannah Kovatnik?"

Clara looked at him determinedly. "Got to be, Benny. Who else?" She turned to Frank. "Oh, yes, I remember Hannah. Everyone remembers Hannah." She glanced at the others. "Remember that time in the meeting hall? That night Schreiber was going on about a strike, and all the girls were there? All of them crowded together. What a noise. Remember that?"

Benny nodded. "Who could forget?"

"Oh yes," Berman said. "Oh God, yes."

"And Schreiber was going on about the defeats," Clara continued, "the weakness."

Benny shivered slightly. "Putting us to sleep, that one. Always whining. I used to say to Leon Jaffe, 'Leon, how come they don't send a big strong man to talk to us? How come always this Schreiber?' Such a sniveler. Always picking at himself. Tics, so many tics." His lips curled down disgustedly. "And I'm supposed to listen to such a person, maybe risk my neck for such a person?" He waved his hand. "Forget it."

Clara seemed not to hear him. "And still, while Schreiber is going on, comes up from nowhere, this girl. What was she? Nineteen? Twenty?" Her eyes darted over to Frank. "Comes up this girl to the platform, and she starts to talking in Yiddish, starts to talking about what's going on in her shop." She shook her head. "Such a speech she made, you wouldn't believe it. Such a speech, without a paper in her hand. Coming from her heart." She looked intently at Berman. "Am I right?"

"Absolutely," Berman said. He looked at Frank pointedly. "You listen to Clara. She knows."

"She was speaking maybe ten minutes," Clara went on, "but it didn't matter. Could have been an hour, no one would have moved. But it was maybe ten minutes, and when it was over, there was such a commotion, you couldn't believe it."

Benny laughed. "And Schreiber didn't know what to do. He looked ridiculous. Like a clown, a fool. This girl had made him look like that."

"But there was nothing for him to do," Clara told him vehemently. "Hannah was doing everything." Her eyes swept back to Frank. "And then, at the end of it, she says, now this was in Yiddish, she says, 'You got to strike. You got to strike. So, tell me, you will strike?' And all the girls, they yell back, yes, they will strike. And Hannah, she puts her hand above her head, and she says, in Yiddish she says, 'Then give me the Jewish pledge.' " Her eyes grew fiery as she repeated it. " 'If I betray you, may my hand wither and my tongue cleave to the roof of my mouth.' " Her eyes widened. "That's what she said. And—boom—that's what they did."

The three old people nodded together.

"That's right," Berman said. "That's what it was like that night."

Frank took out his notebook. "When was that?"

"That was in December of 1935," Clara answered. "I remember because my brother, may he rest in peace, had just died of TB."

"And when did you see Hannah again?" Frank asked.

"After that? Oh, well, after that, we saw a lot of Hannah," Clara answered. She looked at the others. "Some people, they make a stir, then they disappear. But not Hannah. She led the girls, led the strike."

"She led the strike?" Frank asked.

"She started it," Clara said, "and so she finished it. That's the way Hannah Kovatnik was."

"How did she lead it?"

"She worked with the union."

"Which union?"

"The AGW," Benny chimed in. "The American Garment Workers."

"Hannah was a member?"

"Of course," Clara said. "It was a union meeting, the one she spoke at. Schreiber, he was the local bigwig. He was on the Central Committee."

Again, Berman waved his hand. "Such a sniveler."

Clare nodded briskly at Frank's notebook. "Take down his name. Leon Schreiber, a big thing in the union."

Berman shook his head. "He was a *putz*, that one."

"Is he still alive?" Frank asked immediately.

"Leon? No. Been dead for years."

Clara looked at Berman scornfully. "He wasn't such a *putz*, Leon. He worked hard." She glanced back at Frank. "But he was a sort of what you call, what we call, a *schlemazel*."

"You see, a *putz*," Berman yelped. "Just like I said."

Frank continued to keep his attention on Clara.

"A person who . . . who . . . who don't know how to act," Clara explained, "an unfortunate person, always getting messed up."

"That's putting the best light on it," Berman said with a laugh.

Benny touched Berman's shoulder. "Izzy," he scolded, "let Clara talk."

"So anyway," Clara went on, "we saw a lot of Hannah. She was all over the neighborhood. Late at night you'd see her on Orchard Street. Early in the morning, on Ludlow Street, or Hester, maybe, or any of the streets that needed something. Sometimes food, some pumpernickel, a little herring. A little encouragement, maybe. It depended what they needed. Whatever it was, like they say, she did what she could. But she couldn't do everything. Who can? She couldn't make the world over. But like it's written in the Talmud, to make it over, this is not required of a person. But to do what one person can to make it over, this much is a *mitzvah*, a good deed."

"And Hannah did it, that's for sure," Benny said emphatically. "She was like a voice in the wilderness that night in the meeting hall."

"No one ever forgot it," Berman added. "A thrill like that don't come too often." He grinned impishly. "And at my age now, it don't come at all."

"Do you remember her sisters?" Frank asked.

"I remember one of them," Clara said. "She was younger. I forget her name. But she was always with Hannah, always walking next to her." She smiled. "They always looked nice. Hannah always kept herself looking nice. The sister, too. The little girl.

Hannah kept her hair brushed, and always that little white apron. Clean, you know, kept nice."

"And what about the other sister?"

"I don't remember her much. Maybe just a little."

"Was she older? Younger?"

"Near Hannah. Younger, older, who knows?" Clara said. She looked back at the two older men. "You remember anything about the other sister?"

The two old men shook their heads.

"I remember the little one," Benny said. "She was very pretty, but I got no idea about her name."

"What about friends?" Frank said. "From the old days."

"You mean of Hannah?" Clara asked.

"Yes."

Clara stared at the two men thoughtfully. "Friends?" she repeated, almost to herself. "Wasn't there a girl Hannah used to see?" She stopped, trying to remember. "From some little place in Galicia."

The two men stared at her expressionlessly.

"They all came from the same place," Clara went on, "the ones that lived in her building."

"Where was her building?" Benny asked.

"On Rivington Street. Where Clinton comes into it."

Benny nodded his head. "Yes, yes. From Lemberg, Galicia. All those people came from Rivington. That was their *landslayt*." He thought a moment. "She stayed in the union, this girl. For many years." Again he stopped to consider. "Polansky," he said finally. "Etta Polansky."

Clara clapped her hands together softly. "That's the name. Etta Polansky. I remember now."

"And she was a friend of Hannah's?"

"A good friend, yes," Clara assured him. "They were together a lot, those two."

Frank wrote down the name, then looked back up at Clara.

"Do you have any idea where I could find her?"

"So many years," Clara said. "I don't know." She glanced at the others. "You got maybe an idea?"

The two men shrugged helplessly, then suddenly Berman spoke up. "Well, try the phone book."

"That won't help if she got married," Clara said scoldingly. "She would have a different name."

"But could be she didn't," Berman said, almost defensively. "Who knows? Could be an *einzam maidel*."

Clara shook her head. "Talk English, Izzy. He don't speak Yiddish." Then she turned back to Frank. *"Einzam maidel,"* she said. "A woman alone."

11

Frank glanced down at the name and address which he'd copied out of the Brooklyn directory, the only E. Polansky listed in any of the New York City phone books. It was late in the afternoon by then, and the narrow sidewalks of Williamsburg were dotted with people returning to their homes. Large yellow buses, marked in thick black Hebrew lettering, rolled up and down the street, slowly emptying their burden of Hasidic Jews. The men emerged erect and silent, their bodies wrapped in long black coats, their beards flowing down to their chests in tangled strands. As Frank walked among them, he felt like an intruder, for they seemed locked in an immemorial isolation, massed together against the surrounding city as if they knew it was poised to sweep in and engulf them. In Manhattan, he had seen them in such numbers only along 47th Street, the diamond district, where they scurried back and forth, their hands grasping plain black briefcases which were said to contain untold millions in gold and precious stones, and which they sometimes handcuffed to their wrists.

But the Williamsburg section of Brooklyn was entirely different from West 47th Street. It was a grid of streets bordered by small rowhouses which seemed to lean wearily together, as if huddling for warmth against the cold winter air. It gave off a disquieting sense of a people under siege, and as Frank turned right and made his way through the neighborhood, he could feel the heavy weight of the life that was lived around him, tight, enclosed, so utterly self-reliant, watchful and exclusive, that it seemed to wall itself in from the rest of the world, to hold this, its bleak beachhead, as if it were the last on earth.

The house at 2410 Van Kalten Street looked like all the others which surrounded it. It was made of wood which had been covered over with a simulated brick exterior. A small porch spread out from the front door, and just in front of the steps there was a tiny yard, little more than two small squares of green on either side of a cracked cement walkway.

No one answered at the first knock, so Frank waited a moment, then tapped a little more insistently at the door.

It opened slightly, but Frank could see the brass chain as it continued to dangle between the door and the jamb.

"What is it?" someone asked.

"My name is Frank Clemons," Frank said. He took out a card and pressed it through the crack in the door. A small white hand snapped it from his fingers, then stuck it out again a few seconds later.

"I think you must be at the wrong place," the voice said.

"That's possible," Frank said. "But I wonder if you could tell me if an Etta Polansky lives here."

A single brown eye peered out at him through a hazy bar of light. "That's my aunt."

"Is she here?"

"What do you want?"

"I need to talk to her about a friend of hers," Frank said. "A woman named Hannah Kovatnik."

Silence.

"Some people told me that your aunt might have known this woman," Frank said, somewhat more emphatically. "Miss Kovatnik is dead, and we need to let her relatives know."

He could hear the chain rattle softly behind the door, and a moment later it opened slowly. A tall, slender woman stood in the dark interior of the house. She looked to be in her early twenties, and yet her face was drawn and deeply lined, and her eyes had the milky quality of someone who had not been in the open air for a long time.

"My aunt's not doing so good," she said.

"I only have a few questions," Frank said.

The woman stared at him silently. She seemed unable to focus, as if a murky glass divided her from the rest of the world. "I don't know," she said hesitantly. "She may be asleep, you know?"

"No one has come forward to claim Miss Kovatnik's body," Frank explained. "We're looking for a relative, so we can have it buried."

The woman said nothing. Her lean arms dangled from her shoulders like broken limbs, and for an instant she seemed almost to dissolve entirely, crumble into the air.

"Your aunt might be able to help me quite a bit," Frank said insistently. "I'd really like to talk with her a minute, if I could."

"She stays in the back."

"Is she there now?"

"Yes," the woman said. She remained in place, standing rigidly before him, her body like a thin shaft of flesh.

"Would it be all right if I spoke to her?"

"I guess it would," the woman said. She turned and led Frank through the house and into a back room. It was cluttered with books and magazines. Pictures were strewn about the floor, along with jacketless records, paper cups, and an assortment of old pamphlets, dry and yellowing in the dusky light.

"Etta," the woman called as she stepped into the center of the room.

Something stirred to the left, and Frank turned and saw a small iron bed, piled with soiled bedding.

"Aunt Etta," the woman repeated, this time more loudly. She walked to the bed, grasped its metal headboard and shook it violently.

"Etta!" she cried.

A low groan came from the mound of tangled quilts.

"A man's here, Aunt Etta," the woman said dully. "He wants to talk to you about some old friend of yours."

The mound of bedding stirred uneasily again. Then a single gnarled hand crawled over the edge of the covers and pressed them downward to reveal a face that for all its age struck Frank as astonishingly beautiful.

He stepped over to the bed and looked down at her.

"I'm sorry to bother you," he said.

Her eyes were black, utterly black, and they stared up at him without flinching. She did not speak.

"Somebody's dead, Aunt Etta," the other woman said immediately. "One of your old friends."

The old woman nodded, but she did not look at her niece. Instead, she fixed her eyes on Frank. "What can I do for you?" she asked.

"Dead, Aunt Etta," the other woman repeated, "that's what this man's come to tell you."

The old woman's eyes narrowed as they snapped over to the other woman. *"Geh avec,"* she said irritably to her niece.

For a moment the other woman did not move. "I was just trying to help you," she whined.

"Get out, Rachel," the old woman said. "Just go back outside."

The other woman turned feebly and left the room, her bare feet padding softly across the plain wooden floor.

The two black eyes turned back to Frank.

"Sit down," she said.

Frank settled into one of the small chairs which rested near her bed. "I won't be too long," he said.

"You think I care?" the old woman asked with a slight shrug. "If I don't talk to you, I talk to her."

Frank smiled.

"You got children?" the old woman asked.

Frank shook his head.

"I have only the niece," the old woman said bitterly. "Such a prize." She sat up slightly and poked one of her fingers into the soft tissue of her upper arm. "Drugs, you know? There's nothing left of her." Her lips curled down in a deadly snarl. "Such a prize, that one. A gift from God. Used by everybody." The finger plucked at her chest. "Nothing of her own in here."

Frank took out his notebook. "I was down in Chelsea today," he began, "a housing project. A lot of people from the Lower East Side live there now."

The old woman nodded slowly. "From the trade, yes," she said. "Old radicals, some of them."

"I was asking them if they knew a woman from back in the thirties," Frank said.

The old woman stared at him evenly. "A woman? What woman?"

"Hannah Kovatnik."

Suddenly, Etta's eyes drifted down toward a stack of yellowing newspapers, and as she looked at it, a soft wistfulness came into her face.

"Hannah," she whispered.

"She's dead," Frank told her quietly.

Etta's eyes lingered on the dusty pile of papers.

"She was murdered," Frank added.

For a moment, some sort of fierce emotion passed over her face. "Oh, Hannah. Dear Hannah," she said gently. "Who would kill Hannah?"

"The police are looking into it," Frank said.

The old woman shook her head unbelievingly, but she said nothing.

"Her body is still at the morgue," Frank told her. "I'm trying to find a way to get it released for burial."

"At the morgue," the woman said mournfully. "Poor Hannah."

Frank sat back slightly. "The people down in Chelsea, they said that you knew her pretty well in the old days."

The old woman looked puzzled. "I did. But that was so long ago. How could I help her now? She's already gone."

"You worked together, they said," Frank asked.

"Yes," the old woman said. "We worked together, the two of us. In the thirties. At the sewing machines together. That's the way it was." Her mind seemed to drift back effortlessly to that distant time. "In those days, you never stopped. You wanted maybe to eat, to take a bite of something, it was at the machines you did it. You needed to go to the bathroom, it was a big deal." She smiled. "But at least, the way it was, you got to know the person next to you." The second hand emerged from beneath the blanket, its fingers holding gently to a tangled ball of red yarn. "There was a connection, you understand? Between you and the next person." She shook her head despairingly. "Now, it's different. A different world."

Frank nodded. "You remembered her right away," he said coaxingly.

A soft smile fluttered onto her lips. "Who wouldn't remember Hannah? Some memories don't go away." Her fingers gently tugged at a slender strand of yarn. "She had such qualities, Hannah. Such great qualities." Her eyes drifted toward one of the tall stacks of yellowing pamphlets. "She was a born leader. La Pasionaria, you understand? Like that, a voice in the streets. That's what she was. A Rosa Luxemburg, you understand?" Her eyes turned toward the small window. "In those days, everything was possible."

"When did you meet Hannah?" Frank asked.

The eyes lingered on the window, and the small green shutter that closed off the light. She did not answer.

"You mentioned the thirties," Frank said, gently drawing her attention back to him.

"1930," Etta said. She turned to him and smiled. "The fall, I remember."

"Where?"

"Her father, he had died. The rabbi. That's what he was."

"Yes, I know."

"It had been very hard," Etta went on. "They had nothing. And now, the father was dead. What could they do? Who could help them? They had come alone, the whole family, from a little *shtetl* in Poland. The synagogue tried to help, but where there is nothing, there is nothing. Who can give what he doesn't have?" She shrugged. "They stayed in the basement awhile. But they couldn't stay forever." She smiled mockingly. "You know how it is, God must be served. There must be a new rabbi. The prayers must be said. There must be a *shul*. And so, in the end, the children had to go." She straightened herself slightly, pressing her back against the wall. "And so Hannah had to find work," she continued. "She was the oldest. She took on the family, you understand? Everything was on her shoulders. Finally she came down to Orchard Street. There was a sweatshop on the third floor. That's where I saw her." She smiled appreciatively. "She dressed herself up very nice, in a white dress, the only one she had. She looked very good. The manager noticed that. He hired her right away, and they put her at the sewing machine next to mine."

"And that's how you came to know her?"

"Yes," Etta said, "at the machines." Her mind seemed to drift back again, her fingers now turning slowly, spooling the yarn delicately around them. "It was a hard shop. The one on Orchard Street. But they were all hard. A friend of mine, he used to say, 'If the people knew how a coat got to Bloomingdale's, it would break their hearts.' " She looked at Frank intently. "Do you think that's true?"

"I don't know."

Etta waved her hand. "Anyway, it was all piecework, and the bosses were always speeding up the task-rate. You'd start with nine coats in a task, then the bosses would want ten, then twelve. You made twelve, it finished your task. You got paid by the task, so you got the same for twelve coats today that you'd got for nine the day before. That's the way it worked." She shook her head. "You made maybe twenty dollars a week. Sometimes less, sometimes a little more. And if you gave them any trouble, the bosses, you were out."

"Is that what caused the strike," Frank asked, "the task-rate?"

"That was part of it," Etta said, "but it was just the way things were. So bad. Up on the third floor, that's where we worked. Maybe fifteen of us, all girls, all sitting at the machines." She smiled. "They were good girls. Very sweet. Innocent." Then her face darkened. "The owner, he used to walk around, touching them. *Meine vunderbare meydekh*,' he'd say, 'my wonderful girls.' "

"Do you remember his name?"

"Who could forget it," Etta said instantly. "Such a skinny little man. You thought the wind would blow through him. Feig was his name. Sol Feig."

Frank wrote it down.

"It was a 'hotshop,' " Etta said, "Feig's was."

"What does that mean?"

"That it was ready for action," Etta told him. "You know, to be unionized." She shook her head. "The way people were treated, that's what made it hot." She smiled. "There was no ventilation, no shaft for air, so in the summer, the heat was so bad, sometimes you couldn't breathe."

Suddenly the door creaked open and Etta's niece peeped in. "I'm going out," she said crisply. "For smokes."

Etta waved her hand dismissively and the niece crept back slowly, closing the door behind her.

"Smokes," Etta said derisively. "Dope, that's what she'll get. In the park, some dope of some kind. I don't even know what it is. So many. I can't keep up with them." She shook her head. "If you have nothing to live for, you can live for anything." She straightened herself slightly and turned back to Frank. "Where was I?"

"Orchard Street," Frank told her, "the hotshop."

Etta nodded. "Hannah was the first to talk about it. The union. She was the first. And everybody listened, all the girls, because she was a good worker, Hannah was. She was good at the piecework. She had fast fingers." She took a deep breath, and Frank could hear a slight rattling in her chest. "She was a fighter, too," she said. "Made of steel, Hannah."

"What did she do exactly?" Frank asked. "In the shop, I mean."

"She sewed, like me," Etta said. "We made coats. So in that shop you had different people doing different things. You had a baster that kept the cloth moist. You had pressers and a button sewer. There was maybe a trimmer there, and a busheler."

"And you worked together for five years?" Frank asked.

"Close to five years," Hannah said. "We went through the strike together. My God, you should have seen Hannah. She was the leader."

"Of the strike?"

"Our shop. Of our shop."

"This was in . . . ?"

"1935. The winter of 1935," Etta told him. "They'd cut the piece-rate in half, and that meant you could work an eighteen-hour day and barely make enough to live. We walked off when Feig did that."

"And Hannah led the strike?"

"She made speeches," Etta said. "The union paper published one of them, I remember."

"What union was it?"

"The American Garment Workers," Etta told him. "That's the one that made the strike."

Frank wrote it down quickly, then looked back up at Etta. "And Hannah worked with this union?" he asked.

"Oh yes, she did," Etta told him. She smiled brightly. "We had a big rally one day in Union Square. Not just the garment workers, but everybody. What they called an Unemployment

Rally. Hannah spoke for us, for our shop. You should have seen her, the way she stood on that platform. She wasn't big, Hannah wasn't. But on that platform, wrapped up in a big black coat— it was so cold, you know—she looked so big. Like a giant, I mean. She raised her hand when she spoke, always her hand in the air. And her voice, what a wonderful voice. It carried everywhere, like it was on a loudspeaker or something." She looked at Frank intently. "It was something to be there, to see her." She drew in a long breath. "Now, the way it is, you can live your whole life and never hear a voice like that. And what she said. Such great things." She shook her head. "You hear things like that. In a crowd, you know? Everyone together. You don't need to smoke anything, or stick a needle in your arm to make you feel good."

Frank nodded slowly. He could feel the crush of the crowd in Union Square, see its thousand faces lift up toward the small young woman in the long black coat, as her voice began to pour fervently over them. He could hear the people as they continued to murmur inattentively, then grow silent as her voice rose higher and higher, until it finally reached its greatest height and then slid, almost shyly, beneath the thunder of their cheers.

"She did her best," Etta said finally. "Not just for herself. For everybody. For what you call 'the far and near,' the ones you know, the ones you don't."

Frank nodded quickly. "She had two sisters, I understand," he said. "Did you know them?"

"Yes," Etta said. "Gilda and Naomi. She brought them to the shop from time to time. Eventually they both worked there. Gilda was very pretty. All the men were after her, but she wouldn't give them the time of day. I don't think she ever had a man." She shrugged. "Naomi was sort of plain, but she was a nice girl."

"What can you tell me about Naomi?" Frank asked immediately.

"She got married eventually," Etta said. "To a nice man, I heard. He was a teacher, I think." She smiled again. "They were nice girls, the sisters. How are they doing?"

"One of them died," Frank said.

"And the other one?"

"I don't know."

A deep sadness moved into her face. "Gone, too, I guess. Like everything else."

"Naomi's husband," Frank said. "Would you happen to remember his name?"

"No."

Frank held his pencil poised over his notebook. "Would you happen to know if Naomi and her husband ever had any children?"

"No."

"The husband, did you ever hear that he had died, anything like that?"

"No."

"Do you know anything about him?" Frank continued determinedly. "Something that might help me find him?"

"I only saw him a couple of times," Etta said. "He wasn't handsome at all, but he looked sturdy. I guess that appealed to Naomi."

"And you said he was a teacher?"

"That's right."

"Do you know where he might have taught?"

"Maybe public school," Etta said. "Maybe a yeshiva."

Frank wrote her answers down quickly, then glanced back up toward her. "And what do you know about Gilda?"

"She was a beautiful girl," Etta said. "And smart, like Hannah."

"How about Hannah," Frank said. "When was the last time you saw her?"

"She stayed in the shop for a while," Etta said. "After the strike, I mean."

"When did the strike end?"

"March of 1936."

"And you all went back to work?"

"Back to our machines."

"Hannah, too?"

"Yes," Etta said. "She came back to Orchard Street. She was the same old Hannah for a while. She was still working with the union. She wrote articles."

"Articles?"

"For the union paper," Etta said. She reached down to a stack of newspapers that leaned unsteadily beside her bed, pulled one from the top and handed it to Frank. "This is the latest one, but I've kept them all over the years."

Frank glanced down at the paper. "And Hannah published articles in this paper?"

"Yes, she did," Etta said. "Quite a few after the strike. You want to see them?"

"Yes."

For the next few minutes, the old woman rumbled heavily around the room, randomly snatching at the yellowing editions of the union paper that she'd collected over the years. She was able to gather about fifteen of them together before the task seemed finally to overtake her and she slumped back on the bed, wheezing, exhausted, but with an oddly lingering fire in her eyes.

"I hope that'll help you," she said as she handed them to Frank. She smiled quietly. "You can take them with you, I guess. I won't need them anymore."

"Thanks," Frank told her. He tucked the crumbling papers under his arm and started toward the door.

"That's how I saw Hannah the last time, you know," Etta said from behind him.

He turned toward her. "How?"

"With a stack of union papers under her arm," Hannah said. Her mind moved back slowly, gracefully, without fear, as if, after a long and difficult journey, it was returning home. "She was up on Herald Square," she said. "It was around Christmas because I remember there were bells ringing all around her. It was snowing, too, and she was standing in the snow with a rolled-up copy of the union paper in each hand, and she was calling out to the people going by. 'Read this,' she was saying, 'Read this, and keep a place in your heart for justice.' " Her eyes shifted over to the small window, then back to Frank. "I've never forgotten that," she said. "She was so small, but brave." She smiled quietly. "Little Hannah Kovatnik."

"After she left the shop," Frank said, "did she stay in touch with anyone?"

"No."

"Not even you?"

"No," Etta repeated. "She seemed sad all of a sudden. This was just before she left the shop. Very sad. She looked sick. People said, 'Hannah's got TB,' things like that. Then, a little later, she was gone." She shook her head wonderingly. "And she took Gilda with her. Naomi was already married by then. I guess she moved away." She shrugged. "We never heard from any of them again. It was as if all three of them—the Kovatnik sisters—had just dropped off the edge of the world."

12

It was nearly night by the time Frank got off the subway at West Fourth Street. He walked east, through the heart of Greenwich Village, until he reached the Bowery. To the north, he could see the great red facade of Cooper Union, and the little concrete park which spread out in front of it. A few of the evening's small army of street vendors had already begun to display their wares: jewelry, old clothes, and an enormous assortment of books and old magazines. Each night they swept out onto the streets with their varied supply of abandoned goods, and as he crossed the wide square where Third Avenue and the Bowery met, Frank remembered how they'd been on the streets the first night Karen had taken him here, and how he'd stopped at one of them and bought her a small plastic cameo. At first, she'd worn it every day after that, then only from time to time, and finally not at all. He imagined that it was somewhere on the bottom of her jewelry box now, nestled warmly among the emeralds and pearls.

The synagogue was almost exactly where Riviera had remembered it, a square white building only a few paces in from the Bowery. Its outer walls had begun to crack and crumble, and even in the darkening air, Frank could make out the cracked windows of the second floor and the rusty, battered drain which drooped above them.

A short wrought-iron gate blocked the stairs to the second floor, and Frank leaned softly against it as he peered down toward the line of dark basement windows. She had lived down there, Hannah Kovatnik, with her father, the rabbi, and her two sisters, the one so beautiful, the other, as Frank had begun to imagine her, quite plain. In his mind he could hear their voices, high, girlish, speaking in another language as they did their nightly chores or lay together in their bedroom, their three faces lit by gas jets or candlelight. Three sisters, one beautiful, one plain, and the third, Hannah, somewhere in between, lovely in a flowered hat, but plain in a dark scarf, so that perhaps she had come to realize that it was clothes which made the difference, which made her either attractive or ordinary, and out of that, the beginning of a life's devotion.

"You looking for something?" someone asked suddenly.

Frank turned and saw a tall, very thin man eyeing him cautiously from a short distance away. He was dressed in a long blue overcoat, the back of his head covered by a small black yarmulka. His beard was white and it fell almost to his chest. For a moment, he continued to peer at Frank intently. "Are you Jewish?" he asked finally.

"No."

"This is a synagogue."

"I know."

"It is no longer functioning," the man added, in a low, heavily accented voice. "Closed now for many years."

"Did you ever go here?" Frank asked.

"Many times, yes," the man replied hastily. "You are not from New York?"

"No," Frank said. "But I live here now."

The man frowned deeply. "Who would move to such a place, I ask myself?"

Frank smiled. "I followed a woman," he said.

The old man nodded slowly. "And you are staying?"

"I guess," Frank said.

The old man shrugged. "Maybe you're an architect," the man said. "I notice you are looking at the building."

"No," Frank said. "I'm checking on some things about a woman."

"The one you came here with? She lives in the neighborhood?"

Frank shook his head. "No. A Jewish woman. She lived here."

The old man looked astonished. "Lived here?"

"In the basement."

"The basement? Of the synagogue?"

"Her father was the rabbi."

"Ah, yes," the old man said. "This was many, many years ago. No one has lived here since then."

"She was a young girl then."

"And now?"

"In her seventies."

The old man leaned against the gate. He seemed to be going through a series of calculations. "That would have been Rabbi Kovatnik."

"Did you know him?"

"A little," the man said. "He was nice, but nothing in the head. Rabbi, it means 'teacher,' but this one, he had nothing in the head." He nodded toward the gate. "You want to go in? Maybe you would like to look around a little?"

"It's locked."

The old man pulled an enormous ring of keys from beneath his coat. "I manage a few buildings on this block. This one is easy. No tenants." He stepped briskly between Frank and the gate. "Just a second." He fumbled awkwardly with the keys for a moment, then the gate swung open. "Okay, come in." He chuckled to himself. "You couldn't hurt this place, it's been falling down for years."

Frank followed the old man up a short flight of concrete stairs to the door of the synagogue. The old man opened it, then stepped inside, keeping Frank on the walkway.

"Please keep the hat on in here," he said quietly. "It's not exactly a synagogue anymore, but God, He may think it is."

"Of course," Frank said.

"We keep on the electricity in case for a buyer," the old man said as he flipped on the light switch. "Since there's no more Jews in the neighborhood, it's of no use to anyone, this building.

So, we're trying to sell it." He pointed to the ceiling. Dark water stains swept out from the four corners and plaster sagged here and there in large gray flaps. "But as you can see," the old man added, "it's not such a bargain."

"How long has it been closed?" Frank asked as he stepped toward the middle of the room.

"I think maybe fifteen years."

"What happened to the rabbi?" Frank asked.

"The last one? He went to a bigger place. Somewhere in California, I think."

"I meant Rabbi Kovatnik," Frank said.

The old man did not seem to hear him.

"And the people who used to come here, the ones who used to hear the prayers on Shabbas?" he said, almost to himself. "Dead. All dead." He drew an old, badly wrinkled prayer shawl from one of the unpainted wooden pews. "Where have they gone, I ask myself?" He drew his eyes over to Frank. "But who ever hears an answer?" He folded the prayer shawl neatly and draped it over the pew. "You want to see where they lived, Rabbi Kovatnik and his daughters?"

"Yes."

"Come with me."

A narrow wooden staircase led shakily to the basement, its steps creaking loudly as Frank and the old man made their way down.

"For the time, it was not so bad," the old man said as he switched on the light.

The walls were whitish-pink, and paint hung from them like strips of skin. A small pool of filmy water rippled in the far left corner, and Frank could see tiny wet tracks leading out of it and into the dark adjoining room. There was a single table at the center of the room. A menorah rested in the middle of it, along with a stack of crumbling prayerbooks. A rickety stand of bookshelves leaned heavily to the right, its scarred sides bearing down on a small wooden high chair.

"Is there anything interesting in this place?" the old man asked as he looked quizzically at Frank.

Frank shook his head. "Not much."

"You want to see the rest?"

"Yes," Frank told him.

"A regular tour," the man said with a wave of his hand. "But I got nothing but time." He motioned to the right then walked into the next room and turned on the light.

It was the bedroom, and it was not unlike what Frank had briefly imagined as he had lingered outside, leaning on the gate. Three iron beds stretched end to end across the room, their metal springs drooping almost to the ground. There was a paper calendar above one of them. A red *X* had been placed on the date, October 15, 1929, and as Frank stepped over and looked at it, he tried to imagine which of the sisters had put it there and what it had marked: a date, a religious holiday, some upcoming event that had been important enough to signify. He could feel the heaviness of time all about him, the brevity of life, the way it drained away in a quiet rush of days until it was gone, gone as if in one quick, invisible streak.

"He died suddenly, Rabbi Kovatnik," the old man said. "And after that, the new rabbi lived across the street. So they closed the basement."

"When was that?"

The old man squinted toward the calendar. "Right after Rabbi Kovatnik died, I think. Things have been left to go since then." He shook his head despairingly. "What a pity. It's not a bad building. Not a bargain, I admit it. But not such a bad building."

Frank's eyes moved slowly down the bleak row of iron beds. "There were three sisters," he said, as his eyes turned toward the old man. "Do you remember them?"

The old man nodded. "Gilda, I remember. And the oldest one."

"Hannah."

"Ah, yes, Hannah," the old man said. "What her father didn't have in the head, she got it." He looked at him intently. "She was your friend, maybe?"

"No."

"But something to you, yes?"

Frank nodded. "Something to me, yes, she is."

The old man shrugged. "I did not know her very well," he said. Then he turned and pointed down the street. "I lived on Second Avenue in those days. But we came to synagogue here, and so I would see them, the girls." He smiled. "Hannah was the leader. When the rabbi died, she took them away."

"To Orchard Street," Frank told him.

"And did they stay together, the sisters?" the old man asked.

"For a while."

The old man laughed. "Oh yes, I remember."

"Remember what?"

"Was a scandal or something," the old man said. He waved his hand. "I can't remember."

"What kind of scandal?"

"They went to work," the old man told him. "All of them. Even the youngest, the pretty one."

"Gilda," Frank said.

A kind of odd radiance rose in the old man's face. "Yes, Gilda. Such a beautiful girl. She must have been thirteen."

"What about a scandal?"

"For a bachelor, they went to work," the old man said. "Yes, a bachelor, I think it was. People said it wasn't right, him taking in those three girls."

"They lived with him?"

"Upstairs from him."

Frank took out his notebook and wrote it down. "Where was that?"

"Around Orchard Street," the old man said, "but it's all been torn down. Nothing but projects where it used to be."

"The man, what was his name?"

"Feig," the old man said instantly. "Sol Feig." He shook his head. "People said it wasn't right. The rabbi's daughters, you know." He shrugged helplessly. "I don't know. It was the middle of the Depression. People have to eat." He glanced over toward the row of beds. "She was such a bright little thing, Hannah," he said, "always taking charge." He smiled. "The old people still talk about it, how Hannah ran things. Even the rabbi. Around her little finger, that's where she had him." He lifted a single crooked finger into the yellowish air, then made a circle around it with this other hand. "Around her finger," he repeated.

"That sometimes happens," Frank said.

The old man nodded. "Such a smart little girl, Hannah. A quick mind, that one. Everyone said, 'Watch Hannah, she'll go far.' " He cocked his head slightly and looked at Frank quizzically. "Where did she go?"

Frank glanced back toward the row of beds. Their dark gray

shadows seemed to climb slowly up the rough, grimy walls. "I don't know," he said.

"But you are looking for her?"

"In a way."

The old man nodded. "We go, now," he said as his hand moved toward the light.

Back on the street, Frank waited while the old man carefully locked the gate. Then they walked slowly west, toward the Bowery.

"Do you have any idea what happened to the sisters?" Frank asked when they reached the corner.

"No."

"How about any other relatives?" Frank added insistently. "Nephews, nieces, cousins? Anything?"

The old man shook his head emphatically. "When they left this street, we heard only there was a scandal."

"You mean about them living with Feig?"

"Something was bad, something about Feig," the old man said. "Don't ask. I'm an old man. What do I know?"

"But that's all you heard?" Frank asked. "Something about a scandal of some kind?"

"If there was more, it was not for me to hear," the old man said. "I was a little boy. When my parents spoke about such things, they spoke in Polish. Polish they used for secrets."

"But as for yourself," Frank said, "you never saw or heard from them again?"

"Never," the old man said emphatically. "Who knows what happens to people when they leave the neighborhood?"

Frank glanced back down Fifth Street. From the corner it looked like a long black tunnel.

It was a long walk from the old synagogue to the New York City morgue and night had fully fallen by the time Frank got there. Silvio Santucci was the night orderly, and Frank had made it his business to take him out for a drink not long after getting his license. Santucci worked what he called "the graveyard graveyard shift," and Frank had sat in the dark bar for several hours listening to his tales of high-class corruption. "When the Archbishop's sister goes off a roof," Santucci had said toward the end of the evening, and with an air of conclusion, "it ain't a suicide, you know? She may have been depressed. She may even have left a bitchy little note detailing her complaints. But it ain't no suicide. Hell no. The fucking wind blew her off, blew her over a six-foot storm fence topped with another foot and a half of concertina wire." He had then smiled impishly. "I believe that, Frank. But then, what can I say, I'm a fucking fool."

"Hello, Frank," Santucci said now as Frank approached his desk.

Frank nodded.

"So," Santucci said. "Come to wet my whistle again, or cash in on the last one?"

"Cash in."

"Stands to reason," Santucci said. "No such thing as a free drink, right?" He leaned back in his chair. "So what can I do for you?"

"I'd like to see a body."

"Any one in particular?"

"Hannah Karlsberg."

"How come?"

"I'm working on the case."

"That's Midtown North. Got an okay?"

"Not in writing."

"You talk to Tannenbaum?"

"Yes."

Santucci nodded. "Okay," he said. "No big deal." He smiled cheerfully. "Hell, I'd of let you in anyway, Frank, you know that." He stood up and headed down the brightly lit corridor which led to the freezer room.

"Ever been here before?" he asked as he plunged through the wooden double doors.

"Not this one," Frank said. "Others."

"Karlsberg's in number 14," Santucci said as he marched to a wall of stainless-steel refrigerator cabinets. "Here you go."

"Thanks," Frank said.

"Not a relative, right?" Santucci asked. "You said a case."

"That's right."

"Good," Santucci said lightly. "That's the only fucking thing I hate, showing the stiffs to the relatives." He shook his head. "I don't get paid for that. That's cop shit." He grabbed the metal handle and swung open the door. "Heeeeeere's Johnny," he cried with a short laugh as he drew out the carriage.

A huge black bag covered Hannah Karlsberg's body.

"You just interested in the face," Santucci asked, "or the whole thing?"

"Her face," Frank told him softly.

"Easiest part," Santucci said. He reached over and unzipped the bag a few inches. "Looks like a nice old lady," he said as he glanced down at Hannah's face.

"Yeah, she does," Frank said quietly. The skin was very pale, the lips a deep blue, but the face itself seemed soft and kindly. He could imagine how she must have looked in her youth, neither plain, nor beautiful, but a face that could be either, with high rounded cheekbones, large oval eyes, and a full mouth.

"She was slashed real bad," Santucci said, "but I guess you know that."

Frank looked up. "Yes," he said. "And her hand, I know about that."

"That's the psycho touch if you ask me," Santucci said, "that's the thing that lets you know it wasn't her favorite kid with an eye to the insurance."

"Unless it was faked," Frank told him.

Santucci shrugged. "Always a possibility. Is that what Tannenbaum figures?"

"I don't know."

"Want to see it, the hack job?"

For a moment he didn't, then suddenly Frank realized that he had to see it, that it was part of what he had to know.

"Yes," he said, "I want to see it."

"Fine with me," Santucci said. "I've showed a lot worse things in my time, you know?" He drew the zipper down a few inches farther, then reached in and brought out Hannah's lower arm. "There you go," he said, as he laid it across the plastic. "What I call the psycho touch."

The arm was white and smooth, except for the few slits which the autopsy had confirmed as defensive wounds. The hand had been severed at the wrist, and from the look of it, it had been done raggedly, with a twisting, tearing force that had left tattered skin and jagged bone in its wake.

"It looks messy to me," Frank said.

Santucci smiled. "Well, I'll say this, a surgeon didn't do it."
He glanced down at the hand. "Or even a fucking butcher, if
you know what I mean." He shook his head. "This was a yank-
and-pull job, if ever I saw one." He looked at Frank. "Of course,
this guy was probably in a hurry, right?" The smile broadened.
"Not to mention his frame of mind."

"I read the autopsy report," Frank said. "Did anything else
come along after it?"

"No."

"Any visitors drop by?"

"Cops and you, that's all."

"No word from the family?"

"Far as we can tell, this old lady was like the old ME used
to say, 'alone in the fucking universe.' "

Alone, Frank thought, as his eyes once again drew down toward her face. He saw her with her sisters in their bedroom,
then with the other workers in the shop, and finally standing
before the sweeping crowd at Union Square. Alone, he repeated
in his mind, and the word seemed to move through him like a
darkly weaving ribbon.

It was a long walk from the East Village back to midtown,
but he took it anyway. The night was dark and cold, but the
movement of the crowds, the noise, the speeding traffic seemed
to connect him to the city. It was as if the random jostling and
nameless faces provided him with something that worked in
the place of something else that never had, a sense of being
woven, despite his isolation, into an immense, eternal fabric.

He stopped at La Femme Gatée, the small delicatessen at the
corner of Ninth Avenue and 49th Street. A few of the regulars
were there, the old lady with her two pet dogs, the exhausted
night watchman who patrolled the building site across the street,
the Puerto Rican super who read El Diario in the back corner
of the room.

He ordered a coffee, then sat down at one of the large windows
that overlooked the street and began to go through the stack of
old newspapers Etta Polansky had given him. The first was
dated December 12, 1931, and toward the back there was a letter

which had been written by one of the union's younger members, a woman who worked a sewing machine on Orchard Street.

> *When I came to this country in 1927, I wanted to make it on my own, like a good American does. This was my dream. It was the same as most people have. But since working in my shop, I have come to think that this is not the way to think about America, or myself, or about any of the other people in my shop. I think now that we must stand together, and let all the other people stand with us too. We make the clothes the people wear. But we also eat the food they grow. We are in life together, not apart. We are like the body, which needs all its parts to work. We are like the fingers of the hand.*

Nothing by Hannah appeared for almost a year after that. Then, in the spring of 1933, there was another short letter, similar to the first. After that, there was nothing until February of 1936. By then, it seemed to Frank as he read the short article on page sixteen of the paper, Hannah's voice had lost all its girlishness. Now it was strong, self-confident and full of a fierce conviction. He could almost hear it ring in the air around him, feel it flowing over him, as the crowds had felt it in the meeting hall and at Union Square.

> *Justice is not a rally, no matter how big it is. Justice is not a wage, no matter how fair it is. Justice is a way of looking at life. It is a way of seeing every other person, and the rights of that person and the work that that person does for you, and that you do for him. Justice is the way you fit in, and the way you allow other people to fit in. There is no lone justice. There is no solitary justice. There is no work of justice that isolates another person. Justice is the great unifying principle of all life. A single life may look for comfort. A single life may look for love. But all life, when it is lived together, looks for justice.*

It had been written in the middle of a labor struggle that, according to the union paper, had rocked the garment trades for many months. Throughout the paper, there were grainy black-and-white photographs of strikes, sit-ins, lockouts, of men and women gathered in crowded meeting halls, or huddling outside doorways while the police stood at a distance, staring grimly at the crowd.

Frank was nearly halfway through the stack of newspapers when he finished the last of his coffee and walked down the street to his office.

Once behind his desk, he poured himself a single shot of Irish, drank it down, then turned on the desk lamp and began going through the papers once again.

In early March, photographs of strikes and marches gave way to a raw winter violence. Police in thick greatcoats charged into the milling crowds, or rode into them, lashing their horses wildly as they plunged forward.

In the March 14 issue of the union paper, there was another article by Hannah. It detailed the particular difficulties of the sweatshop workers on the Lower East Side, the crowded hovels in which they lived, the exploitation they suffered at the hands of the owners and their brokers. Along with the article, there was a picture of its author, a young woman in a thick sweater, her hair held tightly in place beneath a tattered wool cap, her eyes staring fiercely at the camera from behind a pair of plain wire glasses.

Two weeks later, another picture of Hannah appeared in the paper, this one accompanied by a short article about her which had been written by a man named Philip Stern. It detailed her journey to America, her father's death, her work at the sweatshop on Orchard Street, and finally her continuing commitment to the union. The accompanying photograph showed Hannah at the Union Square rally, her body held high on the platform, her fist in the air, a sea of faces gazing up at her from below in a kind of frozen rapture.

For a long time, Frank stared silently at the photograph. He could almost feel the cold winter wind which lifted her scarf and held it fluttering in the air, hear the roar of the crowd as they cheered her, feel the triumph of her hand in the crisp, biting air, sense the sheer, driving power of her voice as it pealed over them, crying out the words which Stern had quoted:

> *No man lives without other men. No weight is lifted by a single shoulder. No hope is carried on a single voice. Each man lives in another's debt. And the payment of that debt is justice.*

Frank turned the page, then went on to the next issue, and the next. The weeks passed in a sweep of yellow pages. The workers returned to their shops. The machines began to hum again.

And Hannah disappeared.

Frank folded the last of the papers, and stacked it neatly on top of the rest. He stood up and stretched his long arms in the shadowy light. Then he walked over to the small sofa which rested by the window at the front of the room and stretched out across it. For a time, he thought of returning to Karen's apartment, but the idea of padding across its carpeted floor, or sliding in beneath the lush down comforter, did not appeal to him, and so he simply remained on the sofa, his arms behind his head, until light began to break outside his window.

13

Frank had just returned from the corner deli with his morning coffee when Farouk walked through the door.

"You do remember me?" he asked, his enormous frame almost entirely blocking the light from the basement window.

"Of course I do," Frank said.

Farouk nodded. "That is good," he said. "I thought that perhaps the liquor might have erased a few important items."

"It doesn't work that way with me."

"Good," Farouk said. He nodded toward the chair in front of Frank's desk. "I may sit?"

"Of course."

Farouk lumbered over to the chair and eased himself into it. "I make myself available, as you recall."

"Yes."

He smiled. "Well, in such a connection, I have discovered a few things."

"About her business dealings?"

"Her possessions," Farouk said. "She owned the apartment she lived in, along with a small house on Long Island. She was not in debt, and no one was in debt to her. She never declared a dependent on any tax form, which means she supported no one but herself."

"So there are no lost children," Frank said.

Farouk shook his head. "She had no life insurance," he went on, "so no beneficiary. Again, a dead end."

Frank nodded expressionlessly.

"As to her will," Farouk said.

"The American Cancer Society," Frank said. "Tannenbaum told me."

"He is correct," Farouk said.

"Is that all?"

Farouk smiled quietly. "Not quite, no," he said.

Frank stared at him intently. "What?"

Farouk pulled a single piece of lined white paper from an envelope and unfolded it. "One of my professional services, as you might call it, deals with genealogy." He smiled shyly. "If I might say so, I have become quite good at it."

Frank said nothing.

"Do you know what I mean by genealogy?" Farouk asked.

"Tracing families," Frank said.

"This is so," Farouk said. He glanced toward the paper. "I have done some work on the dead woman."

"So have I."

Farouk looked at Frank quizzically. "Is this your usual practice?"

"When I'm looking for a lost relative, it is," Frank told him.

Farouk smiled appreciatively. "Yes, of course." He drew a pair of black-rimmed glasses from his pocket and put them on. "You would like to know what I have found?"

"That her real name was Kovatnik," Frank said. "And that she was the daughter of a rabbi whose synagogue was on the east side."

Farouk looked up from the paper. "This is so, yes."

"And that she had two sisters."

"Again, this is so," Farouk said.

"One of them was pretty. Her name was Gilda."

"That she was pretty is not in the papers."

"And the other one was named Naomi."

"Yes, correct," Farouk said, surprised. "You found all of this from people?"

"Yes," Frank said. "Where did you get your information?"

"From various records," Farouk said. He returned his glasses to his jacket pocket and stared evenly at Frank. "A record is a holy relic. To keep it is a primitive rite. To destroy it is a sacrilege. This is the way it works with records. Not only here. Everywhere. When we take a man's name from the files of the world, we steal his soul away from him, you see?"

"What else did you find out?" Frank asked.

"They came from Poland. A little village not far from Warsaw. The year, if you do not know it, was 1927. Gilda was the youngest, six. Naomi was only two years older. Next came the dead woman."

"Hannah."

"Yes," Farouk said, his eyes still on the paper. "She was born in October of 1910."

Suddenly Frank remembered the calendar. "What day in October?" he asked quickly.

"The fifteenth," Farouk answered. "Why?"

"She had marked it on her calendar."

"Marked what?"

"Her birthday," Frank said. In his mind he could see her doing it, standing on her bed, facing the wall, a red crayon in her hand.

Farouk looked up from the paper. "How do you know this?"

"I saw where they lived," Frank said. "Nothing had really changed very much. Most of the furniture was gone, but there was a calendar."

"I see," Farouk said. "Where was this place?"

"At the synagogue."

"On Fifth Street," Farouk said. "Until their father died?"

"Yes," Frank said. He leaned forward slightly. "Do you know where they went after that?"

Farouk smiled. "Yes," he said. "To a man named Feig. He had a factory on Orchard Street. They lived in the rooms above it."

"Yes, I heard that."

"Something else," Farouk said. He looked at Frank quizzically. "Perhaps something of service, something you did not find yourself?"

"What?"

"This Feig, he is still alive."

"The factory was here," Farouk said as he pointed to a small playground. "This is where they lived."

Through the metal web of the storm fence, Frank could see a bare stretch of ground dotted with swings and seesaws. There was a metal slide at the far corner, and two small children were climbing up it while their mother watched nervously from below. A few feet away, another group of children were moving up and down the climbing dome, one of them screaming triumphantly from its top.

"This playground is a part of the project," Farouk added. He glanced up at the tall brick buildings which towered over them. "If the sisters had had children," he added bleakly, "they might have been living here."

Frank continued to watch the playground. He could remember how Sarah, his daughter, had loved the small playground near their house, how she had climbed higher than anyone else, swung faster, how she had seemed to crave **speed**, motion, height. In those days he had been sure that she had gotten it from him, and that such needs were good, that they would not betray her.

Farouk blew a wide, tumbling cloud of smoke through the fence. "There was no playground then," he said, "no place for a picnic, a walk, nothing." He turned and jabbed the cigarette and ivory holder toward the adjoining streets. "Only the streets, the tenements, the factories." He shrugged. "Such it was, at that time."

"Is it different now?"

"For some," Farouk said with a slight shrug. He turned and pointed down Orchard Street. "Come, let us talk to this Mr. Feig."

They moved north, away from the projects, and as they entered Orchard Street, the crowds seemed to engulf them. On all sides thick herds of people jogged one another mercilessly as they struggled to make their way up and down the street. Wooden display stands spilled out from the small stores, and people stood in tight knots as they picked through the goods. Above them, crude hand-lettered signs advertised in English and Hebrew. There were butcher shops and shoe stores, electronics outlets and haberdasheries, and by the time Frank had jostled his way to the entrance of the retirement home, he had come to think that he could have bought almost anything at some point along the way.

There was a small glass enclosure at the front of the building and Frank followed along as Farouk stepped up to it and nodded to the nurse who sat at a desk behind it.

"I am looking for a Mr. Sol Feig," he told her.

"Are you a relative?" the woman asked.

"No," Farouk said. He reached into his jacket pocket and pulled out a laminated card. "I am from the Social Security Administration," he added, "and it is possible that Mr. Feig would be eligible for certain additional benefits. It is a matter that needs to be discussed with him as soon as it is possible to do this."

The woman looked at the card, then glanced at the small round clock behind her. "Well, you got here just in time," she said. She handed Farouk back the card. "Visiting hours just started." She looked at Frank. "Will you be seeing Mr. Feig, too?"

"Yes, he will," Farouk answered quickly. "Mr. Clemons is my associate in this matter."

The nurse nodded peremptorily. "Room three oh six," she said.

Sol Feig sat in a wheelchair, his face turned toward the small window at the back of the room. His body was curled forward slightly, as if he were reaching for something, and a rounded hump could be seen rising beneath his plain white dressing gown.

"Mr. Feig?" Farouk said as he stepped up to him.

Feig turned slightly, twisting painfully toward them. A gentle palsy rocked his head and shook his two thin hands.

"I am Farouk, and this is my associate, Mr. Clemons."

Feig's small brown eyes darted to Frank, narrowed slightly, then returned to Farouk. "Feig," he whispered gruffly. He blinked rapidly as he labored to straighten himself. "I am Sol Feig. What do you want with me?"

"We would like to speak with you," Farouk added. He nodded

toward Frank. "Mr. Clemons will explain," he said, as he stepped back slightly.

"We're trying to find out a few things about a woman you once knew," Frank began. "We think you might be able to help us track a few things down."

Feig stared at Frank suspiciously. "Woman?" he snapped.

"Her name was Hannah," Frank told him, "Hannah Kovatnik."

Suddenly Feig's lips curled downward. "Hannah," he repeated.

"Yes."

"Hannah," the old man said again, his voice suddenly sharper, more vehement.

Frank knelt down beside the chair. "We understand she worked for you. At your factory here on Orchard Street."

Feig's eyes narrowed into two small, unspeakably hateful slits. *"Sie war eine Hure,"* he snarled.

Frank leaned toward him. "What was that?"

Farouk touched Frank's arm. "Never mind," he said quickly. Then he turned back to Feig. *"Was wissen Sie von dieser Frau?"* he asked sharply.

Feig glared at him bitterly. "Everything," he hissed angrily, "I know everything about her." He spat on the floor. *"Ihr Herz war schwarz."*

Farouk's dark eyes bored into the old man. *"Warum sagen Sie das?"*

"My love," Feig said, again in a low whisper, his voice suddenly breaking over the words. "My dear love."

"What do you mean?" Farouk demanded.

The old man said nothing. He seemed to withdraw into a dark cavern deep within him.

"Did you know her sisters?" Farouk asked quickly.

The old man's eyes drifted toward the window. He did not answer.

"Was wissen Sie, Herr Feig?" Farouk asked.

The old man's eyes swept toward the window. *"Ich weiss nichts."*

"Was wissen Sie?" Farouk demanded sharply.

Feig shook his head resolutely, his lips curling down in a scowl. "No more," he snarled. "No more."

"No," Farouk said with a sudden fierce determination. His body stiffened, and Frank could see a galvanizing passion leap into his eyes. *"Ich will die Wahrheit wissen,"* he said urgently.

The old man did not speak.

"The truth," Farouk demanded.

Suddenly the old man's face twisted brutally. *"Ich muss mit anderen Menschen leben,"* he cried. He wrenched his head to the left, his eyes staring brokenly at Frank. *"Ich habe mit Scham gelebt,"* he said tremulously.

Frank stared helplessly at Farouk.

Farouk glared intently at the old man. *"Die Wahrheit,"* he said.

The old man's face grew stony. *"Fragen Sie Gott,"* he said.

Farouk stepped back slowly, as if giving up. Then he turned and walked into the corridor.

"What was it?" Frank asked as he quickly joined him there.

Farouk stepped over to the elevator and pushed the down button. His face trembled slightly. "Nothing of use," he said, his voice clearly shaken.

"Did he know Hannah?"

"He knew her, yes," Farouk said. He took a deep breath, and let it out slowly.

"Well, what did he say?" Frank demanded.

"He said that he lived in shame," Farouk told him.

"But what did he say about Hannah?"

"He called her his dead love," Farouk answered wonderingly. "And he called her a whore."

"A whore?"

"A whore, yes," Farouk repeated. The elevator door opened and the two of them walked in.

"He said she was a whore," Farouk began again, his voice barely audible above the purr of the elevator, "and that her heart was black."

14

Frank paid the vendor, then tucked the magazine under his arm and headed down 49th Street toward his office. Farouk walked beside him, his eyes surveying the immense rust-colored skeleton of the building which was going up across the street.

"Your rent, Frank," he said. "It will be going up when this is finished."

"Yeah, I know," Frank said.

Farouk's eyes continued to scan the naked maze of steel girders. "The old man," he said. "Feig. He looked like a spider." He turned to Frank. "When the old are thin, they always look like spiders."

"The old man who showed me where Hannah had lived," Frank said. "He talked about a scandal."

Farouk's eyes shifted over to him. "Scandal?"

"Yes," Frank said. "But he didn't go into it."

"Perhaps you didn't press him hard enough," Farouk said.

"I'm not sure it would have done any good."

"Perhaps not," Farouk admitted with a slight shrug.

Frank reached up and absently fingered the pages of the magazine. "She worked for Feig. At least we know that. And she lived above him, in his building."

"And she betrayed him, as well," Farouk said quickly.

"What do you mean?"

"She joined a union," Farouk explained. "She helped to lead a strike against him. It's possible that to Feig, this was betrayal."

"Yes."

Farouk nodded firmly. Then his eyes once again scanned the massive steel building. "That could cause a great deal of bitterness," he said, thoughtfully. "But it wasn't bitterness Feig talked about." He looked at Frank. "It was shame." He considered it for a moment. "He said, '*Ich habe mit Scham gelebt.*' This means, 'I have lived in shame.' "

Frank said nothing.

"Then he said, '*Ich muss mit anderen Menschen leben,* ' " Farouk added.

"What does that mean?"

"It means, 'I have to live with other people.' "

Frank looked at him. "That sounds like Hannah."

"What do you mean?"

"It sounds like something from one of her speeches," Frank told him. "The kind she made during the strike."

"Against Feig?"

"Against him and the others."

Farouk's eyebrows lowered slightly. "Do you think he was quoting the dead woman? Could this be possible?"

"I don't know."

For a little while they walked on silently. Then Farouk glanced at the magazine which Frank had tucked under his arm. "You are interested in interior design?" he asked.

"My client mentioned that someone had done a story on Hannah's apartment," Frank told him. "About how it's decorated. You know, pictures and all. I thought I'd take a look at it."

"Yes, that's good," Farouk said. "I will also look."

Once inside his office, Frank turned on the desk lamp and opened the magazine to the article on Hannah's apartment.

Farouk stood over him, staring intently at the pictures.

"So that is the dead woman," he said as he gazed at the first photograph. It showed Hannah in her study, sitting at her desk, looking pensively at a few fashion sketches. Her hair was pulled tight around the sides of her head and gathered in a bun. She was wearing a dark red blouse that looked as if it were made of velvet. It had a high lacy collar, and seemed a bit too formal for the picture, as if Hannah had decided to dress herself up for the photo session, and in doing so had gone just a bit too far.

"A handsome woman," Farouk said as he looked at her.

Frank remembered her face as it had appeared in the union newspaper, then as he had actually seen it for the first time, white with bluish lips. He turned the page.

The next picture showed the study itself, then the single wall of pictures and awards, all neatly framed and carefully arranged.

"From the look of it," Frank said, "the killer didn't go in here. At least he didn't kill her in here."

Again he turned the page, this time to a large color photograph of Hannah's living room. It looked larger in the photograph, but the subdued elegance was the same. There was the lovely brocade sofa, the polished antique furniture and lush blue carpet, the vases of freshly cut flowers and large glass coffee table.

"This woman lived well," Farouk said quietly as he stared at the photograph.

"Yes," Frank said. For a moment, his eyes held to the picture. Then he turned to the next page.

There was a photograph of Hannah's bathroom, complete with marble fixtures and terra-cotta walls. The accompanying caption gave the dimensions of the room and commented upon its inventive use of so limited a space.

Frank turned the page again, but there were no more pictures of Hannah's apartment, so he flipped back to the beginning again, his eyes lingering on Hannah's quietly contemplative face.

"Was she raped?" Farouk asked.

"No."

"And nothing stolen?"

Frank shook his head. "All her jewelry was there," he said, "and she had a lot of it." He looked up at Farouk. "And she didn't have a safe."

"What do the police think?"

"That it was probably a psycho," Frank said.

"Because of the hand."

"Yes."

Farouk leaned toward the pictures in the magazine. "Where was the body?"

Frank took out the police photo of Hannah sprawled across the living room floor and dropped it onto the open magazine.

Farouk did not flinch as he stared at the photograph. His eyes seemed almost to caress Hannah's contorted body.

"I'm sorry," he said.

Frank's eyes shifted from the stark cruelty of the police photo to the magazine's idealized living room with its soft blue carpet and polished furniture. The two pictures had been shot from almost exactly the same spot in the room, and showed the marble coffee table, the ornately flowered sofa, and then the wall behind it. Slowly, Frank's eyes followed a straight line out from the carpet, then back toward the sofa and up the wall to the neatly arranged collection of photographs.

"Alone," he said after a moment. "In all these pictures. She's always alone." He looked up at Farouk. "It's as if no one knew her."

Farouk straightened himself. "Perhaps the photographer knew her," he said. "Perhaps they talked while he took the pictures."

"It's possible."

"At such a time," Farouk added, "she might have said something about the past."

Frank nodded. "He might have gotten to know her a little. We should talk to him, that's for sure."

"And her killer," Farouk said. "Do you think he knew her?"

Frank shook his head. "I don't know."

Farouk looked at him intently. "So now, you are looking for her killer?" he asked.

For an instant, a swirl of images passed through Frank's mind. He saw Hannah's face at various stages in her life, saw the rooms she'd lived in, the streets she'd walked, heard the words that had come from her pen and her mouth, saw the raised hand in the cold winter air, then the same hand, scarred and mutilated, under the hard light of the morgue.

"Yes," he said. "I am."

*   *   *

The doorman recognized Frank immediately, but he watched Farouk suspiciously as the two of them came through the entrance to Hannah's building.

"I came back to check up on something," Frank told him quickly.

"You're working on the murder, right?"

"Yes," Frank said.

The doorman's eyes shifted over to Farouk. "You, too?"

Farouk nodded silently.

For a moment, the doorman seemed to hesitate, then he shrugged suddenly. "Go on up, then," he said. "I don't care. This is my last day on the job anyway." He stepped into a small adjoining room and returned with a key. "Just don't forget to bring it back to me, okay?"

"Thanks," Frank said as he turned quickly and walked to the elevator.

The crime-scene seal was still on the door as Frank opened it and stepped inside the apartment.

Farouk stepped around him and walked quietly into the living room, turning slowly, his eyes sweeping the four blood-spattered walls. "That is the thing with murder," he said, after he'd completed one languid turn, "it has the look of the thing it is."

Frank walked to end of the foyer and leaned against the wall. "It's all been gone over by ID. Dusted. Vacuumed. Not to mention the pictures."

"The pictures, yes," Farouk said as his eyes came to rest on the swath of dried blood which swept almost to his feet. "They do not tell us how it feels."

"No, they don't," Frank said. "Not about a room like this."

Farouk's eyes peered down the rear corridor, toward the open bedroom door. "In there?"

"Office. Bedroom. No blood. No signs of a struggle."

Farouk's eyes swept back out to the living room. "Everything in here, yes?"

"Everything," Frank said. "But we could still do one more search. Of the whole place, I mean."

"Yes, good," Farouk agreed immediately.

"All right," Frank said, "you take the kitchen. I'll take the back bedroom. We'll work toward each other."

It took them almost two hours to complete a room-by-room search of the apartment, and when it was over, both of them slumped down on the sofa in the living room.

Farouk took a handkerchief from his back pocket and wiped his forehead. "It's been many years since I've done such a thing." He looked at Frank. "And you?"

Frank remembered how he'd meticulously gone through the doll-like room of Karen's sister, searching through the white wicker bureau and neatly ordered vanity for some signal that would guide him to her killer. "Not that long," he said.

Farouk returned the handkerchief to his pocket. "Nothing," he said, breathing heavily. "But this is often the case, yes?"

"Sometimes," Frank said.

"Perhaps, with the photographer, we will have better luck," Farouk said. He stood up immediately, his enormous gray shadow stretching with an oddly protective grace over the stained blue carpet.

The offices of *Homelife* magazine were on the sixty-third floor of one of the towering office buildings that rose above Fifth Avenue.

Frank dropped his copy of the latest issue on the desk of the receptionist. "Is Peter Kagan in?" he asked.

"I believe so," the receptionist said.

Frank took out his identification. "Would you tell him that I'd like to talk to him about the pictures he took a few weeks ago at Hannah Karlsberg's apartment?"

The receptionist's eyes widened. "Isn't she the woman who was murdered?"

"Yes."

"Just a moment," the receptionist said quickly. She disappeared behind a tall gray partition and returned, almost instantly, with a short, stocky man in a thick sweater and blue jeans.

"I'm Peter Kagan," the man said. "I understand this has to do with the Karlsberg shoot."

"That's right."

Kagan looked over at Farouk. "Are you with him?"

"Yes."

"Please come in," Kagan said as he ushered them behind the partition and into a small art room only a few feet away.

"As I told the police," Kagan began, "I didn't know Miss Karlsberg at all. I'd never seen her in my life before that day."

"We're more concerned with any conversation you might have had with her," Frank told him.

Kagan looked surprised. "Conversation? With Miss Karlsberg? Why?" He laughed nervously. "My God, I took those pictures weeks before Miss Karlsberg was killed. We have a three-month lead time on these things."

Frank took out his notebook. "Was Miss Karlsberg with you when you took the pictures?"

"Yes."

"In all the rooms?"

"All of them," Kagan said. "She followed me around the whole time."

"Followed you around?"

"Yeah," Kagan said. "Like a watchdog."

"Watchdog?"

"Like I might steal something," Kagan explained. "Like she was worried about that."

Frank wrote it down. "Did she talk much?"

Kagan's eyes fell toward the magazine. "No. I mean, almost not at all." He shrugged. "She was very stiff. Very quiet. She looked at you in a strange way."

"What do you mean?"

"Like you weren't really there," Kagan said. "It gave you a weird feeling."

"What kind of feeling?"

Kagan thought about it for a few seconds. "It was like you didn't exist, except for that moment. I mean, except for the time that you were with her. It's like you were there for her, and that's all you were."

"As a servant?" Farouk asked. "As if you were there only for her service?"

Kagan shook his head. "No, it was different from that." He smiled. "I mean, I've seen that before. This was different. It was like you didn't even exist for her after you left. You had sort of materialized to do these pictures of her apartment, and when that was over, you just . . .''

"Disappeared?" Frank asked.

"Ceased to be," Kagan said. "Ceased entirely to be."

Frank wrote it down. "How about her life," he asked. "Did she mention anything about her life?"

"No."

"Nothing at all?"

"Nothing."

"How about her past? Anything about that?"

Kagan shook his head. "I didn't even get the idea she had one." He glanced down at the magazine, his eyes lingering on the wall of photographs. "I mean, check this out. All the photographs are in color. Now this woman was what, seventy, something like that?"

"Seventy-four," Frank told him.

Kagan nodded. "Which means that she was a lot older than color photography." He pointed to the wall of photographs. "But all her personal pictures, at least the ones she had on the wall, all in color. That means they were taken relatively recently." He shrugged. "Now maybe she's got a trunk full of old black-and-whites stuck away somewhere. But most people, if they have pictures at all, they have a few from the past, you know." He glanced back and forth from Frank to Farouk, then back to Frank again. "But this woman, it's like she'd been born exactly the way she was."

Frank wrote it down, then stared at the letters silently while Farouk questioned Kagan about relatives Hannah might have mentioned, places she might have been. Exactly as she was, he repeated in his mind, born exactly as she was. But he had already seen her in her youth, seen her with others, seen her in the sweatshops and the snow.

Back at his office, Frank poured Farouk and himself a drink, then settled in behind his desk, his eyes scanning the stack of old union papers.

"She was involved in a strike years ago," he said.

Farouk lowered himself heavily into the chair in front of Frank's desk. "How many years?"

"It was in 1935 and early 1936."

"She was young."

"She sort of led it," Frank told him. He nodded toward the papers. "She wrote things for the union paper. She made speeches."

Farouk smiled quietly. "And so she rose."

"Rose?"

"When you do such things, you rise."

"In the union, you mean?"

Farouk nodded. "What happened after the strike?"

"I don't know," Frank admitted. "I'm not even sure if she won."

"The papers did not tell you?"

"People went back to work at her shop," Frank told him. "I'm not sure why."

Farouk took a sip from the glass, then leaned back slightly in his chair. "It is an old struggle," he said, "and it will not end, as my father used to say, until he who grows the fig can eat it." He took another sip of whiskey, and allowed his eyes to drift back toward the window. "So little light," he added. "You do not find that troubling?"

"I don't really notice it," Frank told him. He took one of the papers from the stack and opened it. "She left the shop not long after the strike ended."

"And where did she go?"

"I don't know," Frank said. "On her application, the one she wrote for her last job, she listed only one job after 1936." He found the picture of Hannah at the Union Square rally and turned it toward Farouk. "This is the way she looked back then," he said.

Farouk's eyes concentrated on the photograph. "Strange," he said, "how you can sometimes feel another person's force." He leaned forward, still staring intently at the picture. "Such conviction," he added. "In my opinion, it is the hardest thing to live without." He shook his head despairingly as he eased himself back into his seat. "Love comes and goes, yes? The same for money. One goes on with it, one goes on without it. But conviction, when it is missing, leaves a hole, I think."

Frank took the application from his pocket and unfolded it on the desk. "She mentions that she worked for Feig," he said, "and she lists one other job. In Brooklyn. At a place called Maximum Imports. But that's all." He handed the application to Farouk. "Other than that, it's been a blank."

Farouk took the paper and perused it casually for a moment. Then he looked up and smiled. "Do not fear, Frank," he said confidently. "In time, we shall fill it in."

15

Farouk had already left on something he referred to only as "other business," when the phone rang in Frank's office.

"Frank Clemons."

"Hello, Frank. It's Imalia Covallo."

"Hello, Miss Covallo."

"I've tried to reach you a couple of times today."

"Is something wrong?"

"No," Imalia said. "I was just wondering if you'd made any progress so far."

"A little," Frank told her. "I found out that Hannah had two sisters."

"Two?"

"Yes."

"Really? Is one of them still alive?"

"I don't know."

"Well, that should be easy to find out, shouldn't it?"

"Yes," Frank said. "If she doesn't mind being found."

There was a long pause. "Mind?" Imalia said finally. "Why would she mind?"

"Well, there's no indication that Hannah was in touch with her," Frank said. "Would you know anything about that?"

"I didn't even know she had two sisters," Imalia said. "As I told you before, the only sister I ever heard Hannah mention was dead."

"Did you know that Hannah had changed her name?" Frank asked.

"Hannah? She changed her name?"

"Yes."

"What was it before?"

"Kovatnik," Frank said. He glanced down at the application which Riviera had given him. "I have something Hannah filled out when she came to work for you," he said. "Sort of an application. It was in with some papers Mr. Riviera gave me."

"What about it?"

"She doesn't list any work between 1936 and 1955."

"She doesn't?"

"No."

"I didn't realize that."

"Did you read her application?"

"I don't think so," Imalia said. "But that wouldn't be unusual. I didn't personally hire Hannah."

"Who did?"

"I suppose Stanley did," Imalia said. "Stanley Burke. He more or less handled things like that in the early days. I remember that Tony brought Hannah in, but it was Stanley who actually hired her. She might have told him about the other places she'd worked."

"I thought you handled everything," Frank said.

"Well, almost everything," Imalia answered quickly. "Stanley did a few things. He was sort of my floor manager for a while."

Frank took out his notebook. "Where would I find him?"

"He lives in Queens," Imalia said. Then she gave him the address.

Frank wrote it down.

"So there's a gap," Frank said when he'd finished the address. "In time, a long gap."

"Well, maybe she was just negligent," Imalia said. "About the application, I mean."

"Well, I never knew Hannah," Frank said. "But from what

I've been able to pick up about her, she wasn't a negligent person."

"Well, maybe it was an interview situation," Imalia explained. "With Stanley, I mean. Maybe she filled him in, and writing it all down on an application form wasn't necessary."

"Maybe," Frank said.

"I mean, if she told him everything, that's all he'd need."

"Did this Mr. Burke ever mention anything she might have told him?"

"No."

"Did he mention anything about where Hannah had worked before he hired her?"

"No, nothing," Imalia said. "All I know is that he said she was very experienced in the trade, and that we could get her cheap."

"Cheap?"

"That's what he said."

"Why cheap?"

Imalia thought a moment. "I don't know," she said finally. "But maybe Stanley can tell you."

It was a large brick house on a lovely tree-lined street, and a nurse in a neatly pressed white uniform answered the door.

Frank showed her his identification. "I'm looking for a man named Stanley Burke," he said.

"Mr. Burke lives here," the nurse told him. "Is he expecting you?"

"I don't think so," Frank said, "but you could tell him that Imalia Covallo sent me."

"Okay," the nurse said. "Come in."

Frank followed the nurse to the rear of the house where an old man sat alone in a large greenhouse.

"Mr. Burke," the nurse said as she slid back the glass door of the room, "this is Mr. Frank Clemons. He says that Miss Covallo sent him over."

The old man raised his head slowly, his watery blue eyes blinking hard against the bright greenhouse light. "Come in, Mr. Clemons," he said.

Frank brushed a thick strand of vine from his path and stepped into the room. It was filled with an assortment of plants. Vines twined up white wooden posts or poured over the sides of their hanging planters. Huge ferns rose from the four corners of the room, their wide green fronds swaying delicately in the moist warm air.

The old man pointed to a small director's chair. "Please, sit down. Would you like something to drink?"

"No, thanks."

"The heat in here will make you thirsty," Burke said. "But I like it. It reminds me of the tropics."

Frank sat down and took out his notebook. "Thanks for seeing me."

Burke laughed quietly. "Well, you know how it is with old employers, you always feel like they're still your boss." His eyes brightened slightly. "She sends me a Christmas card every year."

"How long did you work for Miss Covallo?"

"Just a couple of years," Burke said. "I sort of kept tabs on everybody else in the early days. I did the payroll, hired and fired, that sort of thing."

"When did you do that?" Frank asked immediately. "What years?"

"When she first started out," Burke said. "That was the fall of 1968. I was juggling a lot of things in those days. The whole operation was on a shoestring." He laughed. "Or a hamstring, depending on how you felt about it."

"I understand you hired Hannah Karlsberg."

The old man nodded. "Yes, I did."

"Were you aware that that was not her actual name?"

"Yes," Burke said. "Her real name was Kovatnik."

He watched Frank expressionlessly. "But I only knew her as Hannah Karlsberg."

Frank took out the application and handed it to him. "Do you remember this?"

Burke looked at it casually. "Yes."

"It's not much of an application," Frank said.

Burked handed the paper back to Frank. "Hannah didn't need much of one."

"Why not?"

"Because when one of the grand old men of the rag trade recommends somebody, you hire her."

"Grand old men?"

"That's right," Burke said. "One of the grandest. Like the saying goes, present at the creation."

"And someone like that recommended Hannah?"

Burke nodded firmly. "Not only recommended her," he said. "He brought her to me personally. He was quite insistent, even though he didn't have to be." He smiled. "I mean, in 1955, he was still an old master."

Frank glanced down at his notebook. He could feel his fingers press down on the pencil. "This grand old master," he said. "Who was that?"

"Oh, that was Mr. Bornstein."

"Abe Bornstein?"

Burke looked surprised. "You've heard of him?"

"A little," Frank said. "He was some kind of labor broker down on the Lower East Side."

Burke laughed. "Maybe in years past," he said. "But when I knew Abe Bornstein, he was a lot more than a labor broker."

"What was he, exactly?"

"He was a fixer," Burke said. "A man who made deals. He owned a lot of warehouse space all over the city. He knew people. He got people together."

"And he recommended Hannah?"

"Oh, yes, he did," Burke said. "He came in one afternoon with Hannah and talked to the boss, Mr. Constanza. They had quite a little huddle in the back room, I guess. And when it was over, Hannah had been hired." He shifted slightly in his chair, his finger brushing at a large fern which spread out beside him. "At first I thought somebody was calling in a marker, something like that. But Hannah was not just some ditzy broad that some old man wanted on the payroll. She was a very serious kind of person, and she had a certain look . . . I don't know . . . like she ran things for herself, did what she wanted."

"And this was in 1955?"

"That's right."

Frank glanced quickly at his notes. "But I thought you went to work for Miss Covallo in 1968."

"That's true," Burke said. "But I'd hired Hannah years before that."

"In 1955," Frank said as he wrote the date down in his notebook.

"Absolutely," Burke told him. "I worked for Mr. Constanza then. He owned an operation called Maximum Imports."

"And that was the first time you hired Hannah?"

"Yes."

"For what?"

"I was never really sure," Burke said. "She worked in the office for a while, but I don't think that was the idea."

"What do you mean?"

"I think she was just biding her time there," Burke said. "She was really hired to set up her own thing. From the beginning, I mean. And before long, she'd done it. Hannah was like that. Very determined. Within a year she was running her own operation."

"Her own operation?"

"That's right."

"In Manhattan?"

"No, somewhere in Brooklyn."

"Do you know where?"

"I never found out," Burke said.

"But it was Hannah's, this operation?"

"Well, it belonged to Mr. Constanza," Burke said. "But Hannah was in charge of it."

"What kind of operation was it?"

"I don't know for sure," Burke said. "I just know that Mr. Constanza sunk a lot of money into it. I used to see the bills come in. He bought all kinds of stuff."

"Like what?"

"Various kinds of equipment. A tremendous amount of cloth."

"Cloth?"

"Plain white cloth," Burke said. "Thousands of bolts during the few years I worked for him. All of it went to Brooklyn."

"But you never found out what any of it was used for?" Frank asked.

Burke shook his head. "No, I didn't."

"You weren't curious about it?" Frank asked unbelievingly.

"I was curious," Burke said. "But it was very hush-hush. And you know how it is, when you work for a guy like Constanza, sometimes it pays to know as little as you can."

"Why?"

"Because you never know what he's up to," Burke said. "Or what he's capable of."

Frank looked at him intently. "What did you think it was, the operation in Brooklyn?"

Burke drew in a long breath. "It could have been anything. Absolutely anything. Maybe they made dresses, who knows? Maybe Hannah ran a whorehouse." He smiled knowingly. "With that much plain white cloth, you could cover up a lot of shit."

"Were you there when Constanza and Bornstein talked about her?"

"Just for the first couple of minutes," Burke said. "We were all in the back room, the four of us. Hannah stood in the corner, just sort of glancing around. She was dressed very well, I remember. Elegantly, like she took a lot of pride in herself, in the way she looked."

"Did she say anything?"

"She let Bornstein do the talking."

"What did he say?"

"He told Constanza that she knew a lot about refinishing material. About dyes, sheens, that sort of thing."

"Did she?"

"I never found out," Burke said. "But I got the feeling it was all some kind of code, you know, between the three of them. I was the odd man out."

"Did they talk about what Hannah had been doing during the last few years?"

"No," Burke said, "but one time Bornstein sort of laughed and said, 'And I can assure you that Miss Karlsberg can negotiate with the best of them.' And then Constanza and Bornstein had a big laugh over that." He stopped, his mind drifting back suddenly. "But Hannah didn't laugh," he said, almost to himself. "I remember glancing over toward her, and she was standing in the corner. Very rigid, you know, very cold, somehow."

"Did she say anything?"

"No, nothing," Burke said. "At least not while I was there. A few minutes later, Bornstein said something about ironing out a few problems, and then Mr. Constanza gave me the sign."

"What sign?"

"To leave, the sign to leave," Burke said. "That the rest was all private business."

"And that's when you left?"

"Oh, yeah, absolutely," Burke said emphatically. "With Constanza, the sign meant get out, that it was strictly his own thing. You know, between the interested parties, as they say."

Frank wrote it down quickly, then went on to another subject. "Did you ever meet Hannah's sisters?" he asked.

"No," Burke said.

"But you knew she had two sisters?"

"I knew she had one."

"How did you know that?"

"Because one day we were having some trouble on the line," Burke said. "This was at a shop in the Garment District. Anyway, one of the seamstresses took a few stitches in a finger, and, you know how it is, the whole place came to a stop. The last one to get there was this woman on a crutch. She practically hobbled across the room. Hannah was standing beside me, and I noticed there were tears in her eyes. I said, 'What's the matter, Hannah?' But she just quickly brushed at her eyes. 'Nothing,' she said, 'I just thought of my sister.' "

"When was this?"

Burke's eyes rolled upward gently. "Probably a year after she came to work," he said. "It must have been the fall, because the election was going on. Some sort of election. Everybody was wearing political buttons."

Frank wrote it down. "Did she happen to mention her sister's name?"

Burke shook his head. "No."

"Gilda? Naomi?"

"She never mentioned a name," Burke assured him. "And she let the whole business drop right away. I mean, she just wiped her eyes very quickly and walked away." He stopped, as if trying to find the right words. "Hannah Karlsberg was a complicated person, I think," he said finally. "You would see pieces of her. Those tears. The way she dressed. Little pieces. But nothing fit together in the right way." He smiled. "It's like a pattern. When you tear it, you throw everything off. The lines won't ever fit again. You can sew and rethread, but to a really good eye, it'll always look like a patch-up job."

"And that's the way Hannah looked?" Frank asked.

Burke nodded. "Like she'd been torn into little pieces, and then just sort of stitched together."

Frank thought about it a moment, then let his eyes drift back to the notebook. "So Hannah came to work for this Mr. Constanza in 1955?" he asked.

"That's right."

"And how long did she work for him?"

"I don't know for sure," Burke said. "But she was still working for him when I left."

"When was that?"

"Two years after I hired her. Fall of 1957. I moved to Texas. Some plants were opening up near the border. I was down there for almost fifteen years. But I always wanted to come back. After a while, I could afford to. That's when I hired on with Miss Covallo."

"And hired Hannah a second time?"

"Yes."

"And that was in 1968?"

"That's right, 1968," Stanley said. "The world had changed. Riots in the streets. But in the rag trade, things were like they'd always been, cutthroat. I mean, Miss Covallo was in big trouble."

"What do you mean?"

"Well, she'd started with very little," Burke told him. "And she'd lost most of it during the first two years." He laughed. "Now, everywhere you go, you see that sign, the one with the beautiful woman, and just the words: 'The Imalia Covallo Look.' " He shrugged. "That's the way this business is, full of surprises. I mean, in 1968, when I hired Hannah, I expected Miss Covallo to go under within a year. That's why I left."

"Left?"

"Quit," Burke said. "Took another job. I was jumping ship. Then things changed all of a sudden, and Miss Covallo made a big success. 'The Imalia Covallo Look' was born, but too late for me. I was already working with another company. It's still around, but it's minor league compared to Covallo."

"When did you leave?" Frank asked.

"In December of 1970," Burke said. "I was sure that Miss Covallo was flat busted, that she'd go belly up within a few months." He smiled ironically. "But two years later, she was on top of the fashion world. What a joke."

"So you only worked with Hannah for two years?"

"That's right," Burke said. "And I never got to know her."

"Do you have any idea why she left Maximum Imports?" Frank asked.

"Sure, I do," Burke said with a slight smile. "It closed down a few years after I left."

"Closed down?"

"Constanza ended up in jail," Burke said. "I don't know what happened, exactly. I was in Texas by then. But it was something with the IRS." He smiled. "It always is, right?"

Frank said nothing.

"Anyway, they seized everything but Constanza's jockstrap, if you know what I mean."

"When was that?"

"1965," Burke said. "I know because a few people called me down in Texas to see if there were any jobs."

"Did Hannah call you?"

"No."

Frank wrote it down, then tried to put it all together. "So she was with Maximum from 1955 until it closed about ten years later. Then she came to work for Miss Covallo."

"In 1968, yeah."

"Do you have any idea what she might have done in between?"

"No," Burke said. "But it's possible she might have gone to some other company. Tax records would show that, of course. It's even possible that she went back with the union."

"You knew about the union?"

"Oh, sure," Burke said. "Some of my people used to talk about it. They couldn't believe that she'd gone over to the other side, to the owners."

"They recognized her?"

"Of course," Burke said. "I mean, you can change your name, but you can't change your face. And if time hasn't changed it enough, people recognize it. And you can be sure they recognized

Hannah. I mean, she was considered very radical in the thirties. Very militant. Always making speeches. The word was, that she'd kept the people in her shop out longer than anyone else." He smiled thinly. "Of course—now this is from the union types who remembered her—the guy she worked for deserved to be ruined more than the others, the son of a bitch." He shrugged. "I mean, that's the way my people always told it, that her boss, that he was scum."

"You mean Sol Feig?"

Burke smiled. "Yeah, that's the name. Feig."

"Why did he deserve it more?"

"Because of what he was," Burke said with disgust.

Frank said nothing. He lowered the point of his pencil to the page.

"He attacked a young girl," Burke told him. "Tried to rape her."

"During the strike?"

"Toward the end of it," Burke said. "I was a young man in Cleveland then, of course. All this comes from shoptalk, you know."

"What was the shoptalk?"

"That Feig tried to rape a young woman, and that Hannah found out about it," Burke told him. "The word was that that's how the union beat the old bastard. The people found out what he'd done, you see. And it stiffened their backs a little."

In his mind, Frank could see Sol Feig's broken figure as it curled forward in the wheel chair, his fierce blue eyes staring at Farouk.

"When she worked for you," he said, "did she ever talk about the strike?"

"No," Burke said. "But that would not be unusual."

"Why?"

"Because she'd switched teams by then," Burke said. "It happens a lot, but it always leaves a bad taste."

"Switched teams?"

"Joined the other side," Burke said, "left the union, became a company man."

"But she'd left the union years before she came to work for you," Frank said.

"Years mean nothing when it comes to things like this," Burke told him.

"Like what?"

"Like loyalty," Burke said. "Like betrayal."

Frank wrote it down quickly, then looked back up at Burke. "So there was some resentment?" he asked. "Among the other workers?"

"It was more than resentment," Burke said. "They froze her out. They gave her the shoulder." He smiled sadly. "You see, the way they told it, Hannah had been a lot more than a member, she'd been a leader. And the way they felt, she'd deserted them. So, they did what you'd expect."

Frank nodded.

"You a Catholic, Mr. Clemons?" Burke asked suddenly.

"No."

"Well, if you were a Catholic you'd know about excommunication," Burke said. "Even if you were a Jew, you'd know about that."

"What do you mean?"

"It's like a formal ceremony," Burke went on. "And when it's over, you're cast out of the community forever. Your name can't be spoken. You are one of the living dead."

"And they felt that way—the workers—about Hannah?"

"Yes, they did."

"All of them?"

Burke did not answer right away. Instead, he thought about it for a moment. "Well, maybe not all of them. Maybe all but one."

Frank felt his breath draw in quickly. "Who?"

"Molly Gold," Burke said immediately. "She would talk to Hannah. She took a lot of heat for it. From the others, I mean. But any time Hannah would come into the main shop, the one in Manhattan, the two of them would chat for a while."

"Do you have any idea where she is?"

"No," Burke said. "But she shouldn't be hard to find." He chuckled. "She's got a record as long as your arm."

"Record?"

"Police record," Burke said. His face took on a look of wry amusement. "Molly is one of those people who decided to go her own damn way in the world." The amusement faded abruptly. "And of course, when you do that, life can take some pretty sharp turns."

Frank closed his notebook, glanced about the greenhouse for a moment, then turned back to Burke.

"Why did you tell Miss Covallo that Hannah would work cheap?" he asked.

Burke smiled. "Imalia told you that?"

"Yes."

"She has a good memory."

Frank continued to gaze at him silently. "Hannah had a lot of experience in the business, didn't she?" he asked.

"Yes."

"And she was older by then," Frank added. He did a quick calculation. "Her mid-fifties."

"That's right."

"So why would you think that you could get her cheap?"

"Because no one else would hire her," Burke answered finally. "At least, nobody in New York."

"Why?"

"Because she'd worked for Constanza."

"And he'd been sent to jail."

Burke laughed. "Jail? Christ, that had nothing to do with it. I don't think it even mattered much that he was probably some sort of low-level mobster." He shook his head. "No, the problem with Constanza is that he was a wildcatter, a guy who didn't play by the rules."

"What rules?"

"The rules of the trade," Burke said. "You know, like maybe going with a certain style once in a while, so that everybody has to buy it. Maybe cozying up to a sweetheart union."

"Constanza wouldn't do that sort of thing?"

"No, he wouldn't," Burke said. "And not because he wasn't as corrupt as the next guy. It was just that he was all for himself. He never thought of the interests of the trade as a whole. He didn't grasp the big picture, you might say."

Frank nodded.

"And Hannah fit into that," Burke added quietly.

"Into what?"

"Into that . . . What would you call it? . . . That way of seeing the world," Burke said. "Constanza's way." He shivered slightly, as if in response to a sudden chilling wind. "You could see it in him. In his eyes. Hers, too. I don't know how to say it . . . this icy solitude." He thought a moment, then smiled. "The only person I ever saw cut through it was Molly Gold."

16

It hadn't taken Tannenbaum very long to get back to Frank with
Molly Gold's last known address, but even so, night had already
fallen by the time he made it down to the Lower East Side, and
with the darkness, the whole mood of the neighborhood had
profoundly changed. The teeming street life of the day had given
way to a sullen world of dark, empty streets. Pools of grayish
light gathered beneath the street lamps or hazily illuminated
deserted stretches of the small, untended parks. The shops which
had been so busy the day before were now closed. Thick metal
sheets had been drawn down over their fronts and locked in
place, and the graffiti which had been scrawled across them
gave the entire area a lost and desolate look.

Molly Gold's building was a low brick tenement off Hester
Street. A few squares of yellow light shone from its windows,
but the single bulb in the foyer was dim, and because of that
Frank had to light a match to find her name: Gold M.—Apt.
1-C.

The door of the apartment was scarred and unpainted, and
Frank half-expected that there'd be no answer to his knock. He
tapped lightly, then a little harder, and a voice, old and faintly
irritated, sounded behind the door.

"Nothing. I don't need nothing."

"I'm not selling anything," Frank said hurriedly.

"What do you want?"

"I'm looking for Molly Gold."

"What for?"

"I understand she was a friend of Hannah Karlsberg's," Frank said.

There was a long silence, and from out in the hall, Frank could hear the woman's thin, quick breaths.

"She's dead," Frank added. "Someone murdered her."

A series of locks and chains rattled behind the door. Then it creaked open, and through a thin slant of light, Frank could make out an old woman's face. Her skin was wrinkled and yellowish, a crumpled sack for her head. A stubby unfiltered cigarette dangled from her unpainted lips, and wreathed her head in a pallid ring of smoke.

"Are you Molly Gold?" Frank asked immediately.

"Molly Gold, that's right," the woman said. She plucked the half-chewed cigarette from her mouth and stared evenly into Frank's eyes. "Who are you?"

He handed her one of his cards.

She squinted intently as she looked at it. "What's this?"

"My identification," Frank explained. "I'm a private investigator."

The old woman cackled lightly. "You think I can read this little thing?" She thrust the card back to him. "It's all a blur to me." She laughed again, then stepped back from the door. "Come in."

The living room was cramped, but neatly arranged. There were no cans or bottles strewn about, and the small white tablecloth that had been spread over the little table by the window looked as if it had been recently washed. And yet, despite the cleanliness and order, the room gave off a sense of something moving through the last stages of a long decay.

"Sit down," the old woman said, "unless you'd rather stand. Me, I don't care."

Frank took a seat and waited for her to move uneasily to the table and sit down.

"I'm checking on a few things about Miss Karlsberg," he said.

The old woman wiped a strand of gray hair from her eyes

and peered at him suspiciously. "That little card," she said, "I don't believe that. Whatever it said, I don't believe it." She smiled cunningly. "What are you, local? Local heat? State? Federal? What?"

"None of them," Frank said.

The old woman's eyes narrowed in concentration. "I don't fence nothing. Not one thing. And as far as anything else—no matter what it is—I'm too old for it."

Frank took out his notebook. "Did you read anything in the paper about Hannah Karlsberg?" he asked.

The old woman said nothing. She turned slightly toward the window, parted the shades, and stared out. "You got backup?"

"I'm alone."

"Cops don't come alone," the woman said. She whirled around to face him. "They come in packs," she hissed. "Like wolves. Like hyenas, that's the way they come."

Frank drew in a long, slow breath and returned his eyes to his notebook. "The police are holding her body until a relative comes forward to claim it. That's what I'm looking for, a relative."

Molly stared at him quizzically. "How'd you find me?"

"A man named Burke mentioned you. Stanley Burke."

"He don't know where I live."

"The police do," Frank said bluntly.

"They gave you my address?"

"That's right."

"What for?" the old woman asked tauntingly. "You going to give them something back, right? For their trouble. What are you going to give them? Me?"

"I'm not sure they're interested in you right now," Frank said.

Molly's face soured. "Oh, they're still interested in Molly Gold," she said bitterly. Then she laughed. "You know why? 'Cause they want to know about Nico. Nico and his drugs, how he got them into the country."

"Nico?"

"Constanza. Nico Constanza."

"They may be interested in that," Frank said. "But I'm not."

Molly peered at him doubtfully.

"I'm only interested in Hannah Karlsberg," Frank assured

her. Once again he glanced back down to his notebook. "Mr. Burke said that you and Hannah were friends?"

Molly snuffed out her cigarette. "He said that?"

"Yes."

"We talked a little, Hannah and me," Molly said. "But I don't know if you could call us friends." She shook her head. "She was shy. She kept to herself. She'd changed from the old days."

"You knew her before you worked together?"

"Yes," Molly said. "In the old neighborhood. She was named Kovatnik then."

"Yes, I know."

"She changed her name some time," the old woman went on. "Wanted a more fancy name. Karlsberg's more fancy."

"Yes, it is."

"But it didn't fool anybody," Molly said. "A lot of people remembered her from the old neighborhood. A new name don't mean a thing to them."

"These people," Frank said, "they knew her from her days on Fifth Street?"

The old woman looked puzzled. "Fifth Street? No. Orchard Street."

"You mean, from her shop?"

"She worked in Feig's place," Molly explained. "My shop was a few blocks down. We were both at the sewing machines in those days." She lifted her hands, her fingers bent with arthritis. "See what it does to you? My hands have been this way for almost twenty years." She smiled sneeringly. "But the cops, they don't want to know nothing about that. They just want to know about Constanza, what I did for him." She cackled to herself. "Which was nothing. I told Hannah that. I said, 'I don't do nothing for that pig.'" She stared at Frank intently. "What you do in this world, you do it for yourself," she said vehemently. "Because nobody does nothing for the next guy. Nobody. You understand what I'm saying? Nobody does a fucking thing."

Frank nodded quickly. "When did you first meet Hannah?"

"At this little park," Molly said. For a moment she grew silent, as if trying to recall everything in minute detail. "Where the girls used to go after their shifts," she added finally. "There was a little park, you see, and we'd stand around awhile, sort of breathe the air, loosen up a little from the stooping." She smiled. "Hannah had a way about her in the old days, a friendly way. She liked people, I think." She shrugged. "I was just one of the people she liked. There were a lot of us. She liked groups, joining things, being together. That was Hannah, always around people, talking to them."

Frank saw the pictures on her wall again, a middle-aged woman, alone in Paris, London, Rome. He heard Riviera's voice: *She always kept to herself.* Then Burke's: *She had her own operation.* Then Imalia's: *I didn't know her personally. I'm not sure anybody did.*

"Who was she?" he heard himself whisper.

The old woman leaned forward, cupping her ear with her hand. "What was that?"

"Liking people," Frank said. "Being liked. That must have helped with the union."

Molly nodded firmly. "Oh yeah, it helped. It helped plenty. And Hannah, she could take control of things, too. She liked to take control, and people trusted her." She smiled with a certain carefully controlled pride. "We had a big strike, you know."

"In 1936."

"Lasted for months," the old woman said triumphantly. "But we won it."

"And Hannah was one of the leaders," Frank said, urging her on.

"She stuck it to Feig, that's what," Molly said. "She fucked him good. He never recovered. He had to sell his shop, the bastard. Nobody would work for him, not after that business with the girl." She glanced toward the small kitchen to the right. "Want a whiskey?"

"No, thanks."

She got to her feet. "Me, I'd like one," she said emphatically. Then she walked to the kitchen, poured the drink, and returned to her seat. "I like it by itself," she said. She took a long drink, then wiped her mouth neatly with the paper napkin she'd brought along with the glass. "It's not a Jewish thing, drinking. That's what my mother used to say. 'Go ahead,' she'd say, 'Go drink like the *goyim*.'" She laughed derisively. "I was always a party girl, you know. My mother used to say, 'Molly, you're a party girl, and that's your trouble.'" She shook her head. "We had such fights, my mother and me. That's why I moved out. Went on my own." She took another sip. "Mama was right, you know. She was right about me." She glared at the nearly empty glass for a moment, then lifted her eyes toward Frank. "But what's worth more than a party, huh? What the fuck is worth more than a goddamn good time?" She laughed heartily. "Mama never could answer that one. Worked all day, waited on Papa for the rest of the time. What's the point of that, huh? You tell me."

"Miss Karlsberg had two sisters," Frank said, gently coaxing her mind ahead to the thirties.

The old woman nodded slowly, reluctantly returning to the subject. "Naomi and Gilda," she said dully, her eyes dropping back toward the glass.

"Do you know what happened to them?"

"I heard that Naomi got married," Molly said. "I don't remember hearing much about the other one."

"Do you remember who she married?"

"No."

"After the strike, Hannah sort of disappeared," Frank told her. "Do you have any idea where she went?"

The old woman shook her head. "Unless she went to work for the union people. You could check with them."

"When did you go to work for Constanza?"

"Time flies," Molly said. "Can you believe it, I went to work for Nico in 1957."

"And that's when you saw Hannah again?"

"That's right," Molly said. "She showed up about three weeks later. She came into the office one day. There was a man with her, and the three of them talked for a while not far from my machine. Hannah did most of the talking, but sometimes the other man would say something to Hannah in Spanish."

"Spanish?"

"Yeah," Molly said. She laughed. "It sort of pissed Nico off, the way they'd do that. He was Italian, you know. He didn't speak a work of Spanish."

"But Hannah did?" Frank asked.

"Oh yeah," Molly said authoritatively, "and she sounded like she was real good at it."

"What was she saying to the other man?" Frank asked.

"I don't know," Molly said with a shrug. She took another quick drink from the glass. "The only thing I recognized was the word for money. I remember that. Lots of talk about money." She rubbed her fingers together greedily. *"Dinero, dinero, dinero,"* she said with a laugh. "That's the only Spanish word I know."

"Did you hear anything else?" Frank asked. "I mean, in English."

The old woman shook her head firmly. "Not that I can remember," she said. She slapped her ears lightly with the palms of her hands. "The shops are noisy," she said, "everybody's always bustling around. You get distracted." She snapped a cigarette from the pack on the table and lit it. "That Nico, he was a pig. Everyone thought I was his girl, you know. He had an eye for me. But it didn't work the other way around, no matter what people thought. Never. Not for anything. Not with that pig."

"Did you talk to Hannah often while you worked for Constanza?" Frank asked.

"She was always in Brooklyn," Molly said. "Not Manhattan."

"But when she came to Manhattan."

"Yeah, we would talk," Molly said. "But she was shy. Not like when she was a girl."

"What did you talk about?" Frank asked immediately.

"This and that," Molly said. "I don't remember much of it. She wasn't a party girl, Hannah. Maybe at one time, maybe she could have been. But when she worked for Nico, her party days were over." She smiled. "She dressed in these business-suit dresses. You know what I mean? Little skirt and a plain blouse, and one of those little jackets." She shook her head. "Definitely not a party type."

"What type was she?"

"Strictly business, that's what I'd say," Molly told him. "She looked like she wouldn't take any bullshit." She smiled. "Even in the old days she was like that. You know, like, 'Hey, don't fuck with me.' That kind of person."

Frank nodded.

"Except . . ." Molly added slowly, "except sometimes . . ."

"Sometimes what?" Frank asked.

Molly shook her head, then took another drink, her eyes rolling up toward the ceiling as she finished the glass. "Sometimes she didn't seem like that at all. Sometimes she looked completely different."

"What do you mean?"

"Nico would be talking, and it was like she wasn't hearing him at all," Molly explained. "Maybe the minute before, she was listening real careful, but then, it was like something clicked, and she just tuned out." She looked at Frank curiously, as if she were trying to solve some infinitely involved mystery. "She was like the song," she said finally. "She was lost in the stars. Her mind would wander. You'd be talking to her, and her eyes would shift around, you know, over to the machines, the girls. She looked like she was lost in the stars, like she didn't know who or what she was."

Frank could feel an odd weariness overtaking him as he made his way down the narrow brick corridor to his office. In his mind, he could see Hannah in her sleeping gown as she marked the date of her birthday on the wall calendar, then later, as she had appeared that first day at Sol Feig's shop, dressed in white, and then, still later, wrapped in her thick overcoat, her fist in the air, her voice hanging in the leafless winter trees of Union Square: *Each man lives in his neighbor's debt, and the payment of that debt is justice.*

He fumbled for his keys a moment, found them, then opened the door slowly and stepped into the interior darkness. For an instant, it seemed wholly to engulf him, as if he'd stepped off the edge of the world, and he stood rigidly in place until a sound, very slight, drew his attention, and he felt his hand reach for the pistol at his back, then his own body tense as he felt another hand grab his and twist it firmly.

"Do not fear," a voice said, the mouth so close he could feel its warm breath at his ear. "It is Farouk."

Instantly the light came on, and Farouk released him.

"How'd you get in here?" Frank demanded as he spun around to face him.

"It is not difficult," Farouk said. "I was waiting. I fell asleep on your sofa. Then I heard movement, and I saw only a man in the dark. I was not sure that it was you."

Frank drew in a deep, calming breath. "Well, what do you want?"

Farouk shrugged innocently. "Must there be something?" He smiled. "Perhaps it is only for the companionship."

Frank walked over to his desk and sat down.

Farouk took the chair in front of it. "So, what have you found out?"

"Not a lot," Frank admitted. He took out a cigarette and lit it. "Except that she spoke Spanish."

Farouk's eyes brightened suddenly, as if someone had lit a small candle just behind them. "Spanish?" he asked softly. "She spoke Spanish?"

"Yes."

"Yiddish, this I would understand," Farouk said. "Polish, yes. Perhaps even Russian or German. But Spanish?"

"I don't know where she learned it," Frank told him. "I don't know why she learned it."

"Sometimes, it's only curiosity," Farouk said, "sometimes, a way to spend the hours." He smiled quietly. "Those pictures, the ones in her room. Always alone. This can make you want to fill the time."

"Learning a language?"

"Perhaps," Farouk said. He looked pointedly at Frank. "In my case, also." He lifted his hands helplessly. "For others, it's some other thing. To build a model ship, perhaps. There is sports. There is whiskey."

Frank said nothing.

"Did she speak it well?" Farouk asked after a moment.

"Evidently."

"Like it was learned from others who spoke it well?"

"What do you mean?"

"Not from a book."

Frank shook his head. "She spoke it well, that's all I know."

Something seemed to crawl slowly into Farouk's mind. "This is something I can help with, this Spanish. I can be of assistance."

"How?"

Farouk stood up. "It's late," he said. "And I must help Consuelo."

"Consuelo?"

"Whom you know as Toby," Farouk said hurriedly as he stepped toward the door. He stopped for a moment when he reached it, then looked back at Frank. "It really was for the companionship, you know," he said. Then he turned quickly and walked out the door.

Karen was admiring her new dress in the mirror as Frank walked into the bedroom. She twirled gracefully, and the hem rose in a soft outward wave, then descended.

"What do you think?" she asked.

"Very nice."

"A gift."

"Nice," Frank repeated as he slumped down on the bed. "Who gave it to you?"

"Imalia Covallo," Karen said enthusiastically. "Such beautiful colors." She shifted slightly on her feet, and the long, billowy skirt rocked left and right. "I was just trying it on. I'm not going to wear it to the theater tonight."

Frank glanced toward the window. The night air seemed immensely thick and suffocating, and he thought instantly of the black air of the morgue, the way it must feel inside the sealed refrigerated vaults.

Karen turned briskly again, still admiring the skirt. "I must say I'm tempted, though."

Frank turned back to her. "Tempted to what?"

"To wear it to the theater," Karen said. "But it's much too formal for that." She smiled happily. "Besides, Imalia's giving a benefit for the ballet on Sunday, and I thought I might wear it then."

"Where?"

"At the Museum of American Art," Karen said. "You know, the new one on Fifth Avenue."

Frank nodded.

"Imalia's a Sustaining Member," Karen said.

Frank stretched out on the bed, his long legs dangling awkwardly over the edge. For a moment he closed his eyes, and immediately Hannah Karlsberg's face drifted into his mind, a white oval on a field of black, the blue lips parting slightly, as if she were beginning to stir again, struggling to regain her breath.

"By the way," Karen asked suddenly, "did you find what you were looking for?"

His eyes opened. No, he thought, have you, has anyone?

"You said you were looking for something on a case," Karen told him. "On Seventh Avenue."

"Oh, that," Frank said. "A few things."

She turned from the mirror and smiled brightly. "Anything you can talk about?"

"No."

"You really stick to that, don't you?"

"Stick to what?"

"Confidentiality."

"Yes."

"But it must be difficult sometimes," Karen added. She sat down beside him and ran her fingers across his chest. "Difficult, I mean, to keep it all inside."

He closed his eyes again. "It's just part of the business," he said.

"I guess," Karen said.

He could feel her fingers as they lingered on his chest.

"Want to come along with Jeffrey and me?" she asked.

"No."

"It's supposed to be a very good play."

"No, thanks," Frank said, his eyes still closed.

"We haven't been out to the theater in a long time," Karen added.

"Not tonight," Frank told her. "I think I'll just catch a little sleep."

Karen laughed. "Sleep. You'll be back on the streets by midnight."

Frank rolled away from her slightly. "Maybe."

He felt her fingers as they left him, but only a small and steadily weakening part of him yearned for their return.

17

Frank was waiting outside the doors of the American Garment Workers Union when they opened at nine o'clock the next morning.

The tall middle-aged man who opened them seemed surprised to see him. "You look like you've been waiting here all night," he said.

"Just since eight."

"What's the matter? You couldn't go through the local rep or something?"

"It's not exactly union business," Frank told him.

"No? What is it then?"

Frank took out his identification.

The man looked at it, unimpressed. "Private dick, huh? What's this about?"

"Hannah Karlsberg."

"Who's she?"

"A woman who was once associated with the union."

"Once associated?" the man said suspiciously. "What does that mean?"

"A long time ago."

The man stared at him silently.

"The '35 strike," Frank added.

The man faked a shiver. "Oh, that was a bad one. The old-timers still talk about it. What'd she have to do with that?"

"She was one of the shop leaders," Frank told him.

"Where was her shop?"

"Lower East Side. Orchard Street."

"Heart of the battle, so they say."

"That's what I hear."

"Well, let me see," the man said as he walked a bit farther into the vestibule. "Is this a pension problem, something like that?"

"She's dead."

"Was she entitled to death benefits?"

"I don't think so," Frank said, "but that's not what I'm looking into."

The man turned the corner of the front desk and sat down in the chair behind it. "What's the deal, then?"

"She was murdered," Frank said. "And the police won't release her body until a relative asks for it."

"And you're looking for the relative?"

"That's right."

The man nodded. "Okay," he said. "First I'll send you up to Records. Third floor. Ask for Benny Pacheco. He's the chief paper-pusher up there. Tell him Chickie Potamkin sent you."

"Thanks," Frank said. He walked to the elevator and took it two flights up.

Benny Pacheco glanced away from his computer monitor as Frank entered his office.

"Mr. Potamkin sent me up," he said. He took out his identification. "Frank Clemons."

Pacheco looked at the identification for a moment, then glanced back up at Frank.

"What can I do for you?"

"It's about a woman who once belonged to the union," Frank told him. "Her name was Hannah Kovatnik."

"When did she join?"

"I don't know for sure. She was in the strike in 1935."

Pacheco nodded. "That was a long time ago. Is she still alive?"

"No."

"Do you know how long she was a member?"

"No."

"Well, all the records are here," Pacheco said as he turned to the monitor. "Something should come up." He tapped softly at the keys, his eyes still on the screen. "There it is," he said after a moment. "Hannah Kovatnik. She worked for Sol Feig Clothing Manufacturers from 1932 to 1936." He looked at Frank. "Is that the woman you mean?"

"Yes."

"What do you want to know about her?"

"Anything you can tell me."

"Well, she lived on Orchard Street," Pacheco said. "Looks like it was in the same building as the factory." He looked at Frank. "Did you know that?"

"Yes."

His eyes swept back to the screen. "She had no injuries on the job, as far as I can tell. She didn't file any claims with us." He hit a key on the computer keyboard. "She didn't hold any union office except shop representative, and of course, there was no pay for that."

Frank nodded.

"She remained in the union for three years," Pacheco continued, "and she was severed from it in September of 1936." He turned back to Frank. "That's about it."

"Severed?" Frank asked immediately. "You mean she quit?"

"No, I mean she was severed. She was dropped from the rolls."

Frank looked at him quizzically.

"A union is like anything else," Pacheco explained. "It has its rules. Apparently Miss Kovatnik broke a few of them."

"What rules are you talking about?"

"Well, the big one is dues," Pacheco said. "You don't pay your dues, you don't stay in the union."

"Is that what happened to her?"

"No," Pacheco said as his eyes drifted back to the screen.

"What was it then?" Frank asked immediately.

Pacheco's eyes darted over to the lower left-hand corner of the screen. "She was severed for failure to conform to union ethics," he said matter-of-factly.

"Failure to what?" Frank asked as he took out his notebook.

"Failure to conform to union ethics," Pacheco repeated. He looked at Frank. "That could mean anything," he explained. "It's sort of a catchall. It allows the union to get rid of people it can't deal with for some reason. They could drop you for, say, being a drunk, or for being too violent, too radical, for being a generally abusive person. Hell, it could be just about anything."

"Well, what exactly did it mean in Hannah's case?" Frank asked.

"We don't have that sort of information on computer," Pacheco said. "This is really a status program. Who's in, who's out. Complaints. Medical stuff. That sort of thing." He glanced at Frank. "There's a number code, though, which tells us things in general. Miss Kovatnik's severance, for example, is listed as number seven—which means that it was an ethics violation."

Frank took the union paper from his jacket pocket and opened it to the photograph of Hannah in Union Square.

"I brought this with me," he said. "You mind taking a look?"

Pacheco glanced at the photograph. "Is that her?"

"Yes," Frank said emphatically. "She spoke at that rally. She published in your paper. Somebody wrote an article about her."

"None of that would be on computer," Pacheco told him. "Unless she received some sort of compensation for it."

"I see."

"But that doesn't mean we don't have other records," Pacheco added quickly. "We have plenty of stuff. It's just that most of it is in the archives."

"Where are they?"

"In the Research Department," Pacheco said. "You want to try it out?"

"Yes."

Pacheco reached for the phone and dialed two digits. "Hello, Harry. You got a minute? Yeah. Yeah. I have a Mr. Clemons. He's a private investigator looking into the records of one of our former members. I don't know. Yes. Hannah Kovatnik." He snapped the phone back to its cradle. "He'll be right down," he said.

Only a moment later, Frank turned toward the door of Pacheco's office and saw a tall, elderly man in a light blue suit.

He was muscular and barrel chested, and as Frank looked at him, he realized just what a formidable presence he must have been in his youth. Even now, with silvery hair and slightly crumpled posture, he looked like the sort of man who only said things once.

"Harry Silverman," he said as he offered Frank his hand.

"Harry's sort of the historian of the union," Pacheco said brightly. "Isn't that what you'd say, Harry?"

Harry smiled. "It depends on how much vodka I've had, what I'll say." He looked at Frank. "What's your name?"

"Frank Clemons."

"And what are you looking for?"

"Like Mr. Pacheco told you," Frank said, "I'm trying to trace one of your former members."

"That's usually no problem," Silverman said lightly. "But today's a little different. We got a tip that a certain person is incapacitated for the moment, and I got to cash in on that information right away." He glanced at his watch. "Listen, you don't mind going for a little ride, do you?"

Frank shook his head. "Okay with me."

"The thing is, it's way out in Brooklyn. Around Coney Island. Be back in a couple hours. Is that too much time?"

"No."

"Good," Silverman said brightly. "Let's go."

Frank followed Silverman down the back stairs, out the door, then around the corner to a dark green late-model Ford.

"Get in," Silverman said loudly as he unlocked the passenger door. "It's an American car. One of the few left in New York."

Frank pulled himself into the front seat, then waited as Silverman walked briskly to the driver's side, got in, and pulled away.

"American car," Silverman repeated with a sigh. "We buy American in this union." He smiled wistfully. "We still got a few old ideas hanging around us." He turned east not far from Union Square and headed toward FDR Drive. "Things change, of course," he added. "Used to be, it was strictly a Jewish thing, the garment trade." He shook his head. "Now you got Mexicans, Haitians, Orientals, some legal, some not. Old kikes like me get to feeling isolated." He smiled impishly. "But what the hell, that's the way it works, history. We adjust to it. And we keep one thing in mind. Solidarity. As long as we hold to that, there's a chance for everybody."

"She believed in that," Frank said. "She made a speech about it. Hannah did, I mean."

"Hannah Kovatnik," Silverman repeated thoughtfully. "It rings a bell, that name." He shrugged. "Of course, that calling me the historian of the union is a crock of shit. Historian, that's what they call old punch-drunk organizers who can't cut it anymore." He shook his head. "I'm not quite that bad off yet."

"She was in the 1935 strike," Frank told him.

Silverman's face darkened. "That was a rough one," he said. "Winter and snow and all those bastards freezing their asses off trying to get a living wage. Almost three-fourths of the garment factories had closed by then. So you can imagine the problem." He grimaced. "And the police? Jesus. We'd of been better off dealing with Pinkertons than those fucking micks."

Frank said nothing.

Silverman's eyes swept over to him. "If you're Irish, no offense."

"She worked at one of the sweatshops on Orchard Street," Frank added.

"Like a lot of people."

"She was sort of the leader of it, I think."

"That right?" Silverman said. "What's your interest in her? That'd help me check out the archives."

"She was murdered two weeks ago," Frank said. "The police won't release her body. It takes a relative to make them. I'm trying to find one."

"That doesn't sound hard."

"It wouldn't be, usually," Frank said, "but it is with Hannah."

"Why?"

"The only link is her two sisters," Frank said. "But I can't find them."

"Were they in the union?"

"I don't know."

"You have their names?"

"Naomi and Gilda."

"Last name Kovatnik?"

"At least until they got married it was," Frank said.

"Well, it's a start anyway," Silverman said. "I can have Benny do a routine computer check, and the rest I can handle with my files."

"I'd appreciate that," Frank said.

Silverman laughed. "You a Southerner, or what?"

"From Atlanta."

Silverman shook his head wearily. "You got some hard-headed people down there. You say 'union,' they hear 'atheist Commie bastard.' "

"Yeah."

"We're making some progress, though," Silverman added. "But it's an uphill struggle all the way." He shrugged. "Of course, there's nothing new in that."

Frank nodded.

Silverman returned to the subject. "So," he said, "besides tracking down the sisters, what's the rest of your plan?"

"To sort of work my way through Hannah's own life," Frank said. "See what I can find."

"How far have you gotten?"

"Up to the spring of 1936 in one direction, and back to 1954 in the other."

"Which leaves almost twenty years," Silverman said. "That's a long time."

"For blank space it is," Frank admitted.

Silverman nosed the car into the quickly moving traffic of FDR Drive. "So how can I help you?" he asked.

Frank took out his notebook and began flipping through the pages. "I need to know what she did after the strike," he said. "Who she went to work for, that sort of thing."

"We may not be much help there," Silverman admitted. "When they leave us, they're pretty much on their own."

"Any friends she might have had that she stayed in contact with," Frank added. "Anybody who could fill in the years, maybe know something about the sisters."

Silverman nodded silently as he headed up the ramp and then onto the towering bulwark of the Brooklyn Bridge.

"The thing is," Frank said as his eyes drifted out across the harbor toward the Statue of Liberty and, just behind it, the crumbling ruin of Ellis Island. "The thing is, I don't really know what happened to her. I don't even know what her work was like or why she left it."

Silverman's face darkened suddenly as he stared out across the grim rows of warehouses that lined the harbor. "Well, I can help you with that last one," he said quietly. "At least I can give you a taste of it."

18

Silverman pulled the car into the rear parking lot of a small brick building not far from the whirling rides of Coney Island.

"This is a hotshop," he said as he got out of the car and closed the door. "You know what that is?"

"One with a lot of complaints," Frank said.

Silverman smiled. "How'd you know that?"

"It's come up a few times in connection with Hannah."

"I guess her shop was plenty hot in 1935."

"Yes."

"Most of them were in those days," Silverman said. "But back then about the worst that could happen to you would be you'd lose your job, maybe get cracked over the head by some fucking gun-thug." He shook his head despairingly. "That was bad enough. But it's worse now. With the illegals, I mean. With them, it can be life or death. They start any union trouble, the owners can pretty much hand them over to Naturalization. After that, they can be shipped back to some banana republic where they have to sleep in the streets, beg for water. For a few, it means prison, torture, a bullet in the back of the head."

Frank nodded.

"So in a situation like that," Silverman added, "we're not really talking about complaints, because the people who work here are too scared to go to anybody."

"What are you doing then?" Frank asked.

"Like you, investigating," Silverman told him. "We know a little bit about what's going on around here, but we'd like to know a little more."

Silverman nodded quickly, then headed toward the single metal door at the back of the building. "This shithole is owned by some douchebag out on Long Island. It's packed with illegals, but we don't really give a shit about that. The way they're being treated, now that's another question." He stopped at the door, then glanced quickly at Frank. "Anybody asks you, you're a sewing-machine salesman, okay?"

"Okay."

Silverman rapped noisily at the door, then stepped back as it creaked open.

A large black man stepped out onto the small concrete porch. "Yeah?"

Silverman smiled cheerily and handed the man a card. "My name's Gianelli," he said. "I'm a sales rep with Dothan Garment Machines."

"We're pretty busy right now," the man said suspiciously.

"Yeah, well, that's part of the trade, right?" Silverman said happily. "Not to mention the American way, if you know what I mean."

The black man said nothing.

"You manage this place?" Silverman asked.

"No."

"A guy named Bowler does, right?"

"Mr. Bowler, yes."

"He here?"

"No."

Silverman looked surprised. "No shit? Well, that's funny, because Mr. Cavanaugh—he owns this shop, right? Mr. Luther Cavanaugh? I mean, I may be at the wrong place."

"Mr. Cavanaugh owns it."

"Yeah, that's what the boss said," Silverman told him. "Anyway, Mr. Cavanaugh has expressed an interest in upgrading the equipment here. He asked for a rep to be sent over."

"I don't know nothing about that."

"You don't? Well, Mr. Bowler does. Why don't you give him a call?"

"He's in Florida," the man said. "He had a heart attack down there."

"Really? A heart attack. That's too bad."

"He's in intensive care down there."

"No kidding," Silverman said mournfully. "An older man, is he?"

"Around sixty, I guess."

"Well, my best wishes, you know," Silverman said. "But, like they say, life goes on, and Mr. Cavanaugh asked me to come over and take a look at this place, maybe give an estimate on upgrading the whole thing." He smiled quietly. "I'm surprised Mr. Bowler didn't mention it to you before he left."

"He had a lot on his mind, I guess," the man said.

"Don't we all," Silverman told him. "So, what do you think? Could I take a look around?"

The man stared at him cautiously.

"Just a minute or two," Silverman assured him. "I'm an old pro at this. You won't have to shut a thing down. You won't lose a second of production. I guarantee it."

The man glanced down at the card. "Well, okay," he said hesitantly. "I guess so."

"Thanks a lot," Silverman said as he walked briskly into the building.

The rear of the building was bathed in a deep gray light, and as Frank walked in behind Silverman, he could feel it like a soiled curtain which had suddenly been wrapped heavily around him.

"What do you want to look at?" the man asked Silverman.

"The whole operation," Silverman answered lightly. "I got to get an idea of the pace, you know, cutting, stitching, sorting. You ship out of here?"

"In small lots," the man answered. "No big trucks."

Silverman smiled at him conspiratorially. "I got you," he said.

The man seemed to relax a bit. "Station wagons," he said, volunteering a bit of information for the first time.

"Yeah, that's the best way," Silverman said amiably. "You go to vans, you can end up eating a lot of shit for it."

The man nodded enthusiastically.

Silverman slapped his hands together lightly. "Well, let's have a look-see, shall we?"

The man's hand swept out toward a small, lighted doorway. "In here," he said as he started off toward it.

The darkness gave way suddenly as the man opened the door, and the loud clatter of machinery swept over them.

"Oh yeah, this looks familiar," Silverman said to him as they walked onto the main floor of the shop. He smiled. "Looks like you got some pretty old stuff here." He looked at Frank and chuckled. "What do you think, Mitch?"

Frank nodded. "Old, yeah," he said weakly.

"This is Mitch Donovan," Silverman said to the other man. "I didn't catch your name."

"Pete Crawford."

Silverman stuck out his hand. "Glad to meet you." He looked back out onto the floor. "How long you working here, Pete?"

"Four years."

Silverman drew in a long breath. "Well, I been in rags for almost forty years." He laughed. "Longer than some of these goddamn machines." He stepped forward, his eyes squinting in the hard light. "Looks like you got a pretty good work force here."

"They're okay," Crawford said.

"Got fast fingers, do they?"

"Fast enough, I guess."

Silverman laughed. "Yeah, well, with these old relics, they'd better be." He glanced at Crawford and smiled. " 'Cause if they're not, they'll sew their fucking fingers together, right?"

The two men laughed heartily for a moment, then Silverman moved forward up the central aisle, glancing left and right as he walked.

All around him men and women stood at their machines, their hands flying from the threading needles to the bolts of cloth which lay in piles at their feet.

"These old machines run pretty hot," Silverman said as he continued up the aisle. He turned to Crawford. "They bitch about it in the summer, but in the winter they keep their mouths shut, right, Pete?"

Crawford nodded. "That's right."

"People want it both ways," Silverman added. "That's their goddamn problem."

"We don't listen to much bitching," Crawford said sternly.

A thin smile slithered onto Silverman's lips. "Just ask to see their green cards," he said. "That'll shut them up fast enough." He took a few steps forward, then lifted his head slightly and stared thoughtfully over the room, turning slowly in a broad circle.

"The problem with a shop like this, Pete," he said authoritatively, "is that if you change one thing, you got to change them all." He looked at Frank. "And that's where the money comes in, right, Mitch?"

"Right."

Silverman stroked his chin. "Now, this place can be upgraded," he said to Crawford. "No doubt about it. But it's not going to be cheap, you know what I mean?"

"Everything costs money," Crawford said.

"Yeah, it does," Silverman said. "It sure does. Of course, sometimes if you spend some money, you can save some money." His eyes swept out toward the floor again. "Take the work force, for example. How many people you got working here?"

"Twenty-two," Crawford said.

"You mean on this shift?"

"Yeah."

"How many shifts you got. Three?"

"Two."

"Twelve hours a pop, then."

"That's right."

Silverman pretended to go through a series of calculations. "Well," he said finally, "I could probably fix it up to where you could drop a third of your labor costs. That would mean about ten units, you know." He looked closely at Crawford. "Which would probably put the savings at . . ." He stopped. "What's the hourly, Pete?"

"The average makes about seventy dollars," Crawford answered immediately.

"Per week?"

" 'Bout every nine days they get that."

For an instant, Frank saw something tighten angrily in Silverman's face, but it instantly released, and Silverman smiled sweetly. "Yeah, I could save you some of that," he said cheerfully. "No doubt about it." He glanced at his watch. "Well, I told you I could check it out in about two minutes. I didn't lie, did I?"

Pete smiled contentedly. "No, you didn't."

Silverman turned to Frank. "Got any questions, Mitch?"

"No."

Silverman draped his arm over Crawford's shoulder and guided him back toward the rear door. "Well, we'll be in touch with Mr. Bowler, Pete," he said. "Thanks for letting us in. It would have been a bitch to have come all this way for nothing."

"No problem," Crawford said.

They shook hands again in the parking lot, and then Silverman headed back toward his car. "Want a Coney Island dog, Frank?" he asked lightly as he pulled himself in behind the wheel.

19

Silverman took a bite from his hot dog, then a swig from the can of Budweiser he kept nestled between his legs.

"I like the boardwalk," he said as his eyes scanned it, moving along the line of arcades, freak shows and fast food stands. "People say it's cheap, vulgar." He smiled. "What the fuck do they know about real life, huh, Frank?" He took another sip from the can. "I was born out here, and every time I come back, I remember how my father used to ride the rides with me. It scared the shit out of him, but he did it anyway." He wiped his mouth with the napkin. "Your father still alive?"

"No."

"Mother?"

"I don't know. She went away."

"Up and left, just like that? Usually it's the father who does that."

"This time it wasn't," Frank said. He looked toward the large freak show just behind him. A man in a brightly colored vest was hawking the show to several people who'd gathered around him. A black woman with a large snake stood beside him, along with a hooded man whose arms and chest were covered with tattoos. "She just left one day," he added. "I don't know where she went."

"Probably just as well," Silverman said with a shrug. "My mother died when I was ten. After that, it was just me and the old man. He sold shoes until he dropped from it. He fucking hated shoes. Around the house, he went barefoot."

Frank laughed.

"It's the goddamn truth," Silverman insisted. "First thing when he got home, summer or winter, he'd take off his fucking shoes. And let me tell you something, that's not your ordinary Jew that does that. I mean, taking off your shoes is like sitting *shiva*, mourning the dead." He stopped to watch an old woman as she fumbled through one of the public garbage receptacles, looking for cans or bottles she could turn in for a nickel apiece. "This woman you're looking for," he said, "this Hannah Kovatnik. What do you know about her?"

"Not much," Frank told him. "She was a leader in the '35 strike. She came from Poland, a little village near Bialystok. Her father was a rabbi on Fifth Street. She had two sisters, Naomi and Gilda. When her father died, she took a job on Orchard Street. She led the shop in the strike, then disappeared. Pacheco says she was dropped from the union for some kind of ethics violation."

Silverman waved his hand. "That could be anything."

"That's what Pacheco said."

"The sisters, though," Silverman said. "Did they work in the shop?"

"Yeah, both of them."

"You know for how long?"

Frank shook his head.

"I can check that out when we get back to the office," Silverman said. "Anything else?"

"I'd like to find someone who knew her," Frank said. "Someone who might know where the sisters are."

"You said she disappeared, but she must have turned up again."

"Yeah, in 1955."

"Doing what?"

"Working for a place called Maximum Imports."

"Nico Constanza's operation," Silverman said immediately.

"You've heard of him?"

"Of course."

Frank took out his notebook. "Who is he, exactly, Constanza?"

"He's a douchebag," Silverman said without hesitation. "He's connected, and from time to time he's been known to bring in some muscle to negotiate certain unpleasant labor difficulties. Years back he was just another little prick hanging around Broome Street in Little Italy. You know, watching the old guys play bocci, maybe running a few errands at the racetrack. Then he got into the trade by selling garment hangers. After that, he moved into manufacturing." He smiled. "But like a lot of street thugs, he had trouble controlling himself. One day he personally did a number on one of our people. It so happened that we had a D.A. who owed us a favor, and so Constanza bit off two years. He broke rocks for eighteen months, then hit the streets again."

"But not for long," Frank said.

Silverman's smile widened. "So, you heard."

"Something about the IRS."

"Oh, yeah," Silverman said cheerfully. "That miserable fuck went to Atlanta on an eight-year rap. Did four. Then got iced by some psycho in the communal shower." His eyes brightened. "You can imagine how greatly he was mourned." He finished off the hot dog. "How long did the woman work for him?"

"Until 1968."

"When he went to the federal penitentiary in Atlanta."

"That's right."

"Then what'd she do?"

"She signed on with Imalia Covallo."

Silverman's eyes drifted over to the sea. "Is that who you're working for?"

"Yes."

"What's her interest?"

"Hannah was an old employee," Frank said. "Miss Covallo wants her to have a decent burial."

"She has a heart of gold," Silverman said.

"You know something different?"

Silverman shook his head. "Not really. As far as we know, she runs a pretty clean operation. For the rag trade."

"Meaning what?"

"That it's a nasty world, Frank," Silverman said. "And when

the profit margin is risky and the labor costs are high, well, things get pushed and shoved a little."

"Does Covallo do any pushing?"

"No more than most," Silverman said. "Maybe even a little less. Like I told you, she's as clean as they come, I guess." He drained the last of the beer, then set the bottle down on the wooden bench beside him.

"But no better?" Frank asked.

Silverman looked at him. "Why should you expect her to be? It's the way of the world, my friend. You live in a snake pit, you become a snake." His eyes swept back to the open sea as he laughed bitterly. "You take that little shit-stick who showed us around that sweatshop today; you take him, for example. He's got nothing but that stinking little job. He doesn't live much better than those wetbacks he pushes around. Hell, he probably lives in the same neighborhood they do. Coming home from the shop, he'll probably get mugged by the same psycho. But it doesn't matter. He's Cavanaugh's boy. If Cavanaugh ended up in a car trunk on President Street—you know what I mean, Frank, with a little hole going in and a big hole going out— why, he'd probably cry his fucking eyes out. But if ten illegals drop dead on the floor, he doesn't want to know from that."

He turned away suddenly, as if in disgust, took a deep breath, then let his eyes wander from the sea back to the whirling rides behind him. "That's what people want, for Christ's sake," he said vehemently as he pointed toward the rides. "That's all they fucking want, just to go to the park with the kids, spend a few bucks without having to think about every goddamn penny." He looked at Frank. "Is that so much, for God's sake?"

"No."

Silverman stood up quickly and headed down the boardwalk.

"Back in my day, this whole place was nothing but Jews," he said as Frank stepped up to him. "Like the rag trade, nothing but Jews." He stepped over to a garbage can, dropped the bottle into it, then moved on, slowly ambling toward the great steel chaos of the Cyclone. "And when it changed," he added, "the trade and the neighborhood, I got to tell you, it bothered me a little. But, you know, when I was a kid, my father used to read me this speech from Shakespeare, *The Merchant of Venice*, that part about 'hath not a Jew' this, 'hath not a Jew' that? You know, feelings, hungers. Well, I just put something in the place of Jew. Hath not a spic this, hath not a chink that? And that's all I had to do to get my heart back again."

Frank nodded slowly, then looked up and saw the cars of the Cyclone as they made their first thundering plunge, and as they fell, it seemed to him that the individual screams of each separate person on it blended seamlessly into one long, unending cry.

The library of the American Garment Workers was cluttered, but Silverman clearly knew his way around it.

"We got all the old issues of the union paper here," he said as he pointed to a long line of gray metal shelves. "And we have a lot of correspondence." He pointed to the opposite wall, where scores of filing cabinets were lined up. "Over there, we keep newspaper clippings by year and topic." He walked over to a green metal door. "And in here, we keep the old contracts and stuff." He waved his hand. "But for starters, we can check on the sisters the way Benny checked on Hannah." He stepped over to a small desk in the back corner of the room and placed his fingers on the computer keyboard. "Give me their names again," he said.

"Naomi Kovatnik," Frank said.

"Okay, just a second," Silverman said as he began to type.

Frank stepped behind him and watched the monitor.

For an instant, it went black, then a message appeared.

NO RECORD FOR NAME. CHECK SPELLING.

Silverman looked at Frank. "Got any other names for her?" he asked.

"No."

"Was she ever married?"

"I think she was," Frank said. "But I haven't been able to run it down."

"Okay," Silverman said with a quick shrug. "How about the other sister?"

"Gilda Kovatnik," Frank said.

"G-I-L-D-A," Silverman repeated quietly as he typed in the name.

Again the screen sputtered for a moment, then her name appeared in small amber letters.

"There it is," Silverman said. He leaned forward. "Says she was a member in good standing until 1936." He looked at Frank. "That's when she left."

"Left what?"

"The union."

"That's the same year as Hannah," Frank said. "Did she leave voluntarily?"

"Yes," Silverman told him. "She probably went into another line." He hit a single key, and the screen sputtered once again. "Never joined the union again." He pointed to the lower right-hand corner of the screen. "There's one other thing," he said.

Frank leaned toward the screen. "What?"

"She's dead."

Frank stared at the small D at the edge of the screen, then the date which had been written beside it: SEPTEMBER 12, 1954. Just underneath it, there was a final entry, PD: SAN JORGE COLOMBIA.

"What does that 'PD' mean?" Frank asked immediately.

"Place of death," Silverman told him.

Frank took out his notebook and quickly wrote it down. "How do you know she died?"

Silverman hit another key. "Yeah, that's what I figured," he said, almost to himself.

"What?"

Silverman nodded toward the screen. "Somebody filed a death-benefit application."

"Is that like insurance?"

"It can be, but mostly it's just for some assistance in getting the person buried. You know, some help with the expenses. In this case, she wasn't entitled. Application was denied."

"Why?"

"She hadn't been a member long enough," Silverman said. "Only a few years. That would kill any application for funeral benefits."

Frank's eyes darted instantly toward the screen. "Who filed for the benefit?"

Silverman hit the keys, and a name popped onto the screen: JOSEPH FISCHELSON.

Silverman ran his name through the computer, but nothing came up. "Well, one thing's for sure, whoever he is, he was never a member of the American Garment Workers." He drew in a long, weary breath. "Well, Frank, that's about as far as we can get with the computer."

Frank nodded. "Yeah."

"But we have other ways," Silverman said with a wink.

He stood up immediately and walked into the small cramped room behind his desk. "This ethics problem," he said as he strolled over to yet another line of metal filing cabinets. "That would have been when, exactly?"

"She was kicked out of the union in March of 1936," Frank said.

Silverman pulled out one of the file drawers, riffled through scores of faintly dusty envelopes, then pulled one out and brought it over to the small wooden table that rested near the center of the room.

"This should tell us something," he said as he sat down and opened it.

Frank took the chair beside him, and watched as Silverman's stubby fingers went through the papers.

"It was a disciplinary hearing," Silverman said finally, as he withdrew a single white envelope. He held it up to Frank. Someone had written Hannah's name across it in thick black ink. Under it, in blue ink and somewhat smaller script, someone else had written, Confidential.

"What's a disciplinary hearing?" Frank asked immediately.

"A charge must have been brought against her," Silverman said casually.

"What kind of charge?"

"Could be anything," Silverman said. He turned the envelope over. A dark red X had been drawn over it. "That means secret," he said. "I mean, to outsiders."

"But you can look inside?"

"No problem," Silverman said lightly. He opened the envelope and took out the single sheet of paper it contained.

"This isn't going to help you all that much, Frank," he said as he began to scan it. "It just says that a disciplinary hearing was held concerning Hannah Kovatnik on March 25, 1936. She was charged with a number seven violation, which has to do with union ethics. Like you already knew." His eyes continued to move down the page. "It indicates that Hannah defended herself. Which means she didn't have any kind of attorney. The bottom line is, she lost. She was expelled from the membership." He shrugged. "That's it."

"It doesn't say what the violation was?" Frank asked quickly.

"No."

"Why not?"

Silverman smiled. "That's the interesting part," he said. "Usually it does."

"Then why wouldn't it in Hannah's case?"

"Probably because it would be embarrassing to the union."

"In what way?"

Silverman shrugged. "Who knows? But one thing's for sure. Back in 1936, they wanted to keep it strictly secret. That explains the red *X*, but it also explains why the report leaves everything out." He handed the paper to Frank. "See? Nothing but the bare bones."

Frank glanced at the paper.

"She was accused of something," Silverman said. "And she was found guilty of it."

Frank's eyes continued to move down the page.

"The only other little detail is the name of the guy who brought the charge," Silverman added.

Frank looked at him. "Who was that?"

Silverman took the paper from his hand. "The name in the bottom left hand corner," he said. "That's where it always is." He tapped the paper with his finger. "There it is. Philip Stern."

Frank stared at the name.

"You recognize him?" Silverman asked.

"Yes."

"How?"

"There was an article written about Hannah in the union paper," Frank said. "Sort of a profile. It was full of praise."

"And he's mentioned in the article?"

"No," Frank said. "He wrote it."

"He wrote an article praising her?" Silverman asked unbelievingly.

"Yes," Frank told him, and even as he said it, his mind recalled the portrait which had emerged from Stern's words. He saw Hannah in the fury of her youth, the glory of her commitment, the sheer unbending force of her energy.

"Well, something must have changed his mind," Silverman said offhandedly.

"Do you have his address?"

"I can check it," Silverman said. He tapped the keys, and Stern's name flashed onto the screen.

"Well, look at that," Silverman said as he read the details which appeared under Stern's name.

Frank copied the address into his notebook. "When did Stern leave the union?" he asked when he'd finished.

Silverman's eyes remained on the screen. "He never did," he said admiringly. He looked at Frank. "Now that's what you call an old warrior, Frank, a man who never lost what he had at the beginning."

20

Imalia Covallo had left a message on Frank's answering machine, and as he stood in the dark office, silently listening to it, her voice struck him as oddly vulnerable, as if she could sense that only a thin, almost invisible line separated her from the more desperate world that surrounded her. It was the sort of tone Karen had once had, but had slowly, subtly lost, and for a moment Frank tried to figure out exactly what had been lost along with it.

"I would like to make our afternoon meeting at three P.M.," Imalia said over the soft purr of the machine. "The floor above my shop on Madison. Ask for the private elevator."

He had just begun to rewind the machine when Farouk walked through the door.

"Nice to find you here," Farouk said.

"I was about to head over to see Miss Covallo," Frank told him.

"It is good I came, then," Farouk said. He lumbered over to the chair in front of Frank's desk and sat down. "I have a few discoveries which you might wish to tell her."

"What sorts of things?"

"That the dead woman spoke in Spanish," Farouk said, determinedly moving at his own pace, "this interested me."

"You found something about that?"

"I did, yes," Farouk told him.

Frank slowly lowered himself onto the corner of his desk. "What do you have?"

Farouk took out a single piece of lined white paper. "I have sources in the government," he said.

Frank said nothing.

"I am speaking now of the national government," Farouk added after a dramatic pause.

"Go ahead," Frank said, a little impatiently.

"Well, this business of the blank space in the woman's life, this is troubling."

"Yes, it is."

"Such a large space," Farouk added thoughtfully. "Much time which could have been put to use. Perhaps, during so many years, one might even learn to speak a foreign language."

Frank nodded quickly.

"It occurred to me that if the dead woman had remained in this country, such a blank would be impossible," Farouk continued.

Again Frank nodded impatiently.

"The trail, it is long," Farouk added authoritatively. "There is, of course, the question of taxes which must be paid. Papers must be filed to do this. There is the question of employment. These things cannot be kept secret."

"No, they can't."

"But if the dead woman had gone away," Farouk said, "this is another matter."

"Is that what she did?" Frank asked.

"It is, yes," Farouk said. "And there is a record of it. A passport."

Frank took out a cigarette and lit it. "Go on."

"This is of value?" Farouk asked.

"It might be."

Farouk's eyes returned to the page. "This passport was issued to the dead woman—"

"Hannah."

"Yes, Hannah," Farouk said, his eyes still on the paper. "This passport was issued to Hannah in May of 1936. It was not renewed for many years."

"Where did she use it?"

"South America."

"Colombia," Frank said immediately.

Farouk looked surprised. "You knew of this?"

"Her sister Gilda died there in 1954," Frank said. "Her body was brought back here."

"And buried where?"

"I don't know."

"I can discover this," Farouk assured him. "And, as well . . ."

Frank eased himself to his feet. "I have to meet Miss Covallo," he said.

Farouk did not move. "There is something else," he said. "Of record, I mean."

"What?"

"A license for marriage," Farouk said. "For Hannah."

Frank crushed the cigarette into the ashtray on his desk. "Hannah was married?"

"Yes," Farouk told him.

"When?"

"1954. September."

"What date?"

"September fifteenth."

Frank took out his notebook and flipped through the pages of his interview with Silverman. Then he looked up. "That's only two days after her sister Gilda died," he said. "Where was she married?"

"In Bogotá," Farouk said. "Is that not where Gilda died?"

"No."

Farouk's eyes narrowed curiously. "Where then?"

"In a little village," Frank said. "A place called San Jorge."

"How do you know this?"

"Union records."

Farouk nodded thoughtfully. "I see," he said softly.

"See what?"

"That she was full of contradiction," Farouk said with a slight shrug. Then he smiled quickly. "As are we all, of course," he added.

Frank let his mind drift back to what Farouk had told him. "So she married just before she came back to the United States."

Farouk nodded. "Only a few days before."

"Did the husband come with her?"

"He did, yes," Farouk said. "But it was not a proper marriage."

"What do you mean?"

"They did not ever share the same place."

"They never lived together?"

"No."

"How do you know that?"

"Immigration Records," Farouk said. "According to them the husband lived in Brooklyn. Hannah lived in Manhattan."

"Did they ever divorce?"

"No. At least, there is no record of it."

Frank took out his notebook. "What was his name, the husband?"

"Pérez. Emilio Pérez."

"He was Spanish?"

"South American," Farouk said. "From Colombia."

"That's the man who was with her," Frank said. "With Hannah."

"With her? Where?"

"When she talked to Constanza," Frank told him. "This woman I talked to, Molly Gold, she said that Hannah brought a man with her to see Constanza, and that the two of them—Hannah and the man—spoke Spanish."

Farouk nodded slowly. "Yes, that could be."

Frank pressed his pencil onto the notebook. "Where is the husband now?"

"He returned to Colombia," Farouk said. "I do not know why." He shook his head. "And he did not return to this country."

"Do the police know about all this?"

Farouk shook his head. "They do now."

"You told them?"

"It is not good in my profession to conceal things from the authorities," Farouk said. "But they see no reason for looking into it."

"So Hannah's husband is not a suspect?"

"Not a suspect, no," Farouk said. "As my source put it, 'such a trail is too cold for a crime of such hot blood.'"

"That may be true," Frank said, "but if he were alive, he could get the body released."

Farouk nodded. "It would be a long way for him to come."

"I'm sure Miss Covallo would make it worth his while."

Farouk smiled quietly. "I will try to find him."

"Good," Frank said. Again, he eased himself off the desk and headed toward the door.

Farouk joined him there. "You have found things, too?" He asked as he stepped into the narrow corridor.

"Yes."

"May I know them?"

Frank locked the door of the office and walked up the stairs to the street.

"She had some problems with the union," he said. "Some sort of dispute. She was charged with something. It's still not clear what."

"You are pursuing this?"

"Yes," Frank told him. "But your lead is a lot better." He smiled. "I'll have to settle up with you, Farouk—about money, I mean—when we've finally got the picture."

"We shall do that at the proper time," Farouk told him.

"I just wanted you to know that I owe you," Frank said.

"Owe me, yes," Farouk said. "That is true." Then he smiled quietly, his dark eyes almost black in the late afternoon light. "She is a strange woman, yes?"

"Hannah?"

"Truth," Farouk said softly as he turned very slowly and walked the other way.

The private elevator was in the rear of the building, and it was manned by a single uniformed guard, a tall, bulky man who had a forty-five automatic strapped to his waist.

"My name is Clemons," Frank told him as he stepped up to the bronze-colored elevator doors.

The guard glanced at a notepad, checking for his name.

"Do you have some sort of identification?" he asked when he had finished.

Frank showed him his card.

"Thank you," the guard said politely. "Please step in."

The elevator doors opened onto a luxuriously decorated room, its walls festooned with large photographs of lean, beautiful women wrapped in an assortment of oddly gleaming fabrics. The words beneath the photographs proclaimed "The Imalia

Covallo Look." A large mahogany table sat in the middle of the room bearing a bottle of champagne tilted slightly in an ice-filled cooler. Trays of hors d'oeuvres surrounded the champagne, along with an assortment of wines.

"Hello, Frank," Imalia said as she stepped up to him. She turned toward the room. "Like it?"

"It's very nice."

"This is the exclusive shop," Imalia explained. "It's different from the one downstairs."

"I see."

"Some people prefer to shop in private."

"Is that right?" Frank asked dully.

"Sometimes I go to their homes," Imalia added. "But sometimes they come here." She stepped over to the table. "Would you like something?"

"No, thanks."

Her hand gently grasped the neck of the champagne bottle. "It's a lovely champagne," she said coaxingly. "I always have it around. It's part of the price of doing business. The people who come here expect the best."

"No, thanks," Frank repeated.

"Fine," Imalia said. She walked over to a large velvet chair and sat down. "Well, have you made any progress?"

"Yes," Frank told her.

Imalia smiled. "Good. I'm glad to hear it."

Frank took out his notebook and began to flip through the pages.

"You may sit down, if you like," Imalia told him.

Frank remained standing. "I've found out a few things," he said, "and so has an associate of mine."

Imalia's eyes tensed. "Associate?"

"A guy who's working with me on the case."

"I wasn't aware that you had an associate."

"He's very helpful," Frank assured her. "He knows how to research things, and he's come in with a few important details."

Imalia did not look convinced. "Like what?" she demanded.

"Like the fact that Hannah spent some time in Colombia," Frank said. "And that she was married there."

Imalia sat up slightly. "Married? Hannah?"

"She never mentioned it?"

"No."

"Well, it was over before she came to work for you," Frank said. "The husband went back to Colombia. But technically, they may still be married. And if they are, then he has the authority to get the body released."

"So you're trying to find him, I presume," Imalia said.

"My partner's doing that right now."

"Good," Imalia said. She seemed to relax a bit. "You'll let me know when you find him, of course."

"Yes," Frank said.

"And of course, if he has to come to New York to get the body released, I'll be happy to pay all his expenses."

Frank nodded. "That might be necessary. But I really don't know." His eyes dropped back toward his notebook. "I've also made some progress on Hannah's sisters," he said.

"Really? What?"

"One of them, Gilda, is dead."

"I'm sorry to hear it."

"She died in Colombia in 1954," Frank added. "The body was brought back here. I assume Hannah brought it." He looked up from the notebook. "Someone applied for a death benefit to offset the cost of the funeral. A man named Fischelson, Joseph Fischelson."

Imalia stared at him expressionlessly.

"You never heard that name?" Frank asked.

"No."

"Did Hannah ever mention living in South America?"

"Not that I know of."

"How about the name Emilio Pérez?"

"No," Imalia said. "Who's that?"

"Her husband."

Imalia looked surprised. "She married a South American?"

"Apparently."

"Is it possible that they had children?"

"I don't think so," Frank said. "They don't appear to have ever lived together."

Imalia leaned forward slightly. "But they were married."

"I'm not sure what kind of marriage it was," Frank said.

Imalia struck a worldly pose. "Well, there're all sorts of contracts for living together, of course, but that sort of thing usually comes later, doesn't it?" She smiled. "As they say, 'when love has fled.'"

"Yes."

"But with Hannah and this Emilio," she added, "it was odd from the beginning?"

"He lived in Brooklyn," Frank said. "Hannah lived in Manhattan."

Imalia shook her head wonderingly. "She never mentioned having been married."

"He went back to Colombia," Frank said. "We don't know what happened after that."

Imalia rose from her seat, walked over to the table and poured herself a glass of champagne. "So where does all this finally leave us?" she asked.

"We're moving in two directions," Frank said. "We're trying to trace the one living sister through the union, and . . ."

"What union?" Imalia asked.

"The American Garment Workers," Frank told her. "Hannah was a member until March of 1936. I'm hoping I can find someone who knows something about the other sister."

"Naomi."

"Yes."

"And the other direction?"

"Pérez, the husband. If he's still her husband."

"Two directions," Imalia said thoughtfully. "It sounds very complicated."

"It's a life," Frank said, "so it's complicated." He closed the notebook and returned it to his jacket pocket.

Imalia lifted her arms gracefully. "By the way, I gave Karen one of my dresses. Did she show it to you?"

"Yes."

"Did you like it?"

"It was beautiful."

"They're wonderful, aren't they?" Imalia asked. "Beautiful things."

"Yes," Frank said. He turned slowly and headed toward the elevator.

"But expensive," she added, almost sadly. "Very, very expensive."

"Most good things are," Frank said offhandedly.

Imalia stared at him questioningly. "Do you think that's so, that good things are expensive?"

"Yes," Frank told her. "But not always in money."

Imalia sat back slightly, her eyes boring into him. "No matter what you find out," she said. "About Hannah, I mean. I want to know what it is."

"Of course."

"I want to know everything," Imalia added emphatically. "And I want to know it first." She looked at him commandingly. "Before anyone. Even your associate, whoever he is."

Frank nodded. "You'll be the first," Frank assured her.

Imalia smiled thinly, her long white arms drawing a dark blue scarf languidly along her throat. "Good," she said softly. "Because the customer is always right."

21

It was late in the afternoon by the time Frank got off the subway in the Bronx. He walked down the long flight of metal stairs that led from the elevated tracks to the crowded streets along Sedgwick Avenue.

According to union records, Philip Stern still lived in the Consolidated Housing Project, two enormous brick buildings which the union had built for its members in the fifties, and which, as Silverman had put it when he gave him Stern's address, still housed "the real history of the garment trade."

Stern's apartment was on the sixteenth floor, and the door opened almost immediately.

"My name is Frank Clemons," Frank said to the short, middle-aged woman who stood in the doorway. "Mr. Silverman said he would call you."

"He did," the woman said. "You want to see Papa, right?"

"Yes."

The woman dried her hands on the large floral apron which hung from her neck. "I was fixing him dinner. You like pot roast, you could eat with him."

"No, thanks," Frank said.

"He could use the company," the woman said. "You know how it is with old people, they get into low moods. Papa gets into real low moods."

"Is he here?"

"He likes to sit in the park before dinner," the woman said. She stepped out of the door. "Come on in. I'll show you."

Frank followed the woman through the apartment and out onto a small, concrete terrace.

"There he is," the woman said as she pointed down below. "On the bench next to the street."

Frank could see a small man, bundled up in woolens.

"That's Papa," the woman said. "He's got thin blood. He wears a hat and overcoat all the time."

"Thanks," Frank said as he turned back through the apartment.

"You can have dinner with him if you change your mind," the woman called to him as he closed the door.

Philip Stern sat silently on the small wooden bench, his back very erect, his hands tucked inside the sleeves of his black overcoat. A wide-brimmed gray hat was pulled down tightly over his head, and his throat was wrapped securely in a thick red scarf.

"Mr. Stern?" Frank said softly as he approached him.

Two flashing brown eyes shot over to him. "Yes."

"My name is Frank Clemons. Harry Silverman gave me your address."

"My address?" Stern asked in a deep, steady voice which seemed as dense and powerfully alive as his body. "Why?"

"Mind if I sit down?" Frank asked politely.

Stern nodded toward the bench. "Please."

Frank took a seat beside him and reached for his identification. "I'm a private investigator," he said as he presented his card.

Stern smiled slyly. "Well, I've seen a few of those in my day. Informers, too. Who do you work for?"

"I'm not allowed to say," Frank told him. "But since Mr. Silverman sent me—"

"I can trust you," Stern said.

Frank nodded. "Yes."

"Okay," Stern said. "What do you want?"

Frank returned his card to his coat pocket. "It has to do with a woman named Hannah Kovatnik."

The old man turned away slightly, his eyes drifting up into the reddish leaves that hung above him. He did not reply.

"Mr. Silverman thought that you might help me?"

Stern's eyes remained on the gently trembling leaves. "Help you what?"

"Miss Kovatnik was murdered," Frank said. "The police are holding her body until a relative makes them release it."

"We weren't related."

"No," Frank said. "But you wrote an article about her in 1935."

Stern's eyes swept over to him. "Did Harry tell you that?"

"No," Frank said. "I found the article in one of the old union papers."

Stern smiled wistfully. "I wanted to be a writer back then," he said. "A real writer. The kind who has a feel for things, who cares about something besides his own narrow little life." He nodded slightly, and the bitterness that had inched into his voice suddenly fell away. "There seemed to be so much to write about in those days. The struggle, you know, the sacrifice. Great themes."

Frank took out his notebook and opened it. "That piece you wrote about Hannah," he said. "It was very good."

The old man smiled. "As it turned out, I wasn't a great writer, but I was a pretty good one. And Hannah? Well, a young man couldn't have hoped for better material."

Frank wrote it down quickly.

"I tried to capture her," Stern went on. "Her beauty. Not her body, or her face, or anything like that. Not that kind of beauty. That's for movie stars, fashion magazines. I wasn't after that. I was after Hannah, herself. Not the way she looked, but the way she acted, the way she made people feel."

"Her hand in the air," Frank said.

"Yes, that's what I mean."

"You did it, I think," Frank told him.

Stern nodded. "I think so, too," he said with a sudden muted pride. "A man can write well when he's inspired." He smiled. "That's the only time a man can write well. Everything else is just some kind of bad faith, as the French call it. Inauthentic nonsense."

"And you were inspired by Hannah?" Frank said, returning him gently to the subject.

"Yes," Stern said firmly. "Very much. And I wasn't the only

one either. You must have seen that picture, the one of her giving that speech in Union Square."

"Yes, I did."

"Those faces, looking up at her. Didn't they look inspired?"

"Yes."

"Well, there you have it then."

"Were you at that rally?"

"Of course," Stern said. "You don't cover the world in an office, you know." Something seemed to strike his mind. "You said you were looking for a relative?"

"That's right."

"Well, she had two sisters," Stern told him. "She was sort of their guardian, you might say. The father was dead."

"Yes, I know."

"Gilda was beautiful in her face," Stern added. "But Hannah, she was beautiful in her mind, her heart, what she thought about and wanted. These things were beautiful in her." He shook his head wonderingly. "It's hard to imagine it."

"When did you meet her?"

"While the strike was going on," Stern said. He shivered slightly. "It was a bad winter. There was so much snow." His eyes drifted over to the large reservoir which faced him from across the street, its surface rippling lightly in the cold winter breeze. "The wind off the East River was like a sheet of ice, and I can remember how Hannah stood in it hour after hour with that little sign she'd painted. Justice, it said. That's all. Just one word. In red. Justice."

Frank wrote it down. "This was in Union Square?"

"Orchard Street," Stern told him. "In front of her shop."

"The one Sol Feig owned."

Stern nodded silently. "Sol Feig, yes," he said finally.

"Hannah was the leader of that shop, wasn't she?"

"She was the leader," Stern said. "Absolutely. And she was a damned good leader, let me tell you. She had a gift, a wonderful gift. She could make you believe in something as powerfully as she believed in it herself." His eyes flashed suddenly, with a kind of odd, liquid fire. "Do you have any idea what a great gift that is?"

Frank said nothing.

"In a leader," Stern added, "it is the greatest possible power." He lifted one of his hands from its covering sleeve and drew it into a tight fist. "It's the gift of inspiration," he said fiercely. "It's the power to inspire people to do more, suffer more, than it seems possible for them to do."

In his mind, Frank suddenly saw and heard Hannah Kovatnik in all her brief and glowing splendor, saw her eyes staring wildly into the cheering crowds, her body drawn taut in the freezing air, her voice ringing through the bare, leafless trees, blistering, furious, overwhelming.

"I had never seen anything like her," Stern said, his own voice suddenly high, tremulous, but not breaking. "She made everything seem possible. More than that. She made a *great thing* seem possible."

"Justice," Frank said.

"Yes."

Frank could feel a strangely ancient sorrow suddenly move through him, a deep, silent mourning for everything that goes wrong.

"What happened?" he asked quietly.

Stern shifted his shoulders slightly. "What do you mean?"

"With Hannah."

For a moment, Stern seemed to move away from him, sinking back into an impenetrable solitude. Then he suddenly straightened himself slightly. "She won," he said darkly.

"Won what?"

"The strike," Stern said. "Her shop won."

For a time, Frank allowed the silence to lengthen between them. Then, abruptly, he broke it.

"But that's not the end of it, is it?" he said.

"For most people it was."

"But not for Hannah."

Stern shook his head. "No, not for Hannah."

"She was expelled from the union not long after the strike," he said.

Stern's eyes swept back to the gently shifting waters of the reservoir. He did not speak.

"There was a hearing of some kind," Frank added, as he continued to watch the old man closely.

Stern's eyes closed slowly, and his hand crawled back beneath the sleeve.

"A charge was made against her," Frank continued.

Stern's eyes tightened.

"You brought that charge."

The old man's eyes opened slowly, still staring straight ahead. "How do you know that?"

"There's a paper in the union archives," Frank went on. "But it leaves a lot out."

A thin smile rose on Stern's face. "Of course it does," he said with an edge of bitterness.

"What do you mean?"

Stern looked at Frank pointedly. "Do you think it was easy to make a union in those days?" he asked fiercely. "Do you think it was something you did with your hands in a pair of white gloves?"

"No," Frank answered immediately.

Stern laughed coldly. "You should have been there in the winter of 1935. You should have seen what the papers wrote about us. You should have seen the police charging us on horseback. Like cossacks. Like in Poland." He shook his head wearily. "Then you would have some idea of what Hannah felt."

"About what?"

"About what she did," Stern said, his voice still hard, yet strangely weary. "And why she did it." He turned away, as if to regain control of himself. "But still," he added after a moment. "But still, there are limits. There have to be limits."

"On what?"

"On us," Stern told him. "On what we're willing to do."

Frank pressed the tip of his pen against the notebook. "And Hannah went beyond them, the limits?"

"Yes."

"How?"

The old man stared at Frank hesitantly. "What does it matter? What are you looking for?"

"The truth."

"About what?"

"About Hannah."

Stern turned away again, a single hand grabbing at the red scarf, plucking at it nervously.

Frank leaned toward him slightly. "What did she do?"

"She broke a commandment," Stern said simply, crisply, as if he would say nothing more.

"Which one?"

Slowly the old man turned back toward Frank and stared squarely into his eyes. "The ninth commandment," he said.

Instantly Frank remembered his Bible-thumping father, how he'd raged from the pulpit, going through the commandments one by one until the dusty congregation had been all but pressed to death by their agonizing weight. It was then that he had learned them, one by one, as they seemed to fall like great black stones from the rocky ledge of Sinai.

"Thou shalt not bear false witness," he said.

Stern's face suddenly took on an oddly muted anguish. "Yes."

"She lied about someone?" Frank asked immediately.

"Yes."

"Who was it?"

"Sol Feig," Stern answered immediately, as if the last of his old resistance had given way, and the past was now sweeping back over him, thundering like a wave.

"The man she worked for," Frank said.

"Yes."

Frank could see Feig as he now lived, locked in his room on Orchard Street, crumpled in his chair, his watery eyes glaring toward the squat red tenements that faced him from the window.

"Sol Feig was a greedy man," Stern began. "And he ran a greedy shop. It was also very profitable, and a few people hoped that the strike would break him, cause him to sell at a loss." He stopped, and his eyes drifted out toward the water once again. "One of them was a man named Abe Bornstein."

In his mind, Frank could hear Bornstein's voice as he leered at Hannah from his bench in the park: *She's the rabbi's daughter. She don't open up her legs for nobody.*

"Bornstein wanted to take over Feig's operation," Stern went on, his voice now fully controlled. "He wanted to break him, and he wanted to use the strike to do it. That's why he came to Hannah."

"Why Hannah?"

"The strike had been going on for a long time by then," Stern explained. "People were beginning to break. They couldn't buy food or coal. You have to understand what it was like in the winter of 1935." He shook his head. "Hannah was working desperately to keep everybody going, but even a woman like her, even a person with that kind of force, can't do everything. She couldn't keep her people warm at night. She couldn't keep food in their stomachs. And without things like that, the fire goes out." He shivered slightly as a lean wind blew around them, sweeping a line of rust-colored leaves over their feet. "The fire was going out," he repeated. "Hannah could see it. And so could Abe Bornstein. That's when he came to her."

Frank could see them in the park together, just as Riviera had described them, huddled beside a slender wooden bench, while in the distance, a knot of unemployed men fed wooden slats into a flaming drum.

"Bornstein had a plan," Stern went on matter-of-factly. "He had an actress who was willing to claim that Feig had tried to rape her. He knew that a charge like that would put some steel back in the strike. Hannah's job was to broadcast it throughout the union, let it loose in the neighborhood. The Lower East Side was like a little village in those days. Feig would be ruined. The strike would win. Bornstein would buy Feig out, and once in control, he'd deal with the union in a better way."

"Is that what happened?" Frank asked quickly.

"More or less," Stern said. "But things got badly out of hand. The rumor finally got to Feig's daughter." He stopped. "Feig had nothing but his daughter. Except for the shop, she was his whole life."

Frank could feel a terrible tension growing in his body, pressing outward, as if trying to explode.

"Her name was Marta," Stern said. "She was only fifteen." His eyes returned to Frank. "She worshipped Feig. And after this came out—on Christmas day, as a matter of fact, 1935—she hanged herself in her bedroom closet."

Frank's eyes swept out toward the looming towers which rose on the other side of the reservoir.

Stern watched him closely. "Can you imagine what that did to Feig?" he asked. "The suicide of his only daughter?"

Frank kept his eyes on the twin gray towers. "Yes."

For a time, they sat in silence, then Stern shifted slightly in his seat, massaging his knees rhythmically. "Circulation problems," he explained.

Frank turned toward him. "How did you find out about what Hannah and Bornstein did?" he asked.

"The oldest way in the world."

"What way is that?"

"Someone told me."

"Why?"

"Because this person thought that Hannah had gone too far, that she'd compromised the struggle, that if it was ever discovered that some union-planted lie, some vicious slander, had ended up causing a young girl to kill herself—that if that ever became known, it would be the end of the union."

"So he told you about it?"

"Yes."

"So that you could bring the charge."

"That's right."

"Why didn't he bring it himself?"

"He couldn't."

"Why not?"

"Because blood is thicker than water, Mr. Clemons," Stern said bluntly. "It's thicker than almost anything."

"What do you mean?"

"Hannah had only one real friend in the world," Stern said. "One person she could tell everything to."

Frank waited, his pen bearing down on the pad.

"Her sister," Stern said finally. "Naomi."

"And Naomi told you?" Frank asked immediately.

"No," Stern answered quickly. "Naomi's husband. He'd overheard it all."

"This husband, what was his name?"

"Fischelson. Joseph Fischelson."

Suddenly, Frank saw the name as it appeared on the request

for death benefits for Gilda, little amber letters on a dead black screen.

"So it was Fischelson who came to you?"

"Yes," Stern said, "because he couldn't bring the charge himself. He gave me all the information I needed to pursue it. I started with the actress. She was a rummy. She broke fast. Then Bornstein tumbled. I had all the facts. And so I brought the charge."

"And that's when they had the hearing?"

"Yes."

"Did Hannah defend herself?"

"Not really," Stern said. "She sat at the end of the table. She was staring straight ahead. She looked different, like something had been drained away from her, some kind of moisture. She looked hard. She looked like she'd never care about anything again."

"Where was this hearing?"

"A small room in the back of the union meeting hall," Stern said. "It was off Delancey Street. It's all been knocked down for high-rises."

"Who was there?"

Stern thought for a moment. "Beidelbaum was there. Sidney Beidelbaum, the head of the local. I was there, with all my information. Karl Fisk. Norman Vladeck." He shook his head. "They're all dead."

"When it was over, what happened?"

"They swore her to secrecy," Stern said. "Then they told her to withdraw from all union activity."

"And she agreed to do that?"

"With a little nod," Stern said.

"Did she say anything?"

"Not until it was over," Stern said. "Then she stood up. She'd been sitting at the end of the table. It was a real inquisition type of setup. Hannah alone at one end of the table, all these bearded men at the other end." He frowned harshly. "It was an awful thing. Even the way it looked was awful."

"But when it was over, she said something."

"Yeah," Stern said. "She stood up. Very stiff. Full of pride. She stood up and she said the old words they use when they issue the final divorce decree in Orthodox Jewish marriages. She stood up and she said—and this was in Hebrew—she said, I cast you out. I cast you out. I cast you out. Three times, just like that. According to the rules of Jewish law."

Frank wrote it down. "Then she left?"

"That's right," Stern told him. "She turned on her heels, and walked out the door. None of us ever heard from her again."

22

For a long time after he returned to his office on 49th Street, Frank simply sat at his desk, smoking one cigarette after another until the ashtray was overflowing and the air had become so thick and rancid that he could barely stand it. He thought of Karen, and he realized that he would not be able to go home at all tonight, that there were too many sleepless things shuffling about inside him. He could hear Sheila's voice, reminding him of the twenty-first birthday their daughter would never have, and he thought of Feig's daughter, her body swaying in the closet, and then the old man himself, hunched over and wheezing, living in the utter isolation a single lie had brought him.

It was past midnight by the time he finally walked out onto the street, turned left and headed toward Tenth Avenue. The late afternoon cold had deepened with the night, and as he strolled down 49th Street, Frank thought of the snows of 1935, of Hannah's sign flapping loudly in the wind off the river, of the lines of pickets who huddled along Orchard Street while Feig stared down at them from his office high above. He heard the ringing speeches, felt the ground tremble as the horses charged down the uneven brick streets, sensed the greed and sacrifice, all the frozen hopes and fatal fire of those tumultuous wintry days.

\   *   *   *

Farouk was already seated at his usual table when Frank walked into Toby's. He nodded silently as Frank came through the door, then motioned him over to the one empty seat at the other end of his table. He looked more weary than he had before, a hunched, gigantic figure, his enormous hands wrapped around a small glass, his large round eyes staring off into the distance as if he were peering out across desert reaches, or back into his hidden youth.

"Good evening, Frank," he said quietly.

Frank nodded.

"What would you like?"

"An Irish."

"Fine," Farouk said. He made some sort of hand signal to his wife, and she immediately deposited a full fifth of Bushmills on the table.

"This will do?" Farouk said as he opened it.

"Fine."

Farouk poured each of them a shot, then lifted his in toast. "To whatever," he said softly.

Frank touched his glass to Farouk's. "Right."

Farouk's dark eyes seemed to glow out of the shadowy light that surrounded him. For a moment, he watched the others in the bar as if he were guarding them in some distant way, or simply taking down their stories in his mind.

"Well," he said at last, as he returned his glass to the table, "did you find a relative?"

"Not exactly."

"But something?"

"There's a brother-in-law," Frank told him. "A man named Joseph Fischelson."

"A brother-in-law to Hannah?"

"Yes."

"And the sister is living?"

"I don't know."

Farouk nodded. "And this brother-in-law, he lives where?"

"I don't know for sure," Frank said. "But he should be easy enough to find."

"If he wishes to be found."

"No reason why he shouldn't," Frank said. "At least as far as I know."

"Some people prefer the shadows," Farouk said.

"Like you?"

Farouk smiled. "It is possible to know too much, to divulge too much," he said. "Perhaps that is why I live alone."

"Don't you ever get tired of it?"

"The other way tires me more," Farouk said bluntly. Then he shrugged. "One begins everything with a great passion, then it fades away. That is what breaks the heart, Frank, the way time wears everything down." He took another drink. "You think you can outrun it. You take the caravan to the port city, then a steamer across the sea. In a strange land, you ride the trains until you know where you are by the way the boxcars shift around the curves. Even the rails become familiar."

"Is that what you did?"

"For many years."

"Why not forever?"

"Because the drifters do not hold the secret," Farouk said with a slight smile.

"Who does?"

"The ones who most believe in what they've done," Farouk said matter-of-factly. He eyed Frank pointedly. "Was Hannah one of those?"

"For a while she was."

Farouk nodded quickly, then took another sip from the glass. "And have you learned anything new about her?"

"Maybe."

Farouk's eyes widened, but he did not speak.

"You remember that she was kicked out of the union in January of 1936," Frank said.

"Yes."

"I found out why."

Farouk continued to stare at Frank silently.

"She was in a conspiracy, you might say. With a guy named Bornstein," Frank told him.

"Bornstein?"

"He was a labor broker, among other things," Frank said. "He was interested in taking over Feig's shop."

"The Feig of Orchard Street."

"Yes," Frank said. "They cooked up a story about him trying to rape a woman. Bornstein had an actress who was willing to back them up."

"But this rape was a lie?"

"Yes," Frank said. "It was all a lie, but Feig's daughter believed it, along with everybody else."

Farouk took a sip from his glass.

"She killed herself," Frank added. "She was fifteen."

"*Ihr Herz war schwarz,*" Farouk said, almost to himself.

"What does that mean?"

"It's what Feig said," Farouk told him. "Her heart was black." He looked down at his glass. "He meant Hannah's heart."

"It was a bad time," Frank said. "Bad things happened."

Farouk nodded quickly. "And this lie," he asked, "it was discovered?"

"Discovered, then hushed up. By the union, I mean."

"Of course," Farouk said.

"Anyway, Hannah was brought before some kind of committee. It wasn't exactly a trial, but it ended up with her being bounced from the union."

"And Bornstein?"

"He'd already bought Feig out," Frank said. "A real fire sale."

Farouk stared at his glass thoughtfully. "And this was in January, 1936."

"Yes."

Farouk took a quick drink, then returned the glass firmly to the table. "Hannah's passport," he said, "was stamped in Bogotá on February seventh, 1936."

"Just a few weeks later."

Farouk nodded. "I am thinking of money."

"To get to Colombia, you mean?"

"I am wondering where it came from."

"Yes."

"And for what reason she would go there."

"That, too," Frank said.

Farouk's eyes slid over to Frank. "To bury her is not enough."

"No, it isn't," Frank said.

Farouk smiled. "But to discover her, to do it for the thing itself," he said, "this is what matters, is it not?"

"I think so," Frank said.

Farouk poured Frank another drink. "This Bornstein is alive?"

"No," Frank said. "He died in 1959. But before that, he brought Hannah over to work for a guy named Constanza."

Farouk pretended to shiver. "*El ojo malo*," he said at the mention of Constanza. "The evil eye."

"So I've heard."

"Now dead."

"Murdered."

"The air is cleaner," Farouk said, "much cleaner since that day." He finished his drink, then poured himself another. "We must see the brother-in-law."

"He tried to get a death benefit to help bury Gilda," Frank said. "That was in 1954."

"She was only in her thirties, Gilda," Farouk said. "This is young for death."

"Yes, it is."

"Why did she die?"

"I don't know."

"I can find that out," Farouk assured him. "But I think we must see the brother-in-law. What do you know about him?"

"Nothing more than what I've told you," Frank admitted. "And the fact that it was Fischelson who turned Hannah in."

"Turned her in?" Farouk asked.

"For the plot against Feig."

"That's odd, don't you think?" Farouk asked. "That he would do such a thing."

"Maybe."

"But you know only that he did it?"

"Nothing else."

Farouk thought about things for a moment. "Did Hannah not return with her sister's body?" he asked finally.

"No."

"And the reason?"

"I guess you'd have to say that she stayed behind to get married."

"To Pérez."

"Yes."

Farouk's eyes narrowed somewhat. "A quick marriage, would you not say?"

"It has that look."

"And then a quick return to New York," Farouk added immediately.

Frank nodded.

Farouk leaned back heavily in his chair. "Perhaps she did not mourn her sister?"

"It's possible that she didn't," Frank said.

"Possible, yes," Farouk said in a slow, calculating voice, "if, as Feig would have it, *'Ihr Herz war schwarz.'* "

For a while they sat together in silence. Across the room, Toby paced back and forth from one side of the bar to the other, wiping a wet cloth along its surface with each pass. She had the look of someone immensely strong and self-reliant, and as Frank watched her, he could feel a strange admiration sweep out to her, to Farouk, to all the strange, indecipherable rogues who gathered in such places during the gray after-hours of the world.

"Maybe she changed," he said finally. "Hannah, I mean."

Farouk took a toothpick from his jacket pocket and slid it into the corner of his mouth. "What she had was good."

"What do you mean, her life?"

"Her belief," Farouk explained. He picked at the large gap between his two front teeth. "Love? A man can live without it. And money? Most people do." He withdrew the toothpick from his mouth and stared dully at its frayed point. "But belief? This you cannot live without." He shrugged lightly as he watched Toby pocket the night's receipts and lumber toward him, the barcloth hung loosely around her neck. "You can go on, this is true. Like a plant. But live?" He shook his head. "No, you cannot truly live."

Toby nodded tersely as she passed, and Farouk immediately got to his feet. "Closing time," he said, as he turned his hand gently under Frank's shoulder. "Come, we will walk you home."

Frank got to his feet, and the two of them followed Toby to the door, waited as she locked it, then walked downstairs and turned to the left, heading slowly southward down Tenth Avenue for a while, then east, toward midtown.

"You should sleep, Frank," Farouk said as they came to the corner of 49th Street.

Frank glanced toward the little iron gate which fronted his office. "Yeah."

Farouk looked at him pointedly. "You are sleeping there?"

"I think so."

"From now on?"

He saw Karen cocooned in her ice-blue silk sheets, saw the pink room and the deep, lush carpet, and realized with a sudden anguished recognition that he would never be with her again.

"From now on," he said as the first light broke along the avenue.

23

Farouk was waiting for him when Frank came out of the offices of the American Garment Workers and bolted across 16th Street and into the newly renovated elegance of Union Square Park.

"This place was once a shooting gallery," Farouk said as Frank sat down on the bench beside him. "To walk through here was a dangerous undertaking."

Frank saw the park differently, through a grainy photograph of a freezing crowd huddled beneath the bare limbs of winter trees. "This is where Hannah made her speech," he said. His eyes perused the oddly domesticated landscape, the gently rounded knoll, the small, compact playground of swings, slides and sandboxes. "I guess it was her last one."

Farouk nodded. "Yes." He drew his eyes over to Frank. "What did you find out?"

"I talked to Silverman," Frank said. "We looked up a Naomi Fischelson in the union files. She was there. She'd been a member in good standing since 1935."

Farouk smiled delightedly. "Hannah's sister. She is still alive?"

"No," Frank said. "She died last year."

"And the husband?"

"Still alive as far as anybody knows," Frank said. "At least he's still drawing on his wife's union pension."

"Which means they have his address?"

"Yes," Frank said. "Some place in Brooklyn. The Heights. Heard of it?"

Farouk nodded vigorously. "Yes, I know it," he said as he rose quickly and headed toward the subway. "Come, I will take you there."

The building in which Joseph Fischelson lived was one of the few on the street that still seemed somewhat run-down. Everywhere else, the brownstone facades had either been restored or were in the process of restoration. Metal scaffolding dotted the long, tree-lined street, and the sound of hammers and drills rang continually in the early morning air.

"Four-C," Frank said as he pressed the buzzer in the building's foyer.

A harsh crackling sound came from the wall speaker, but the voice could still be heard above it.

"Who is it?"

"Frank Clemons," Frank said loudly. "I think Mr. Silverman called you this morning."

"Yes, all right," the voice replied. Then the buzzer sounded, unlocking the second door, and Frank and Farouk walked into the building.

Fischelson's apartment was at the top of a four-story walk-up, and the two of them were both out of breath by the time they reached the door.

It opened immediately, and a small, white-haired man stared at them from over a gently drooping length of brass chain.

"Mr. Clemons?" the man asked.

"Yes," Frank said. He nodded toward Farouk. "And this is Farouk, my partner."

The old man continued to stare at them, his eyes lingering on Farouk.

"You're Mr. Fischelson?" Frank asked.

The old man did not answer, but he opened the door.

"I was sitting on the terrace," he said as they stepped into the room. "I like the view. Would you mind?"

"Not at all," Frank assured him.

Fischelson led them through a living room whose walls were

covered with framed photographs of Fischelson and a woman Frank assumed to be his wife, Naomi. For a moment he stopped and gazed at one of them.

Fischelson stared at him wonderingly. "Is there something wrong?" he asked tentatively.

"Oh, no, not at all," Frank said. He pointed to the photograph. "Is this your wife?"

"Yes."

Frank continued to look at the photograph. "It's just that I've heard her name so many times. It's nice to see her face."

Fischelson nodded. "She was a fine woman."

"Do you have a picture of Gilda?" Frank asked immediately.

Fischelson pointed to a second photograph, which hung just a few inches above the first. "There," he said. "That's Gilda."

The picture showed a woman in her late teens with dark eyes and dark hair.

"Gilda was quite a beauty," Fischelson said, "but she didn't know it. That was what was so wonderful about her. She really never knew how beautiful she was."

Frank nodded. "Yes."

"Well," Fischelson said after a moment, "shall we begin?"

He turned and led Frank and Farouk out onto a small enclosed terrace. A wrought-iron breakfast table sat in one corner, and a few lawn chairs were crowded into the other.

"The view," Fischelson said as his arm swept toward the large windows. "Beautiful."

"Yes, it is," Frank said. Outside the window, the great gray expanse of New York harbor swept out for miles. To the north the towers of Manhattan loomed in such enormity that they dwarfed the Statue of Liberty and miniaturized the huge gray ramparts of the Brooklyn Bridge.

"It's why I stay here," Fischelson said. "The view. The place is crawling with up-and-comers now. They're always redoing things, stripping paint, putting in saunas." He smiled ironically. "Wall Street types. Not one of them has ever seen the Lower East Side." He nodded toward the distant shore of Manhattan. "Not like Naomi and I did, when there was nothing between you and a billy club." He smiled. "But then, I guess Harry told you all about that."

"You mean the strike of 1935?" Frank asked. "You were in-volved in that?"

"Up to my neck," Fischelson said. "So was Naomi." He glanced down at the small glass-topped table. "Every night we had din-ner here," he added as he sat down behind it. "We weren't perfect together. Who is? But we were good enough for it to last."

"I'm sorry about her death," Frank told him.

"Part of life," Fischelson said stoically. "Her life was good. No one expects it to go on forever." He looked at Farouk. "Are you Jewish?"

"No," Farouk said. "Arab."

Fischelson smiled. "Then we are both Semites."

Farouk nodded expressionlessly.

"Isn't that the way we should try to look at it?" Fischelson asked.

"Where one comes from," Farouk said indifferently, "what does it matter?" His eyes drifted over to the flat gray bay. He waved his hand. "We all come from over there," he said. His eyes shot over to Fischelson. "You are from Poland?"

"Maybe Russia. Maybe Poland," Fischelson told him. "What it was depended on which day of the week you left."

Farouk laughed.

"The borders were always changing," Fischelson said. "I was nine years old. What did I know from any of it?"

"Your wife," Frank began slowly, "she was from a village near Bialystok."

"Yes."

"Along with her two sisters."

"Gilda and Hannah."

Frank took out his notebook. "I presume you know about Hannah."

"Mr. Silverman told me when he called."

"You didn't know before then?"

"I had read about a woman being murdered," Fischelson said. "But that was another name. When I knew Hannah, her last name was Kovatnik." He shrugged. "There was no picture in the paper. What would I know from Karlsberg?"

"You hadn't seen her since she changed her name?" Frank asked.

"No."

"When was the last time you spoke to Hannah?"

Fischelson leaned forward slightly. "You know about the hearing, or whatever you would call it?"

"Yes."

"Everything?"

"I know that you spoke to a man named Stern, and that he brought the charges against Hannah."

Fischelson sat back again. "Then you know everything," he said. "As for Hannah, she never knew."

"That you had talked to Stern?" Frank said.

"She never knew that," Fischelson said. "She never had any idea that I even knew about it. And she never suspected Naomi. They were sisters, after all."

"So you stayed on good terms with her even after the hearing?" Frank asked.

"For a while," Fischelson said. "As long as it was possible."

"What do you mean?"

"Until she went to work for Bornstein," Fischelson said. He thought about it for a moment. "But even before that, it was different."

"In what way?"

"She was different," Fischelson said. "Cut off, you might say. She was cold." He shook his head. "It was like the old Hannah had died, and this new one had taken over her body." He smiled sadly. "She had such hopes, you know," he added. "During the strike, I mean. And when this business with Feig happened, and then, later, with the hearing, Hannah sort of withdrew from the rest of us." He raised his hand, fingers stretched out, then let them droop forward limply. "She went like that. She lost something. I don't know what you'd call it, whatever it was she lost. Spirit, maybe. She had a great spirit." He smiled suddenly, his eyes brightening visibly, as if small lights were turning on inside his memory. "Did you read her speech? The one she made at Union Square?"

"Yes."

"You see what I mean by spirit?" Fischelson asked. "That's what she had while she was in the fight. After it was over, that's what was missing."

"And that's when she went to Bornstein?"

"She was cut off from something," Fischelson said, "so she went to something else. Sometimes with people, it can be just that simple."

"In Hannah's case, she went to Bornstein," Frank said.

Fischelson nodded. "He was part of it. But not the whole thing." He thought about it for a moment. "She was disconnected from what had mattered to her." He looked at Farouk. "You could tell by her eyes, her voice. Something was dead." He glanced back to Frank. "Bornstein had an eye out for her. He offered her a job. She needed one, so she took it. That's just the way it was." His eyes turned back toward the bay. "It was a big thing for a while, her going to work for him. Nobody knew about the hearing. That had to be kept secret. So she couldn't tell anybody that she'd been kicked out. It had to look like she'd just left and joined the other side, gone from that speech in Union Square to being Bornstein's girl."

Frank glanced down at his notes. "She left New York in March of 1936."

"Coldest day you could imagine," Fischelson said. "We went to the boat with her. Gilda was there too, of course, the two of them were just standing there in front of that boat, shivering. I'd never seen Hannah look so lost, so alone. Gilda would come over and put her arm around Hannah's shoulder, but she'd just brush it off with this look in her eye, this cold look."

Frank wrote it down.

"But she had no choice but to go," Fischelson said. "Hannah, I mean. She couldn't stay in New York. How could she stay here? I mean, with the way people thought of her, like she was a traitor."

"So she went to South America," Frank said. "To Colombia."

"That's right," Fischelson said. "We got a few letters from her."

"Where did they come from then?"

"Some place called San Jorge," Fischelson told him. "I'd never heard of it. But I got the idea it was some little village in the jungle. That's where she went."

"What was she doing there?"

"Something for Bornstein."

"She never told you?"

"Something in the garment trade, like here," Fischelson said. "But I don't know what it was." Again, he shrugged softly. "For a few years, maybe five, she wrote to us. But after that, there was nothing."

"What about Gilda?" Frank asked immediately. "She went to Colombia with Hannah, didn't she?"

"Yes."

"Why?"

"Because she worshipped Hannah," Fischelson said. "Hannah was almost like a mother to her."

"So she never thought of staying in New York?"

"No," Fischelson said. "I don't think it ever crossed her mind to live without Hannah."

"Did you hear from Gilda?"

"Often, yes," Fischelson said with a sudden delight. "She wrote about the people there—in San Jorge—about what they were like." He smiled quietly. "You got the feeling that she sort of fell in with them."

"Fell in with them?" Frank asked.

"Started to live like they did," Fischelson explained. "Like she was one of them, not a foreigner anymore."

Frank wrote it down. "What did she write about?"

Fischelson thought for a moment. "She talked about the way they fished and bathed in the river. You got the feeling it was very primitive, but that Gilda had come to love it anyway, the place and the people. Everything."

"Did she mention what Hannah was doing there?" Frank asked.

Fischelson shook his head. "Just something for Bornstein," he said. "She never said what it was." He smiled quietly. "Her letters were strange," he added thoughtfully. "Very peaceful. Full of love, you might say. It was a short life, but from her letters, it sounded like a good one."

Frank wrote it down in his notebook, then looked up. "What did Gilda die of?" he asked.

"Some sort of tropical thing," Fischelson said. "I don't know what."

"How did you find out about her death?"

"From Hannah," Fischelson said. "Just a little telegram. It

said something like: 'Gilda dead. Sending body.' Just like that. Very . . . very . . . well, businesslike. You know, like she was shipping a crate of bananas." He shifted slightly in his chair. "It really infuriated Naomi, the way Hannah acted."

"What do you mean?"

"Well, for one thing, there was no body," Fischelson said. "Hannah had her cremated. All we got was a little box of ashes."

"And that's what you buried?"

"We didn't know what else to do with it," Fischelson said. "I know some people keep them. In a little vase, you know, on the mantle. But we just couldn't do that. So we ended up burying it just like a body."

"So you had a funeral?"

"If you could call it that," Fischelson said. "It was just Naomi and me." His face grew strained. "Naomi was furious with Hannah. Not only for the cremation, but because she didn't even come home with the ashes. As a matter of fact, we never heard from Hannah again. That telegram about Gilda was the last thing we ever got from her."

"So you didn't know that she got married?" Frank asked.

"Married?" Fischelson asked wonderingly. "Hannah got married?"

"Yes," Frank told him. "Only a few days after Gilda died."

An oddly pained expression rose into Fischelson's face. "No, I didn't know that," he said. "I didn't know Hannah had gotten married."

"Did you know that she'd come back to the United States?" Frank asked immediately.

"I suspected it," Fischelson said. "But only recently."

"When?"

"About two months ago."

"Did she contact you?"

Fischelson laughed. "Well, not directly," he said. "But maybe, in her own way, she was trying to do that."

"What do you mean?"

"Well, Naomi and Gilda are buried side by side," Fischelson explained. "And every week I go out to visit the graves. About two months ago, flowers—fresh flowers—started showing up on Gilda's grave. Nothing fancy. Just a single rose. But I didn't put it there."

"So you thought it was Hannah?" Frank asked.

"I couldn't think of anyone else who might do it," Fischelson said. "Naomi was dead. Who else would do it?" He waved his hand. "I mean, she'd been out of this country since 1936. Nobody knew her, except maybe the people in that village. When Gilda left here, she had only Hannah. When she left that little village, she left everything else." He shook his head determinedly. "It had to be Hannah. Maybe out of some sort of conscience."

"So you never tried to trace the flowers back to her?" Frank asked. "Find out where she was, maybe get in touch?"

"No," Fischelson replied emphatically. "Why should I have done anything like that? Naomi was dead. I hadn't even heard from Hannah in thirty years." He glanced at Farouk helplessly. "And besides, what was I supposed to say? 'You know, Hannah, I'm the one who betrayed you. I'm the one who sent you to Colombia, who sent Gilda to her death.' Not even Naomi knew that." He laughed bitterly. "Sometimes, there's nothing left but silence."

"Sometimes," Frank said, as he closed his notebook and put it back into his jacket pocket. "Did Mr. Silverman tell you why I wanted to talk to you?" he asked.

"Just that Hannah had been killed, and that you were looking into her life."

"That's partly it," Frank said. "But there's also been a problem in getting her body released for burial."

"Why?"

"It's a police matter," Frank said. "But they would have to release it if a relative requested it."

"So?"

"Well, the way the law looks at it," Frank said, "you're a relative."

"And you want me to do that?" Fischelson asked. "Get her buried?"

"Yes."

"But I'm just her brother-in-law. There's no blood between us."

"You'll do," Frank assured him.

For a moment, Fischelson thought about it, then, suddenly, a curious relaxation swept into his face. "All right," he said. "I will." He glanced back and forth from Farouk to Frank. "I mean, after all this, maybe I can make it up to her a little." His eyes moved toward the window and the immense gray wall of Manhattan. "You know," he said, "I was never really sure that I'd done the right thing."

"What do you mean?"

"In talking to Stern," Fischelson said. His eyes softened delicately and he seemed to reach deep down into himself, grasp something tenderly, and draw it out. "I've lived with this too long," he said finally.

"With what?"

"With this secret," Fischelson said. "This dreadful secret."

"What secret?"

Fischelson hesitated a few seconds longer, then began.

"It was love," he said. "You see, I was in love with Hannah. Terribly in love with her. I was married to her sister, but I was in love with her. She would have nothing to do with that, of course, so after a while I gave up." He shrugged. "Then I found out about Feig, about what she'd done. I told Stern that I'd overheard it, but really, Naomi told me all about it. I don't know how she felt about it, but I thought that what Hannah had done was a terribly reckless thing, and so I went to Stern." He glanced toward the bay. Far in the distance a great cruise ship inched its way out from behind the tip of Manhattan. "Maybe it was because I was really trying to save the union. But maybe it was because I wanted to destroy Hannah." His eyes shifted over to Frank. "To this day, I don't really know." He looked at Farouk. "I don't suppose I ever will."

Frank put his notebook in his pocket and stood up. "I want to thank you for being willing to request Hannah's body," he said.

Fischelson smiled sadly. "Under the circumstances," he said, "I think it is probably the very least that I could do."

It took them only a few minutes to reach the Midtown North precinct house on 54th Street. Tannenbaum was waiting for them upstairs, and sat at his desk patiently while Fischelson filled out the necessary forms, then signed the final request for Hannah's body.

"Well, that'll do it," Tannenbaum said as he gathered up the papers and placed them in a small folder. He stood up and offered Mr. Fischelson his hand. "Thanks for coming in."

Fischelson shook Tannenbaum's hand, then disappeared back down the stairs.

"Nice man," Tannenbaum said to Frank as he sat back down behind his desk. He glanced quickly at Farouk, then turned his eyes back to Frank. "Well, I guess you've done your job," he said.

"Yeah," Frank said.

"Miss Covallo will no doubt throw in a nice bonus," Tannenbaum added. Again, he glanced briefly at Farouk before looking back to Frank. "Anything else?"

"How soon will the body be available?" Frank asked.

"By this afternoon," Tannenbaum said. "That soon enough for your client?"

"I guess it is."

"Good," Tannenbaum said matter-of-factly. He leaned back in his chair and folded his arms over his chest. "Anything else?"

"No," Frank said.

"Okay," Tannenbaum said. "Then, if you'll excuse me, I'll get back to work." He looked at both of them pointedly. "Because I'm just a flatfoot in plainclothes, and so I still have a murder to solve."

24

Frank was leaning on the black wrought-iron gate when Imalia's car pulled up to the curb a few hours later. The rear door swung open immediately.

"Hello, Frank," Imalia said. She scooted back on the seat. "I'm off to the airport. Can we talk on the way?"

Frank pulled himself into the car and closed the door behind him.

"Sorry for this inconvenience," Imalia said lightly as the car made a left-hand turn on Ninth Avenue. "But I have to be in Washington tonight. It's quite a rush. I have to be back in New York tomorrow morning. I'm planning a huge party at the American Museum of Fashion for Sunday night."

Frank nodded.

"Would you like a drink?"

"No, thanks."

"I hope you don't mind if I have one," Imalia said. She pulled gently at a silver handle in front of her, and the bar swung into place. "I understand you have some important news," she added as she dropped a single ice cube into her glass.

"Nothing I couldn't have told you on the phone," Frank said.

"I don't like the phone," Imalia said crossly. "It's too impersonal. I guess it comes from working with fabric. I like the personal touch." She poured a scotch, then sat back comfortably in her seat. "Now, what is it?"

"As you know, Hannah had two sisters," Frank began. "Both of them are dead. But one of them, Naomi, was married, and her husband is still alive."

"Really? Where?"

"Here in New York."

Imalia looked at him excitedly. "You've located him?"

"Yes."

"That's wonderful, Frank."

"He lives in Brooklyn," Frank told her. "I spoke to him this morning."

"Can he have the body released?" Imalia asked anxiously.

"He already has," Frank said. "We went to Midtown North earlier today. He signed all the forms. Hannah's body will be ready for burial whenever it can be arranged."

"Excellent, Frank," Imalia said. "Just excellent. I mean it."

"Mr. Fischelson—that's the brother-in-law—he said something about having her buried next to her sisters."

"And where are they buried?"

"A Jewish cemetery in Brooklyn."

"Fine," Imalia said without hesitation. "That's certainly up to him, wouldn't you say?"

"Yes."

"As for the expenses, I'd be happy to pay them."

"He might appreciate that," Frank said. "I don't get the idea that he has a lot of money."

"Consider it done," Imalia said briskly. "Absolutely no problem. It would be an honor, really."

"I'll tell him."

"You do that."

"Do you want to know where it is?"

Imalia looked at him, puzzled. "Where what is?"

"The funeral," Frank said. "The time and place."

"Oh, sure," Imalia said. "Just leave it on my machine if I'm out."

"Okay."

"Good," Imalia said crisply. She lifted her glass. "Sure you wouldn't like to toast your success?"

Frank shook his head.

"Well, let me at least say that you've done a wonderful job on this, Frank," Imalia told him. "Karen must be proud of you."

Frank said nothing.

Imalia took a long drink, then returned her glass to the tray. "Of course, gratitude is not enough, is it?" she asked with a smile.

Frank glanced out the one-way window of the limousine. They were moving into a world of sleek boutiques and exclusive restaurants and toward the naked steel girders of the 59th Street Bridge.

"I mean your fee, of course," Imalia said. "How would you like it?"

Frank continued to stare out the window. Blocks of art galleries swept by, along with scores of shop windows stocked with the very best that could be bought, hand-tooled leather, velvet, satin, fine wines and Russian caviar, the finest things on earth.

"Your fee, Frank," Imalia said. "How would you like it?"

Frank did not look toward her. "It doesn't matter," he said.

"Check? Cash?"

"It doesn't matter," Frank repeated.

"And the amount?"

Frank looked at her. "Two thousand dollars."

Imalia took out her checkbook. "Plus a bonus," she said as she began to write it.

Again Frank turned back to the window. The car moved smoothly along Madison Avenue, then took a slow, graceful right turn onto 57th Street.

"Here you are," Imalia said as she held the check toward him. "As you can see, I've added an extra two thousand."

"That's not necessary," Frank told her.

"It is, if you really want service," Imalia said brightly. "And after all, that's what it's all about, don't you think?"

Frank pocketed the check.

"May I drop you somewhere?" Imalia asked.

"Drop?"

"Well, I don't suppose you want to ride all the way out to La Guardia, do you?" Imalia asked.

"No."

"Next corner all right?"

"Yes," Frank said.

Imalia gave the order, and the car drifted over to the corner of 57th Street and Third Avenue.

Frank got out immediately.

"And once again, thank you so very much, Frank," Imalia said as he stood on the busy corner. "I'll recommend you to all my friends." She smiled sweetly, and for an instant, Frank could see the girl she had once been, small, pale, her slender legs dangling from a fire escape above the teeming streets of Little Italy. For a moment he wanted to freeze her face just as he saw it, study it for hours, try to find the road that had taken her from Prince Street to the swank boutiques of the Upper East Side. It was a desire that she seemed to sense almost as quickly as he had felt it, and with a single, sudden movement, she closed the door between them, as if to block the purpose of his eyes.

It was not a very long walk to Karen's apartment, but he walked it slowly, thoughtfully, trying to come to terms with the vague uneasiness that always overtook him when a case was over. It was as if everything lived on the surface of something much deeper and more mysterious, a murky, shifting undercurrent. There were times when he wanted to dive deeper and deeper into it, define its limits, and then return to the upper reaches with an infinitely expanded sense of what lurked below, its dark, unreachable depths.

He was still thinking vaguely of Hannah, still lost in the hazy emptiness of a completed assignment, when he opened the door to the apartment and found Karen in the living room, her arms folded sternly over her chest, staring at him with her light blue eyes.

"I missed you last night," she said.

"Sorry."

"I decided not to go to work today," Karen said. "I decided to wait for you. To wait as long as it took for you to come home."

Frank said nothing.

"I am not an insecure woman, Frank," Karen added.

"No, you're not."

"I don't cling to people, you know that."

"Yes."

"And I won't cling to you," she added flatly.

"I know."

"But respect matters to me," Karen said. "My self-respect matters." She shook her head. "Maybe it was when we met. The way we met. Maybe I was just too vulnerable. Angelica and all that. Maybe you were. About Sarah. About Sheila. Both of us, too vulnerable."

She waited for him to answer, and when he didn't, she added, "Maybe I made a big mistake, Frank."

"Maybe we both did," Frank said. "That's usually the way it happens."

"So something's wrong," Karen said. "It's not just been my imagination."

"No."

"It's not just some case you're on."

"No, it's not."

She stood up slowly. "What is it then?"

"I don't know," Frank said. "Time, maybe. Change."

"We've only been together for a year."

"Something else, then. I don't know."

"Love," Karen said bluntly. "What else could it be?"

"I suppose," Frank admitted.

A terrible sadness moved into her face, but even as he saw it, Frank knew that it was not specifically for him, but for the way things were, their complications and disappointments, the way life came, lingered awhile, then passed away before you could ever hope to learn how to live it.

"You were coming back for your things, weren't you?" she said.

"Yes."

"Your two suits. What else?"

"Socks. Razor. Do you want a list?"

"Where are you going?"

"My office."

"You're going to live there?"

"For a while."

"Are you sure you want to do that?"

"Yes, I'm sure, Karen," Frank said.

She looked at him affectionately. "So am I, Frank. I can't help it."

"Why should you even try?" Frank asked. He smiled. "You're not a liar, Karen. You never have been." He shrugged. "We tried something. It didn't work. Sometimes, that's all there is to it."

She started to say something, thought better of it for a moment, then decided to go ahead. "Do you have . . . somebody?"

"No."

"I wish you did, Frank. I truly wish you did."

He did not answer her, and for a few seconds they simply gazed at each other as if they were strangers once again, just as they had been that first day, she in her paint-spattered jeans, he in his dusty brown suit.

"I do," Karen said finally. "Have someone."

"Lancaster," Frank said. "I know."

Karen nodded. "We haven't . . . but still . . ."

"It doesn't matter, Karen."

"No, I suppose not," Karen said. She turned away for a moment, her eyes fixed on the terrace. Then, after a time, she faced him once again, "Listen, Frank, if money's—"

"No," Frank said quickly, "I just got paid, as a matter of fact. Your friend, Imalia."

"You're finished with that case?"

Frank nodded.

"How did it come out?"

Frank smiled softly. "What difference does it make, Karen?"

Something in her face softened inexpressibly. Then she walked over to him and gathered him into her arms. "Sorry," she whispered. "So sorry."

He allowed his own arms to embrace her loosely. He felt the warmth of her body, the cool of her hair, and something already half-lost within him moved yet a little deeper into the enveloping shade.

The phone was ringing as Frank came through the door of his office. He quickly laid his bundled clothes and supplies on the desk and answered it.

"Frank, it's Leo," Tannenbaum said in a voice that seemed less dismissive than before. "I just wanted to let you know that we've released the body. Formally, I mean. All the paperwork's been done."

"Thanks."

"No sweat," Tannenbaum said. "The trail is too cold to fight over it."

"Did you call Mr. Fischelson?"

"Yeah," Tannenbaum said. "He said he'd arrange for it to be picked up this afternoon."

"Okay," Frank said. "Thanks."

He hung up the phone, then picked it up again, and called Fischelson.

"I understand the body's been released already," he said. "I want to thank you. I mean, on behalf of my client."

"I was happy to do it," Fischelson said. "Like I said before, it was the least I could do."

"When are you planning to bury Hannah?"

"Tomorrow afternoon."

"Where?"

"Beth Israel," Fischelson said. "It's a cemetery in Brooklyn. I arranged for the burial to be at three o'clock." He stopped, as if thinking about something for which he could not find the appropriate words.

"As you know," he said finally, "I wasn't in touch with Hannah."

"Yes."

"As a matter of fact, you probably know more about her than I do."

"Maybe."

"So, I was wondering," Fischelson went on hesitantly. "Did you get any idea about her being religious, anything like that?"

"No."

"I mean, she was Jewish. Born Jewish. You know about her father?"

"Yes."

"Well . . . What do you think? . . . Should I get a rabbi?"

"Did you have one for her sisters?" Frank asked.

"Yeah, I got one," Fischelson said. "Mostly because of their father."

"Well, he was Hannah's father, too," Frank said with a sudden sense of lingering allegiance.

"Yeah, he was," Fischelson said. Then he hung up.

Frank lifted his suit from the desk and hung it in the small closet next to the front door. Then he deposited his toothpaste, brush and shaving gear in the cramped little bathroom. It was all he had, but it did not really strike him as so little.

For a few minutes he stood by the front window, his eyes lifted slightly to watch the people who passed along the sidewalk. Then he walked back to his desk and sat down. For a long time he sat in silence, his eyes staring at the unlit lamp that Karen had given him. The late afternoon light glowed faintly along its polished bronze surface, and for an instant he saw its beauty as Karen herself must have seen it, the carved base and slender, curving neck, the multicolored shade with its intricately woven pattern of stained glass. It was beautiful in the care that had been taken to create it, in the mind that had conceived it and the hands that had shaped it with a beauty that was incontestably grave and good, full of that imperishable labor which, it seemed to him, bestowed the one true value on all man's worldly goods.

25

The Beth Israel Cemetery was an enormous expanse of jutting gray stones, large and small, some ornately sculptured, some plain and featureless. The two which rested in the far right corner of the grounds were modest, but dignified, and they seemed to impose a respectful silence on the few people who gathered around the open earth of Hannah Karlsberg's grave.

Imalia stood off to the side of the grave. She was dressed in a long black dress, with matching hat and veil, and she kept her gloved hands primly at her sides.

Riviera was only a few feet away, the afternoon sun shimmering radiantly in his long white hair.

Fischelson kept his place at the foot of the grave. He nodded as Frank stepped up beside him, but his eyes remained on the black-coated man who stood at the head of Hannah's grave, praying quietly in Hebrew while he rocked gently back and forth, along with several other men who were dressed in the same black coats and hats.

When the rabbi had finished, Fischelson threw a handful of broken earth onto the casket, then paid first the rabbi, then the others.

"I never liked this, you know," he said to Frank as the last of the men had taken the money and headed quickly back toward the gate of the cemetery.

"The way they hang around the cemeteries."

"Who?"

"The religious ones," Fischelson said contemptuously, "the aging yeshiva boys." He nodded toward the men who'd stood with the rabbi, and who could now be seen threading among the dark gray stones. "They stand there with their prayerbooks. Stand at the gate. Like vultures, if you ask me. They pray if you pay them." He glanced angrily at Frank. "You call that religion?"

Frank said nothing.

"Ah, maybe I've just gotten old and bitter," Fischelson said as he looked back toward the three graves. "Life, you know. It doesn't work. It just doesn't work. I don't know why."

Imalia walked over quickly, nodding politely to the two of them. She offered her hand to Fischelson.

"I'm very sorry," she said, as she lifted the veil from her face and folded it back over the top of her hat. "Hannah was a wonderful person."

Fischelson nodded silently.

"I wish I had known her better," Imalia added. "But I can tell you that I certainly respected her, and that she'll be missed by all of us."

"That's certainly true," Riviera said as he walked up behind her.

Imalia smiled quietly, then drifted away, moving slowly toward the limousine which waited for her a few yards away.

"Just a terrible thing, what happened to Hannah," Riviera said as he stepped closer to Fischelson. "Terrible thing." His eyes moved over to Frank. "But at least now, she's at peace," he said. He looked back at Fischelson, quickly shook his hand, then walked briskly away and disappeared into the limousine.

Fischelson gave a final glance toward the three graves, then headed slowly toward the gate, his shoulders slightly hunched against the cold. Frank walked along beside him.

"What should I have done?" Fischelson said as they neared the entrance to the cemetery. "Tell me that. Huh? What should I have done about Hannah? If it had been found out—this business with Feig, with Bornstein—if it had been found out, the whole union would have been destroyed."

Frank nodded.

"It was reckless, what Hannah did," Fischelson said vehemently. "It was stupid."

Frank said nothing.

"But what I did destroyed her," Fischelson added mournfully. "It was like I took a knife and cut out her heart. It was the same thing."

Far to the east, a wall of impenetrable gray clouds was approaching the city, the sort Frank remembered from his youth, heavy with snow and the hard winter winds.

"It's over," he said. "She's in the ground."

Fischelson's eyes darted over to him. "I wish she'd died during the strike," he said fiercely. "I wish some gun-thug had shot her in Union Square, shot her while she was still standing there with her hand in the air." His voice suddenly broke. "I loved her," he said. "What I told you before, it's true." He looked at Frank pointedly. "You know what I mean, don't you?"

"Yes."

"In love," Fischelson said passionately. "In love with your wife's sister." He laughed joylessly. "I told a guy about it once, a guy I worked with. Eddie Panuchi. I told him all about it, and he just draped his arm over my shoulder, and he said, 'You know, Joe, when I hear something like this, I think of what my mother used to say about the same sort of situation, "Hey, it could have happened to a bishop." ' "

"Did you ever tell anyone else?" Frank asked.

"Besides Eddie? Of course not," Fischelson said. "It was just between me and Hannah." He shook his head wonderingly. "It was during the strike," he went on. "I couldn't stand it anymore." He lowered his head slowly, as if to receive the blow he thought he must deserve. "I went to her, to Hannah. I told her how I felt." He stopped, and leaned tremulously against a single gray stone. "I loved Naomi. I really did. But with Hannah, it was this fire, this awful fire. Uncontrollable." He looked at Frank beseechingly. "Do you know what I mean?"

"Yes."

Fischelson smiled helplessly. "Do you know what Hannah said?" he asked. "This will tell you all you need to know about her." He pushed himself away from the stone, straightening his body. "She put her hand on my face, and she said, 'Joseph, one love at a time.'" His eyes turned to Frank. "She meant that a person could handle only one devotion, not two, and that if you couldn't put all your heart into something, I mean, the whole thing, you were nothing." He shrugged wearily. "Maybe that was what made me tell them what I knew. Tell Stern, I mean. Maybe I wanted to take that one devotion from her, so that she would come to me." His eyes drifted back toward the corner of the cemetery where the Kovatnik sisters lay, three of them together, as they had once shared their single room beneath the synagogue. "I really don't know if that had anything to do with it," he added quietly, "the fact that she couldn't love me back." He drew in a long, tormented breath. "But I can tell you this, Mr. Clemons, it's the only thing I've really thought about for the last forty years."

They walked the rest of the way out of the cemetery in silence, then stood in silence until the bus arrived at its stop a few minutes later.

When the doors opened, Fischelson stepped on quickly and deposited his token.

"Thanks for your help," Frank told him.

Fischelson smiled sadly as he turned toward Frank for a final word. "Do you think she's at peace?" he asked.

Frank did not answer, and in an instant the doors of the bus closed between them in a shrill hydraulic hiss.

For a time, Frank lingered on the corner, his hands sunk in his pockets, the collar of his coat pulled up against the increasingly chill wind. He didn't want to go back to his home, or office, or whatever it was now. He didn't even want to go back to the neighborhood which surrounded it. The bars didn't appeal to him, nor the grim hotel lobbies, nor the glittering arcades.

Instead he wandered back through the dark iron gate of the cemetery, back through the gray stones, to where Hannah's grave still lay open, waiting to be covered, a reddish trench stretched out between her sisters. For a while, he leaned against a neighboring stone and gazed into the gutted earth, toward the elegantly polished coffin. He smoked a cigarette pleasurelessly, found no place to put the butt, shoved it finally into his jacket pocket, and lit another. For a time, he watched the gray overhanging clouds, then the city of stones, the distant wrought-iron gate, and finally, the single red rose that waved coldly over Gilda Kovatnik's grave.

Frank was staring absently at his uncluttered desk when he heard someone coming through the door of his office, looked up, and saw Farouk.

"I'm sorry," Farouk said as he closed the door behind him.

"About what?"

"The funeral," Farouk said. "I had wanted to come."

"It doesn't matter," Frank told him. "I didn't expect anybody but Fischelson."

"I wanted to come," Farouk said. "I'd meant to. But there was a call."

"It doesn't matter, Farouk," Frank assured him. He lit a cigarette, then reached into the top drawer of his desk. "I have some money for you."

"Money?"

"For your help," Frank said.

"Ah, yes," Farouk said, as if the whole question of payment had slipped his mind.

"The total fee was two thousand dollars," Frank told him. "Plus a bonus."

"Bonus?"

"Another two thousand."

Farouk smiled. "Miss Covallo is very generous."

"Yes, she is," Frank said. He opened the envelope and drew out the stack of bills. "She gave me a check. I cashed it on the way back from the funeral." He slid the bills across the desk. "Take your share."

Farouk looked at the money wonderingly. "How much is that, my share?"

"I don't know."

Farouk stroked his chin thoughtfully. "Perhaps ten percent. That would be four hundred dollars."

"Whatever you say," Frank told him. "Just peel off what you want."

Farouk drew four one hundred dollar bills from the stack, then slid the money back to Frank. "Thank you," he said.

Frank put the rest of the money in his jacket pocket, then reached for the bottle that rested, half-empty, on his desk. "Want a drink?"

"Yes, that would be good," Farouk said. "To break the chill."

They were on their third drink, and the basement shadows had deepened into a gray half-light when the door to the office opened once again.

Tony Riviera stopped instantly, his body in full silhouette against the brick wall of the corridor.

"I assume you're open for business," he said.

Frank nodded slowly.

"Good," Riviera said. He closed the door behind him, then pulled a chair up to Frank's desk. "I'm glad to find you in," he said. His eyes drifted briefly toward Farouk, then shot back to Frank. "I've just come from a long talk with Miss Covallo. We were talking about the job you'd done on tracking down Mr. Fischelson. I don't have to tell you how pleased she is."

Frank said nothing.

"We were thinking," Riviera said, "that you might want to stay on the case a little longer."

"Stay on the case?"

"That's right," Riviera told him. He hesitated. "You must have guessed what I'm talking about."

"Her killer," Farouk blurted.

"Yes," Riviera said. "That's exactly right. The fact is, he's still out there. Hannah may be at peace, but . . . somehow it's not enough."

Frank and Farouk exchanged glances, but neither of them spoke.

"You know, in Spain . . ." Riviera began. Then he stopped and looked pointedly at Farouk. "I'm from Spain."

Farouk nodded. "Yes, I thought so."

Riviera looked pleased. "Really? Why?"

"The accent," Farouk explained. "It is truly Spanish."

"Yes, it is," Riviera said. "You're very perceptive."

"My ears are good," Farouk said. "But then, I have traveled. I have often heard English spoken by Castilians."

"Castilian, yes," Riviera said delightedly. "Purely Castilian." He smiled at Farouk appreciatively for a moment, then returned his eyes to Frank. "In any event," he said, "Miss Covallo is interested to know if you"—he glanced quickly at Farouk—"you *two* would be willing to work a little longer on the case."

"Purely as a murder case," Frank said.

"That's right," Riviera told him. "Something that's much more in your line, I'm told."

"I don't really have any leads," Frank said. "I'd have to start pretty much from scratch."

"That's no problem," Riviera assured him. "As a matter of fact, Miss Covallo expected that. After all, nobody's asked you to find Hannah's killer." He stopped and glanced back and forth from Frank to Farouk. "Until now."

"Have the police made any progress?" Farouk asked.

"Not that we're aware of," Riviera said. "That's why Miss Covallo is interested in your continuing to work on it. She doesn't think the police are doing very much."

"What do you think?"

"I think the trail is very cold by now," Riviera said. "And when that happens, people have a tendency to put their attention on other things." He waited for some response, then added, "Miss Covallo wants someone to put all their attention on Hannah. It's just that simple. Same fee as before, no time limit."

Frank looked at Farouk. "What do you think?"

Farouk nodded slowly. "I am willing, of course. But I must leave it to you."

"All right," Frank said as he returned his attention to Riviera. "We'll look into it."

"Very good," Riviera said as he stood up. "I'm glad you can stay on it." He turned and offered his hand to Farouk. "I think the sooner we find the lousy *bicho* who killed Hannah Karlsberg, the better off everyone will be."

For a moment Farouk looked at Riviera oddly, then he pumped his hand twice, and released it.

"Yes, of course," he said.

Riviera turned to Frank, shook his hand, and walked quickly to the door. "Well, good luck," he said, as he opened the door and stepped into the corridor. "You can report whatever you find to Miss Covallo."

For a few minutes after Riviera left, Frank and Farouk continued to sit silently in the steadily darkening air of the office, each sipping slowly at what was left of his drink.

"We don't really have anything, do we?" Frank said at last.

"Don't have what?"

"Anything," Frank said. "A single lead."

"Nothing," Farouk agreed.

"We're back to the beginning."

Farouk nodded heavily. "Yes. The beginning."

"Or the middle," Frank added. "Or the end." In his mind, he saw Hannah Karlsberg's life run like a speeding film before him, the murderous journey across the sea, the arrival in a foreign land, the basement apartment on Fifth Street, the sweatshop on the Lower East Side, her body in a white dress, then a wool coat, her hand in the air, then on a marriage license, then gone entirely, lost in a bloody stump, and finally just an open grave between two others, with nothing to adorn them but a rose.

26

Frank drew the small white vase out of his coat pocket and turned its base outward, toward the man behind the counter.

The man gazed casually at the small adhesive label which had been attached to the bottom of the vase. "Yes, that's ours," he said.

Frank took out his identification, showed it to the man, then indicated Farouk. "My associate."

"Hello."

"We'd like to ask you a few questions, if you don't mind."

"Go ahead."

Frank set the vase down on the counter. "You use a lot of these?" he asked.

"Of course," the man said. "It usually has a single flower in it. An orchid, sometimes. A tulip. A rose. Where did you get it?"

"Off a grave."

The man smiled. "Well, that's a little odd, but it can happen."

"Do you deliver flowers?"

"Of course."

"To cemeteries?"

"Anywhere."

"If this were delivered, would you have a record of it?"

"Absolutely," the man said. "Where did you find the vase?"

"Beth Israel."

"Any particular person?"

"A woman named Kovatnik," Frank said, "Gilda Kovatnik."

The man nodded peremptorily, then disappeared into the back of the room.

"A nice place," Farouk said as he stared about, his eyes glancing from one flower or fern to the next. "To work with flowers wouldn't be so bad."

"I guess not," Frank said.

Farouk sniffed the air appreciatively. "And the sweetness, that is also good." He smiled. "Like a bakery."

The man returned with a large gray ledger. "That's a regular delivery," he said as he placed the book down on the counter.

"What do you mean?"

"It's a standing order," the man explained. "We deliver a single red rose once a week." He read the details from the book. "To Beth Israel Cemetery, the grave of Gilda Kovatnik, Row 11, Plot 72."

"Paid in advance?" Frank asked.

"Yes."

"How?"

Again, the man's eyes fell to the book. "Cash."

"Man or woman?"

"It's a man."

"Can you describe him?"

"An older man. Very tall. He comes in here once a month."

"And orders a flower?"

"Yes."

"Do you have a name?"

The man shrugged. "It's a regular American long-stem rose."

"I mean for the person who pays the bill," Frank said.

"Oh," the man said. He laughed lightly. "Sorry." He looked at the book for a moment, then back up at Frank. "Kincaid," he said, "Benjamin Kincaid."

Frank and Farouk exchanged glances instantly. Then Frank turned back to the man behind the counter. "You wouldn't happen to have an address, would you?" he asked.

"Of course," the man said lightly. "Twenty-five fifty-seven Parkman Street."

Frank started to take out his notebook, but Farouk grabbed his arm. "There is no need," he said. "I know where that is."

"It is in Boerum Hill," Farouk said as he and Frank emerged from the subway on Clinton Street. "Near my old home." He smiled pleasantly. "Come, I will show you."

They walked south along Clinton until they reached Atlantic Avenue.

"Here it is," Farouk said as he glanced up and down the street, "the place of my youth."

It was the small, closely knit Arab quarter, a world of crowded shops where fresh dates and cashews were sold from enormous barrels and burlap sacks. The raw meaty smell of kibbee mingled with the sweetness of halvah and honeyed cakes, and as Farouk strolled slowly eastward, sniffing the air, he seemed to return to a time that was even more distant than his youth, when the desert tribes still wandered over the featureless sands.

"When you are in exile," he said as they stopped for a traffic light at the corner of Court Street, "there is a strangeness to it . . . a not-here-ness, you know?"

"Yes."

"So, you also miss your home?"

"No," Frank said. "Something else. I don't know what." He lit a cigarette. "You lived around here, Farouk?"

Farouk nodded toward an ornately decorated Middle Eastern restaurant on the opposite corner of the street. "On the third floor," he said. "There was no restaurant on the street then. It was a store for spices. Garlic. Clove. It is the way our apartment smelled."

"I remember the smell of cotton poison," Frank told him. "The bush pilots used to fly over the fields, spraying this white powder. It had a dry, sweet smell." He shrugged. "It's hard to describe it."

The light changed and the two of them strolled on down Atlantic Avenue until they reached Parkman Street.

"This way," Farouk said as he guided Frank to the right.

It was a street of dilapidated brownstones whose crumbling, graffiti-strewn facades looked down on littered sidewalks and gutted automobiles, and yet, as Frank walked along it, he could feel the simple life that sustained it. Despite the cold, a knot of teenagers gathered on a broken stoop and listened to the blaring music that came from their enormous silver radio. Across from them, two old men trudged forward against the slicing wind which swept in off the bay. In the distance, a couple quarreled loudly, while only a few yards behind them, a young child, wrapped in heavy clothes, spun round and round on a small rusty tricycle. It was all of this that gave the street and its surrounding neighborhood a sense of deep reality and concreteness, of being cradled in a network of interwoven experiences, and as Frank made his way through it, he thought again of Hannah, as she sat alone at the end of the table, staring back at the three stern-faced men, of the second exile which they had imposed upon her, and of how she now reminded him of Ruth, whose Old Testament story his own father had so often related to his stricken congregation; Ruth, stripped of her homeland and her people.

"She should never have left," Frank said suddenly, almost to himself, as he stopped at the front of 2557 Parkman Street.

Farouk looked at him. "Who?"

"Hannah."

"Left what?"

For an instant, he started to answer, "New York. She should never have left New York." But then he saw her in the steaming shop again, saw her in the snow of Orchard Street, and finally, as she stood before the crowds of Union Square; and suddenly he realized that it was more than New York that she had left behind, more than Orchard Street.

"Left what?" Farouk repeated.

"Her one devotion," Frank answered quietly. "Her one and only love." Then he started up the stairs.

Farouk reached for the buzzer to apartment 3-B, then stopped, his stubby finger held motionlessly in the air. "Do you have any kind of weapon with you, Frank?" he asked.

Frank nodded. "You?"

Farouk patted under his left shoulder. "Always," he said grimly. Then he pressed the buzzer.

Silence.

He pressed again.

Silence.

"Perhaps the super?" he asked.

"Okay."

Farouk pressed the buzzer for apartment 1-A, and almost immediately the door just beyond the entrance opened and a slender, well-groomed black man came to the door.

"Yes?" he asked as he opened the door.

Frank produced his identification.

The man eyed it casually. "As I understand it, you have no legal authority," he said.

"What?"

"No legal authority," the man repeated. "I have to understand these things, because many times people in these buildings are sought after by certain people. Some have legal authority. Some do not. You, for example, do not. Naturalization, that is another matter. As are agents of the Internal Revenue Service. But a private investigator has no legal authority in the state of New York." He stopped. "Now, what are you doing, collecting bills, or something of that nature?"

Frank said nothing.

"That would not surprise me," the man went on, "because we certainly have a few people in this neighborhood who do not pay their bills."

"This isn't about a bill," Frank said.

"A Mr. Kincaid," Farouk said. "In apartment 3-B?"

"What about him?"

"Someone close to him has died," Farouk said. "We are here to inform him of it."

"Did you ring his bell?" the man asked.

"Yes," Frank said.

"He didn't answer," Farouk added.

"When does he usually come home?" Frank asked.

The man shook his head. "Whenever he wishes. I do not keep track of a man his age."

"He is an old man?" Farouk asked.

"Yes," the man said. "But he looks quite well."

"Does he have a job?"

"Job? I do not think so," the man said. "But he does keep busy, I believe."

"Doing what?" Frank asked.

"Working at the settlement house," the man said. "He does some teaching there. For the immigrants."

"The Brandon Street Settlement?" Farouk asked immediately.

"Yes," the man said. "Do you know it?"

"In the past," Farouk told him. He smiled pleasantly. "How long since you were in Port-au-Prince?"

The man smiled back instantly. "Long time," he said, "but I have not missed it."

"Much oppression," Farouk said.

"They are dying in the streets," the man added.

Farouk nodded quickly. "Terrible thing, for the people of Toussaint."

"We shall finally have a good land," the man said determinedly. "Though perhaps not in my lifetime."

Again Farouk smiled sweetly. "Well, as they say, 'if not for me, then for my children,' yes?"

"That is how it must be seen," the man agreed.

Farouk stepped back slightly. "This Mr. Kincaid," he said. "You said he works at the Brandon Street Settlement?"

"I have seen him go over there," the man said. "I have heard he teaches there."

"What does he teach?" Frank asked.

The man shrugged. "I am not sure. It could be anything. These people are right from the boat, as we say. They know nothing of this country. It is always a new crop. Every six months. They live at the settlement, but they know nothing of America." He smiled. "Perhaps that is what he teaches them, how to be good Americans."

Frank took out his notebook. "How long has Mr. Kincaid lived here?"

"About a year," the man said.

"Has he ever had a job?"

"No," the man said. "Just down at the settlement house. You cannot really call that a job. It is an act of charity, perhaps. Or perhaps he merely wishes to keep himself busy."

"Do you know where he lived before he came here?"

"No, mon. He did not say," the man told him, "but he speaks Spanish very well. It is only Spanish people at the settlement house."

"From Spain?" Farouk asked.

The man laughed. "Spain?" He laughed again. "No, these ones are from across the border. They come in vans. Not from over the water. They live in the settlement house for a while, then they go back home."

"And Mr. Kincaid works with them?" Farouk asked.

"Yes."

"Does Mr. Kincaid have regular hours?" Frank asked.

"Regular?"

"Times when he comes and goes," Frank explained. "Regular times."

The man smiled broadly. "He is like the moon. In the morning he goes. In the evening he returns. This is his schedule."

"When does he usually get home?"

"Before night," the man said.

"Okay, thanks," Frank said as he closed his notebook. "We'll be back later." He turned toward the stairs, motioning Farouk along with him.

Farouk did not move. He smiled quietly, his eyes still on the superintendent. *"Est-ce possible de visiter l'appartement de Monsieur Kincaid?"* he asked, almost kindly, as one colonial exile to another.

The superintendent smiled back. *"Pourquoi?"* he asked.

Farouk said, *"C'est quelquechose de très grave."*

"C'est quoi, cette affaire si grave?"

"Une maladie des tropiques," Farouk told him grimly. *"Je vous assure. C'est grave."* He reached into his jacket pocket, fumbled around for a moment, then pulled out a laminated card that identified him as an agent of something called the International Center for the Control of Contagious Disease.

The man read the card quickly, then stared at Farouk worriedly. *"Cette maladie, est-elle vraiment contagieuse?"*

"Oui," Farouk said, nodding gravely. *"Très contagieuse."*

The man stepped out of the door instantly, his eyes flashing over to Frank. "Please, this way," he said.

27

The room was dark and musty, and as soon as he walked into it, Frank could feel the heavy burden of a life lived far away. There was the curious smell of unusual herbs, plants, spices, of skins dried under different suns, leathers tanned by unknown processes.

But the light which swept in from the hallway revealed a strangeness that his other senses had only guessed, and from which, Frank noticed as he glanced back toward the door, the Haitian superintendent shrank.

"*Lieu des diables,*" he whispered as he edged himself from the door and slipped back down the stairs.

Farouk's eyes slid over to Frank. "Place of devils," he said.

Frank turned and looked at the room, and as he did so, a chill swept over him, haunting and inexplicable, a sense that the world had suddenly shifted in its flight, edged itself a little deeper into the engulfing darkness.

He took a short, hesitant step to the right, his fingers gripping the small table which rested near the center of the room. Its feel of cold metal reassured him, and he stepped forward once again, his feet edging into the layer of parched brown stalks and dried leaves which covered the floor.

"Take care," Farouk said softly from behind.

Frank took another step, his eyes turning toward the wall nearest him. It was covered in enormous flat leaves which had been strung on barbed wire and which now hung like small brown bodies from the barbs. A rectangular reed mat lay beneath the curtain of leaves, along with a few earthenware bowls and vases. In his mind, Frank could see Kincaid as he curled up on the mat, sleeping there through the humid summer nights or shivering through the winter ones, his feet half-hidden in the leafy covering of the floor. He looked at the clay water pitcher beside the mat and the small cup beside it, and he could see Kincaid in his thirst and desperation, see his hand wrapped around the bowl, his tongue licking at its rim.

He turned slowly, his eyes scanning the room while Farouk remained at the door, his hand already curled around the grip of his revolver.

"What is it that you see?" Farouk asked after a moment.

Frank did not answer. He continued to let his eyes work for him in the way they always had, in silence, in solitude. He saw a picture of a beautiful woman, which Kincaid had hung with reeds and fronds, and he knew that it was Gilda, now browned by the tropical sun, thinner, less robust, but Gilda nonetheless, staring vacantly at the camera from the veranda of her jungle hut. A small table rested like an altar beneath the photograph, and Kincaid had arranged it with candles, a beaded necklace, a single wooden spoon. A handmade crutch leaned against it, and he had placed ribbons along its sides, stringing them upward in a bright red spiral. A small bit of torn cloth, stained with red, hung from the arm, its tattered edges drooping toward the floor.

"This is not love," Farouk said, as he moved farther into the room, his eyes peering wonderingly at the crutch and its bloodstained cloth. "This is worship."

Frank's eyes continued moving steadily around the room. There were pictures, some hung in ribbons, some in garlands of dried leaves, of brown women in dusty tattered dresses, brown men in buttonless shirts and battered straw hats, brown children staring wide-eyed at the lens, naked or half-naked, their bodies framed by the thick wall of jungle which inevitably rose like an immense green wave behind them.

"This is a man who remembers," Farouk said as he took another step into the room. Idly, he picked up a small paper box from the table near the door and turned it slowly in his fingers. "It is filled with teeth," he said to Frank as he returned it to the table.

Frank walked into the next room and found it completely bare. There was no furniture, no clothes in the single closet, no source of light or heat, only the bare unswept floors and blank, water-stained walls.

Together, Frank and Farouk moved into the kitchen. Another mat lay across the floor, dirt and leaves scattered around it, along with an assortment of bowls and cups. A large water pitcher rested beside it, still faintly damp from the morning.

Farouk walked over to the stove and absently turned on one of its gas eyes. It did not ignite.

Frank opened the small, squat refrigerator, but no light came on.

"This man," Farouk said, "lives in his own world."

"Yes."

"He doesn't heat his food," Farouk added, "or keep anything cold."

"I guess not," Frank said as he closed the refrigerator door.

"Perhaps it's poverty," Farouk said. "Perhaps he couldn't pay the bills."

"Maybe," Frank said as he wandered back into the front room. "But all these plants," he said. "What are all these plants?"

Farouk followed him into the room. "I don't know," he said as he stepped over to the small table. His eyes moved from the tip of the crutch up to the bloody cloth, then over to the tiny framed picture which had been hung next to it. He leaned forward, eyeing it carefully, staring at Gilda, at the dress which hung loosely from her shoulders. "It is the same one," he said.

Frank looked at him. "Same what?"

"The dress in the picture," Farouk said. He touched the tattered piece of cloth that hung from the arm of the crutch. "This came from it."

Frank glanced at the cloth, then stepped over and looked closely at the photograph. "Yes, it did."

Farouk's finger touched the torn scrap of Gilda's dress tenderly. "This is a man who keeps things," he said solemnly. Then he looked at Frank. "We must wait for him."

Night had entirely fallen by the time they heard footsteps trudging up the stairs toward the apartment. The ragged quilts that Kincaid had hung over the cramped square windows blocked even the small amount of refracted light that might otherwise have alleviated what was now an impenetrable interior blackness.

From his place on the floor, Frank could hear Farouk's breath catch suddenly as the steps creaked in the hallway. Then he heard his large, ponderous body shift heavily and rise with a quiet groan.

"You okay?" Frank asked.

"I am well, yes," Farouk replied.

Frank got to his feet quickly and rolled his shoulders to ease their tension. He could hear the man outside as he topped the last step and headed for the door of the apartment. He straightened himself, touched the grip of his pistol as if to reassure himself that it was still there, and then allowed his hands to fall loosely at his sides.

"Take care," Farouk whispered from somewhere across the room.

The door opened slowly and a rectangle of light swept into the room, then disappeared abruptly as the man quickly closed the door behind him.

In the darkness, Frank could hear him rustling about, a hand in a pocket, an awkward shifting of papers, then the sound of a match, a sudden white glow of light near the door, and after that a yellowing in the air around him.

Kincaid had lit a candle, and as he turned back toward the room its pale orange glow caught the surprise in his eyes. For a moment, he stood absolutely still, his arms cradling a number of books and papers, his eyes resting first on Frank, steady, even, unflinching, and then moving over to Farouk with the same calm suspension.

"Yes," he said, but Frank could not tell whether it was a question or a statement, and because of that, the three men simply stared at each other motionlessly, eerily, like the points of a triangle.

The man turned and placed the books on the small table beside the door. For a moment, he seemed to hold himself in that position, his back to them, as if waiting for them to do whatever it was they had come to-do to him.

"My name is Clemons," Frank said softly. "Frank Clemons. I'm a private investigator."

The man rotated slowly toward them but said nothing.

"This is my associate," Frank added, pointing to Farouk.

Kincaid stared at him expressionlessly. "The time has come," he whispered.

"What?"

Kincaid nodded toward the mat of reeds. "May I sit?" he asked.

There was a kind of strange tenderness in the question, and it took Frank entirely by surprise.

"Sit?" he asked.

"On the floor," Kincaid said.

"Of course," Frank told him.

Kincaid walked over to the sleeping mat and lowered himself onto it, locking his legs one under the other, Indian-style. Then he picked up a small earthen bowl and rolled it softly between his open hands. His skin was very brown and leathery, and it looked as if it did not belong to him, but to some animal from which it had been stripped, then dried, then laid across his naked bones.

"Are you Benjamin Kincaid?" Frank asked.

Kincaid kept his eyes on the bowl.

Frank felt his fingers crawl slowly toward the pistol in his belt. "Are you Benjamin Kincaid?"

Kincaid's long brown fingers nestled the bowl tenderly.

"Yes, I am," he said.

"And this is your apartment, Mr. Kincaid?" Frank asked immediately.

Kincaid raised the bowl to his lips and gently kissed its rim.

Frank glanced questioningly at Farouk.

Farouk shrugged gently, but said nothing.

"Is this your apartment?" Frank repeated, this time more sternly.

"Yes," Kincaid answered without hesitation.

"We looked around a little," Frank said cautiously. He waited for some kind of response. When there wasn't one, he added, "You have an interesting place here."

Kincaid said nothing. He glanced toward the quilt that hung from one of the windows, his eyes following the jagged red line that slashed across its middle.

"I said, you have an interesting place," Frank repeated, still trying to draw him out. "All these bowls and candles. These plants on the floor."

Kincaid laid the bowl down on the edge of the mat, took up a small vase and poured an amber liquid into it. He did not look up.

"We've been looking into a murder," Frank added, this time with an edge in his voice, hard, firm, ready to act. "Hannah Karlsberg's murder."

Kincaid nodded. "Hannah Kovatnik," he said.

Frank took out his notebook immediately. "Did you know her?" he asked.

Kincaid said nothing. Instead, he placed the small green vase among the parched reeds and leaves that were gathered around the mat.

"What can you tell me about her, Mr. Kincaid?" Frank asked stiffly.

Kincaid's eyes drifted over to the photographs which he had arranged on the opposite wall. "There was once a beautiful village," he said. "A perfect village in a perfect world." He smiled sweetly. "Can you imagine that?" he asked, his eyes shifting first to Frank, then to Farouk. "Living as you do, living in this place, can you even begin to imagine such a place?"

No one answered.

Kincaid caressed the bowl again, neither more nor less tenderly than before. "Do you know what misery is?"

No one spoke.

"The loss of paradise," Kincaid said. He smiled sadly. "You think this is paradise, this city, this country, the way we live? For a long time, I thought it was. Then the Church sent me to Colombia." He shook his head mockingly. "They sent me to help the people who lived there to become like us." He threw out one arm, then drew it slowly around the room. "But as you can see, I became like them. I loved the things they made and ate and wore. I loved the life they lived better than the one I was trying to force on them."

Frank's eyes moved over to the pictures, and he could see the life that they portrayed, one that was neither lost nor desperate, not lived in isolation. He could see its changeless reality in the fruit trees and the river, the play of light on brown and green. In his mind, he could feel the warmth of its air, the sheer blue expanse of its overhanging sky, the vast eternal peace its jungle wall ensured.

"Do you know what it means to join humanity?" Kincaid asked as he took another vase and began to pour yet another liquid, this one faintly blue, into the bowl. "I mean, to feel that you are a part of it, that you cannot separate yourself from the smallest, most insignificant part of its destiny?" He mixed the two liquids with his finger, then brought the finger to his mouth and sucked it softly. "Of course you don't," he said as he drew the finger from his mouth. His eyes narrowed. "How could you, living as you do? One tiny atom in a world of tiny atoms. Each man his own god. Separated from the world, from your neighbor. What can you know but your own mind? What can you feel but your own suffering?"

For a reason he could not imagine, Frank suddenly saw Hannah at Union Square, aflame in her resolve, then in the photographs on her wall, cheerless, solitary, a woman who now seemed entirely bereft, isolated, cut off. What was her armless hand still reaching for?

He shifted nervously, then asked a question which, even as he heard it, struck him as utterly distant, lost, unreal: "Did you love Hannah?"

"No," Kincaid said. He rotated the bowl in his hands. "Her sister."

"Gilda," Frank asked.

Kincaid returned the bowl to its place before him on the mat. "Yes." He took a brown stalk from the floor and plucked a few of its parched leaves from the shaft. "It is an old story: the serpent comes into the garden." He crushed the leaves in his fingers and sprinkled them onto the liquid. "Hannah."

"The serpent?" Frank asked immediately.

"She came with money," Kincaid went on. "Came into paradise. Into a little village in the jungle."

"San Jorge?" Frank asked.

"San Jorge," Kincaid told him. "She came with money, lots of money."

"Why?" Frank asked, his pencil holding steadily over the notebook as he prepared to write Kincaid's answer down.

"To find something wonderful," Kincaid said. He stirred the crumbled leaves into the liquid. "The miracle potion, the jungle magic that would make the world beautiful."

"A drug?" Frank asked.

Kincaid laughed softly. "She found a place to make it," he went on. "Later, she paid a man to bring the people in."

"Pérez?" Frank asked.

Kincaid looked at him quizzically.

"I'm talking about Hannah's husband," Frank added, "Emilio Pérez."

"They found the jungle magic," Kincaid said, "but it was from the Devil." His eyes fell toward the bowl. "From the mouth of hell."

Frank stepped toward him slightly. "What was this 'jungle magic'?" he asked.

Kincaid did not seem to hear him. "And so they began to get sick," he said. "They grew weak, and their bones grew twisted. Their skins broke and a yellow ooze poured out of them." He drew in a long, painful breath. "Then they began to die. And so we stacked their bodies by the river." Something in his eyes darkened almost imperceptibly. "Hannah would come out on the veranda and watch them from a distance. She would stand in her long white dress and watch Pérez lead more of them into the factory that made the jungle magic. They would work, then they would die, and we would stack their bodies by the river."

"What bodies?" Frank asked immediately.

Kincaid did not answer. His eyes drifted toward the crutch, and the bloodstained cloth that hung from it. "Hannah had lost her soul. Her eyes were dead." He looked at Frank, and a strange pride swam into his face. "But not her sister's eyes. Not Gilda's."

"What about Gilda?" Frank asked quickly.

"She went into the factory every day," Kincaid said with a

sudden, luminous smile. "You would have to be an exile to
understand how much I loved her." His voice seemed to break
on the last words, but he stopped, regained himself, then went
on. "She knew. She knew. She allowed herself to know."

"Know what?"

"That the jungle magic was from hell," Kincaid said. He
picked up a small pouch from the head of the mat and sprinkled
its contents, a dull greenish powder, into the bowl. " 'I will show
you,' she said, and she worked with the people every day after
that, until she got like them."

"What do you mean?"

Kincaid shook his head. "I made a crutch for Gilda."

Frank drew his eyes over to the crutch which still leaned
against the wall beside the small table. In his mind, he could
see Gilda as she hobbled along the riverbank or simply stood
beneath the low-slung branches and stared out into the jungle
depths.

"She kept after Hannah," Kincaid continued, his voice suddenly grown dark, grim. "She never let it rest. She threatened
to leave the village." He looked vehemently at Frank. "Then she
died," he said. "But her crutch was still beside her bed."

"The drug, the magic," Frank said. "It killed her?"

"Yes," Kincaid said matter-of-factly. "They took her body and
burned it by the river."

Frank could see the fire as it licked slowly at Gilda's dress,
then consumed it. He could see the black smoke that rose from
it, coiling upward into the thick, overhanging limbs.

"Was she murdered?" Frank asked.

"By her heart," Kincaid replied. He dipped his finger into the
bowl, then lifted it to his face, and raked it across his forehead,
leaving a long, pinkish line. "There are two good times to die."
He dipped his finger into the bowl once again. Then he drew it
slowly down the right side of his face. "You should die when
your heart is dead." The finger continued down the side of his
face, etching his bony jaw and halting at his chin. "Or when it
has finished with its work." He closed his eyes for a moment,
then he opened them. "Such a year," he said mournfully. "Such
a year for death, for assassination." He shook his head. "I should
have known that one death must always lead to another."

For a time, there was only the silence of the room and the three motionless figures who remained within the shadowy light of the candle.

"Pérez," Frank said, this time pressing harder, insistent, determined. "Was he the first?"

Kincaid seemed to come back into the room from a great distance. "What?"

"Emilio Pérez," Frank said. "Did you kill him?"

"Yes," Kincaid said. "He left, then returned. It was for his mother's funeral." Once again he dipped his finger into the bowl. "Revenge can be its own reward."

"For Gilda's death?" Frank asked.

Kincaid's mind seemed to detach itself from Frank's question. He took a small yellow seed from a brown earthen bowl which rested at the head of the mat and chewed it slowly. "They had a beautiful story, the people of the village," he said.

"Revenge for Gilda's death?" Frank repeated emphatically.

Kincaid continued to chew the small yellow seed. He did not answer.

"Is that why you killed Pérez?" Frank demanded. "And Hannah?"

Kincaid glanced about the room, his eyes suddenly very steady as they gazed first at one object, then another. It was as if each object bore its own secret message, and he was collecting them methodically, gathering them for storage in some final, but undetermined home.

"When did you come back to the United States?" Frank asked sternly.

"A beautiful story," Kincaid began again, obliviously. He closed his eyes, and painted each lid with the mixture on his finger. "A story with a moral," he added. His eyes flashed open, glittering wildly in the shifting light. "That revenge is the only justice for the dead." He leaned forward, as if in an act of prayer, and swiftly pulled a machete from beneath the mat. "When your work is over," he said, "it is time to die."

Frank reached for his pistol. "Put that down," he said coldly as he pointed to the machete.

Farouk drew his gun, wrapping both hands around the grip and sighting down the barrel. "Do not move," he said.

But Kincaid was already moving toward them, the machete whirling over his head.

Farouk dropped to a kneeling position, the barrel of his pistol pointed steadily at Kincaid's head. "Do not move," he shouted.

Kincaid took a small step forward, lifting his face toward the ceiling, his eyes following the whirling blade. "I come!" he cried.

Frank stepped back and cocked the hammer of his pistol. "Drop it!" he screamed.

The blade continued to whirl above Kincaid's uplifted head, swinging over him, turning to flame in the flickering candle. For a moment he seemed frozen in a terrible suspension, then he stepped forward with a sudden, galvanizing determination and in one smooth movement drew the machete across the bare, brown flesh of his throat. A dark red wave spilled over its wide blade as he staggered to the right.

Frank dropped his pistol and rushed toward him, blood spurting across his chest in rhythmic crimson geysers from Kincaid's throat.

"*Call an ambulance*," Frank screamed as the two of them sank helplessly to the floor.

Farouk holstered his pistol and ran from the room, his heavy body thundering down the stairs.

Frank could feel the warm spray of Kincaid's blood as it pumped upward from the wound. He pulled a handkerchief from his pocket and pressed it hard against the gaping cut which ran in a deep valley across Kincaid's throat. He felt the warm flow as it soaked through the handerchief, then ran down it in a stream that grew thinner and thinner with each passing second, until Kincaid's eyes rolled upward and his chest grew still, and the blood on Frank's grasping fingers slowly thickened and grew dark while he rocked Kincaid gently back and forth, cradling him in his arms like a child.

28

Frank's body bolted upward at the sound of the knock, his eyes focusing on the disarray that surrounded him, the dusty, unswept floor, the cluttered desk, the bloodstained clothes that hung from the chair at the other side of the room.

He stood up, pulled on a pair of pants and walked to the door.

Tannenbaum nodded expressionlessly. "Hope it's not too early for you, Frank."

Frank rubbed his eyes roughly.

"Had some trouble sleeping lately?" Tannenbaum asked.

"What do you want, Leo?" Frank said.

"Well, you know how it is, Frank," Tannenbaum said. "Things have to be settled, so we're going to have to ask a few more questions."

Frank nodded.

Tannenbaum smiled politely. "May I come in?"

"Yeah, okay," Frank said dully. He stepped out of the doorway and let Tannenbaum pass in front of him. "You want a cup of coffee?" he said.

"No, don't bother," Tannenbaum said, waving his hand dismissively. "I'm just here to clear up a few last details." He shrugged. "I mean, there's no question about what happened yesterday. The suicide, I mean. You know that."

"So what do you need?" Frank asked as he eased himself down behind his desk.

"Well, it's about the Karlsberg murder," Tannenbaum said. "We'd like to put the lid on that one, too."

"Yeah."

"But we have to be absolutely sure that Kincaid was our man," Tannenbaum added. He took out his notebook and opened it to the first blank page. "You understand the procedure, right?"

"Yes."

"Just a few details, that's all I'm here for," Tannenbaum said as he sat down in the chair in front of Frank's desk. "Now, according to what you told the officer on the scene, Kincaid said something about revenge. Could you go over that with me?"

"What part?"

"Well, for one thing, did you suggest the subject to him?"

"The subject of revenge?"

"Yes."

Frank shook his head. "No, I didn't."

"How did it come up?"

"He was talking about Gilda, about her death," Frank said, straining to remember the exact details.

"That's when he mentioned revenge?"

"Yes."

"What did he say?"

"That it could be its own reward," Frank told him. He took a cigarette from the package on his desk and lit it. Then he offered one to Tannenbaum.

"No, thanks," Tannenbaum said. "Too early." He glanced back down at his notebook. "Did he say anything else about revenge?"

"Yes," Frank said. "Something . . . I . . ." He pulled open the drawer of his desk and brought out his notebook. A few of its pages were stuck together by Kincaid's blood, and he had to pry them apart carefully. "Here it is," he said finally. Then he read from the page. " 'Revenge is the only justice for the dead.' "

Tannenbaum copied it quickly into his own notebook. "Don't throw that notebook away until everything's closed on the Karlsberg case," he said when he'd finished.

"I won't," Frank assured him.

"Did Kincaid say that he killed Pérez or Miss Karlsberg out of revenge?"

"No."

"Did he say he killed Emilio Pérez?"

"Yes, he did," Frank said, casually allowing his eyes to drift toward the drawn shade of the front window.

Tannenbaum looked at Frank pointedly. "Did Kincaid tell you that after killing Pérez, he cut off his hand?"

Frank's eyes shot over to Tannenbaum. "No," he said.

Tannenbaum wrote it down.

"Did he cut off Pérez's hand?" Frank asked immediately.

"Yes, he did," Tannenbaum replied with a slight smile. "At least that's what the Colombian police have told us." He wrote something in his notebook, then looked back up at Frank. "Saved it, too."

"Saved it?"

"We found the skeletal remains of a human hand in one of Kincaid's closets," Tannenbaum said. "It was male, so we figure it must have belonged to Pérez." He handed Frank an envelope. "We found a lot of stuff in his apartment. Here's a copy of the inventory."

"Thanks."

Tannenbaum nodded peremptorily, then went on to another subject. "That village," he said. "San Jorge. It's gone."

"Gone?"

"A ghost town. Since 1954."

"So that stuff about poison," Frank said. "It was true?"

"That's right."

"What was the poison?"

"They still don't know," Tannenbaum said. "We told them about what Kincaid said, a magic drug. They grow some weird stuff in the hills up there. It could be that Hannah was trying to refine it somehow, get some extra strength in it." He smiled. "People are always looking for a better lift. Out in California, they got this new drug they call 'ecstasy.' " He laughed. "Can you believe that?" He looked back at his notebook. "When Kincaid made that crack about revenge, what did you take it to mean?"

"I took it for his motive," Frank said matter-of-factly. He snuffed out the cigarette. "It's as good as any."

Tannenbaum laughed lightly as he wrote it down. "Well, it's an old one, right?"

"Hannah had caused Gilda's death," Frank said. "Along with Pérez. That's the way Kincaid saw it."

Tannenbaum nodded in agreement. "Tell me this, Frank: Do you think Kincaid had come back to the United States specifically to kill Miss Karlsberg?"

"I don't know."

"Do you think there might be any other targets? I mean, in this country?"

"He didn't mention any."

"Did he say how he found out where she was?"

"No."

"Well, like they say, Frank, it's a big country."

Frank said nothing.

"And she'd changed her name," Tannenbaum added.

"He didn't say anything about how he found her," Frank told him.

Tannenbaum flipped a page of his notebook. "He worked at this settlement house, right?"

"That's what the super told us."

"Us?"

"Me. Farouk."

Tannenbaum smiled. "Oh, yeah, Farouk," he said. "How'd you get involved with him?"

"We met. At a bar."

"No kidding?" Tannenbaum said brightly. "Which one?"

Frank said nothing.

Tannenbaum smiled thinly. "Maybe that little illegal after-hours dump on Tenth Avenue?"

Frank did not answer.

Tannenbaum laughed. "No need to get nervous, Frank. We've known about that little dive for years. Who gives a shit, huh?" He returned to his notebook. "This settlement house business," he said. "We've checked that out, too. Kincaid worked there, all right. Strictly voluntary. Always with Latinos." He shook his head wonderingly. "He loved the Hispanics, I guess." His eyes wandered over to Frank. "A lover of humanity, right?"

"In a way," Frank said.

"That what you think?"

"Yes."

"Slashed her up pretty good, though," Tannenbaum said darkly.

Frank said nothing.

Tannenbaum closed his notebook and stood up. "Well, I guess that's it," he said. "Everything checks out."

Frank walked him to the door.

"We checked Kincaid's machete, too," Tannenbaum said as he stepped into the hallway. "It could have been the one that killed Hannah."

"Could have been?" Frank asked.

"Well, it only had Kincaid's blood on it," Tannenbaum said. "He'd had plenty of time to wash it. But as far as the wounds on Hannah's body, it fit them pretty well."

"That's not the same as evidence," Frank said.

"No, but Kincaid's machete was a homemade affair," Tannenbaum added. "They make them in Colombia. Mostly for the cane fields. They're not imported here." He smiled. "Which means you just can't go down to Times Square and pick one up." He dropped his hand onto Frank's shoulder. "Thanks for the help," he said. "I mean it. Nobody's happier than me to put this case to bed." Then he nodded quickly and headed for the stairs.

Frank walked slowly back to his desk, took out the bottle of Irish and poured himself a drink. For a while he sat silently, his mind drifting wearily back over the preceding hours. Once again he saw Kincaid rise from the mat, the machete dancing over his head until it finally sliced downward and Kincaid staggered forward, his knees bending slowly as he fell into Frank's astonished arms.

After that, it had been long hours of talk, as the ambulance arrived, then the police, and finally the Brooklyn homicide detectives who'd kept him in the small brown grilling room at the precinct house. They had paced around methodically, as he had paced around so many others during the days when he was, himself, a homicide detective, firing questions, then repeating them, until they had finally settled for the fact that neither Frank nor the "big Arab"—as they continually referred to Farouk—had murdered Benjamin Kincaid.

Dawn had already broken over the city by the time he'd returned to his office, and so he'd simply slumped down on the sofa and twisted about fitfully until Tannenbaum had delivered him from a sleep far worse than waking.

Now, as he lit a second cigarette, Frank knew that he could not return to the sofa. Instead he opened the envelope Tannenbaum had left, drew out the papers, and spread them across his desk.

Wearily, he read what the police department had been able to gather on Kincaid during the last fifteen hours. They had traced his life in its broad details, his birth in California, his ordination as a Catholic priest, his service in South America, and his final residence in the remote, jungle outpost of San Jorge. It was there that he'd lived until 1954, the year Pérez was murdered. For the next few years, he'd wandered about South America, working as a teacher in the slums of Lima, Bogotá and Santiago. He had returned to what was left of San Jorge in 1968, stayed for a few months, then begun what appeared to be a long, meandering journey back to the United States, drifting up the jagged coast of Central America, living for a while in Mexico City and Monterrey, then finally crossing the border at Nuevo Laredo in 1981. During the following years he'd continued to follow the coast along the Gulf of Mexico and then northward, with short stays in Savannah, Charleston, Baltimore, Philadelphia, and finally New York. He had worked in all these places, always as a teacher, always in the slums. In New York, now an old man, he had finally retired.

Frank folded the paper, then went through the others, an autopsy, an inventory of Kincaid's possessions, such as they were, a statement by the Haitian superintendent and a few of his neighbors which traced his general movements, habits, and character traits. It was all routine, and he'd seen such papers hundreds of times in the past. Still, he resisted the impulse to return them to the envelope, seal it, and drop it into one of his file drawers. And so, for a long time, they remained scattered across his desk while his mind wandered about as if detached in some odd way, and yet profoundly engaged by the lingering mood of Hannah's death, and Gilda's, the brown bodies by the river, Kincaid with his head held back, offering his throat to the whirling blade. He could hear Farouk's body as it plunged down the stairs, feel the warmth of Kincaid's blood as it soaked through the shirt which still hung from the chair across the room.

He stood up, walked over to the shirt and picked it up. For a moment, he glanced about, looking for some place to put it, a paper bag, a plastic can, and then, suddenly, he heard a voice in the gray air: *This is a man who saves things.* He draped the bloody shirt over the chair, walked to his desk and sat, staring back at it until the dark red stains seemed to write their own insistent message in his mind.

It was nearly noon when Farouk came into the office. "Are you all right?" he asked as he sat down on the small sofa by the window and drew out a cigarette.

"I'm okay," Frank said. He returned his eyes to the scattering of documents and reports, which still lay strewn across his desk.

"It is difficult," Farouk said in a voice that was low, considered, oddly mournful, as if something besides justice had been served by Kincaid's death, a malicious appetite for the sorrowful and ironic. "There was some goodness in this man's heart."

"Yes, there was."

"Until he came back here."

"To New York, you mean?"

"Yes."

"Do you think he came back to kill Hannah?"

"It's possible."

"It's possible," Frank admitted. "But if he did, how did he know to come to New York in the first place?"

Farouk shrugged.

"And once he got to New York," Frank went on, "how did he find her?"

Farouk stared at Frank evenly. "I don't know."

"According to the interviews the police have done," Frank said, "Kincaid went from his apartment to that settlement house every day. He stayed there for several hours, then he went back home. That was his day. That was all he did."

Farouk said nothing.

"And another thing," Frank added. "Kincaid had been in New

York for several months. He lived in a Queens apartment for a
while, then moved to Brooklyn. That's when he started showing
up at the settlement house."

Farouk nodded.

"Why did it take him so long to kill her?" Frank asked emphatically.

"I do not know," Farouk said.

Frank's eyes bored into him. "Do you remember what your
friend at the police department said? About Hannah's husband,
I mean?"

Farouk nodded slowly. "That it was too old a trail for a crime
of such hot blood."

"What if he was right?"

Farouk remained silent, but Frank could see a slowly building
intensity in his eyes.

"And something else," Frank added. "When we were in his
apartment, you looked all around and then you said that whoever
lived here was a man who saved things."

"That is true," Farouk said.

"Where is Hannah's hand?" Frank asked. He nodded toward
the police inventory of Kincaid's apartment. "He had bones in
his place, teeth, plants and seeds. He had a bloodstained cloth,
and old pots. Stalks of something, dirt from places."

"But no hand," Farouk said.

"No, there was a hand," Frank said. "Look at this." He handed
him the police inventory. "Tannenbaum brought it over. It's a
list of everything that was found in Kincaid's apartment."

Farouk's eyes drifted down the column until it struck the
single item Frank had already marked in red.

"The hand," Farouk whispered.

"A human hand," Frank added. "That's right. But it isn't
Hannah's. It's too old. It must have once been attached to Emilio
Pérez."

"Pérez," Farouk repeated as his eyes settled firmly on the
paper Frank had handed to him.

"Kincaid cut off Pérez's hand when he killed him years ago."

"And saved it all these years," Farouk added.

"Yes," Frank said. "But there was only one hand. Not two."
He waited a moment, then drew the paper slowly from Farouk's

fingers. "There's no more money in this case, Farouk," he told him softly. "Not a dime. I can tell you that."

A strange smile broke over Farouk's dark face. "That is the odd thing about money," he said.

"What?"

The smile dissolved. "That it's what you always take in the place of what you need."

29

The Brandon Street Settlement House was a large wooden building which rested on a run-down street in the Boerum Hill section of Brooklyn. It had been freshly painted, and because of that, it looked considerably less dilapidated than the much smaller row houses which surrounded it.

"It was here when I was a child," Farouk told Frank as they walked up the stairs together. "It was here that I learned English."

"It's the only place we can begin," Frank said matter-of-factly as he headed up the stairs, opened one of the large double doors and walked in.

The building seemed almost entirely deserted, and for a moment the two of them stood alone in the empty lobby. Large portraits of Brandon Street Settlement's past benefactors hung from the recently painted walls, and small rectangular bronze plates identified some of them as having been members of New York's most prestigious families.

"It was always a favorite charity," Farouk said as he stared about. "They were always coming around, the people who gave the money." He smiled. "They came in big black cars, and the people on the steps, the immigrants, they would think that someday they would have such cars, too."

"What went on here?" Frank asked.

"It was a place to help foreigners," Farouk answered. "Help them to adjust, you might say, to the new country."

"Adjust how?"

"To the place, to what was required," Farouk said. "To learn English, so you could get a job."

Frank nodded silently while his eyes glanced about the empty lobby. "Was it usually this deserted?"

Farouk laughed. "No. It was full of life. We were always having parties, festivals. People wore their old clothes, the ones from their native countries. There was music. There was dancing." A bright, playful light filled his eyes. "It was a good place. People gave assistance." He paused a moment, his eyes glancing about the silent lobby. His lips parted, and he started to go on. But suddenly the silence was broken by the sound of footsteps, and both Frank and Farouk glanced quickly to the left, and saw a group of men and women heading toward them from the end of the corridor.

"*Arriba*," someone said harshly from the end of the line. "*Vamos*."

The men and women moved on down the corridor, their heads slightly bowed, their brown faces vacant, silent, unquestioning. They carried battered suitcases or simple cloth bundles, and they speeded up noticeably each time the voice cried out from behind them.

Frank stepped to one side of the corridor and Farouk to the other, so that the line of people passed between them, then moved on to the rear of the building and disappeared behind a set of heavy metal doors.

"What can I do for you?" someone asked suddenly.

Frank turned back toward the corridor and saw a muscular man in jeans and a light blue sweatshirt.

"We're just closing down," the man said.

"Closing down?"

"The settlement house," the man explained. "It's being closed down." He gave Frank a quick glance, then allowed his eyes to settle on Farouk. "Are you the new owner?"

"No," Farouk told him.

"I thought, with all the Arabs in the neighborhood . . ."

"We don't have anything to do with the settlement house," Frank said. He took out his identification.

The man gave it a perfunctory glance, then looked up. "What do you want?"

"You know a man named Kincaid?" Frank asked. "Benjamin Kincaid?"

"Yeah, he's the old guy who offed himself, right?"

"Yes," Frank said.

"Yeah, I knew him a little," the man said. "But I've already told the police everything I knew about him." He shrugged. "Which wasn't much. The guy was creepy. He didn't say much, except to the *campesinos*."

Frank took out his notebook. "What did you tell the police?" he asked immediately.

"That he did some sort of teaching around here. He'd come in and hang out with the people from the neighborhood, teach them stuff."

"Like what?" Frank asked.

"I don't know," the man said. "There's a school set up downstairs. It's got desks and stuff. It's for some of the neighborhood kids."

"Just kids?" Farouk asked as he stepped to Frank's side. "What about the people who just went by? Did he teach them?"

"No, he didn't," the man said. "That's not allowed. Those people are more or less boarding here. School's not for them."

"You mean they live here?" Frank asked. "Those people?"

"That's right," the man said. "Until they get shipped out."

"Shipped out?"

"Back to where they came from."

"They're illegals?" Frank asked.

The man laughed. "No, of course not. We don't deal with illegals. We don't want the trouble. These people are on six-month visas. They need a place to stay for just that long. Then they head back to wherever they came from." He nodded toward the rear doors. "That bunch is heading back now."

Farouk smiled thinly. "Heading back. How are they heading back?"

The man's eyes narrowed. "Who are you?"

Farouk said nothing, and after a moment, the man turned

his attention back to Frank. "You looking for anything in particular about this Kincaid guy?"

"We're just looking into what he did here at the settlement," Frank said.

"Well, nothing illegal, I can tell you that," the man said earnestly. He shifted slightly on his feet. "I mean, Brandon Street Settlement's been around since the turn of the century."

"But in the past, it was not a boarding house," Farouk told him.

"No," the man said, "but that just means it's changed with the times."

"How has it changed?" Farouk asked insistently.

"Well, in some ways it's still like it was in the old days," the man said. "At least, as far as the teaching goes."

"But in other ways it's like a hotel?" Frank asked.

"Yeah. Except there's no charge," the man said. He laughed slightly. "I mean, these people, the ones you just saw, they couldn't afford a hotel."

Frank wrote it down.

"You want to look around?" the man asked brightly. "Go ahead. It's not the Waldorf. But then, for these people, it's free." He smiled politely. "So go ahead, check it out. Just don't steal anything." He nodded quickly, turned on his heels and headed off down the corridor.

A moment later, two vans, both of them filled with the people who'd marched down the corridor, rumbled out of the driveway, turned right, and barreled down Brandon Street.

Frank's eyes slid over to Farouk. "What do you think?"

Farouk shook his head. "I don't know."

Frank looked at the single flight of stairs that led up to the second floor. "Wouldn't hurt to look around, would it?"

"I don't think it would hurt, no."

Together they moved up the stairs to the second floor. Like the rest of the building, it appeared entirely deserted. Small rooms lined both sides of the hallway, each with its own bed, desk and water basin. A small plaster image of the Virgin Mary sat on the window sill of each room, along with two votive candles and a plain white doily.

"It looks just fine," Frank said.

Farouk nodded quickly. "We should look downstairs as well."

The two of them headed down the wide staircase which led back to the lobby, then moved on down the more narrow one which led to the basement.

A large room had been set up with desks and a blackboard.

"This is where Kincaid taught," Farouk said as he stared at the fews words which had been written in yellow chalk across the board. Someone had tried to erase them, but they could still be seen faintly against the black background of the board. Two columns, one in Spanish, one in English, of three words each, both columns under the heading: *Palabras importantes.*

"Important words," Farouk said quietly. Then he read them. "*Verdad.* Truth. *Libertad.* Freedom. *Justicia.* Justice." For a moment, his eyes lingered on the board, following the words once again, staring at them intently, as if trying to discover some elusive richness in their meaning. Finally, he gave up, and turned from the board, his eyes shifting over to Frank. "What do you say of one who writes such things?" he asked.

Frank shook his head slowly. "I don't know." He looked around silently. "It looks fine here. Clean. Very nice."

Farouk did not seem convinced. "In the day, perhaps," he said. Then he smiled knowingly. "But the true detective watches through the night."

It was almost night when they got back to 49th Street, and by that time the army of flannel-shirted construction workers who lounged along the street had been replaced by knots of teenagers, homeward-bound pedestrians and a few well-dressed suburbanites who rushed nervously toward the distant, glittering lights of the theater district.

"Well, we didn't find much," Frank said, as he opened the door of his office, then stepped aside and let Farouk pass into it.

Farouk nodded. "No, we didn't."

Frank turned on the light, walked to his desk and pulled out the bottle of Irish. "Want one?"

"Yes," Farouk said without hesitation. He lowered himself into the chair opposite Frank's desk. "It is an odd thing, memory," he said. "I remember the settlement house as such a big place. Big rooms. Big windows. This is the way a child sees everything."

Frank poured two drinks, and handed one of them to Farouk. The two drank quickly, without a toast, then Frank poured each of them a second.

"We're at a dead end, Farouk," he said as he lifted his glass to him.

Farouk nodded slowly. "Yes, we are."

"Maybe it's all been solved," Frank added. "The whole thing."

"Perhaps," Farouk said. "But there is the matter of the hand."

"Maybe Kincaid was through collecting things," Frank told him.

"But all his life, such a single-minded man," Farouk said. He took a quick sip from the glass. "Does such a person change, do you think?"

"It's possible," Frank said. He took out his notebook, turned it to the notes he'd written while talking to Kincaid, and began to scan them casually. In his mind, he could see the room where he'd written them, its windows covered with tattered native quilts. He could smell the dusty, pungent odor of foreign herbs and hear the crackle of drying stalks and leaves as he'd gotten to his feet and watched the strange, bent figure open the door, then close it, then light the single candle on the table by the door.

"I tried to get everything down," Frank said.

Farouk's eyes lifted toward him from the rim of his glass. He did not speak.

Frank continued to look through his notes, his eyes moving methodically from one line to the next. "He said that Hannah was a serpent in the garden," he said. "That she'd brought in a lot of money and made a place to find—"

"To find the jungle magic," Farouk said. "Yes, I remember that." He shook his head. "It would make the world beautiful, this drug, the one she'd found."

"And then, later, she'd brought in a man to make it."

Farouk nodded thoughtfully. "Pérez," he said.

"And to bring the people in," Frank concluded.

"A man to bring the people into the factory, or whatever it was," Farouk concluded.

"Then we talked about Pérez, and Kincaid admitted killing him," Frank went on, his eyes still fixed on his own tiny script.

"Then his death," Farouk said. "Kincaid's."

Frank nodded. "Yes." He finished his drink and lit a cigarette.

Farouk did the same, and for a few minutes, the two of them sat in the smoky silence, each going back through all he remembered of the case.

"I think Hannah was into something," Frank said finally. "I think this whole business with clothes was a front for something else."

"The jungle magic," Farouk said pointedly.

"Some sort of drug," Frank said. "Maybe that was her connection to Constanza."

"And when he was put in prison, she went into business for herself?" Farouk asked.

"Something like that."

"It's possible," Farouk said musingly.

Frank snuffed out his cigarette and began going back through his notebook, reading each page slowly, carefully, while Farouk watched him silently.

"But maybe it was in stages," he said after a moment, as he looked up from the notebook.

Farouk leaned forward slightly, his large brown eyes squinting through the tumbling smoke. "Stages?"

"Three stages," Frank said. He flipped back through the notebook. "Listen to this: First Hannah builds a place to find the drug. That's the beginning. Kincaid says that later she found a place to make it, and that after that, she hired a man to bring the people into it."

Farouk stared at Frank expressionlessly.

"That's three stages," Frank explained.

Farouk nodded slowly. "Yes."

Frank thought an instant longer, then snapped up his notebook, flipped through the pages, and glanced back up at Farouk. "Kincaid said, 'I didn't think it could begin again.'"

"What?"

"And he said that it was 'such a year for death, for assassination,'" Frank added quickly. "That was the year it began again, a year of death, of assassinations."

"Which would be?"

"Well, it could be 1968, couldn't it?" Frank said. He thought a moment. "That's also the same year Constanza went to prison."

"1968," Farouk repeated quietly.

"That would be the 'year of death' Kincaid talked about."

Farouk nodded. "Yes, it could be," he said. "But suppose he was talking about South America. Which is where he was at the time."

Frank said nothing.

"Of course, we could check on that," Farouk added. He seemed to consider his next question carefully. "That man, Riviera," he said finally, "you know him well?"

"No. Why?"

"Perhaps he might know if this 'year of death' refers to South America," Farouk replied.

"Riviera? Why would he know about it?"

"Because he knows Colombia."

"How do you know that?" Frank said. "Riviera's not from Colombia. He's not even from South America."

Farouk stared doubtfully at Frank.

"Riviera's from Spain," Frank insisted. "He's a Spanish Jew. Remember? He made that clear right away."

"Perhaps he is what he claims, a Sephardic Jew," Farouk said, his eyes narrowing. "But he knows South America. This I can tell you with certainty."

"What makes you so sure?"

"Because when he was at your office, he called Hannah's killer a *bicho*," Farouk said. "In Spain, this can only mean 'bug.'" His eyes seemed to darken slowly. "But in Colombia, it is a word of great contempt. A vulgar word for the penis. In English, you would call it 'prick.' This is what he called Kincaid."

"But he could have picked that up in New York, couldn't he?"

"It is possible."

Frank stared intently at Farouk. "But it could also be a lie."

"A lie, yes," Farouk said softly. His face grew very concentrated, and for a long time he did not speak. Then suddenly, his eyes brightened. "A lie," he said. "Which is sometimes where the truth begins."

30

"There were more lies than one," Farouk said as he walked up to the park bench where Frank sat waiting for him. He smiled. "But the truth is in the hall of records."

"What truth?"

"Well, for one thing, that Riviera is a man of property," Farouk said. "In this country, that is a hard truth to conceal."

"What kind of property?"

"The Brandon Street Settlement," Farouk said. "The records show that he owns the building." He smiled cunningly. "And since he does not rent it, but turns it over for a charitable use, he pays no taxes."

"When did he buy it?"

"The year of death," Farouk said. "The spring of 1968."

Frank took out his notebook. "Go on."

Farouk lowered himself onto the bench, then turned up the collar of his overcoat. "It's getting colder. There will be snow tonight, I think."

"You said something about more lies than one," Frank said.

Farouk blew into his hands, then rubbed them together rapidly. "He is from Spain, this much is true," he said. "But other things are wrong with what he told you. For example, he has been to Colombia forty times since 1968."

Frank wrote it down quickly. "Forty?" he repeated, astonished. "When was the first time?"

"He went there in October of 1968," Farouk said from memory.

"To Bogotá?" Frank asked.

"That is the interesting thing," Farouk said. "He did not land in Bogotá. He went instead to the northern part of the country, along the slopes of the Andes."

"San Jorge?"

"The one airport nearest it, yes," Farouk said. "He went again in the spring of the next year. Then again in the fall. He has been doing this, two trips a year—one in April, one in October—he has been doing this for twenty years."

Frank wrote it down. "Why twice a year?" he asked, almost to himself. "Why the spring and the fall?" He thought a moment, his mind moving back through everything he knew, all his cases, his entire past, ranging over all of it in a kind of instantaneous rush. Then, from nowhere, he heard the distant rumble of the old propeller plane, saw the clouds of white powder flow out from beneath its tail, smelled the sickly sweet odor of the poison that drifted down over the gently shifting cotton fields. "Crops," he said. "The planting and the harvest."

Farouk smiled. "Yes," he said immediately. "That could be it. The jungle magic."

Frank looked at him. "Marijuana?"

"Perhaps," Farouk said. "It is grown in Colombia."

"Anything else?"

"The leaves of the coca plant are processed there."

"Cocaine?"

Farouk nodded.

Frank thought for a moment, then flipped back through his notebook. "Here it is," he said, when he'd found what he was looking for. "Kincaid said that she, meaning Hannah, that she found a man to make it."

"Someone to grow the marijuana," Farouk said. "Or to process the cocaine."

Frank continued to stare at his notebook. "Maybe Pérez was killed, maybe that man was—"

"Riviera," Farouk said. "It is possible." He glanced toward the notebook. "What else did Kincaid say?"

Frank read from his notes. "Someone to bring them in."

"The shipments," Farouk said. "Of the drug." His eyes drifted out toward the bare trees of the courtyard. "But what drug?"

"The growing season should tell us that," Frank said. "Whatever it is, it has to be planted or harvested in the spring or fall."

Farouk lifted himself heavily from the bench. "Well," he said, puffing slightly in the cold air, "this will not be difficult to discover. From Colombia, it could only be marijuana or cocaine."

Frank stood up beside him. "How do you know?"

"Because Colombia is the homeland of my wife," Farouk told him. Then he headed off through the small park, his eyes fixed on the subway station at its northern edge.

"Cocaine or marijuana," Farouk repeated, as he and Frank stood on the wide steps of the New York Public Library. He looked up at the massive marble facade of the building. "All the secrets are here," he said with a kind of strange awe, "if one knew how to find them." He headed slowly up the stairs, mounting them one by one while Frank followed at his side.

"In this building there is a strange room," Farouk added once the two of them were inside the immense lobby. He looked at Frank. "Room two two eight. It is a place of great interest."

"What's in it?"

"Government documents and reports," Farouk said. "I have spent many hours looking at them. Everything is there. If you look closely at them, they will tell you how everything works."

"Will they tell us about Colombia?" Frank asked.

"That is the very least they will tell," Farouk said. He turned quickly to the right and proceeded up the gently curved staircase.

Room 228 was the least imposing of the many rooms they passed on the way to the northern corner of the library. There was a narrow entranceway, with two small rooms on either side. A few modest bookshelves ran along either side of the hallway, but Farouk did not move toward them. Instead, he walked quickly to one of the computer terminals at the front of the room, sat down immediately and began typing. Frank stood above him, his eyes staring at the screen as the words began to flow across it: NATIONAL NARCOTICS INTELLIGENCE COMMITTEE REPORT.

The screen flickered slightly, then the call number for the book appeared. Farouk jotted it down on a call slip, then took it into the room at the left and handed it to one of the clerks.

"There will be a short wait," he said as he turned back to Frank. "We will wait in the other room. The book will be brought to desk number sixty-four."

It arrived only a few minutes later, a small gray volume of little more than a hundred pages.

"Now we are ready," Farouk said delightedly. He opened the book first to the table of contents, perused it quickly, then turned to the index.

"Cocaine," he whispered as he flipped through the pages of the index, found the citation, then turned to it.

Frank leaned over and read what appeared on the page:

Cocaine, a bitter crystalline alkaloid $C_{17}H_{21}NO_4$. Obtained from the leaves of the coca (Spanish; Quechua, kúka) plant, a shrub grown in South America, genus Erythroxylon, family Erthroxylaceae. The coca plant is grown in the higher elevations of South America. It requires an extended mean temperature of approximately 65 degrees Fahrenheit and is best grown in the hilly terrain along the slopes of the Andes.

Farouk turned the page quickly, his eyes scanning the page with a steadily increasing speed.

"Here it is," he said after a moment. Then he read aloud in a low whisper. "Cocaine is harvested three times a year. First in the *mediados de marzo* (March), then in the *mediados de San Juan* (June), and finally in the *mediados todos los santos* (November)."

"Those aren't the right dates for Riviera's trips," Frank said when Farouk had finished.

Farouk said nothing. He returned to the index, looked up *marijuana*, then turned to the indicated page and read the entry slowly, while Frank looked on. "Cannabis, the dried leaves and flowering tops of the pistillate hemp plant, is cultivated year-round, particularly in Colombia, where the leaves are blended with coca paste (cocaine) to produce a third, highly intoxicating drug known locally as *bazuco*."

Farouk looked up from the book. *"Bazuco,"* he said thoughtfully. "Maybe that's the jungle magic."

"Maybe," Frank said as he sat down beside him. "But the growing season still isn't right for Riviera's trips."

"No, it isn't," Farouk said as he closed the book. "Nothing fits."

Frank leaned forward slightly, his eyes drawn to the long rows of books which ran along the four walls of the reading room. "He goes every six months," he said.

"Without fail," Farouk added. "For the last twenty years, every six months, yes." He glanced down at the book. "But nothing grows during that time." He shook his head in exasperation. "Nothing is harvested in April or October." He slid the book across the table. "Cocaine is harvested three times. But Riviera goes only twice to Colombia. And marijuana is harvested year-round." He thought a moment longer, then turned to Frank. "It could not be these drugs."

Frank looked at him. "Maybe it's some new drug." In his mind he could see the small yellow seeds that had dotted the floor of Kincaid's room. He could hear Kincaid's voice as he spoke again, his voice as dry as the bed of stalks that covered his floor: *And later another man came to bring them in.* "Or maybe the shipment's made differently," he said.

Farouk stared at him. "Differently? How?"

"Kincaid said that a man came down to Colombia to bring them in," Frank said.

"Them, yes," Farouk told him, "the shipments."

"Or people."

"People?"

"Whatever the drug is, maybe Riviera is just the mule."

Farouk watched Frank intently. "Meaning what?"

"Maybe Riviera is the one who gets the shipments here," Frank said. "And maybe he uses people to bring them in."

"People?" Farouk asked again.

Frank nodded. "That's right. And these people, maybe he puts them up at the Brandon Street Settlement."

Farouk's eyes narrowed, but he did not speak.

"On six-month visas," Frank added.

"And that would be the cover for the shipments?" Farouk asked immediately. "The people at Brandon Street?"

"I don't know," Frank said. But in his mind he could see them as they trudged down the long corridor, their heads bent forward, silent, while the man screamed at them from behind. They seemed to weave together in the white, windless space of the freshly painted hallway, brown like the stalks that covered Kincaid's floor, a withered human harvest disappearing behind a large gray door.

31

It was early the next morning when Farouk arrived at Frank's office. For a time, he sat in the shadowy light, waiting for Frank to finish shaving, his eyes moving slowly about the room, while the smoke from his cigarette curled up toward the water-stained ceiling.

"It is early, yes," he said as Frank emerged groggily from the small bathroom. "But we must be there before he comes."

"And we don't know when that is," Frank said. He pulled on his jacket, then his long black overcoat. "Does it still look like snow?"

"For tonight, they say it is coming," Farouk told him. "A big storm from the north."

"That could make things difficult," Frank said.

"We will stay close," Farouk assured him. "Snow or not, we will be near."

"Okay, let's go," Frank said as he buttoned the last button of his coat. He walked to the door, let Farouk pass in front of him, then followed him up the stairs to 49th Street.

"I brought my car," Farouk said as he guided Frank to the right toward Eighth Avenue. "We cannot do this thing from underground." He pointed to a battered late-model Chevrolet. "The heater is not working, but that is its only problem."

"Does Riviera have a car?"

"I don't know," Farouk said. "But if he does, we will need one for ourselves."

They got in quickly, then drove silently down Ninth Avenue, turned left on 34th Street, and headed toward the heart of the Garment District.

"We will park in front," Farouk said, as he guided the car up the curb just opposite the underground parking garage of Riviera's building. "If he has a car, we will see him go in." He reached for the small red-lettered sign which lay on the seat beside him. "This will keep the police away," he said as he turned the sign toward Frank. It read: NEW YORK CITY POLICE DEPARTMENT OFFICIAL BUSINESS.

"Where'd you get that?" Frank asked.

Farouk hooked the sign to his sun visor, then lowered the visor into position. "My cousin, Hassan, owed me a favor. With this, he returned it."

Frank nodded quickly, then eased himself back into the seat. "This was the part I always hated," he said.

"You must not think of it as boring," Farouk told him. "If you do, a stakeout is unbearable." He shook his head. "You must think of it as a moment of great anticipation. You must say, 'What I do not yet have, I anticipate.' " He smiled. "This is the way to see it, as the instant before the panther leaps."

Frank took out a cigarette and lit it, his eyes lingering on the dark tunnel of the underground garage. "If we don't see him go in by nine, I'll call him on the phone. If he's there, we'll know he didn't use a car."

"Of course," Farouk said. "And we will abandon ours."

"We can just park it in that garage."

"Of course," Farouk repeated. "You see what freedom we have, my friend? We can take a car, or we can leave it." He smiled mockingly. "The world is boundless, yes? Beautiful and boundless."

Frank took a quick draw on the cigarette and watched the crowds as they thickened steadily along the sidewalks. He could feel his own inner time moving at the same darting pace as the people around him, and he began to tap his foot rapidly against the floor of the car.

Farouk eyed him curiously for a moment. "As I once said, you are very restless, Frank."

"It's my nature," Frank said. He took a long draw on the cigarette, then crushed it in the ashtray on the dashboard.

"Perhaps you have some ideas to go with it," Farouk added. Frank shook his head.

"Too bad," Farouk said with a slight, dismissive shrug. "It is good to have ideas about the way you live."

Frank's eyes shifted over to him. "What's yours?"

Farouk took a deep breath. "To do good to the good, and bad to the bad."

Frank smiled. "You want him, don't you? You want Riviera."

"If he is using these people to mule in the drug," Farouk said, "if this is his way, then yes, I want him." He shook his head. "A man should get what he wants in life by himself. He should not use others."

"So that he who grows the fig, should eat it," Frank told him. "Isn't that what your father said?"

Farouk smiled broadly. "Yes."

Frank returned his eyes to the entrance of the underground garage. "It's getting late," he said. "Maybe I should make the call. Riviera may already be in his office."

Farouk nodded. "Yes, he may."

Frank opened the door and started to pull himself out of the car when something glinted in the corner of his eye, and he saw Riviera's gleaming silver hair. He was driving a dark blue station wagon, his eyes staring straight ahead until he neared the garage, then slowly guided his car into it.

"Did you see him?" Frank asked immediately as he quickly got back into the car.

"The license plate number is BR7-5570," Farouk said casually.

Frank reached for his notebook.

"No need," Farouk told him. He tapped his finger against the side of his head. "It is safe in here."

It was almost midnight before Frank saw him again. He leaned forward quickly and nudged Farouk from his sleep.

"He's leaving," Frank whispered.

Farouk straightened himself immediately, his eyes searching the gray interior of the garage for Riviera's silver hair.

"Ah yes," he said when he saw him.

From behind the dusty windshield, Farouk could see Riviera as he made his way briskly to the station wagon, then got in and quickly drove out of the garage.

They followed him as he turned left and headed east, then took another right on Park Avenue, moving southward between the office buildings that lined the avenue on both sides.

"Perhaps he is going home," Farouk said, as he speeded up slightly to remain just close enough to keep Riviera's car in sight.

Frank did not speak. He kept his eyes on the blue station wagon, watching closely as it moved into the East Village, then through it, the car heading easily past the brightly lit restaurants of Little Italy and then into the dense tenement blocks of Chinatown.

"He's going to the bridge," Frank said, as the station wagon curved easily around the jutting gray wall of the Municipal Building and then gently nosed up the entry ramp to the Brooklyn Bridge.

Farouk pressed the accelerator slightly, and the old car sputtered wearily, but jerked forward, its faded yellow headlights beaming onto the ramparts of the bridge.

Once across the river, the station wagon exited immediately, then veered to the right and headed out toward a dark, secluded area of abandoned warehouses.

Farouk glanced at Frank and smiled. "I don't think he's going home," he said.

The smooth pavement gave way to bricks and cobblestones as the station wagon made a quick left and moved out toward the river.

Farouk eased his foot off the accelerator, slowing down immediately. "We should not get too close. In traffic, it would not be so bad. But here, it is too obvious."

Frank nodded. "Don't burn it," he said. "Don't burn the tail."

Riviera's car continued toward the river, then abruptly turned right and headed down a dark, unlit road.

"We can't follow him in the car, Farouk," Frank said. "It's too deserted. He'd pick up the tail right away."

"Yes," Farouk agreed reluctantly. He wheeled the car over to the side of one of the buildings and stopped. "We'll have to try to keep up with him on foot."

They got out immediately and began trotting toward the corner. The air was cold, and as they ran, jets of condensed air shot out in front of them. The smell of the river was deep and musty, and it reminded Frank of the lazily flowing southern streams in which he swam away his childhood, then of that other river, deep in the Colombian jungle, where the bodies had been stacked like cords of wood along the muddy banks.

As they rounded the corner, Frank could see the taillights of Riviera's car like two tiny red eyes. They moved to the right, then stopped.

Farouk stopped too, gasping noisily as he tried to get his breath. "I cannot run like this," he said, puffing wildly, his huge hands plucking at his coat. "I am not a deer."

"He's stopped," Frank said, his eyes fixed on the taillights.

Farouk dropped his fists to his sides and stared out into the darkness.

The taillights flashed off, and it was as if an impenetrable black wall had suddenly thrust itself toward them. For a moment, the two of them stood in the darkness, still trying to regain their breath.

"Ready?" Frank finally asked.

"Yes," Farouk said.

They moved over toward the building and walked quietly alongside it. Frank could feel the rough texture of the brick and mortar with his fingertips, and as he continued forward, he took a strange, inexpressible comfort in that single bleak sensation.

Suddenly, in the distance, a square of light shot toward them, and Frank could see that Riviera had opened up the tailgate of the station wagon, throwing on the light inside the car. He could see Riviera's hair gleaming, almost magically, in that light. His large brown hands were wrapped around a small metal drum, and he leaned forward carefully and slid the drum into the back of the car, then turned quickly and disappeared into the building, leaving the tailgate open, the single light still glowing hazily in the cold winter air.

"The drug," Farouk whispered. "Do you think it is the drug?"

Frank did not answer. He pressed his shoulders against the

side of the building, scraping it softly as he continued forward. One step at a time, he inched his way toward the light, until he was almost at the door of the building. It was then that he glanced back and realized that Farouk had disappeared into the thick harbor darkness. For an instant, he wanted to call him, and as he stopped himself, he realized that he wanted Farouk at his side, not because he wanted help, but because he didn't want to die the old scriptural death of the lost, alone save for the presence of his enemies.

He started to step forward, then heard a long, slow breath behind him.

"I am fine now," Farouk whispered vehemently. "But my breath, I had to get it back."

Frank turned back toward the car, took two steps, then drew back at once.

Riviera stepped quickly out of the building once again, walked over to the station wagon, and slid in a second small green drum.

Frank stepped out of the darkness, and as Riviera turned and saw him, he noticed that the old man's face was oddly beautiful in its deep lines and full, unparted lips, and that there was something about him that seemed to tower over the car, the street, the buildings, rise up and over all these things, until it stood in its own dreadful solitude, cold, bloodless, beyond the call of human needs.

"Did you follow me?" Riviera asked suddenly.

"Yes."

"Why?"

"To check out a few things."

Farouk stepped into the light, his shoulder almost touching Frank's.

"I see you brought your partner," Riviera said to Frank.

Frank said nothing.

Riviera lifted his head slightly and took in a deep breath. The whistle of a tugboat broke the air around him, but he did not seem to hear it. "I didn't know that you were still working on the case," he said. "After that man died, I thought it was over. Are there still some other things Miss Covallo is interested in?"

"A few that we are," Frank said.

"What things?" Riviera asked immediately.

"They have to do with Hannah," Frank said.

Riviera smiled. "In one way or another, everything does."

Frank stared at Riviera expressionlessly. "What does that mean, exactly?"

"Her death calls things into question," Riviera said.

"What things?"

"What her life was worth," Riviera told him. He glanced at Farouk. "What anything is worth." He smiled slightly, then turned back to Frank, his eyes moving slowly up and down Frank's body. "You could use a new overcoat, Mr. Clemons. Would you like to have one?"

"Some of what I found out about Hannah has to do with you," Frank told him.

"That doesn't surprise me," Riviera said matter-of-factly. "The world is very interconnected, if you know what I mean."

"I don't."

Riviera's body stiffened. "What are you after, Mr. Clemons?" he demanded impatiently. "I'm a busy man, as you can see."

Frank glanced toward the small green containers. "What's in those cans?" he asked.

"Solvent," Riviera answered. He nodded toward the building to his left. "This is a refinishing plant. We're closing it down. Certain materials have to be removed."

"In the middle of the night?"

"This is a difficult trade," Riviera said. "We don't always play by the rules." He glanced toward Farouk, then back to Frank. "The government has very strict regulations about disposing of certain chemicals. The procedures are very expensive." He smiled. "We sometimes try to avert the cost."

"By dumping things at night?"

"Yes."

"Is that what you're doing, dumping it?"

"Transferring it," Riviera said. "You know, to a safer place." He smiled thinly. "At least for a while."

"You seem a little high in the chain of command to be doing that kind of work," Frank said.

Riviera laughed. "Just the opposite," he said. "Only someone very high could be trusted to do it." There was a strange distance in his voice, a sense of falling away, as if something in him had suddenly plunged over a cliff.

"You go to Colombia pretty often," Frank said. "You go in April and October."

Riviera said nothing.

"Twice a year for the last twenty years," Frank added.

Riviera stared expressionlessly into Frank's eyes.

"Hannah was in Colombia for a while," Frank said. "A village called San Jorge."

Riviera remained silent, but Frank could see something building like a fire behind his eyes.

"That's near the slopes of the Andes," Frank added. "Drug country."

Riviera's face relaxed slightly. "Drug country?"

"That's right," Frank said. "Marijuana. Cocaine. A mixture called *bazuco*." He looked at Riviera pointedly. "Maybe something else. Something new."

Riviera smiled mockingly. "You think I'm a drug dealer?"

Frank did not reply.

Riviera laughed lightly. "Well, if I'm a drug dealer, how do I get this whatever-it-is into the country?"

"Through a building you own," Frank told him. "The Brandon Street Settlement."

Riviera laughed again, a hard, dry laugh, mocking and ironic, which seemed to slash at the thick darkness which surrounded him.

"Well, you have found enough," he said, at last. "You have stumbled upon enough in your stupid way."

Frank glared at him. "Enough what?"

"Enough to die a fool," Riviera said, as he pulled the pistol from his jacket. "Do you think I haven't killed before?"

Frank felt his heart like a cold stone in his chest. He glanced at Farouk, who stood motionless beside him, his face paling as he glared at the pistol.

"Hannah," Frank said.

"Before that, too," Riviera said. He lifted one of his large gnarled hands. "With this." He laughed again. "Do you know how to make it in this world?" he asked. "Not by hard work. That's bullshit. Everyone works hard. No. You make it by being willing to do anything you have to do." His face grew flushed in the cold air. "If you live in a sewer, you eat the sewer rats." He glanced at the small green cans. "Drugs? Ridiculous."

"What is it?" Frank asked.

Riviera looked at him almost admiringly. "You really want to know, don't you? Well, it can't hurt now." His eyes softened. "Something amazing," he said, his voice full of wonder. "Not a drug, but something amazing." He pulled a plain white handkerchief from his back pocket. "Something that you take from a little yellow seed, and you refine it, and you put it on this handkerchief, and, you know, it will seem to glow."

Frank's lips parted. " 'The Imalia Covallo Look,' " he breathed.

Riviera smiled. "It was discovered years ago by a chemist in Colombia. A genius. His name should be famous."

"Emilio Pérez," Frank said.

"That's right. He found that a little pod from a very common herb could make ordinary cloth more beautiful than you could imagine. It's all in the sheen it gives to the material. It wraps you in light. When you wear a dress, it illuminates you. You are clothed in stars. You look like a goddess." Riviera looked mournfully at the two small cannisters. "And that's the last of it," he said. "There'll probably never be any more. Kincaid saw to that." His eyes shifted back to Frank. "He was there when Bornstein sent Hannah down to refine and produce it." He smiled almost wistfully. "We called it the *magia de la selva.* "

"The jungle magic," Farouk whispered.

Riviera glanced at him, then turned back to Frank. "It was magical, all right," he said. "But is was also poisonous. At least at one stage, the processing. It had no color, no taste, no odor. But during that time, it could be absorbed in almost any way. From the air, through the skin. There was no way to stop it."

"And Kincaid knew that," Frank said.

"Yes," Riviera said. "He killed Emilio because of it. Cut off his hand and simply disappeared into the jungle." He shook his head. "Hannah always thought he must have died there." He smiled. "You can imagine how she must have felt when he showed up at her door."

"He found her?"

"He ended up at Brandon Street," Riviera said. "That's where he saw the seed. Probably only one of them, clinging to some *campesino*'s shirt. That was all he needed. He went to Hannah, thinking that she knew about it."

"She didn't?" Frank asked.

Riviera shook his head. "Of course not. She thought we had found a way to process it safely. She would never have used the extract, not after what happened in San Jorge." He smiled. "I told her that we'd found a way to control it, that we were always changing the workers who worked with it, just to make sure that no one would be harmed." He cocked the pistol. "She wanted to believe that, and so she did."

"Until Kincaid came to her apartment," Frank said.

"That's right."

"But he didn't kill her."

"No," Riviera said coldly. The barrel of the pistol inched out slightly. "I did."

"Kincaid told her about how the whole operation worked," Frank said quickly.

"You're stalling, Clemons," Riviera said.

"I want to know what happened."

"Well, you're right, of course," Riviera said. "Kincaid told Hannah how whole batches of workers arrived at Brandon Street every six months. How they came from everywhere, so that when they went back home, got sick and died, no one would ever be able to figure out that the one thing they all had in common was a short stay at Brandon Street." He smiled. "We figured it all out very well."

"We?" Frank said.

"Don't be stupid," Riviera said. "Imalia Covallo is the sort of person who wants to make it." He laughed derisively. "She thought Kincaid killed Hannah, and that if he weren't found, he'd kill her, too. That's why she hired you. To find Kincaid, so that I could kill him. It was a stupid thing to do, but she panicked." His eyes grew dark. "But it was Hannah who really betrayed me. I set her up with Imalia. I gave her a job when no one else would touch her. Then she betrayed me, threatened to expose everything." He smiled at the irony of her death. "It's like she suddenly went back to the way she was in the old days."

In his mind, Frank saw Hannah once again at the meeting hall, her hand in the air as she cried out the ancient Jewish curse: *If I betray thee, O Jerusalem, may my right hand wither, and my tongue cleave to the roof of my mouth.*

"So I killed her," Riviera said flatly, "and tried to make it look like Kincaid, just in case he went to the police with what he knew, or, later, in case you ever found him." He smiled. "But as it turned out, I didn't have to kill Kincaid." He lifted the barrel slightly, his eyes narrowing slowly as he did so. "No more talk," he said in a flat, stony voice. "Time to die."

"You can only shoot one of us at a time," Frank said.

"I only intend to shoot one of you," Riviera said. He glanced at Farouk. "I presume that's all that will be necessary, Farouk?"

Farouk nodded. "Of course," he said calmly.

Riviera smiled. "I heard you were realistic about things like this," he said. "That's why I hired you. I'm glad it was true."

Frank stared at Farouk. "You were working for him?"

"Yes," Farouk said, his eyes suddenly very cold and distant, as if he were peering back at Frank from the other end of a long narrow tunnel.

Frank felt something at the very center of himself break achingly.

Farouk bowed his head slightly, then stepped away, moving far to the side, then around, until Frank could see his face watching him mercilessly from just over Riviera's shoulder.

"Goodbye, Mr. Clemons," Riviera said.

Frank pressed his back against the hard brick wall, and it was if he could feel every grain of its rough surface against his flesh. He could hear the wind as it twined softly along the deserted streets, and feel the dark eternal flow of the river. He glanced upward at the cloud-covered moon, and he imagined the vast intricacy of the stars, the black unending night, the dark hazards of the world, its most secret corners, and he realized with a sudden astonishing clarity that he did not want to leave these things behind, that, barren though they seemed, conscienceless and void, they were still held inseparably within the fabric of his life.

He heard Riviera say once again, as if it were a chant, *"Time to die,"* and he closed his eyes and waited.

"The *campesinos*," he heard Farouk say suddenly, "they are still dying of this poison?"

Frank kept his eyes closed tightly, still waiting.

"Yes," Riviera said.

Then he heard the pistol fire, and he felt his head slam against the brick, but he did not fall.

"*Bicho!*" he heard Farouk whisper vehemently.

Then he opened his eyes and saw Riviera stagger forward, a huge red plume of blood flooding over his chest, a look of inhuman astonishment on his large brown face.

"*Bicho,*" Farouk said again, as he watched Riviera fall forward, slamming face down onto the street.

Frank continued to stand rigidly in place, his back still pressed flat against the brick wall.

Farouk looked at him. "I did not know of this," he said, "of the deaths." He returned his pistol to its holster and stepped over to Frank, peeling him gently from the wall. "Come now, my friend," he said softly. "It is not time to die."

32

Farouk stopped at the little iron gate which led down to Frank's office.

"I will see you tomorrow, yes?" he asked.

Frank nodded quietly. "Sure."

They had just walked the few blocks from the Midtown North headquarters to 49th Street, where they'd dropped off the two green canisters and told the whole story to Tannenbaum. Almost two hours of questioning had followed before they were finally released. Then they'd headed down Ninth Avenue, the icy wind off the Hudson pursuing them all the way.

Frank lifted his collar against it and took a step down toward his office. "Take it easy, Farouk," he said.

Farouk looked at him sadly. "I did not mean for it to be so close," he said for the third time since Riviera's death, "but I did not know the whole story."

Frank looked at him pointedly. "When did he hire you?"

"The day before I introduced myself at Toby's," Farouk told him. "He said that Miss Covallo had hired an investigator, and that he wanted to make sure that this person could be trusted."

"And you believed him?"

"I had no reason not to," Farouk said. "As you know, investigators are not always reliable. They pad their accounts, charge for time they do not spend on a case." He shrugged helplessly. "You might have been such a person."

"I understand," Frank told him.

"Riviera asked only that I follow you," Farouk added. "But he told many lies, and they began to rise around him. After that, I wanted to stay with you."

"To protect me."

Farouk nodded slowly. "To do good to the good," he said. Then his eyes swept down toward Frank's office. "This is not a place for a man to live for too long a time."

"No, not for long," Frank assured him.

"Perhaps, tonight, you might wish to stay at my place," Farouk added.

Frank shook his head. "I don't think so."

Farouk took a step away, then turned back toward Frank. "Tomorrow, they will deal with Covallo."

"Yes."

Farouk looked at him a moment, then offered his hand. "Tomorrow we shall go on to other things."

Frank nodded gently, but did not answer. Instead, he simply waved half-heartedly, then walked down the stairs and into his office.

For a while he tried to sleep, tossing fitfully on the sofa, until his anxiousness overtook him and he stepped over to his desk and lit a cigarette. Its billowing smoke enveloped him, and he thought of the people of San Jorge, of Hannah as she had watched their bodies grow weak and trembling, their smooth brown skins erupt in boils, of Gilda and Kincaid, sacrifice and vengeance, and as he thought of these things, he could still hear Hannah's voice ringing over the bare wintry trees, and it struck him that deep in his own soul he had heard her at that moment in her life, heard her like the others who'd gathered in the cold and pressed their faces into the wind and listened as she spoke, watched as her hand lifted like a torch into the air.

He finished his cigarette, then lit another, pulled on his old brown overcoat and walked out onto the street.

The first winter snow had begun to fall, already outlining the naked steel girders of the unfinished building across the way in a silvery lace. It swept along the avenues in bitterly piercing sheets, but he walked on through it determinedly, his eyes staring straight ahead as it swirled around him, then fell to earth in gentle slopes along the curbs and beside the buildings.

It was almost an inch deep by the time he made it over to Fifth Avenue, then turned north. The great manicured forest of Central Park was white and gleaming in the street lights which dotted it, but in his mind, Frank could see only the green river lined with brown bodies, and as he walked steadily northward through the deepening snow, he could hear the gentle, gurgling sound the bodies made as the still surviving villagers slid them mournfully into the water.

The snow lay in a thick white blanket over everything by the time he reached the doors of the museum.

"Excuse me, sir," the doorman said as Frank stepped up to the entrance. "The museum is closed for a private function." He smiled sweetly. "It will be open to the public tomorrow morning."

"I'm here to see Imalia Covallo," Frank told him.

"Is she expecting you?"

"No," Frank said. He took out his identification. "Just tell her I'm here."

The doorman looked at the card, then glanced back anxiously toward the crowd behind him. "Look, I suppose you can go in," he said after a moment. "I really can't leave my post." Then he stepped back and opened the door.

The building's large, spacious rotunda was filled with well-dressed patrons, and as Frank edged his way through them, he thought again of Hannah, and wondered how often she had come to such places, mingled with such people, observed the astonishing sheen in a dress worn by someone across the room and thought of San Jorge, of Gilda, and then, later, in one sudden cruel realization, of the long lines of people who had already been moved facelessly through the lethal triangle that Riviera had established for Imalia Covallo. Once again, he saw her in her youth, a young woman bent over a sewing machine, her fingers dancing around the glinting needle, her feet pumping incessantly at the pedal on the floor, and it seemed to him that all her hope for mercy still lay bound up in those days, closed within their noble grip like something still held within the grasp of her severed hand.

"Frank?"

He turned and saw Imalia moving toward him, her eyes watching his questioningly. She was dressed in a long black gown, and wrapped within its folds, her body seemed strangely pale and fleshless, hardly there at all.

"What are you doing here?" she asked as she stepped up beside him.

"I came to make a last report," Frank said, his voice barely louder than the hum of the crowd.

Her eyes widened. "Last report? I thought it was all settled."

"Not quite," Frank said.

She smiled sweetly. "I'm sorry I couldn't invite both you and Karen to this party. I really am. But I had heard that . . ." She glanced about, her eyes darting from the bar at her left to the table of hors d'oeuvres which rested a few yards beyond it. "There's Karen."

She was dressed in the shimmering black gown Imalia had given her, and as Frank looked at her, he could hear Etta Polansky once again: *If you knew how a coat got to Bloomingdale's, it would break your heart.*

"Anyway," Imalia said brightly, "I'd heard that you and Karen, that you were . . ."

Frank stared at her.

"Of course," Imalia added nervously, "I'm happy to have you here."

Frank looked at her closely, his eyes sweeping over her dress, taking in its lustrous sheen. "Nice dress," he said.

"Thank you," Imalia said. "I didn't expect you to notice."

"Nice color," Frank added. "It seems to glow."

Imalia watched him intently, her eyes narrowing. "I'm glad you like it," she said, her voice now strangely lifeless.

"A color like that . . ." Frank began.

She seized his arm. "Frank," she said, "we should talk, don't you think?" She nodded to the left. "Let's talk, Frank. Really." She stepped to his side and tugged him toward her. "Please, Frank," she said in a fearful whisper.

"No."

She stepped back around to face him. "This is not the place for any more discussion."

Frank shrugged. "It's as good as any." He glanced around for a moment, taking in the other people. Then his eyes drove into her. "Do they know?"

Imalia's face paled. "Please, Frank. We can work something out."

"Do they know what they're wearing?" Frank repeated, his voice now hard, insistent.

Imalia said nothing. Her lower lip began to tremble.

"Do they know?" Frank demanded, his voice now loud enough to draw a few quick glances from the people crowded around him.

Imalia's body shuddered. "Frank, for God's sake." She grasped his arm. "Please."

He pulled it free and shoved her backward toward the door. "Do they know?"

Imalia stumbled into the crowd around her, breaking a heel, then slumping awkwardly to the left. "Please, Frank," she pleaded. "Please, don't."

He pushed her backward once again.

The people parted around them, staring wildly as Frank shoved her again, this time driving her through the glass door and out into the snowy air.

"No, Frank," Imalia cried. She stood in the snow, her dress blowing in the winter wind, her long thin arms gathering around her against the cold. "Please, Frank," she pleaded as she sank down in the gray slush of the sidewalk, "please." She leaned forward, her head drooping toward her splayed legs, her hair hanging in a tangle at her shoulders.

Frank stood over her, staring down mercilessly. He could feel people gathering around him, hear voices crying for the police, but he did not move, and after a while he heard the first peal of the siren as it came toward him through the snow, felt the arm of the officer as he was led away, glimpsed the steady silver light that shone toward him from the badge.

It was almost dawn before he heard footsteps coming down the corridor, looked up, and saw Farouk staring at him from behind the bars of the holding cell.

"Our names are connected," he said quietly.

"Somebody called you?" Frank asked.

"Tannenbaum," Farouk told him. "He said that you had been arrested for disturbing the peace, and that I might want to make myself available." He smiled. "Come. There are things to be signed. But I have paid your bail."

Within a few minutes, they were on the street together, strolling slowly down Ninth Avenue, the snow now deep and lovely along the deserted boulevard, silent in its impossible innocence.

"She did not deny it," Farouk said after a moment.

"Imalia?"

Farouk nodded.

"I didn't think she would," Frank said.

"Everything has been discovered," Farouk added.

Frank stopped suddenly, and drew in a long slow breath. "One mistake," he said quietly. "She made only one mistake."

"Imalia?" Farouk asked.

"Hannah," Frank told him. For a moment he stood motionlessly, his long dark shadow stretching out across a field of white. Then, without a word, a signal, a reason of any kind, he began moving forward once again.